# The Apocryphal Napoleon

# The Apocryphal Napoleon

by
**Louis Geoffroy**

Translated, annotated and introduced by
**Brian Stableford**

A Black Coat Press Book

ISBN 978-1-61227-579-6. First Printing. December 2016. Published by Black Coat Press, an imprint of Hollywood Comics.com, LLC, P.O. Box 17270, Encino, CA 91416. All rights reserved. Except for review purposes, no part of this book may be reproduced or transmitted in any form or by any means, electronic or mechanical, including photocopying, recording, or by any information storage and retrieval system, without permission in writing from the publisher. The stories and characters depicted in this novel are entirely fictional. Printed in the United States of America.

# *Introduction*

*Napoléon et la conquête du monde, 1812-1832, Histoire de la monarchie universelle* was initially published anonymously in 1836. A second edition was published in 1841 bearing the title *Napoléon Apocryphe* and bearing the signature Louis Geoffroy, and a third appeared in 1851, after the election of Louis-Napoléon as president of the Third Republic; after a pause, it was "rediscovered" in 1896, and it has been regularly reprinted thereafter. It is here translated as *The Apocryphal Napoléon*, a previous translation published in Oklahoma City in 1994 always having been exceedingly difficult to obtain.

"Louis Geoffroy" was an abbreviated version of the named of Louis-Napoléon Geoffroy-Château (1803-1858), a magistrate in the civil tribunal of Paris. He was the son of Marc-Antoine Geoffroy-Château (1774-1806), an officer in the engineering corps who had attracted the attention of General Bonaparte while fighting in the division commanded by Jean Lannes during the Egyptian campaign, but subsequently died in battle in Europe in 1806, as recorded in the text of the story. Like all the children of officers killed in action, Louis—who was not yet three years old—was then formally adopted by the Emperor, in accordance with his decree of 6 May 1806, but it is not certain that he ever met his adoptive father.

The text of the novel also refers several times to the biologist Étienne Geoffroy Saint-Hilaire (1772-1844), who was Marc-Antoine Geoffroy-Château's older brother, both of them being among the children of the advocate    Jean-Jacques-Gérard Geoffroy (Saint-Hilaire was a village where their father owned a house, and their other two brothers also added arbitrary suffixes to their surname). Geoffroy Saint-Hilaire, who is likely to have played a far more active role in young Louis' upbringing than his notional adoptive father, was a colleague of the Chevalier de Lamarck, and carried forward the latter's theory of evolution, which did not involve the notion of a common descent of all living forms by gradual variation from a single ancestor, but an unfolding of latent potential within various types by virtue of adaptive responses to environment. He too accompanied Bonaparte to Egypt, as part of the scientific mission attached to the military one, alongside other scientists and artists mentioned in the present story as playing a similar role in the Emperor's hypothetical expeditions of the 1820s. He was elected to the Académie des Sciences in 1807.

Unlike the materialist Lamarck, Geoffroy Saint-Hilaire was a deist, and his notion of evolution includes a strong emphasis on the notion of divine design that was absent from Lamarck's *Philosophie zoologique*, which might be of some significance with regard to the account of the world's political and social evolution offered in Louis Geoffroy's novel. Although the novel is certainly somewhat tongue-in-cheek, there is also a good deal of serious speculation in it, and the author—then anonymous—added a brief preface to the first edition claiming that he had been carried away by his own fantasy and had ended up "believing" in it, "as a sculptor who has just completed his marble sees a god in it, kneels down and adores it."

That remark too is ironic, but it does convey something of the force of the utopian ideal enshrined in the story, in a fashion so completely over the top that when Napoléon is crowned as Universal Monarch, two stars are obligingly extinguished in order to reconfigure the constellation of Orion so that it can be renamed in his honor. There is a point at which the absurd becomes sublime, and Geoffroy's *Napoléon apocryphe* seems to have reached that point, perhaps without the author quite intending to—something that helps the novel acquire the status of a masterpiece. There is a strong sense within it of the unfolding of a latent design, an evolution toward perfection, and the notion of adaptation to circumstance might help to explain some of its more striking implausibilities, including the agreed capitulation of the Americas and the unanimous conversion of the Jews.

Little more is known about the author than the data summarized above; he only signed one other work (with his full surname), and merely as editor—*Le Farce de maistre Pierre Pathelin, précédée d'un recueil de monuments de l'ancienne langue française, depuis son origine jusqu'à l'an 1500* [The Farce of Master Pierre Pathelin, preceded by a collection of monuments of the ancient French language form its origin to the year 1500] (1853)—although it is conceivable that he might have published other anonymous texts before or after issuing this one in 1836, to which he never had the opportunity to add his signature in subsequent editions. Whether that is so or not, however, the present work entitles him to a highly significant place in literary history. The novel is nowadays celebrated as the first extended exercise in alternative history (or, as some have it, "alternate history"), which survives and thrives both as an intellectual game played by historians and as a rich literary subgenre partly affiliated to the genre of science fiction. Insofar as history is theoretical, involving notions of cause and effect, and sometimes the notion of repetitive patterns, its theories can only be "tested" by means of thought-experiments, because the past can only be re-enacted in the imagination, time itself being recalcitrant to re-setting.

Geoffroy's *Napoléon apocryphe*, like most exercises in alternative history, is not experimental in the sense that it is a dispassionate logical extrapolation of a premise, but few experiments in science are genuine in that sense, most of them being designed to support a conviction rather than test it—but Geoffroy, as a magistrate as well as the nephew of a leading scientist, would have known full well that honesty in trials is mostly appearance. Napoléon, in Geoffroy's account of his alternative career, is not so much a working hypothesis following a plausible logic of events as an instrument of a utopian dream, and the implausibility of his facile conquests is really a comment on the difficulty—perhaps the hopelessness—of dreams of political progress toward any kind of universal harmony. Unlike most utopian fantasies, previous and subsequent, Geoffroy's does not simply leap to a consummated *modus vivendi*—indeed, it has very little to say about the pattern of life in the perfected world that Napoléon creates—but focuses on the historical steps that would have to be taken in order to get *there* from *here*, and the kinds of obstacles that would have to be overcome. By flattening those obstacles as summarily as he does, the author highlights by means of manifest unlikelihood the true magnitude and insurmountability that those obstacles present in the tragically real history in which we find ourselves stranded.

It might be significant that Geoffroy published his novel only two years after Félix Bodin published *Le Roman de l'avenir* (1834; tr. as *The Novel of the Future*),[1] which also pioneered, or attempted to pioneer, a new genre, that of *roman futuriste* [futuristic fiction]. There had, of course, been fictitious visions of the future before, but Bodin argued that they all fitted into one of two categories: utopian images of social amelioration or apocalyptic vision of doom, painting hopes or fears but not producing works of fiction that represented a potential future as it might seem to the people living it, dealing imaginatively with the future as Walter Scott had dealt imaginatively with the past. Geoffroy does not attempt something similar in the sense that he tries to set a conventional novel in his alternative world—his is definitely a fictitious narrative history—but he is similarly attempting something new and unprecedented by tinkering with the previously taken-for-granted "rules" and conventions of fiction, to remove it from the straightjacket of mimetic representation, and might have taken some inspiration from Bodin.

There is, too, a sense in which Geoffroy's novel is futuristic, even though it is set in the past, because the past it describes, having branched away from the recorded past, advances and evolves more rapidly into its own future, overtak-

---

[1] Black Coat Press, ISBN 978-1-934543-44-3.

ing ours in its amelioration, not only politically but scientifically and artistically. The geographical and scientific discoveries made in the world of the text are all discoveries that remained unmade but potentially makeable in the 1836 in which the novel was issued. Hindsight informs us that very few of them came to pass—that there is no inland sea in the heart of Australia, no buried city of antediluvian antiquity in Mexico, no Tower of Babel in the ruins of Babylon, and that the methods of steering balloons and enhancing the human sensorium described in his chapter on scientific advances under the aegis the Universal Monarchy were pipe-dreams—but that is not the point; the point is that the story does look forward to a wonderland of as-yet-untapped possibility awaiting human effort, and although the specifics of that vision are mostly mistaken, the fundamental assertion is true and the emphasis the author put upon it entirely justified.

In fact, Bodin's exercise and Geoffroy's were both products of a new surge of thought and literary endeavor, which were certainly not typical, but nevertheless firmly rooted therein, and perhaps deserve to be reckoned among its finest achievements. Geoffroy's novel clearly illustrates and pays homage to that affiliation. Unlike the real Napoléon, Geoffroy's makes the effort to reconcile himself with one of his most high-profile critics, Madame de Staël, not only seducing her with his sudden goodwill but ordering the Académie Française to admit her as a member, immediately, with no regard for a constitution that has no scope for female admission. In so doing, the Emperor credits his conversion to his reading of two of her books, one of which was one of the leading exemplars of the French Romantic Movement, while the other gave it its name. When he lists the important publications of the 1820s in his alternative history he includes masterpieces (all unknown in our history) by Alphonse de Lamartine, Victor Hugo, Alfred de Musset, Charles Nodier, Honoré de Balzac, Stendhal and Jules Michelet—all leading participants in the French Movement—as well as adding works by the English Romantics Lord Byron and Walter Scott, written in French following the addition of England to the French Empire, and the "final and most eccentric" work by J. W. Goethe.

When he published his *Napoléon*, Geoffroy would have been aware that Balzac had dedicated the ground-breaking *Père Goriot* (1835) to Geoffroy Saint-Hilaire, identifying a link between Romantic literature and Romantic philosophy and science that was one of the key features of the Movement. Even though there is nothing Balzacian about Geoffroy's narrative method and strategy, there is an evident kinship in his own mind between what he was doing and what the key members of Charles Nodier's famous *cénacle* were trying to do. As to whether Geoffroy attended meetings of that *cénacle* himself, we can only speculate, but a biographical note on his father in a book co-authored by Nodier mentions that Marc-Antoine Geoffroy-Château left behind several unpublished manuscripts, and Nodier might well have got that information from Geoffroy. Prior to becoming the first classic novel of alternative history, therefore, Geoffroy's work is primarily, essentially and spectacularly an embodiment of the spirit of Romanticism, and its utopian dreams and excessive glorification of its hero need to be seen in that light if they are to be fully understood.

The novel has mostly been seen, in retrospect, as an earnest glorification of Napoléon, and if its author ever took his theoretical status as the Emperor's adoptive son seriously, he reason enough for hero-worship, but its most conspicuous feature is its sharp wit; although straight-faced, it is in places an exceedingly sarcastic text, and also deliberately shocking in places, in describing its hero's occasional inclination to vengeful violence, not merely in his savage slaughter of civilians in Afghanistan, but also in his ruthless destruction of the adherents and monuments of Islam. Its rhetoric is sometimes difficult to evaluate—it is not at all certain whether the reader is intended to sympathize with the Emperor or General Oudet in the digression describing their strange encounter—but we can be reasonably certain that its perennial fascination with rank, pomp, the height of thrones and the dimensions of monuments is not straightforwardly sincere.

Although it is difficult, in consequence, to measure the exact depth of its satire, it remains the case that the publication of the book in 1836 and again—this time with the author's signature—in 1841, was not without bravery. Louis-Philippe was not as repressive a king as Charles X, but he was not unready to banish people who offended him, and Bonapartist sympathies were definitely one of the things that was liable to offend him—Louis-Napoléon, the future Emperor Napoléon III, spent a lot of time in exile or in prison, although his habit of trying to organize conspiracies and coups certainly contributed to that unpopularity. It is probably significant, as a symptom of diplomacy, that Louis-Philippe and Louis-Napoléon are both relegated to its unspecified background, while the leading architects of the July 1830 "revolution" are treated relatively kindly, but that still leaves plenty of material in the story to which Louis-Philippe or his agents might have taken exception. That aspect of the book's history also needs to be borne in mind if it is to be appreciated fully, and its achievement accurately measured.

The novel's classic status is not in doubt, and it is one of the key works in the evolution of French *roman scientifique*, but it is by no means merely of historical interest. It does need to be read in historical context (I have tried to fill in the bare bones of that context with footnotes, admittedly at the cost of overloading the text somewhat in its early chapters) but if it is read with an awareness of that sort, it reveals itself as a rich and profound work that still has a great deal to offer the contemporary reader, and still has a challenge to pose to ideas and ideals of social progress.

This translation was made from a copy of Tallandier's facsimile reprint of the 1896 edition, published in 1983.

Brian Stableford

# THE APOCRYPHAL NAPOLEON

## BOOK ONE

### Chapter One
### MOSCOW

Old Russians have more than love for their ancient capital; it is devotion. For them, Moscow is the holy city, and its sight reminds them of God; so, when they arrive on Mount Salvation and they perceive their Jerusalem, they kneel down and salute it by making the sign of the cross.

The French army, arriving on the fourteenth of September on the summit of that mountain, had something of the enthusiasm of the Muscovites; and when the Emperor, having moved a few toises ahead of the silently climbing army, was the first to set foot on the topmost ridge, and he shouted "Soldiers! Behold Moscow!" that cry was repeated like thunder, and the last ranks, who could not see anything yet, also cried: "Behold Moscow!"

It was there, that city, with its thirty-two districts, its thousand bell-towers, its golden cupolas ; its Oriental, Indian, Gothic and Christian spires; an immense city undulating among the numerous hills on which it rests, as if a caravan of all the peoples in the world had paused there and erected its tents.

The French army, deploying over Mount Salvation, contemplated that magnificent spectacle, parading dazzled eyes over the heavy towers of the Kremlin with the great bell tower Ivan sparkling.

"There it is!" said the Emperor, spurring his white horse, and he traversed the ranks with the splendor of the conqueror illuminating his face.

Meanwhile, the army continued its march.

"Halt!" he cried; and his order tumbled like a cascade over all the ranks, a thousand obedient voices, from Maréchal to sergeant, shouting "Halt!" in their turn.

The generals gathered around him, and he held council before the holy city.

It appeared calm and submissive, like a vanquished enemy, trembling, but perhaps too silent.

The general was waiting for it to speak.

"They're not coming," he murmured; and he marched rapidly into the midst of his men, who stepped back as he approached, on the lookout for whatever thought escaped his lowered eyes.

Then, a quarter of an hour later, as he grew tired of waiting for something, he asked King Murat[2] what the calm signified.

"Who would have thought," he said, "that some boyar would not have come out of the capital with the useless golden keys of the city?"

At the same time, an orderly officer appeared; he announced that General Miloradovich[3] had evacuated the city and that his rearguard had already left.

---

[2] Joachim Murat (1767-1815) was Napoléon's brother-in-law, married to his sister, Catherine; he captured the canons that fired Napoléon's famous "whiff of grapeshot" in 1795 and fought beside him from then on; he was appointed King of Naples, or King of the Two Sicilies, in 1808. In our history he attempted to hold on to his crown after Napoléon's fall but was defeated in battle, and fled to Corsica; he tried unsuccessfully to organize an insurrection in Calabria, but was captured, charged with treason and shot.

[3] Mikhail Miloradovich (1725-1798) negotiated the surrender of Moscow in the wake of the battle of Borodino.

Another officer came then with a few Frenchmen found at the gates of Moscow; they told him that it was deserted.

Two hundred and fifty thousand Muscovites had withdrawn from their Jerusalem.

Moscow was deserted.

"Forward march, then," said the Emperor. "It's for my army to repopulate it."

## Chapter II
## ROSTOPCHIN

Napoléon liked to sleep in the beds of other kings and to repose in the palaces from which his appearance exiled them. The army received the order to remain in the outlying districts, while he went straight to the Kremlin, and there, when evening came, he strolled in the highest towers, alone and silent, gazing at the calm of a city devoid of life and a sky devoid of sun; all that was bleak and dolorous for such an active soul.

He saw his army, established in the distant districts; in the city, a long silence reigned, and calm everywhere, except for a few scattered palaces that seemed to be animated by the presence of generals who had chosen them for their dwellings.

Only the barbaric cries, Scythian voices, were audible at intervals; one might have thought that they were responding to one another.

Midnight chimed. The horizon turned red. From the middle of the city flames rose up; it was the bazaar that was burning, then the churches, then the houses, and then the suburbs; fire burst forth everywhere; Moscow reappeared in the darkness, sparkling, with its thousand flaming bell-towers and its cupolas of fire.

The Emperor understood that disaster; he remembered Wilna, Smolensk and the burning villages that had strewn his route.

"Let it die, then!" he cried, and he gave orders for the army to leave the infernal city immediately.

The soldiers had already woken up before that order. The cry of "Fire!" resounded everywhere, but only uttered by French voices, and the first sleep in the conquered city had been troubled by the horror of the conflagration.

The orders were carried out. At five o'clock in the morning, the troops fell back outside Moscow and reclimbed the slope of Mount Salvation. Scouts had penetrated as far as

Petrovsky, a palace of the czars a league from the capital, preparing it for the Emperor, who went there with his general staff, and, half a league further on, a manor of grandiose appearance having been identified, General Kirgener[4] went there with the engineers in order to take possession of it and fortify the position.

Within view of the manor, however, only a few rifleshots away, swirls of smoke were seen escaping from it, followed by bright flames and partial explosions. The magnificent habitation, enveloped completely, soon appeared to be nothing but an immense hearth. In the distance, a few carriages were drawing away with great rapidity. General Kirgener ordered their pursuit, but they were so far ahead that there was no chance of catching them, and they were already disappearing from view when they fell into the midst of a party of Frenchmen. Other soldiers arrived and took them to the general.

In the principal carriage there was a middle-aged man, tall and thin, with a grave face and a high forehead; at the first attack he had tried to defend himself, but, seeing that longer resistance was vain, he surrendered and appeared before General Kirgener, who, not recognizing any external sign on the stranger, asked him his name.

"What does it matter to you?" replied the unknown man.

Irritated by that response, which he thought insolent, the General was already thinking that he ought to take vengeance for it when the unknown man said to him: "My position is such, Monsieur, that it is to the Emperor alone that I ought to speak and make myself known."

The general hesitated, but the man's self-confidence caused him to give in, and he sent him to Petrovsky.

The Emperor was visiting the posts of that residence and traversing one of the courtyards when the unknown man's carriage came into it. An officer who was following it dismounted and made known the circumstances of the capture

---

[4] François Joseph Kirgener, Baron de Planta (1766-1813).

and the prisoner's intention only to explain himself to the Emperor.

Napoléon looked at the stranger fixedly, gave the order to evacuate the courtyard, and, when he was alone with Duroc[5] and the man he asked: "Who are you?"

"A man who thought he could escape Your Majesty's vengeance but who, charged with an immense action, has no fear of rendering himself responsible and making himself known. I am the governor of Moscow, Rostopchin.[6]

"And what is that action?" demanded the Emperor, going pale.

"Your Majesty knows that and can see it." And Rostopchin indicated with his arm the lake of fire on which the holy city was drowning.

"The fire!"

"Yes, Sire."

"It's the work of a barbarian, Monsieur; your consciousness of the crime ought to divine the punishment."

"It will be my last sacrifice, Monsieur; I await it calmly."

"A sacrifice! What do you mean?"

"I had my entire fortune in Moscow and in my manor house; it was in my own home that the fire was first set. I have sacrificed everything for my fatherland; all that is yet lacking is my life."

"Say that you have sacrificed your fatherland by inundating it with the flames that are reducing it to ashes."

"Since it is only flames and ashes that Your Majesty cannot vanquish!"

---

[5] Géraud Duroc, Duc de Frioul (1772-1813) was the Maréchal responsible for measures taken to secure Napoléon's personal safety, in France and on campaign.

[6] Fyodor Rostopchin (1763-1826) ordered the evacuation of Moscow after Borodino, but left a contingent of police behind with orders to burn the city—he subsequently denied having done so, but eventually admitted it.

The Emperor strode back and forth rapidly, his lips pale and quivering. "What rage!" he said. "What madness! You wanted to be the Russian Brutus, Monsieur, but are they not your children that you have killed?"

"It is for my fatherland to judge me, Sire."

"Your fatherland!" He stopped, looking at his with glittering eyes. "Your fatherland! But what tells me that it is not a horrible holocaust that you have made to your sovereign? What tells me that it is not the sacrifice of Moscow to Petersburg, the old Muscovy that you are immolating to the new Russia?" Drawing nearer to him, he said, with a bitter smile: "How much did he pay you for your fire?"

Rostopchin frowned and went pale, perhaps with anger. "Russia will judge me after Your Majesty, and people will speak of me differently, Sire, when I have been shot."

"A firing squad is the execution of the brave, Monsieur, and fire..."

"Can only be a cowardice?"

"An infernal mystery!" murmured Napoléon, stepping back in astonishment. A few seconds later, he added: "If there's nothing in all that but blind patriotism..." He did not complete the sentence.

"Your Majesty has judged me," said Rostopchin, joyfully. "I can die."

"No! You don't deserve it, nor is it worth the effort, probably. Give him a safe conduct. Go, Monsieur, your action remains entirely yours, but whatever it might be, doubt will wither it. Go."

Rostopchin left, and the Emperor went back into the palace.

## Chapter III
## *THE ARMY'S DEPARTURE*

The French army had appeared before Moscow sooner than the Russians expected, so, instead of finding it in ashes, the fire had hardly started when it arrived. The military stores had not been consumed, and immense resources were still found in the city, where the Grande Armée could rest and wait for reinforcements.

Meanwhile, the Emperor, who did not want to let time go by uselessly and who wanted to take advantage of the season, still favorable, ordered the departure for the twentieth of September, and after having assembled a council he decided to march on Petersburg.

On the morning of the twentieth, the Grande Armée, which had been joined by the corps of Eugène and Poniatowski,[7] set forth, numbering one hundred and sixty thousand men and four hundred pieces of artillery. Before its departure it witnessed the last sighs of Moscow; the sea of fire had devoured itself, and the palpitating city was only throwing off a few swirls of smoke and ash here and there. The Emperor, showing it to the army disdainfully, and for the last time,

---

[7] Eugène de Beauharnais (1781-1824) was Napoléon's stepson, the son of the Empress Josephine; he was appointed Viceroy of Italy by Napoléon and was in command of the Fourth corps during the Russian campaign; in our history he took command of the retreating army after Napoléon and Murat left it. Prince Jozef Poniatowski (1763-1813) was in command of the Fifth Corps during the Russian campaign; his Polish troops were the first to enter Moscow on 14 September, and he fought in the rearguard during the retreat.

said: "There is only one capital of Russia now; let's march on it."[8]

---

[8] In our history, Napoléon stayed in Moscow for a month, trying to negotiate a peace with Alexander I, unsuccessfully. He then advanced on Kaluga, but the Russians refused to commit themselves to a pitched battle, continuing to harass the exhausted French army until it was forced to retreat; hunger and cold devastated the forces, which eventually suffered fatal casualties well in advance of three hundred thousand, with a further hundred thousand taken prisoner—losses from which it never recovered.

## Chapter IV
## THE BATTLE OF NOVOGOROD

The order had been given to all the divisions of the French army disseminated in the various Russian provinces to rally to the road from Moscow to Saint Petersburg. Forty thousand Prussians and Austrians joined the Emperor at Volokolamsk. Further on, the divisions of Grouchy and Latour-Maubourg[9] joined the corps of the King of Naples, of which they became part, and after them the troops of the Kingdom of Italy and the Germanic Confederation arrived.

It was on the road to Saint Petersburg that the Battle of Klin took place on the twenty-third and the Battle of Twer on the twenty-sixth, where the Russians lost five thousand men. The following day, another division of the French army, commanded by General Montbrun, beat them again at Staritza. In the latter affair, General Montbrun was mortally wounded and immediately replaced in his command by General Caulaincourt.[10]

Meanwhile, the Grande Armée, ever victorious and two hundred and fifty thousand men strong, traveled toward Saint Petersburg with great celerity. For his part, the Emperor Alexander had recalled all the forces of the Empire to him. The Royal Prince of Sweden, Bernadotte, his ally, had joined him

---

[9] Emmanuel de Grouchy (1766-1847) was commander of the Third Cavalry during the Russian campaign; he commanded the escort squadron during the retreat. Victor de Fay de La Tour-Maubourg (1768-1850) was in command of the Fourth Cavalry.

[10] Louis-Pierre Montbrun (1770-1812) was actually killed at Borodino while commanding the Second Cavalry. Armand Caulaincourt, Duc de Vicenza (1773-1827) was Napoléon's Grand Ecuyer during the Russian campaign, in charge of maintaining his horses and riding at his left side.

with thirty thousand Swedes.[11] In addition, he had received via the Baltic ports a reinforcement of twenty-five thousand English troops. He concentrated his formidable forces in Novogorod and its environs, had the city fortified, and waited, with an army at least equal in number to the French army, for the Emperor Napoléon, who was advancing from victory to victory along the magnificent road between the two capitals.

On the seventh of October, on a cloudless sunny day, the two great enemy armies perceived one another and deployed to face one another. The movement of those immense forces having taken a long time, however, night fell and God postponed his decision of the destiny of Europe until the following day.

The next day, the eighth of October, arrived, and the great battle took place. What a battle! And what a victory! Europe and the world know them, and there is no need to give other details here than those that the Emperor dictated himself in the rapid bulletin that we shall transcribe here:

### Bulletin of the Grande Armée

*Novogorod 9 October 1812.*

The day of 8 October will be glorious among all the days of glory.

The Grande Armée has fulfilled the Emperor's expectations; the Battle of Novogorod will make it forever illustrious.

Three hundred thousand Russians, Swedes and Englishmen had taken up positions under the walls of the city and in the plain preceding it, around the road to Twer.

---

[11] Jean Bernadotte (1763-1844) was appointed a Maréchal of France and Prince of Pontecorvo while serving under Napoléon, but broke with him in 1810 when he was elected Crown Prince and effective Regent of Sweden, founding its royal dynasty; in 1813 he allied Sweden with Napoléon's enemies.

The French army, two hundred and fifty thousand strong, occupied the whole of the left side of the road and the three hills overlooking Novogorod.

The battle commenced at nine a.m.; by four p.m. it was all over.

Sixty thousand men of the enemy army are dead, more than seventy thousand have been taken prisoner; the rest have drowned in the lake or dissipated before us.

At two p.m. Maréchal Kellermann, at the head of his division, was hit by a cannonball in the lower abdomen and died on the battlefield.[12]

Emperor Alexander and Maréchal Bernadotte, placed on one of the heights to the right of the road were outflanked by General Compans and have been taken prisoner.[13]

Of twenty-five thousand English troops, scarcely two thousand were able to escape death.

The Grande Armée has lost about six thousand men and has eight thousand wounded.

---

[12] François-Étienne de Kellermann, later Duc de Valmy (1770-1835) was on sick leave during the Russian campaign, so he survived in our world to lead the Fourth Cavalry and then to fight at Waterloo, where the futile cavalry charges he ordered were considered by some later analysts to have helped lose the battle. He was a fervent opponent of the Bourbons in the peers' Chambre during the Restoration, after succeeding his father there.

[13] Jean-Dominique Compans (1769-1845) rose through the ranks after enlisting as a volunteer in 1789, and continued his military career after Napoléon's initial fall, serving on Louis XVIII's council of war after the Restoration. Although he supported Napoléon during the Hundred Days he refused the command that would have involved him in Waterloo and was subsequently awarded a peerage by Louis XVIII, opposing the Duc de Valmy in the Chambre.

The Emperor has continued forward toward Saint Petersburg, taking the Czar and the ex-Crown Prince of Sweden with him.

The enemy army has lost the English commander-in-chief, three field marshals and twenty-two general officers.

We have to regret, as well as Maréchal Kellermann, the brave General Friant and several other generals.[14]

Generals Grouchy and Rapp have been wounded.[15]

Soldiers, your bravery and your conduct have been admirable; I thank you for that.

Napoléon

Such was the bulletin, a faithful and still confused expression of the miracles of that day; it had been a long time since history had witnessed such a disaster, and the catastrophe of two sovereigns falling into the power of a victor.

Without deigning to see them, the Emperor continued his rapid march with his army toward Saint Petersburg; it was there that he wanted to treat with his enemies.

---

[14] Louis Friant (1758-1829) was seriously wounded at Borodino and left behind, only rejoining the army during the retreat. He was colonel-in-chief of the Old Guard grenadiers during the Hundred Days and was wounded again at Waterloo.

[15] Jean Rapp (1771-1821) was another heroic general who rose through the ranks. He was wounded at Moscow, and again while fighting a rearguard action during the retreat. He commanded the Fifth Corps during the Hundred Days, but was otherwise engaged during Waterloo. He attempted to leave the army thereafter, but his resignation was refused.

## Chapter V
## SAINT PETERSBURG

On the fifteenth of October, the Emperor, with the Grande Armée, advanced on the walls of Saint Petersburg. Half a league from the city an immense cortege was seen; it was the Senate, followed by all the authorities and the people, with Prince Constantin at their head, who had come to bring Napoléon the golden keys to that capital city of Russia.

The Emperor received them gravely and without response. He did not permit the Senate and the Czar's brother to communicate with the Imperial prisoner; it was only in Saint Petersburg that he wanted to make his intentions known.

He entered it that same evening, and his officers prepared the Imperial Palace for him, where he slept.

Emperor Alexander was lodged in Prince Constantin's palace and Bernadotte was relegated to one of the wings of the Imperial Palace, under guard.

The entry of an immense and victorious army into the magnificent city of Saint Petersburg had attracted a crowd and general admiration. The newspapers of the day recounted the addresses, the flatteries and the brilliant fêtes that welcomed the French, but the Emperor refused all the tributes and did not want to receive anyone until he had settled the interests of the empires.

On the next day, the seventeenth of October, he had an interview with the Emperor Alexander announced; Bernadotte was summoned to it. The Emperor appeared there with the King of Naples and Prince Eugène. The interview lasted two hours and took place in the palace of the Czars. Three seats were arranged at a table; Napoléon, Alexander and Murat occupied them; Bernadotte and Eugène remained standing.

"Finally," said the Emperor," speaking first, "this war is over, and you are both my prisoners; but I distinguish between your actions. You, Sire, were fighting for Russia, for your country. You, Monsieur le Maréchal"—he was addressing Bernadotte—"have forgotten that you were French and have taken up arms against France!"

Bernadotte wanted to reply, and said that, Sweden having become his fatherland, he had been obliged to forget everything in order to devote himself entirely to her.

"Silence!" said the Emperor, severely, and added: "Well, that new fatherland is no longer yours; you have become a Maréchal de France again, Monsieur, and it will be up to you not to forget it again. The Duc de Valmy's division no longer has a commander; you will replace him. You are no longer Prince of Sweden; remember that I give you orders and no longer treat with you. Go."

Maréchal Bernadotte went out with Prince Eugène. The King of Naples followed them a few minutes later.

Left alone, the two emperors talked with a coldness and constraint that bore little resemblance to the brilliant and amicable conversation at Tilsit.[16]

Napoléon spoke as a victor; the Czar, a prisoner and defeated, scarcely disputed the concessions that were imposed on him as orders. Soon, the Ministers of State came in and drafted the bases of a treaty that the Emperor wanted to keep secret, for it was then, for the first time, that he promulgated as a decree emanating from himself alone the results of treaties that he had signed with the other powers.

His decree was delayed by the communications that had to be made with Sweden and Denmark, after the forced assent of those two crowns and that already obtained from Austria and Prussia.

It was decreed:

That the kingdom of Poland was reestablished in its integrity, such as it had existed before the first division;

---

[16] The treaty Napoléon signed with Alexander at Tilsit on 7 July 1807 was the first of two, the second being with Prussia two days later; their terms gave Napoléon control of Central Europe.

That Finland was returned to Sweden, which ceded Norway to Denmark;

The Duchy of Holstein was reunited with the Empire and divided into three French départements;

The dignity of the Crown Prince of Sweden was withdrawn from Maréchal Bernadotte, with the consent of the Emperor and the states of Sweden;

The King of Sweden was to pay France an annual tribute of five million francs;

The Emperor of Russia, in addition to an indemnity of a hundred and fifty million rubles for the expenses of the war, would also contribute to the treasury of the Empire an annual tribute of twenty million francs;

The prisoners taken by both sides would be returned.

Those were the principal dispositions of the famous Decree of Saint Petersburg, a decree crushing for the vanquished States, of which two articles were not made known, kept secret in order to avoid a final humiliation for the two sovereigns.

That was to put at the disposal of the Empire two fleets, Swedish and Russian, and a part of the military forces of the two States.

Napoléon's politics followed, everywhere and incessantly, his idea of the conquest of England.

## Chapter VI
## *PONIATOWSKI*

Napoléon knew what strength he as giving himself in the north of Europe by reestablishing the Kingdom of Poland. It was in him that the chivalrous nation in question had hoped, which, for fifty years, had been seeking to reunite the disparate limbs of the fatherland. Their hope changed to adoration when they saw their Poland reborn, as complete and as strong as it had been before the conquests and the dismemberments.

If anything could increase their gratitude further, it was the name of the king that Napoléon had chosen for them.

Poniatowski, without a throne, without Estates and without a scepter, was still the King of the Poles; he was the nephew of Stanislaw August, their last sovereign, and the great name of Poniatowski had a charm for them that the glory of the young hero, who bore it so well, further increased.

Prince Poniatowski had not quit the French army during the war. He was with the Emperor at Saint Petersburg when the principal members of the most illustrious families of Poland arrived there, in response to orders they had received in advance. On the twentieth of October, Napoléon summoned them to the palace of the Senate; he appeared in the midst of those palatines himself, accompanied by the young prince, and, amid expectation and profound silence, he said:

"Poles, Poland is reborn; she reappears powerful among the other States of Europe. For a long time I have been meditating the moment of her resurrection.

"Poles, your devotion to my person and your admirable courage have inspired my gratitude. Today, I am paying my debt. You have a fatherland, and here is your king!"

At that moment, Napoléon lowered his hand upon the head of Poniatowski, who was standing beneath him. It was thus that he designated him, and that gesture and those words were greeted by cries of enthusiasm and admiration.

He added: "Your constitution was old, and discordant with the order established in Europe. I have occupied myself with its revision, as a father who will always regard you as equals of his other children. Let this day forever be a festival among you, for it is that of the restoration of Poland!"

These final words were received with less enthusiasm: a kind of silent stupor contrasted, in some, with the enthusiasm of others. In fact, the last words informed Poland that her old privileges were annulled, and that henceforth, she was no more than a vassal of France—but in sum, she existed, and the joy was great.

Napoléon had noticed the mixed impression that his speech had left, but without appearing to take exception to it, he beckoned to Prince Poniatowski to approach.

Having climbed a few steps, the latter knelt down before the Emperor and deposited his sword, that of a French general, in his hands. The Emperor received it, lifted him to his feet, and gave him a golden crown, and the two of them embraced. Then, having traversed a gallery, they reappeared together on a balcony of the palace, where they were rejoined by Emperor Alexander, who had abstained until then in appearing at the investiture of a kingdom he was losing.

Thus was Poland reestablished.

## Chapter VI
## THE YEAR 1813

Napoléon wanted to stay in Saint Petersburg throughout the winter; he was glad to annihilate by his presence the imperial enemy that he had taken ten years to defeat. Now that he reigned in its empire, and was resident in its palace, he prolonged at his leisure the great effect of his victories, perhaps in order to make the Russian nations understand more fully that above their czar there was an even more formidable omnipotence, and that Napoléon was between Alexander and God.

Saint Petersburg was, in any case, an admirable city in which to reside: a new city, expressly designed to be a capital, without the remnants of an old city having mastered the action of those who wanted to regenerate and embellish them, as in the other cities of the world. There, a great sovereign, scarcely a century before, had traced the lines, marked out the squares and indicated the edifices, and suddenly, at his will, marvelous constructions had come in an obedient host to aggregate and line up in that desert, and maneuver in that space, like an army of palaces and temples, with an admirable order. An immense population had immediately arrived, and the young capital of Europe already had all the characteristics of human eternity.

What creation had made at a stroke in Saint Petersburg, what fire had half-achieved in London, it had required all the slowness of centuries to effectuate in Paris, but Napoléon was strong enough to compress time in his hands, and he promised himself the prompt regeneration of his cherished city, in the midst of his studies of the conquered city.

Meanwhile, the Russian troops, dislocated, so to speak, were disseminated throughout the Muscovite empire, and above all toward the Oriental extremities, while the Grande Armée was aggregated within the walls of Saint Petersburg and occupied the coast from Riga to Cronstadt, as well as the provinces and cities neighboring the capital. The Emperor also ordered the occupation of Stockholm by the Junot and Régnier divisions,[17] which the Russian fleets transported over the sea; and, master of the capitals of the North, surrounded by his forces, he assigned his armies the coasts of the Baltic for their winter quarters, and, from the height of submissive Europe, he set about governing France.

In that epoch, three unknown generals, Malet, Lahorie and Guidal attempted by an insensate conspiracy, whose cause and range have never been fully understood, to overturn the imperial government. It was in the prisons that the men had woven their plot, which expired, so to speak, on the threshold of their cells. Napoléon took pity on that mad attempt and, by an act of disdain, ordered the three men to be set free—"in order that they can conspire in the open air," he said.[18]

However, decrees arrived incessantly in France from Saint Petersburg, regulating everything and administrating everything with the great wisdom that is so useful when it emanates from such a high power. The kingdoms that had become French, the interior départements, and the various administrations received organizations that always ameliorated the existing state of things, without too rapid a disruption of the past, which had to enter to a considerable extent in what was being regenerated.

---

[17] Jean-Andoche Junot, Duc d'Abrantès (1771-1813) rose through the ranks to command the Eighth corps at Borodino; rumor has it that he might have faked his death and gone to America. The Régnier indicated cannot be the administrator Claude-Ambroise Régnier, or either of the two Napoleonic Generals of that name, both of whom died before the Russian campaign, so the reference remains enigmatic.

[18] The so-called Malet conspiracy, named for Claude-François de Malet, produced an attempted *coup d'état* on 23 October 1812, which failed dismally. In our history the leading conspirators, including Victor La Horie and Maximin Guidal, were executed.

Paris, above all, was the constant object of his thought; it was there that all the magnificence, luxury and grandiosity of his ideas were accumulated; it was like a poetry in the midst of his labors. He took pleasure, so far from his capital, in creating numerous squares there, in radiating plantations in the middle of new streets in all directions, and in sowing public fountains and statues in bronze and marble of the great men of the fatherland. The decree of 5 December determined the opening and the immediate construction of the famous Rue Impériale, projected since Louis XIV, which was concluded in 1816, a magnificent French thoroughfare departing from the Louvre and progressing in a straight line all the way to the Barrière du Trône, twenty-four feet wide, planted with four rows of trees and bordered, throughout its extent, but superb and symmetrical palaces with galleries under two lines of arcades and columns.

In the midst of those works, the omnipotence deployed with so much splendor in the vanquished nation, and a more mysterious but no less decisive diplomatic action that increasingly submitted northern Europe to the politics of the French Empire, the year 1813 dawned brilliant with glory for Napoléon and showed the situation in Europe, in his regard, as follows:

*Countries under the direct domination*
*of the Emperor Napoléon:*

France
Holland
Hanover
Oldenburg
Italy
Illyria

*Under the domination of his family:*

Spain

Naples
Portugal
Westphalia

*Under his indirect domination:*

The confederation of the Rhine, Bavaria, Wurtemburg, Saxe, Baden, etc.
Switzerland
Poland, vassal
Sweden, tributary
Russia, ditto.
Austria, ally furnishing troops and money
Prussia, ditto.
Denmark, ditto.

*Remaining outside that influence:*

Sardinia
Turkey
England

Which is to say that there were now only two nations in Europe: the first and last on the list, France and England.

## Chapter VII
## HAMBURG

The Emperor left Saint Petersburg and Russia at the beginning of April 1813. He had thought about leaving an army of occupation in the capital, but, yielding to the pleas of Alexander, and satisfied in addition by other important guarantees, he had the city evacuated by his troops, left considerable forces in Cronstadt, and embarked in that port for Stockholm.

The Czar had accompanied Napoléon to Cronstadt. Charles XIV, the King of Sweden, also came to meet him with the keys to his city, for it seemed to him that he already had none but kings for guards. He entered the capital as victor and master and only the tricolor flag floated over all its edifices, in order that everyone would know that Stockholm was filled by Napoléon.

He thus accomplished his destiny of setting his foot on all the capitals of the world.

His sojourn in Stockholm was short; that city, agreeable but mediocre in population and in power, soon bored him. Sweden is a nation that has no strength of its own and can only place a weight in the balance of European coalitions. That satellite politics had such scant importance in the Emperor's eyes, especially in that epoch, that he thought he ought not to occupy himself in measuring it or weakening it, and, soon disengaged from his futile relations with Charles XIV, he embarked for Danzig.

He did not stop for long in that city and went on almost immediately to Hamburg, where he had convened for 11 May a conference of continental kings.

All the kings had already arrived, having brought the magnificence of their courts with them, fusing them all to make a single court and a magnificence worthy of Napoléon. He soon arrived himself with the Kings of Naples and Westphalia,[19] and his reception in the main hall of the Senate Palace had the incredible feature that there were only sovereigns waiting there to welcome him.

There were the emperors of Austria and Russia, the Kings of Prussia, Bavaria, Saxony, Wurtemburg, Sweden and Poland.

In a preliminary room were the sovereign princes of the Confederation of the Rhine, the ambassadors of Turkey and Switzerland and the prime ministers of the powers. Napoléon traversed that first room slowly, and the High Chamberlain, opening the door of the one where the sovereigns were, said in a resounding voice: "The Emperor!"

At that name, the two emperors and the kings rose to their feet and, by a simultaneous homage, seemed to recognize his omnipotence

Napoléon, having sat down in the middle of them, immediately got down o business, explained the purpose of the conference and fixed the bases and the hours of the sessions. He concluded by sending them to the splendid feasts that the marshal of the palace had prepared on is orders.

From that room the Emperor passed into a long gallery and, conducted by the Emperor of Austria, entered an admirable room where the most dazzling spectacle came to delight his gaze.

On a throne was the Empress Marie-Louise,[20] with her son the King of Rome, and around her, as if she were laden

---

[19] The King of Westphalia was Napoléon's youngest brother Jérôme (1784-1860). In our history he served in several official roles during the Second Empire.

[20] Marie Louise, Duchesse de Parma (1791-1847) was the eldest child of Emperor Francis II of Austria, who became Napoléon's second wife in 1810 in a political marriage designed to cement peace between France and Austria, which had long been in conflict. In our history she ruled Parma and two other duchies after Napoléon's exile, and after his death in 1821 she married twice more.

with diamonds and sparkling ornaments, were the Empress of Austria, six queens and the Emperor's sisters. The most resplendent of all of them were the Princess Borghèse and the beautiful Queen of Prussia, slightly confused, whose cheeks were tinted with bright incarnadine.[21]

But Napoléon only saw his wife and his son; he embraced them warmly. That surprise was worth a triumph for his heart, and he expressed his gratitude tenderly for an unexpected meeting prepared with such gracious mystery. He stayed for quite some time in the midst of that court of queens, and the whirlwind of pleasures commenced that same evening.

Every morning was reserved for the sovereigns' political conferences. The ministers were sometimes summoned to them. In the evening there were continual fêtes, sumptuous feasts, firework displays over the Elbe and in the gardens, and finally balls ad spectacles of a marvelous magnificence.

French and Italian actors had been summoned to Hamburg to enchant that flower-bed of kings. During a performance of *Cinna*,[22] Napoléon received a letter, which he opened and read. A flash of joy was observed in his expression, immediately suppressed by a somber frown; he had just learned of the death of Monsieur Pozzo di Borgo.[23]

---

[21] Princess Borghèse was Napoléon's sister Pauline (1780-1825), whose second marriage—another political affair—was to Camillo Borghese, Prince of Suimona. In our history there was no Queen of Prussia in 1812, Friedrich Wilhelm III's wife, Louise of Mecklenburg-Strelitz, having died in 1810

[22] Pierre Corneille's tragedy of 1771.

[23] The Corsican politician Carlo Andrea Pozzo di Borgo (1764-1842) was closely associated with Napoléon when he was a delegate to the French National Assembly in the early 1790s, but his family and the Bonapartes belonged to different clans with a long history of feuding, and they fell out. Pozzo accepted the presidency of the island when it became a British protectorate; for the rest of his life, as a peripatetic diplomat, he was one of Napoléon's bitterest enemies, helping to negoti-

There was between Napoléon and Pozzo di Borgo an implacable hatred, a Corsican hatred born with them and not even extinguishable by death. For ten years Pozzo di Borgo had been running around Europe fleeing before the treaties and conquests, always taking refuge where there was an enemy of Napoléon, in order to stir up hatred and inspire him to war: a sublime vendetta in which the ambush and the dagger were battlefields and armies.

Pozzo di Borgo had left Saint Petersburg a few days before the Emperor's entry; he had been going to England, where the ship that was carrying him was wrecked within sight of Scotland, without any rescue being possible.

That death was a victory for Napoléon, who could not dissimulate his joy at first. Was the somber emotion that followed it regret for an involuntary joy or for an incomplete vengeance?

The splendid fêtes continued, however; those in Dresden, which in the same month of the previous year had been so brilliant, could not be compared to them. The Emperor of Russia and the King of Sweden, lacking then, enemies that were to be vanquished, augmented the crowd today, vanquished and tributary.

Napoléon appeared in the first rank everywhere, and people were already accustomed to naming him the king of kings.

For him, that pomp and ostentation only occupied his thoughts marginally; he had other concerns, and beneath that splendor he was agitating the destiny of England.

---

ate Bernadotte's alliance with Alexander. In our history he fought for Wellington at Waterloo and then supported the restored Bourbon monarchy.

## Chapter IX
## SPANISH AFFAIRS

Every people has its genius, and it is that genius which it is necessary to subdue, even more than it power, to assure a conqueror of its domination.

In Russia, Napoléon had tried to compress the thought of aggrandizement; he had taken Poland back from that empire; he had driven back Germany, and in the North he had withdrawn important provinces. He had not been able to do more then, because the Orient remained outside his politics, but he probably sensed that everything was not settled in that direction.

In England, that other great enemy, it is the monopoly of world commerce that is her politics and her genius, and while awaiting more, the Emperor developed and made sure more vigorously than ever of the execution of the Decree of Berlin regarding the continental system.[24]

But Napoléon was not unaware that he still had in the south of Europe two formidable antagonisms that his victories had not been able to weaken, and whose development his politics had not been able to stop.

In Spain, there was the fanaticism of religion and the former royalty, with which a few principles of liberty were beginning to be allied.

---

[24] Napoléon's Berlin Decree of 1806, following the French victory over the Prussians at Jena, forbade the importation of British goods to countries dependent on or allied with France; it was a significant innovation in economic warfare, reinforced by the Milan Decree of 1807, but it misfired badly; the French navy could not police it adequately on the high seas and it prompted international smuggling on a colossal scale, ultimately doing less damage to the British economy than that of France.

In Italy, and even in France, the captive and fulminating papacy held peoples in suspense, refusing them their priests and bishops, and simultaneously inspiring terror by means of its excommunications and pity by its miseries.

Thus, after the subjugation of the north of Europe, three forces still remained to be vanquished: England, the Pope and Spain.

Spain, overturned five years before by the civil war, burned and bloody, was nevertheless proud of her long rebellion. She lifted up the hearts of her children with the triple cry of her religion, her captive kings and liberty, and, so strong herself, she felt herself powerfully supported by the English armies under the command of the Duke of Wellington.

The position of the Peninsula was very grave then, the royalty of Joseph[25] very unsteady, and although Napoléon's success in Russia assured him of much preponderance in the North, Spain remained outside that influence and that atmosphere of victory. The French armies that were fighting there laboriously had been driven back everywhere after considerable disasters, and in spite of signal but sterile victories.

At the beginning of 1813, Portugal had been evacuated by French troops for the third time. The Duc d'Abrantès, obliged to give way before Lord Wellington's superior forces, had withdrawn to Extremadura, where he succeeded in joining up with the army corps of the Duc de Raguse,[26] but in that

_____

[25] Joseph Bonaparte (1768-1844), Napoleon's older brother; he was King of Naples and Sicily from 1808-1808 and King of Spain from 1808-1813; in our history he returned to France in 1813 but spent most of the rest of his life in the United States before returning to Europe in 1932, when, following the death of Napoleon's son, he was regarded by Bonapartists as the rightful Emperor of France, although he did not support that claim and left it to his nephew to adopt the title of Napoléon III

[26] Duc de Raguse was the title given by Napoléon to Auguste de Marmont (1774-1852). He was gravely wounded at the

province again, fate favored the combined armies of Spain and England; the French were driven back to Ciudad-Réal, where an important battle was fought and won by the English general, who, having dissipated two corps of the French army, marched on Madrid and took possession of it, justly proud of having turned the tide of fortune for the first time in twenty years and finding himself, in consequence of his unexpected successes, master of Portugal and half of Spain.

The sublime exaltation of the Spaniards, which cannot be called fanaticism when it is a matter of a sentiment causing one to die for the fatherland, aided those results admirably. In the kingdom of Léon, the Comte de la Romana, at the head of twenty thousand men had defeated the corps of Maréchal Jourdain under the walls of Valladolid, in spite of the heroic efforts of the old warrior, and driven the French out of that part of his territory.[27]

But the successes of the enemy stopped there. The entire east of the Peninsula, from the Pyrenees to Gibraltar, remained submissive to King Joseph. Maréchal Suchet, whose glory in that war will remain imperishable, by means of a series of sieges, like that of Tarragona and the memorable capture of

---

Battle of Salamanca in July 1912 and had to return to France; in our history he returned to action there but switched sides in 1814 when he saw that France could not win, and remained loyal to Louis XVIII during the Hundred Days. He tried to put down the July Revolution of 1830 and was exiled thereafter. The verb *"raguser"* became a synonym in France for betrayal.

[27] Jean-Baptiste Jourdain (1782-1833) was yet another Napoleonic general who rose through the ranks; forced to abandon Madrid after the Battle of Salamanca he and Joseph Bonaparte had to retreat to Valencia, but did turn the tide for a while, until Wellington's crucial victory at Vitoria in June 1813, which wrested Spain completely from French control. In our history he supported the Restoration until he joined Napoléon during the Hundred Days, but then knuckled under again and went into politics.

Valencia, liberated Andalusia and the kingdom of Valencia, while Maréchal Soult, incessantly victorious, never ceased to occupy Catalonia, Aragon and a part of Castille.[28]

That state of things is easily explained. During his gigantic expedition in Russia, Napoléon had withdrawn from Spain in order to gather the formidable forces of his army together, and since their removal successes had been divided, the Anglo-Spanish armies even gaining an incontestable advantage. After having quit Madrid, Joseph had retired to Valencia; it as there that he heard the disastrous news of the Battle of Arapiles, won by Wellington over the Duc de Raguse, which gave the victor the kingdom of Léon and Navarre.

Such was the state of affairs in Spain at the beginning of 1813, when an extraordinary event complicated them further.

---

[28] Louis-Gabriel Suchet, Duc d'Albufera (1770-1826) and Jean-de-Dieu Soult, Duc de Dalmatie (1769-1851) also rose through the ranks. After the victories at Tarragon and Valencia, Suchet was driven back again permanently in our history. He supported the Bourbons initially but incurred the wrath of Louis XVIII when he joined Napoléon during the Hundred Days and was stripped of his peerage. Soult is nowadays notorious for plundering Andalusia while he was its military governor. He also supported Napoléon during the Hundred Days. After 1930 he declared himself a partisan of Louis-Philippe, and had a glittering political career, still in full swing when Geoffroy wrote the present text, serving as Minister of War and Prime Minister. After 1848 he declared himself a Republican, but died a week before Louis-Napoléon's *coup d'état*, thus missing the opportunity to turn his coat again.

## Chapter X
## THE FLIGHT OF FERDINAND VII

At that time, France had become the prison of several sovereigns. Pius VII was a captive at Fontainebleau, Charles IV at Compiègne, the ex-queen of Etruria in Nice and Ferdinand VII and his children at Valençay, a magnificent château belonging to Prince de Talleyrand.[29]

The political police of the Empire maintained a particularly attentive watch on the last residence. It has been thought at first that Ferdinand was disposed to flee and rejoin the English army and his people, but those suspicions had calmed down. During a four year sojourn at Valençay, King Ferdinand, occupied with frivolous concerns, distancing all political ideas, having not made any attempt or manifestation, had ended up reassuring the anxieties of his watchers. He had even resisted with a passive energy whose range it was difficult to estimate the proposition of a carefully-planned escape.

In 1810, Baron Kolly, a Piedmontese and agent of England, had succeeded in reaching Ferdinand, under the disguise of a diamond merchant; he had urged him fervently to flee; everything was prepared to reach the coast of Gascony rapidly, where an English frigate was waiting to transport him to Gibraltar. But Ferdinand, either because he suspected a trap or because he then preferred the repose of his prison to the agi-

---

[29] Charles Maurice de Talleyrand-Périgord (1754-1838), who was Prince de Bénévent before being Prince de Talleyand, was unable to pursue a planned military career because of lameness; he went into the Church instead but then became a diplomat, acting for Napoléon until 1805 but then working against him and working covertly to thwart his ambitions; in our history he negotiated the Bourbon Restoration and then worked for Louis-Philippe, thus earning himself of a reputation as a career turncoat and/or diplomatic genius.

tated risks of flight, rejected any participation in the plot; he did more, and denounced Baron Kolly's steps to the Emperor, with the result that Kolly was arrested in Orléans and shot.

Since that event, the captivity of the prince had been considerably softened; his frequent correspondence with Napoléon set aside any idea of flight; he reproduced two pleas incessantly therein: an alliance with one of the Emperor's nieces, Lucien's elder daughter; and a change of residence, for the sojourn at Valençay had become intolerable to him.

Suddenly, in the early days of February 1813, the news spread through France that Ferdinand VII had disappeared from the Château de Valençay. The searches of the Imperial police were impotent to discover the traces of his flight. Indications cleverly managed by the accomplices of the intrigue encouraged the belief that the prince had taken the road to Lyon or that to Bayonne. The police directed all their efforts in those directions, which the skill and mystery of Canon Escoiquiz, the leader of the conspiracy, rendered fruitless.[30]

In the meantime, the fugitive, unrecognizable in the garments of a woman of the people, headed for Tours and, steering clear of main roads and towns, reached the Atlantic coast, opposite the Île de Noirmoutier, where an English brig was waiting to transport him to Spain.

He disembarked at Santander with his liberator Escoiquiz. He immediately headed for Burgos, where he was received by Generals Wellington, Moore, Mina and Castanos, the Ducs de San Carlos and de l'Infantado, and the grandees and authorities who had remained faithful to his party. He

---

[30] In our history, Napoléon released Ferdinand in December 1813, and he returned to Spain with his close confidant Juan Escoiquiz (1762-1820), with whom he soon fell out. Ferdinand found his rule—now a constitutional monarchy rather than the absolute monarchy he had enjoyed before—a difficult business, complicated by wars of independence in Spain's American colonies, but he clung on to power until his death in 1833, which immediately precipitated a civil war.

reviewed the armies in the city, distributed titles and promotions, and set himself at the head of the English and Spanish troops. On 7 May 1813 he made his entry to Madrid, to enthusiastic cries from the people and the clergy.

Meanwhile, during the previous months, several corps of the Grande Armée in the North had resumed the road to France and had returned to the heart of the Empire. Napoléon, after having settled in the Russian war the destinies that had been at stake there, quit Hamburg and returned to Paris, where he immediately decided on a new expedition in Spain, with considerable forces of which he would take command.

France was immediately agitated by preparations for war; the passages of troops and materiel heading south succeeded ne another without respite, the army corps of the Prince de la Moskowa[31] and the King of Naples met up in the Pyrenees while the troops of the Confederation of the Rhine, entering via Bâle, went into the plains of Toulouse to join forces with those of the Kingdom of Italy. Those formidable forces were only waiting for their Imperial commander to cross the Pyrenees.

Napoléon had returned to Paris on 5 June, but without any great publicity, and had only stayed there for a few days. When the Senate and the great bodies of State came to congratulate him on his latest triumphs, he replied, like Caesar, that nothing was done while things still remained to do.

During that brief sojourn he remained constantly enclosed in the Tuileries, working incessantly and with an indefatigable activity. The major general of the army, Prince de

---

[31] One of the titles created by Napoléon for Michel Ney (1769-1815), the most famous of all the generals who rose through the ranks, dubbed "the bravest of the brave" by Napoléon. His trial for treason and execution by firing squad after Waterloo—in stark contrast to the fate of the other generals who had supported Napoléon during the Hundred Days, some of whom voted for his execution in the peers' Chambre—was one of the great scandals of the era.

Wagram,[32] several Maréchals, the Ministers of War, the Administration of the War and Finance, did not quit the château, where they had established their temporary residence. The other ministers also worked with him frequently. Delivered to such cares he refused any audience, reception fête or ceremony.

It was learned with surprise, however, that that there a marked exception as made to that rule for a celebrated sculptor. Canova[33] was often received by the Emperor, who had already summoned him to Hamburg. No one was unaware of the affection for him borne by the Holy Father; his travels between Fontainebleau and Paris became so frequent and his conferences with the two sovereigns so continual, that public attention was keenly excited and no one doubted that some important result was being prepared by his intermediation.

That opinion was further fortified when it became known that during the Emperor's fifteen-day sojourn in Paris, the King of Naples, Cardinals Fesch and Maury and the Minister of Religion Monsieur de Préameneu[34] had made several successive journeys to the Château de Fontainebleau.

-------------------

[32] Louis-Alexandre Berthier, Prince de Wagram (1753-1815) was Major-General of the Grand Armée until the defeat of 1814, but hesitated over rejoining Napoléon when the latter returned to France and died in suspicious circumstances that have never been explained.

[33] Antonio Canova (1757-1822) was the greatest neo-Classical artist of the era. Napoléon gave him several commissions. In our history he created his most famous work, the *Three Graces*, in 1814 and became the Pope's plenipotentiary minister in 1815, tasked with recovering works of art that Napoléon has taken to Paris.

[34] Félix Bigot de Préaumeneu (1750-1825) was Minister of Religion from 1808-1814, Napoléon made him a peer during the Hundred Days but he lost everything thereafter and retired from public life.

## Chapter XI
## POPE PIUS VII

Napoléon left Paris on 22 June 1813, taking with him the King of Westphalia and the viceroy of Italy. In the carriages of his retinue were the two Ministers of War, the Duc de Bassano,[35] the Prince de Wagram and Cardinal Fresch. The presence of the cardinal was such a great singularity that it became the object of all the conversations in Paris. The imperial cortège, did not follow the road to Spain via Étampes and Orléans, but took the road to Fontainebleau, where the emperor arrived at about three o'clock in the afternoon.

The Minister of Religion and Cardinal Maury had already arrived that morning. The latter, immediately admitted to an audience with the Pope, had had a long conference with him and had notified him of Napoléon's intended arrival. Thus, when a courier came to announce the imminent arrival of the cortege in the courtyard of the palace, Pius VII came down from his apartments, followed by his cardinals, confused and trembling in anticipation to the scene that was about to unfold between the excommunicating pontiff and the excommunicated sovereign.

The pope had just set foot on the perron when the imperial carriage came to a halt. Napoléon got out and, followed by the two kings, the Cardinal and Prince Eugène, climbed the steps and, having arrived before he Holy Father, he removed

---

[35] Hugues-Bernard Maret, Duc de Bassano (1763-1869) was the Minister of Foreign Affairs from 1811-1813, although he was replaced in our history by the Marquis of Caulaincourt in November of the latter year. He then became Napoléon's private secretary, remaining with him until Waterloo and during the Hundred Days, after which he was exiled until the July Revolution cleared the way for his return; he served a brief term as Prime Minister under Louis-Philippe.

his hat and addressed the following speech to him, in a slow and solemn voice.

"Holy Father, the fatal circumstances that have caused our dolor have ceased. I have deplored them as much as Your Holiness must have done. France and Europe know what my respect for the Catholic religion and its virtuous pontiff has always been. My first act, on receiving power from God, was to restore its altars. And in the temporal difficulties that have arisen between the Holy See and my Empire, my veneration for Your Holiness has never weakened.

"Time has marched on, and I have known that the interests of the Catholic religion could not be displaced from the capital of the Christian world. Rome is yours, Holy Father, and that city will be returned to you. The patrimony of Saint Peter, which Charlemagne, my predecessor, conceded to the Holy See, must be attributed to it again, with a new organization that the times and needs of my empire have necessitated.

"I therefore beg Your Holiness to forget the past, and actions in which my will has been misunderstood, and to return, if you please, to the capital of Italy, which requires so much courage and virtue!"

"My son," replied the venerable pontiff, his eyes bathed with tears, "this striking step fills my heart with joy and gratitude. May the God of armies bless your arms and your power forever, and may He forget the invocations that I have been obliged to make in my dolor."

Raising his hands to the heavens, Pius VII added: "Omnipotent God, may my prayer rise to your throne, and may the destiny of his great prince be filled with the glory and happiness of which you are the divine and inexhaustible source!"

At the moment when Pius VII lowered his hands, trembling with emotion and prayer, Napoléon seized them, and, bowing, was about to kiss the fisherman's ring when the Pope, in a surge of joy, opened his arms and closed them in an embrace: the extraordinary reconciliation of two great powers.[36]

Both of them went into the palace, in the midst of the tumult of joy that had gripped all the witnesses of the scene.

When they reached the main reception room the Pope and the kings had just sat down with the Emperor when Napoleon suddenly stood up and commanded silence with an imperious gesture. The Holy Father and the kings got up too, and a few seconds of awkward expectation were followed by this further allocution by the Emperor:

"Holy Father, the hope of this welcome, so worthy of you and of me and so desired by our peoples, is not the only thing that has brought me to Your Holiness. I have also brought the greatest tribute that the Church of which you are the head can receive that this moment."

No one in the illustrious assembly, even the Pope and the kings, expected those words or understood their mystery, so there was a movement of amazement.

"God, who has protected me in my victories," Napoléon continued, "has inspired in me the result that ought to follow them. Russia, Holy Father, in a part of our treaties that I have kept secret until now, has renounced forever its protectorate of the Greek religion. The Czar has ceased to be its spiritual leader; at my request he has consented to return to Your Holiness those strayed sons, in order that they will no longer recognize any but the one Father and Pontiff of Christianity."

---

[36] In our history too, Pius VII, who had been elected pope in 1800 due to the negotiations of the French Cardinal Maury, signed a Concordat with Napoléon in 1813, in the negotiations for which Maury and Cardinal Fresch—Napoléon's uncle—probably played a leading role, but it was not nearly as dramatic, or as sweeping in its scope, as this one. The Pope eventually returned to Rome in 1814, where he received a hero's welcome, and immediately revived the Inquisition and the Index of Forbidden Books.

"O Caesar," cried Pius VII, in his exaltation, with an entirely Italian vivacity, "you are rendering to God what God had given to Caesar!"

"At this very moment," Napoléon added, "proclamations that the Czar has communicated to me are being read in all the churches of the Russian Empire, and have also been addressed to the Greek churches of Turkey and Asia Minor. In all of them, all Christians are being adjured to rally the sons of Christ beneath your sole and holy pontificate, and it remains to your wisdom, Holy Father, to direct and decide the great movement of Christianity in the East."

"Never, since Charlemagne," exclaimed Pius VII, "has the Lord received a more magnificent tribute from men. Never has a holier victory been won in his name. Come, Sire, come; let Your Majesty, His sword and His law, accompany me into the sanctuary where we shall go to bless Him and glorify Him!"

Then, with a rapid stride that his old age would have refused him, but which the enthusiasm of his joy allowed him to find again, the venerable pontiff headed swiftly toward the chapel, and, raising his hands to the heavens, in the midst of those sovereigns, cardinals and great men of the earth, he sang the *Te Deum* in a voice suffocated by tears of joy and glory.

The emperor spent that day and the next and Fontainebleau. During that time, he had continual conferences with the Pope, sometimes one-to-one but more often with the kings, the ministers and Cardinals Fesch, Gonsalvi, Maury and Paca. It was in those conferences that the bases were laid of the concordat and decrees that we are about to detail.

Canova, who had been a skillful intermediary between the Emperor and the Pope, and who had been able to attract the esteem and affection of both by the dignity and amenity of his character, took part in those conferences, and was named a Grand Officer of the Légion d'honneur, and created a Comte of the Empire, on the evening of the first day.

## Chapter XII
## THE CONCORDAT AND DECREE OF
## FONTAINEBLEAU

It was with the bitterest dolor that the Emperor Alexander had obeyed the victor in that abandonment of the protectorate of the Greek Church. Of all the conditions of the victory, that was the most humiliating and the most fatal; it had, at least, been the most disputed; and the Czar, forced to submit, had obtained that it would remain secret for a few months, in order to prepare minds or its promulgation in his Empire. Alexander had offered several provinces rather than resign that right, for it went to the future destiny of Russia and destroyed at a stroke the politics of four centuries.

Napoléon knew that as well as Alexander did. In fact, when the Greek Empire fell under the blows of Mohammed II there existed in the North a power almost unperceived until then, but which the Empire coveted, perhaps dreaming of the domination of the world.[37] That was Russia. She picked up the crown of the Orient that had just been broken and placed it on her head. The Greek religion was vanquished and subjugated; she welcomed it, and became its ally and support.

Since then, the idea of the Empire of the East, based on the domination of the Greek Church, had been incessantly pursued. Ivan the Great founded the new Empire at the moment when the first fell. A century later another Ivan took the title of Czar or Caesar, reserved until then by the Russians to the emperors of the Lower Empire. A few years went by, and Czar Feodor, freeing the Russian Church from the patriarchate of Constantinople, created a national patriarchate in his empire. Another century went by, and Peter the Great, going further, declared himself the leader of the Greek Church; and

---

[37] The Ottoman Emperor Mehmed II had conquered Constantinople and put an end to the Byzantine Empire in 1451.

since then, armed with the two bonds of religion and power, mingling them and braiding them, so to speak, the Russians had marched at a constant pace toward the Empire of the Orient, the Byzantium that every Czar and Empress had promised their successor.

But Napoléon, already Emperor of the Occident, while awaiting the Empire of the World, had clearly seen that knot of politics; his sword had sliced through it violently, and the holocaust of the Greek schism had confirmed his power as well as the sovereignty of the Roman Church.

The day after that great interview, on 23 June 1813, at three p.m., the Emperor and the Pope signed the bases of the new concordat, which repealed the dispositions of the concordat of 15 July 1801. The decisions of the Council of Paris in August 1811 were annulled, notably those that gave metropolitans the right to proceed with the institution of bishops when a year has passed since their nomination, without the Pope having accorded that institution in the meantime. Six new archbishops and thirty-three bishops were created in the former France. The circumscriptions of dioceses were fixed in the States that conquest had aggregated to the Empire. Ecclesiastical endowments were augmented, the liberties of the Gallican Church maintained and implicitly recognized. The conditions of mixed marriages between Catholics and Protestants were fixed. In sum, the dignity of the Holy See, by the skillful redaction of those preliminaries, seemed increased, without the power of the Emperor being diminished in consequence.

That concordat became definitive on 8 September 1813 and it was effective from that date that it was promulgated as a law of the Empire.

An additional article, that was never rendered public, was thus conceived:

*The organization and administration of the Estates of the Church (the départements of the Tiber and the Trasimene) are fixed by common accord in conformity with the dispositions of the decree of 23 June 1813.*

In fact, the Emperor issued a decree that same day from Fontainebleau in which, without renouncing the civil and military administration of the Church Estates that were to conserve their new organization, he seemed to restore to the Pope and his successors a part of the sovereignty of those Estates. Thus, the Pope conserved all property in the pontifical domain—which is to say, all the castles, palaces, land, forests, collections of art and riches belonging to the Holy See. He recovered the direct and exclusive nomination of bishops and all the ecclesiastical charges and functions in his Estates. The police of the city of Rome and its revenues belonged to the Holy Father, as well as a quarter of the revenues of the former Roman States, with the sole charge of provision of endowments to cardinals, bishops, functionaries and ecclesiastical establishments.

The sovereign right of granting mercy in the same circumscription belonged equally to the Pope and the Emperor, who could each exercise it independently.

Thus the entirety of religious power and a part of the rights of sovereignty were returned to the Pope, the wealth of the Holy See and its possessions were restored to him, revenues more considerable than they had had before that new state of things were attributed to him, and all the expenses of his Estates were left to the public treasury of the Empire.

Such a concordat and the accompanying decree were unhoped-for in the circumstances in which the head of the Church was then placed. He believed that he had served God and his conscience well in accepting conditions that restored the grandeur of his tiara. He did not wait for the promulgation of the concordat to give the nominated bishops the institution that he had previously refused and to change into a brief of praise and actions of grace the sentence of excommunication launched against the great Emperor who had now repaired the outrages and brought the Church the solemn present of the reunion of the Greek communion.

Not everything that had taken place in those brief conferences at Fontainebleau was made known then. The unexpected arrival of King Charles IV of Spain, who came from Compiègne on the morning of 23 June and took part in a discussion gave the two courts that then populated the old château of François I a great deal to think about.

On the evening of that day, Napoléon took his leave of the Holy Father and, taking the road to Orléans, headed for Spain.

## Chapter XIII
## THE SPANISH CAMPAIGN

The campaign had opened before the Emperor's arrival. Already, the army corps of the Prince de la Moskowa and the King of Naples had crossed the Pyrenees and descended into Navarre, while the German and Italian troops headed toward Saragossa, where the general aggregation of the various army corps was to be effected by conjunction with the troops of Maréchals Soult and Suchet.

The ensemble of those forces was formidable, amounting to no less than two hundred and thirty thousand men.

The enemy had tried to oppose that movement of combination. Castanos,[38] in Castille, had tried to stop the Duc d'Albuféra's march, but, beaten at Moya and almost crushed at Cuença his army had scarcely saved its debris, crossing the river and returning to Madrid.

Almost at the same time, the Duc de Dalmatie destroyed the corps of the Marquis de La Romana at Lerida, a glorious defeat in which La Romana, the noble fugitive of the Baltic, died as he had lived, a hero.[39]

Weakened by those two defeats, the Anglo-Spanish army under the command of Lord Wellington nevertheless remained equal in number to the French army. It was camped to the south of Segoia, with the mountains behind, in control of the passes that led to Madrid. Having nothing to fear from that

---

[38] In our history, Francisco Javier Castaños, Duque de Bailién (1758-1852) was at the head of the army that was ready to invade France in 1815, although that became unnecessary after Waterloo.

[39] This is an anachronism; the most trusted of Wellington's Spanish generals, Pedro Caro y Sureda, Marquis de La Romana (1761-1811), had died before the junction of the alternative histories, not in battle.

direction, it was reinforced from day to day by scattered troops that the English general, in the expectation of a large-scale and decisive battle, recalled from Portugal, Extremadura and Castille.

In that part of Spain there had been no serious engagement for some time. Wellington agglomerated his forces with his consummate prudence, maintaining his positions, covering Madrid, and with a powerful and rested army, in the midst of bellicose and enthusiastic populations, awaited fortune.

Meanwhile, the operations of the French troops were effectuated. Their general aggregation took place near Aranda, where the immense rendezvous had been arranged, and where the Grand Armée, aggregated beyond Duero, awaited the Emperor's arrival.

Napoléon was traveling like a thunderbolt. He was at Bayonne on the twenty-seventh of June, Pampeluna on the twenty-ninth, and was in the midst of his army on the first of July.

King Joseph immediately handed over command to Napoléon, and the meeting of the two brothers, after such diverse fortunes, took place within the sight of the troops, who burst forth in transports of joy and enthusiasm.

The day of 2 July was spent in the deliberations of a long council of war, to which all the generals and chiefs of the various services were summoned in succession. The resolutions made were immediately put into execution.

The next day, Napoléon passed his entire army in review, and addressed the following proclamation to it:

*Soldiers, you are about to find yourselves facing your veritable enemies. For four years the English leopard has been running around this unfortunate country, tearing it apart and devouring it. A war of assassinations and treasons has blocked your efforts until now. I have been aware of your miseries and I have come to you in order to put an end to them. Your brothers, the victors of Novgorod and Moscow, are accompanying me; they have come to unite their heroism with yours. Soldiers of the army of Spain, a few more days and the rebellion will be confounded, England vanquished, the Peninsula pacified, and the legitimate King of Spain will reenter his capital at your head.*

*Tomorrow, the Grand Armée will cross the river.*

*Issued at the general quarters of Aranda, 3 July 1813.*

*Napoléon*

On 5 July the army corps of the Prince de la Moskowa took the road from Valladolid to Segovia to prevent the junction of General Raleigh, who was bringing twenty-two thousand English and Spanish troops from Asturias and Galicia to Lord Wellington's general quarters. An engagement took place—a veritable battle—in which the enemy lost five thousand men and its artillery, and was forced to retreat in disorder toward Valladolid.

On the eleventh, the French army, commanded by the Emperor, was extended and developed in the plain within sight of the bell-towers of Segovia.

Meanwhile, the English army had remained motionless in the positions in which it seemed to have been waiting, for more than three weeks, for the approach of the French. Napoléon's arrival having not determined any movement in it, nor any retreat, it became evident that Lord Wellington was disposed to accept battle if it were offered to him.

The days of the eleventh and twelfth passed in that apparent torpor; no partial attack or hostility was launched on either side, as if the two generalissimos were afraid that the slightest shock might disturb the conditions of a battle that would necessarily be decisive.

The Anglo-Spanish army, commanded by Lord Wellington and by Generals Castanos, Black, Moore and Palafox under his orders, counted an effective force of a hundred and eighty-five thousand men.

Napoléon's army, more than a hundred and eighty thousand strong, was divided into six corps, under the commands of the King of Naples, the Viceroy of Italy, the Princes of

Essling[40] and de la Moskowa, and the Ducs de Dalmatie and d'Albuféra.

The artillery was equal on either side, but the enemy cavalry was superior.

On 13 July, at six a.m., the French Grande Armée moved off. Immediately, a similar movement took place in Wellington's army; the two formidable corps approached one another, like two gigantic monsters. The first collision was terrible, and the most furious and murderous battle was immediately engaged.

The action continued for eight hours, with varying fortunes, approximately equal in sum. Enthusiasm and bravery worked miracles on both sides, but at two p.m. a movement ordered by Napoléon decided the victory.

It was the corps of the Viceroy of Italy that, crossing the river twice and outflanking the enemy's left wing, commanded by Wellington in person, fell upon it rapidly, surrounding it and rendering it impotent to fall back, while the Imperial Guard, kept in reserve until that moment, was launched forward, fresh and terrible, broke through the English general's lines, placed him between two fires, crushed him without any hope of flight, and forced him, after a disastrous combat, to lower his arms and surrender.

At the same time, the right wing, commanded by General Moore, was smashed and dissipated by the King of Naples, and General Moore, hit by a cannonball, died at that moment on the battlefield.[41]

---

[40] André Masséna, Duc de Rivoli and Prince d'Essling (1758-1817). Once Napoléon's favorite among the generals who rose through the ranks, he lost that favor in our history when he was forced to retreat from Spain, and did not serve again; he did not support Napoléon during the Hundred Days.

[41] This too is anachronistic; Lieutenant-General John Moore (1761-1809) had been killed fighting Soult at Corunna before the division of the alternative histories.

From then on the rout became general. The French army, victorious at all points, no longer had anything before it but cadavers and enemies who asked for mercy and were taken prisoner. The carnage had been particularly horrible at the center, where the Spanish troops were, who, determined to vanquish or die, were obstinate in an insensate resistance. They fell in droves under the fire of the French artillery. Nineteen thousand perished thus; Generals Castanos and Palafox were killed and Mina, taken prisoner, was taken to the general quarters.

General Wellington's army corps had lowered arms and capitulated, as reported. They amounted to thirty-three thousand men, and the General himself, taken prisoner at the head of his troops, whom he did not want to abandon, was taken before the Emperor.

Napoléon had a brief and curt conversation with Wellington. He received his sword coldly, and without returning it to him. The English general, beaten but still dignified, concluded the interview with a few vague words and was taken away by a detachment of Bavarians.

The results of the victory were immense; the English troops, killed or taken prisoner, had been annihilated, and the Spanish forces, fallen on the battlefield or fugitive, completely destroyed, leaving no element of aggregation and resistance henceforth.

Such was the Battle of Segovia, one of Napoléon's most glorious triumphs, which annihilated at a stroke the national rebellion and the support of England, and recaptured Spain.

The French army had suffered lightly, eight thousand men being rendered incapable of combat, but no important loss had been signaled in the general staff.

If we do not report the bulletin of that great battle it is because we have just summarized the most remarkable particularities.

On 6 July 1813 the Emperor made his entry to Madrid at the head of his troops and with an apparel of war and victory that was imposing in its magnificence.

First he went to the Church of Saint Jago where he was received solemnly by the clergy; he witnessed the *Te Deum*, while the thunder of cannons mingled with the city's bells in all directions.

That first step by Napoléon, rendering glory to God for his own glory, had a great effect on that religious population, and those who were there recognized a clever calculation on the part of the victor, praising its deference to the sentiments of the country.

Napoléon was not unaware of the utility of that influence, which he continued carefully; he even augmented it by the proclamation posted as soon as he arrived in Madrid and soon spread throughout Spain.

*Spaniards,*

*God has put an end to the cruel war; His Providence has blessed my armies, and has wanted by me to snatch Spain from the horrors of the civil war stimulated by the perfidious alliance of England. Your eyes have been opened, Spain, and you have recognized the cunning and egotism of those heretical merchants. I have not come here to conquer Spain but to pacify and regenerate it. Your ancient institutions are dear to you, and will be maintained; your religion, which is mine, will be respected, and my brother, who knows and shares my thoughts, has returned to your midst in order to share your glory and your happiness.*

*From the Royal Palace of Madrid, 17 July 1813.*

*Napoléon.*

From the first moments of his sojourn in Spain, the Emperor had the provinces occupied by his troops, which did not meet any resistance anywhere. Maréchal Soult entered Lisbon without firing a shot, and the fourth occupation of Portugal by the French armies was definitive.

It was in one of those troop movements that Ferdinand VII was arrested near Toledo and taken back to Madrid, from which he had fled on learning of the loss of the Battle of Segovia.

He was taken to the Emperor, who, overwhelming him with his gaze, said to him: "So here you are, a fugitive in Spain as in France, trembling here as there, only having the strength to hurl into the abyss of civil wars the great nation that cannot and does not want to be yours. A bad son and a bad king, what do you expect? If I were a tyrant and a tiger, as you have said in your insolent proclamations, I'd have you shot. Your father has advised me to do that, and never to count on your word. Tomorrow, you'll be taken back to France."

It was in the midst of the court, the grandees and the generals, that the Emperor let his anger burst forth. Ferdinand threw himself to his knees and, with a sort of solemnity, told him that he was unworthy of the throne and unworthy of forgiveness. He renounced his rights to Spain forever. He was ready to salute and recognize Joseph as king. He asked for mercy and begged the Emperor not to send him back to the Château de Valençay.

"Poor nature!" exclaimed he Emperor, secretly delighted by such abasement. "Remain here, then, and we shall decide our fate later." And, turning toward several Spaniards, he asked: "Well, Messieurs, what would you have done with this king?"

Napoléon's vengeance stopped there. Satisfied to have debased the fugitive of Valençay so publicly, he did not want to go any further, and sent away the crowd of witnesses; left alone with Ferdinand VII his conversation became milder, and made compensations to the prince that effaced the humiliation with which he had just been covered.

The Emperor reproached him with an almost affectionate vivacity, for his flight, his relations with Escoiquiz, his maneuvers and his proclamations. He made him understand that, at the very moment of his departure, his position was about to be fixed and relieved; he added, with an apparent emotion, that his rebellion had destroyed projects of alliance that he was on the point of realizing.

Ferdinand, still under the terror of his first reception, was confounded by joy and gratitude. For five years he had been soliciting an alliance with the daughter of Lucien Bonaparte, and in such a circumstance, instead of the scaffold that his fear had caused him to glimpse, the victor seemed to be adding to his pardon the favor refused before the crime.

He threw himself at Napoléon's knees, renewing his formal resignation of the crown of Spain, and the most urgent request for an alliance with the imperial family.

Napoleon concluded the interview by augmenting his hopes; then he left with Ferdinand. As they traversed a gallery where they found the crowd of lords and generals, he said aloud: "Messieurs, I alone have the right to complain of the prince, but no one here will forget that he is the son of Charles IV, who could have been King of Spain himself."

## Chapter XV
## AN ASSASSINATION ATTEMPT

Spain was pacified; the guerillas, dispersed and devoid of energy, had returned to their hearths; the English had disappeared; religion, protected by the Emperor and King Joseph, returned to them in influence what it received from them in support; the clergy calmed national passions. Furthermore, an extraordinary rumor began to spread, of an unexpected event that Spain would never have dared to expect: the Pope, it was said, was to traverse the Peninsula and spend a few days there before returning to Italy.

That rumor took one increasing consistency; the senior clergy, which had never ceased to maintain communication with the sovereign pontiff, received frequent news confirming that hope. It was said that Pius VII, in order to close the abysm of the Spanish revolutions, would come to consecrate the new dynasty in person and appease the agitations of the countries by his benedictions.

Meanwhile, the Emperor organized the kingdom, reassured the people, rallied the grandees to the new dynasty, also attaching the priests to it by skillful condescension, revived the old institutions and, while augmenting his power, satisfied popular needs and passions.

King Joseph stood aside before the Emperor, but seconded him with his activity.

A single event burst forth in the midst of these great endeavors.

On 5 August 1813 Napoléon was returning from the Escorial, fatigued by that long journey, and dismounted from his horse a few moments before arriving at the Royal Palace of Madrid. He was accompanied by the Duc de Dalmatie and

General Bertrand;[42] he was advancing on foot toward the gate and was about to enter the first courtyard when suddenly, from behind two columns, a young woman launched herself toward him, shoved General Bertrand away violently, and struck the Emperor with a dagger-thrust, which, fortunately, thanks to a movement on Napoléon's part, was arrested by the thickness of his garments and only inflicted a slight scratch on him.

The young woman immediately fell in a faint after that act of fanaticism.

At the moment when the soldiers of the guard ran forward toward the unknown woman, seized her and carried her into the palace, another young woman ran up and, in spite of the efforts of the witnesses, came to throw herself at Napoléon's feet, crying: "Mercy! Mercy, Sire! Mercy for my sister!"

The two women were taken into the palace. Napoléon had the second—the one who had begged for mercy—brought to him.

She came in. She was a young woman of great beauty; there was something angelic in her physiognomy. Her eyes, full of tenderness and tears, were shining beneath the thick tresses of her hair, by which her visage as covered.

"Oh, Sire," she cried, embracing his knees, "forgive my sister! Mercy for an insensate! She has not conceived the crime; her will did not enter into it; it's misfortune that has betrayed her reason. Mercy, sire!"

"Who are you?" asked the Emperor.

"We are both the daughters of Colonel Herreira. My father, whom we adored, Sire, was killed five months ago near Cartagena. The French shot him; he was our support, our hap-

---

[42] In our history Henri-Gatien, Comte Bertrand (1773-1844) accompanied the Emperor to Elba, returned within him for the Hundred Days and then accompanied him to Saint Helena; he was granted an amnesty after Napoléon's death that allowed him to return to France, where he was briefly elected to parliament after the 1830 revolution.

piness. My poor sister was driven almost mad by it, and God has abandoned her in inspiring her to vengeance."

"How do you come to be with her?"

"I knew nothing of her plan, Sire; for two months she has been silent and wanted to be alone, but I as frightened to see her so somber; my mother was also afraid of her grief. We suspected some mystery. I did not lose sight of her, and attached myself to her footsteps."

"What is your mother doing?"

"Sire, she is in profound misery, ill and inconsolable."

"Where does she live?"

"Near here, in the street of the Incarnation. I wish that she were here Sire; you would have mercy on her dolor."

"Go away."

She was taken away in spite of some resistance and her repeated cries of "Mercy for my sister!"

The Emperor summoned an orderly officer, said a few words to him in a low voice, and had the guilty party brought in.

She was pale; her dark eyes were dry and her icy lips tremulous; her beauty had disappeared under the convulsions of her terror.

"Send for a priest," said the Emperor, in a muted voice.

"Oh my God!" said the young woman. "To die! To die!"

"You fear death," Napoléon said to her, bitterly, "but you wanted to give it to me! What is your name?"

"Rosalie."

"Your action was barbaric and infamous. You do not believe in God, since you wanted to assassinate me."

The Emperor's wrath was terrible, and the scene too much. Rosalie fell in a faint, uttering a groan.

When she recovered her senses she saw by her side the old and austere face of a Dominican who was leaning over her, and Napoléon, who was looking at her with an expression of pity.

"To die—it's necessary than that I die!" cried the young woman. "Oh my father! Oh Sire, mercy!"

A door opened and the orderly officer appeared. He brought with him a thin and suffering woman, whose astonishment at the sight of the scene was evident proof of her ignorance of what had happened.

"My daughter!" she cried, running to Rosalie.

"Mother!" And the two women confounded their tears, for the mother had already sensed some new misfortune.

"Madame," said the Emperor, "your daughter has committed a great crime."

There was a moment of terrible silence.

"Father," he added, turning to the Dominican, "I had you summoned here to tell this young woman that our religion is a religion of forgiveness, not of murder." And, addressing the mother, who was almost dead of terror: "As for you, Madame, take this unfortunate child away. I shall forget her crime; I do not want to delve into it. I know your name and your misfortunes; Colonel Herreira's widow ought not to be living in poverty. I shall mention you to the King and I shall not forget you. Let your daughter live with her remorse; for myself, I forgive her. Take her away."

Without waiting for the effect produced by that magnanimous action, Napoléon left the room swiftly, leaving everyone, especially the mother and daughter, in an inexpressible emotion of gratitude and joy.

That sublime act of clemency soon caused an extraordinary sensation in Madrid and throughout Spain, and people everywhere said: "Napoléon forgives in the name of God."

## Chapter XVI
## PIUS VII IN SPAIN

On 8 August 1813 King Joseph addressed a letter to the archbishops and bishops; it informed them that the Holy Father was coming to Spain, entering via Pampeluna and passing through Burgos, Valladolid, Segovia, Madrid, Toledo, Badajoz, Seville, Grenada, Valencia and Tarragona, where he would embark for Civita Vecchia and Rome.

The Pope's sojourn in Madrid would be prolonged by a great ceremony, which everyone divined would be the consecration of the new monarch. The king also summoned all the clergy and the monastic orders to come to meet the Pope, in the course of his itinerary. He also announced that the passage thought Badajoz had been determined in order to gather the clergy of Lisbon and Portugal in that city at that time.

That appeal to the religion of the people of the Peninsula produced the greatest effect. The hopes of the clergy and the nation were realized. Thus, the prelates, the priests, the convents and the entire population prepared to receive the sovereign pontiff in the midst of a religious triumph.

Pius VII thus kept the promise he had made to Napoléon at Fontainebleau, to come in order to appease agitations by his presence, ensuring the victory and consecrating the new monarchy.

King Joseph, accompanied by the Viceroy of Italy, went to the frontier to receive the Holy Father personally, who was accompanied by the former King of Spain, Charles IV. The latter only had one brief interview with King Joseph, and departed immediately for Madrid, where he was to meet the Emperor and Ferdinand VII.

Everything had been anticipated and organized in order for the sovereign pontiff to be surrounded by a cortege of a magnificence worthy of him. After a series of carriages carrying King Joseph, the archbishops of Toledo, the primate of

Spain, of Santiago and Saragossa, the bishops of Léon and Oviédo, the latter two being directly linked to the Holy See, and a host of prelates, leaders of orders and abbés, the Holy Father's vehicle appeared; it was draped in red velvet and resplendent with gold and precious stones. It was harnessed to eight mules caparisoned in cloth of gold. An innumerable clergy and a great deployment of Spanish and French military forces completed the majesty of the triumphal march.

In every town and village through which it passed, and even on the roads, the Holy Father found entire populations, sometimes having come from more than fifty leagues away, preceded by their clergy, with crosses and fluttering banners.

His progress was incessantly slowed down by the enthusiasm and the prayers that rose up as he passed. His sojourn in Burgos was prolonged for two days. On his arrival in Valladolid he found the Archbishop of Braga and the entire clergy of northern Portugal.

From Segovia he headed for the Escorial, where Napoléon was waiting for him, accompanied by the King of Naples and Kings Ferdinand VII and Charles IV. It was there that an imposing ceremony took place on 22 August.

That day, at ten o'clock in the morning, in the superb church of the palace, the Pope being enthroned before the altar, in the presence of Napoléon, placed on a platform with King Joseph and the French and Spanish courts, the two former kings Charles IV and Ferdinand VII, followed by all the children and princes of the House of Bourbon, came successively to resign their rights to the Spanish throne, invoking the name of God.

The two kings and the princes made the oath of abdication, after which the Pope said mass. A witness statement of that solemn act was drawn up and sent to all the municipalities of the realm.

Then next day, with the cortege of kings, which Napoléon had thought he ought not to join, the sovereign pontiff made his entry to Madrid in the midst of an excitement difficult to depict.

Everything had been ready several days before for the coronation of King Joseph. The constituted bodies, the civil authorities, the grandees of Spain, the military leaders, the nobles, the municipalities and the senior clergy had been summoned. On 25 August, in the midst of ringing bells and firing cannons, the religious investiture of the kingdom of Spain was given to Joseph in the presence of the Emperor Napoléon.

Pius VII remained in Madrid until 30 August; then he continued his voyage via Toledo as far as Badajoz, where he received the archbishops of Lisbon and Evora, with the Portuguese clergy. He stayed for two days in Seville. He passed through Grenada, Alicante, Valencia, Tarragona, and, knowing that the Emperor and his court of Kings would come to meet him again in Barcelona, he returned as far as Catalonia.

It was from Barcelona that Pope Pius VII quit Spain. When he set foot on the ship that was to take him to Italy he raised his hands to the heavens and blessed the land where he had been almost adored, and, in a final invocation, he prayed the Almighty finally to make peace and concord succeed the five years of war in that land, and the misfortunes hat had desolated it.

King Charles IV went with the Holy Father to Rome. The next day, Napoléon separated from King Joseph after having fixed in a final council the duration of the occupation of the peninsula by the French army. He departed on 14 September on a ship that took him to Marseille, where he disembarked with the King of Naples and Ferdinand VII.

In that short space of time Spain had been vanquished, conquered and pacified, and Napoléon had appealed to religion to destroy all the fanaticism so long engendered by rebellion and war, in order to secure peace, his politics and his power there.

## Chapter XVII
### LUCIEN BONAPARTE

While Spain was being calmed and organized under Joseph, who had finally been accepted as her king after the solemn abandonment of the House of Bourbon; while the sovereign pontiff, intoxicated by his triumphant progress in Spain, was finding the same triumphs and the same joys in Rome; and while the Emperor was flattening all the obstacles, destroying them one after another, satisfying the sentiments and the passions of peoples, he was attaining a goal that the dignity of his family and the needs of his heart still lacked.

Lucien Bonaparte, the sole member of the imperial family who was still named Bonaparte, in consequence of his quarrels with Napoléon, had thought he ought to escape his wrath; he had taken refuge in London with his wife and children. There, he probably deplored in secret the position in which his wounded dignity and former political opinions—weakened by time, which marches so quickly, and the catastrophes of empires—retained him. His amity for his brother still subsisted, however; Lucien was still the superior man who, on the eighteenth Brumaire, dominating the storms, had saved Napoléon's life at the risk of his own. But he was also a brave man, who had not wanted after that to sacrifice to his brother's omnipotence a separation from a cherished wife, whose virtues seemed preferable to him to the royal grandeurs that the emperor had wanted to impose on him.

The double condition of Lucien's divorce and the marriage of his daughter to King Ferdinand had been rejected, and the fear of a facile vengeance had caused him to flee to England.

He, the second by merit among the Emperor's brothers, lived very quietly in the midst of his family. He cultivated letters, and the strength of his compressed genius spread forth in poetry and literature; he had just published an epic poem, *Charlemagne*.

In spite of that long quarrel, the two brothers understood one another and loved one another, and Napoléon felt that he ought to yield first, because he was the greater.[43] A correspondence was established between them via the intermediary of Monsieur de Las Cases, who carried Napoléon's offers.[44]

The Emperor recognized Lucien's marriage and added to that document, which satisfied the husband's heart and mind and smoothed everything over, the following propositions:

The kingdom of Portugal was given to Lucien.

His eldest daughter was to marry Ferdinand VII.

The provinces of Braga and Tras-los-Montes, on the right bank of the Douro, were recovered from Portugal and returned to the crown of Spain.

In compensation for the increase, Spain ceded Catalonia to France.

Lucien felt the last glimmers of his democratic opinions extinguishing before these magnificent offers; a charming

---

[43] In our history, he did not, expunging Lucien (1775-1840) from the imperial almanacs from 1811 onwards, but Lucien returned to France in 1814 following his brother's abdication, where titles were conferred on him by the Pope. During the Hundred Days, however, Lucien rejoined his brother, and was consequently banished after the Restoration. He was living in Italy when Geoffroy wrote the present text.

[44] Emanuel, Comte de Las Cases, or Las Casas (1766-1842) also rallied to Napoléon's cause during the Hundred Days, although he had been a very minor figure during the Empire; he then served as an intermediary between the defeated Emperor and the British, accompanying him to Saint Helena and serving as his secretary there; his memoir of that exile is a precious but not entirely reliable historical document. He was expelled before Napoléon's demise but made a great deal of money from the memoir when he was allowed to return to Paris after the latter's death.

letter from the Emperor to the wife of the new king, in which he treated her both as a queen and a sister, touched him even more, and decided him completely. He immediately replied to his brother that he accepted the regal propositions with gratitude, and that, henceforth linked by amity and politics to the Emperor's destiny, he could do no better in order to make him understand that than by signing his response with his new names as king: Lucien-Napoléon.

That sacrifice of the name of Bonaparte was an homage that the Emperor felt keenly. So, when he returned to France, after having escaped the watchful hospitality of England, the new King of Portugal reappeared in the midst of the family from which he had been separated for so long, and received a welcome there as royal as it was fraternal, especially for the Queen, the sister-in-law for whom Napoléon dispensed the treasures of his god grace and grandiosity.

After a few days of fêtes, the marriage of Ferdinand VII with Lucien's daughter was celebrated at Rambouillet. That château and its dependencies were given to the two spouses during their residence in France, but Ferdinand VII did not remain there for long, and took his new wife to Venice, where he usually resided in the palace of the Viceroy of Italy.

After the celebration of the marriage Lucien-Napoléon soon left himself for Portugal. He stopped off in Madrid, where he was glad to see his brother Joseph. In that city they signed the treaty of delimitation of their territories, in conformity with the bases that the Emperor had fixed.

On 15 January 1814 King Lucien-Napoléon and the Queen of Portugal made their entry into Lisbon, their capital, to the unanimous acclamations of the people, for there are always acclamations for events that have grandeur and novelty.

The reunion of Catalonia with the French Empire did not produce in Spain the painful effect that might have been expected. The acquisition of the Portuguese provinces granted in exchange flattered Spanish pride considerably. In any case, Catalonia, incessantly occupied by French armies for five years, had separated its politics from the rest of the Peninsula and manifested more than once its desire to be reunited with France. During Napoléon's brief sojourn in Barcelona, that manifestation had been renewed with the greatest urgency. Napoléon had not taken long to satisfy the desire, for it went well with his politics of having a foot on the threshold of all the States of Europe.

Catalonia was divided into five départements; that of the Bouches-de-l'Èbre, which did indeed contain the mouths of that river, was not the least important.

The republic of Andorra, a small State forgotten by its neighbors, by time and even by geographers, was extinguished by that readjustment of provinces; its magistrates were removed and it reentered the general organization; ten centuries of independence and obscurity could not shield it from the gaze that saw everything and molded everything.

Thus, victor in the North, pacifier of Spain and Portugal, at peace with the Holy See, and reconciled with his family, having calmed the anxieties of peoples, Napoléon, henceforth free of those accomplished tasks, found himself face to face with his veritable enemy, and was able to devote himself entirely to his unique thought: England.

# BOOK TWO

## Chapter I
## ENGLAND

England, which Napoléon detested; England, for which he had invented his continental system, that solemn exile of a nation to which water and fire were refused on the continent; England, which he had fought in Sweden, in Russia, in Hanover and in Spain; England, ever present or hidden with her cunning and her gold, a hydra with renascent heads that incessantly spat their poisons over the flamboyant thunderbolts of his eagle; England, finally, which filled his heart with hatred and vengeance, and which he wanted to vanquish, humiliate and annihilate at any price!

The victory of Segovia had been decisive. Spain, entirely purged of the English, was pacified. King Joseph, master in Madrid, reigned there tranquilly.

However, vanquished in Russia and expelled from Spain, proud England still remained queen of the Ocean, from which she challenged the master of Europe.

Weary of that endless struggle, the Emperor had sent General Lauriston to England from Saint Petersburg, charged with offering a truce of sorts and bring a few preliminaries of peace.[45] He thought that in the midst of his victories and his power, his dignity would not suffer from that step.

---

[45] In our history Jacques Lauriston (1768-1828), the French ambassador to Russia prior to the Russian campaign, helped cover the retreat from Moscow, but was eventually captured and help prisoner until the Empire fell. Then he returned to France and entered the service of Louis XVIII, to whom he remained faithful during the Hundred Days.

The English ministry, for its part, had sent an already-famous diplomat, Mr. Canning, who came to Napoléon with instructions of a similar nature. But those two secret missions, with no definite character, did not lead to any result. An equal pride on either side rejected the concessions demanded, and England withdrew from the negotiations first, believing that she was as unbreakable in her homeland as the rocks of her islands.

It was therefore necessary to continue the war: a war of extermination henceforth without respite; a duel to the death between the two nations, or rather between Napoléon and her, in which it was necessary that Napoléon or England should perish.

The Congress of Hamburg opened in those circumstances, with its external mask of festivities, and the constant thought within of taming the rival nation. An offensive confederation was formed there of all the maritime powers of Europe, under the direction of France. All the fleets of those States were put at the Emperor's disposal. Soon, the Atlantic ports, from Cadiz to Cronstadt, were animated by an unaccustomed activity, and a decisive expedition was scheduled for the spring of the following year.

After having pacified Europe, the Emperor did not believe that all the forces on the continent were too many, and an entire year of preparations too much, to ensure the success and the glory of such a great conquest, and the rest of the year was thus spent with that sole thought and in that endeavor, without any event of any importance signaling it.

For the first time, England, which, on the other side of the sea, knew everything and saw everything, doubted her destiny.

## Chapter II
## *PREPARATIONS FOR WAR*

During the Emperor's sojourn in Russia, the Empress Marie-Louise had brought a daughter into the world named Clementine-Napoléon.[46] On that occasion the Emperor issued a decree to the effect that his children would have, from birth, the title of King or Queen of the blood of France, reserving for himself the right to attach to that title the determination of Estates and Realms, as he had done or his first-born, the King of Rome.

We shall doubtless speak again about that young queen, the memory of whom has remained so dear to France.

A third child, named Gabriel-Charles-Napoléon, born in February 1814, also had the title of King on his cradle, but it was expected that a more significant title would designate him in Europe. That vacancy of a word was more noticeable then than the most striking deed, as there was no action of the Emperor that did not have its reverberation, his silence as well as his decision.

Meanwhile, since the Congress of Hamburg, the Atlantic coasts, in the north and the south, had come to life with the prodigious activity imprinted on maritime affairs. During the winter, squadrons, all bearing continental standards, came successively to unite in the Elbe, between Hamburg and the sea; transport vessels were constructed in the ports of Holland, and the Elbe fleet, incessantly increased by all the navies of Europe, and which the fleets of Antwerp and the Baltic came to join in April 1814, counted at that epoch sixty ships of the line, a hundred and forty-four frigates, a large number of other warships and a prodigious quantity of ships for transport and disembarkation.

---

[46] A fictitious character—no such daughter was born in our history, nor was a second son of the marriage to Marie-Louise.

The King of the Two Sicilies, Grand Admiral of the Empire, departed in the company of Duc Decrès, the Minister of Marine,[47] to inspect those immense preparations; at the same time, two hundred thousand men of the land armies, who had been gathering for months in Mecklenburg and Westphalia approached Hamburg in order that everything would be ready for a sudden embarkation.

England, keeping watch unrelentingly on the slightest movements of Europe, could not see those formidable armaments without anxiety, and without opposing obstacles to them. In several engagements, her vessels had tried to prevent the junction of different squadrons in the Elbe, but partial combats, in which the advantages had been uncertain and never important, could not prevent the complete unification of all the naval forces of Europe on the coasts of Holstein.

She too, in the expectation of an invasion, had raised up all her power and, believing that she had discovered the places designated for the landings, had moved the greater part of her means of defense there.

Nothing as yet, however, allowed Napoléon's intentions to be known in a certain manner. The month of April was almost complete without any official declaration having appeared, and Europe awaited the fatal moment in silence and stupor.

That mysterious calm was broken suddenly by this decree, dated 22 April 1814:

*Napoléon Emperor of the French, etc., etc.*
*Has decreed and decrees the following:*
*Article 1. Our beloved son Gabriel-Charles-Napoléon will henceforth take the title of King of England.*

---

[47] In our history, Denis Decrès (1761-1820) briefly resumed his firmer post as Minister of Marine during the Hundred Days. He died in a fire started deliberately by one of his servants.

*Article 2. Our Ministers of Foreign Affairs, Justice and the Interior and the Secretary of State are each charged with what concerns them in the execution of the present decree.*

*Given in our Imperial Palace in Hamburg, 22 April 1814.*

*Napoléon.*

*Seen by us, Arch-Chancellor of the Empire.*

*Cambacérès,*
*Prince-Duc de Parma*[48]

*On behalf of the Emperor:*

*The Secretary of State.*
*Duc de Bassano*

---

[48] Jean-Jacques-Régis de Cambacérès, Duc de Parma (1753-1824), who was Second Consul when Napoléon became First Consul, is nowadays remembered as the author of the Napoleonic Code promulgated by the Emperor in 1804. In our history he served as Arch-Chancellor of the Empire until Napoléon's fall and was recalled during the Hundred Days; he was exiled in 1816 but his civil rights were restored in 1818; he used the title of Duc de Cambacérès thereafter, the Duchy of Parma having reverted to Marie-Louise.

## Chapter III
## LANDING IN ENGLAND

It was thus that the imperial gauntlet was thrown down; that was the forfeit that he gave for the pledge of battle, and the division of the country to be vanquished was his proclamation of war.

Undoubtedly there are in similar challenges reported by history a hint of unpleasant arrogance, and all too often a negative or contrary result has shown up all the vanity and ridicule of emphatic proclamations of that sort, but in this one there was a difference: twenty years of combat, political skill, preparations, and above all, hatred, were summarized in the decree, so serious that England trembled; she saw that everything was henceforth finished for her; that Napoléon had burned his boats, and that it was necessary for one or the other to die in the contest.

As we have already said, only the form of the decree could be surprising, for such a war had been gestating for a long time, and for a long time her provinces had been arming themselves with all their defensive forces. But her anticipations were partly mistaken, both with the regard to the precise timing of the imperial expedition and the landing places.

Scarcely had the decree of 22 April burst forth, however, than the fleets had already set forth, and that formidable expedition quit the continent and headed for England.

Such was the rapidity of the events that the English government had not foreseen them. Two months did not appear to it to be sufficient for what taken less than a week to accomplish; and, as if everything were to frustrate its penetration, instead of steering into the Thames estuary and toward the coasts from Portsmouth to Ipswich, the French fleets, favored by the winds, came to operate their disembarkation on the coast between Boston and Yarmouth.

The disembarkation was effected in two days, without any obstacle. From the first day, the third army corps, under the command of the former Crown Prince of Sweden, returned to being Maréchal Bernadotte, marched on Norwich, took possession of it, in spite of a stubborn resistance, and established itself throughout the county of Norfolk while waiting the for the other army corps to come to join it in the environs of that city. Soon, the military movements of the French army were executed; two successive battles were disputed furiously in the regions of Hertford and Ipswich, but the French army continued moving forward.

A third battle, even more considerable, took place under the walls of Colchester. Generals Belfour and Harris, of the English army, were killed there; twelve thousand Englishmen remained on the battlefield, and the French army also had to deplore, in the midst of its victory, considerable losses and the death of the brave General Lepic, killed by a shell at the commencement of the action.[49]

But those combats, which would have been decisive in other circumstances, were only preparations for the prodigious Battle of Cambridge.

The English government had not ceased, since the first news of the disembarkation, to deploy the greatest activity. The battles of Ipswich and Colchester had served in its calculations, and had delayed, in spite of their victories, the progress of the French troops. In the meantime, the English troops withdrew to various points and frontiers, where the Duke of York,[50] the generalissimo, had dispersed them. They headed

---

[49] Louis Lepic (1765-1827) rose through the ranks to earn his promotion to general in 1813, but retired in 1814. He was made a Comte by Louis XVIII in 1815, and did not join Napoléon during the Hundred Days.

[50] Frederick Augustus, Duke of York and Albany (1763-1827), the second son of George III; he was the younger brother of the Prince Regent, who became George IV in our history. Undistinguished on the battlefield, he nevertheless

for Cambridge at a forced march, and gathered in a matter of days in the environs of that city into a formidable army of more than two hundred and twenty thousand men.

Napoléon had not prevented that junction of English armies, and perhaps he was glad to prolong the apparent inertia in which he left his own troops for a few days in order to finish with the partial combats that did not resolve the problem, and to put in confrontation at a single point the destinies and the accumulated forces of France and England.

The Duke of York did not want to quit the environs of Cambridge; he resolved to wait for the enemy there, and his determination became all the more assured when he discovered that the general was advancing toward that city with his entire army.

It was on 4 June 1814 that the gigantic battle took place.

On one side, the Emperor had the kings of his family and the King of Saxony,[51] and on the other, the Prince Regent and the Dukes of York and Cambridge[52] were present. The English army had been reinforced the day before by the arrival of the army corps of the General Marquess of Anglesey,[53] at the head

---

brought about vital reorganizations of the army while he was its commander-in-chief.

[51] Frederick-Augustus I of Saxony (1750-1827) remained loyal to Napoléon in our history even after the disastrous Russian campaign, when most of his former allies switched sides.

[52] In our history, Prince Adolphus, Duke of Cambridge (1774-1850), the seventh son of George III, the great-grandfather of the present queen, Elizabeth II, was the Military Governor of Hanover in 1814, having previously been colonel-in-chief of the Coldstream Guards.

[53] In our history Major-General Henry Paget (1768-1854) was excluded from active duty in 1814 because he was involved in an adulterous relationship with the wife of Wellington's brother, but he was allowed back for the Hundred Days, famously losing a leg at Waterloo. He was not made Marquess

of ten thousand Scotsmen, and had thus risen to two hundred and thirty thousand men. The French army counted no more than a hundred and ninety thousand; the artillery was formidable on both sides, and the English cavalry had the numerical advantage.

The encumberment of the Duke of York's troops, the result of the extraordinary rapidity of events since the landing, led to great disorder, and constrained the commander-in-chief to precipitate his movements of attack. Than circumstance favored Napoléon's plans singularly; he was thus able to lead the combat in to the terrain that he had reconnoitered and chosen.

The action, engaged at sunrise, concluded with the day, but everything was terminated before nightfall. The results were immense. At nine o'clock in the morning the English troops, under the command of the Duke of York, devastated by the French artillery, saw their commander-in-chief struck dead by a cannonball. At half past nine the Duke of Cambridge was wounded himself, and severely. Widowed of those two generals, deprived of command and in the greatest confusion, the English army was surrounded on all sides, crushed and destroyed.

The intensity of war had never been greater; never had such a great struggle arisen between such great peoples. England and France were there as nations rather than armies, and their old national hatred overflowed in fury and slaughter; but Providence had decided once again that conquest by Napoléon. Overwhelmed and falling in thousands, the English soldiers died in their lines, without yielding their positions, and when, at the end of the day, reduced to despair, their battalions in shreds could no longer do anything but die without defending themselves, they finally withdrew, uttering a great howl of dolor, which concluded the battle. That cry was the last sigh of England, and the fall of the giant shook the world.

---

of Anglesey until 1815, so the use of the title here is anachronistic.

Along with the Duke of York, its generalissimo, the enemy army had lost twenty-two generals. Fifty-four thousand men had perished, the rest were wounded or taken prisoner. Scarcely forty thousand fugitives had escape the carnage, heading for Bedford. All of the artillery remained in the power of the victor, and the Duke of Cambridge, wounded and a prisoner, had been taken to the Emperor.

The losses of the French army amounted to more than fourteen thousand men. The King of Naples had received a slight wound in the left arm. Maréchal Ney and General Compans had also been wounded, the latter so grievously that they despaired of his life for several days.

Everything was decided by that incredible victory. England was more than vanquished, she was destroyed and erased from the world; like her army, the nation no longer existed.

The Emperor entered Cambridge that evening, where he only stayed for one day. Two days later, on the sixth of June, he marched with his army directly upon London, and entered it as victor on the ninth of June, the day when the Imperial flag flew from the Tower, the Monument and public edifices.

Parliament, since the Battle of Cambridge, and in the midst of that national crisis, had been in permanent session. Scarcely had he arrived in London than Napoléon went to Westminster; coolly, he entered the chamber of the House of Commons—which had been joined by the Lords—and marched rapidly to the Speaker's chair. There, he declared in a resounding voice that the parliament was dissolved—"and destroyed," he added.

At the same time, the troops that had accompanied him evacuated the hall, after which the Emperor had the doors locked, and took away the keys himself. Having driven his horse to the middle of Westminster Bridge, he threw the keys into the Thames forcefully, shouting: "There is no more parliament! There is no more England!"

There was no more England! It was the second time that a sovereign and his army, emerged from France, had conquered that country. The battles of Hastings and Cambridge had been equally decisive, but what had been a kingdom for William, Napoléon only wanted to see as a province.

There was no more England! She did not even think of struggling. The rapidity of the conquest had stupefied the English to such an extent that they were no longer able to do anything but submit; the ports and the interior cities received the victors silently, and the nation, no longer having any faith in her destiny, impotent and devoid of hope, waited for what Napoléon would do with her.

The day after the Battle of Cambridge the royal family had withdrawn to the Northern provinces; they learned in York of the entry of the French into London. The Prince Regent sent Lords Castlereagh and Liverpool to the Emperor as ambassadors, but the latter refused even to receive them, saying that he could not treat with such enemies, and that, vanquisher of England, he wanted to remain her master.

All the skill of those diplomats failed before Napoléon's rigor, and their political illusions were scarcely extinguished when the decree you are about to read informed them how the victor would dispose of the vanquished nation.

## Chapter IV
## THE DECREE OF LONDON

*Napoléon, Emperor of the French, King of Italy, Protector of the Confederation of the Rhine and Mediator of the Swiss Confederation, etc., etc.*

*Has decreed and decrees the following:*

*Article 1. The seas are free; the various States of Europe will take back the colonies that they possessed before 1789.*

*Article 2. England is reunited with the French Empire.*

*Article 3. The House of Brunswick has ceased to reign over England.*

*Article 4. King George III will take the title of vassal king of the united kingdoms of Ireland and Scotland, with the charge of paying annually to France a tribute of five million francs, and furnishing a contingent of war in troops and money to be fixed in due course.*

*Article 5. The English parliament is suppressed.*

*Article 6. England has no other constitution than that of the French Empire of which it is a part.*

*Article 7. England is divided into twenty-two départements.*

The numerous articles that followed in the decree contained the judiciary, administrative and military organization of the new province.

Forty peers of the most illustrious houses were summoned to the French senate, and a hundred English députés were appointed to the elective chamber, for it was the spirit of the decree, as well as the will and politics of Napoléon, to fuse the two nations, in order that they should no longer be more than one State, France, into which England had been absorbed.

Arch-Chancellor Cambacérès was appointed Viceroy of England, and charged with creating the new judiciary and administrative organization.

The Maréchal Duc de Dalmatie came to take command of the military forces and establish the military system.

The English were maintained in their charges and functions, insofar as the new dispositions permitted.

The debris of the English army, collected and treated without much exigency and rigor, were, after having crossed the sea, transported to Holland, France and Italy in order to be distributed and gradually fused with the French troops. Thus placed under the command of French officers, that army became unimportant and devoid of danger, at the same time as it augmented the Emperor's military forces in a useful manner.

For three years there were only French garrisons in the twenty-two new départements.

Commerce breathed; the seas had become free again. England recovered from its depression, its interest accustomed it to being French, and its pride buckled under the mildness and skill of the new domination.

King George III, without troops and without means of resistance, accepted the fragment of royalty that was thrown to him in compensation for the loss of his empire, and went tranquilly to establish his court in Glasgow.

It was, in fact, the case that the moral strength of England no longer existed. The moment that that unbreachable land had been breached, the charm was broken; it became an ordinary nation, and could be vanquished.

All of its colonies were united with the French Empire except for Dominica and the Lucayan Islands in the Antilles Sea, English North America and the island of Ceylon in India, which were assured to the King of Scotland and Ireland.

Thus, India, New Holland, the African islands, the Cape of Good Hope, Malta, Gibraltar, Jamaica, the Antilles, Newfoundland and the other English colonial possessions became integral parts and colonies of the French Empire.

The islands of Jersey and Guernsey became a subprefecture dependent on the département de la Manche, the chief place of the arrondissement being fixed as Guernsey. The new French laws replaced in those islands the ancient customs and Norman laws that they had conserved until then.

The East India Company was dissolved and Asian commerce rendered free.

England's national debt remained to its charge and separate from that of France.

A primate archbishop was established in London; he had the spiritual supremacy of the Church of England. The immense revenues of the clergy were attributed as amortization funds for the payment of public debt and the members of the clergy were, like those of the French clergy, paid fixed salaries drawn from general State funds.

London also became the seat of a Court of Cassation, a Polytechnic School and a Law School. The Universities of Oxford and Cambridge became academies. The English University was established in London.

French laws were translated and became obligatory from the first of January 1815.

And few years had gone by when England, vanquished and dissolved, found itself reconstituted as a province of the Empire and sensed that it was French.

## Chapter V
## HARTWELL

The Emperor Napoléon, wanting to render the results of his conquest complete, did not consent to cede the smallest part of it without imposing the seal of his suzerainty thereupon. Thus, he made it known that he would go to Glasgow in person to give the investiture of the united kingdoms of Scotland and Ireland to the dispossessed king of Great Britain. That action had a great political importance in his eyes; it was to lower the status of the king given those two kingdoms and manifest his own power to the nation he had just founded.

On the road from London to Glasgow is the town of Aylesbury, and a few miles from that town is a manor house named Hartwell. It was there, curved under the blows of a terrible destiny, that the old royal family of the Bourbons lived; there too lived a King of France, sacred in blood, crowned by misfortune, whose vain royalty was no longer anything but a name and a few sterile homages of faithful servants.

At the approach of the French army, the friends of the exiled king had invited him to flee; they represented to him he dangers he would have to run if he fell into the hands of the man known in that place as the usurper. There was talk of the possibility of a great crime. There was, it was said, a legitimacy to be acquired by a few murders, and that the sacred head of the king would be the first to be struck.

Louis XVIII turned away from this advice to the aged Prince de Condé,[54] who was at Hartwell at that moment. "And you, cousin?" he asked him.

_____

[54] Louis-Joseph de Bourbon, Prince de Condé (1736-1818) had headed an army of émigrés after the Revolution, becoming the leader of the *ancient régime*'s opposition to it, but the army was disbanded in 1801 and he lived quietly in England

Monsieur de Condé replied that for him, he could only see grandeur in the remaining to face the Emperor, and waiting for him.

Louis XVIII shook the old man's hand affectionately. "That's what I think, cousin," he said. "We'll see whether there's anything in a King of France that can stop the blade of a murderer."

He was mistaken in his dolor; he misunderstood the grandeur of Napoléon's soul, whose politics was too noble to dream of a crime that would, in any case, be pointless.

Having arrived in Aylesbury, the Emperor wanted to go to Hartwell. The presence of the Bourbons on that estate surprised him, and perhaps he admired their courage. He deviated from his route, quit his cortege and, only accompanied by the Duc de Dalmatie and General Rapp, headed for Hartwell House at a fast gallop.

His unexpected arrival caused the greatest agitation in the house, and it was with a kind of fear that Monsieur de Blacas[55] came to announce the news to Louis XVIII.

"It's a visit," said the King, smiling. And with his usual presence of mind, he added: "It would be bad form not to receive him; I am at home, Monsieur, and you can show General Bonaparte in."

The appellation "General" applied to the Emperor drew tears from that faithful old aristocrat; he did not know what might come from such a meeting, if the legitimate and dispossessed King of France refused a sovereign title to the powerful Emperor of the French.

Napoléon was introduced, accompanied by his two generals. Louis XVIII, having sent away his court, remained alone with the Prince de Condé, and the following conversation took

---

thereafter; in our history he returned to Paris with Louis XVIII after Napoléon's fall.

[55] Pierre de Blacas d'Aulps (1771-1839) was the master of what was left of Louis XVIII's household during his exile.

place between the two sovereigns, which was recorded by General Rapp in his memoirs:

Louis XVIII, rising to his feet as Napoléon arrived: "General, I had not expected this good fortune, and your visit to this house astonishes and is precious to me."

At these words, Napoléon went pale and bit his lip. He replied: "Misfortune has rights to all homages, Prince, and I did not want to pass so close to such illustrious Frenchmen without seeing them. The sovereign of France likes to meet his people wherever they are."

Louis XVIII: "People! Doubtless you mean to say your King?"

Napoléon, smiling: "Your Highness does not think so."

Louis XVIII, with dignity: "Nor your subjects, undoubtedly?"

The Emperor fell silent and, drawing the armchair in which he had just sat down closer to that of the King of France, he looked him in the face and said to him: "All these formulae are vain. I know Your Highness' wit, and my time is too full for me to battle with it on a terrain where I would be at too great an advantage; I ought to explain myself clearly.

"Your Highness still conserves the title of King of France, but twenty-five years of misfortune ought to have convinced you of its vanity. I, and I alone, am the veritable sovereign of France, which I have enlarged to the borders of Europe, and the world, which does not know you, does not even know whether any Bourbons still exist. Twenty-five years of misery has dried up their memory.

"However little concern I might have for a resignation unnecessary to my designs, it is for you to wonder, Prince, whether it might not be appropriate to quit that sterile title of King of France, which another title and my power has absorbed.

"However, your house has been royal for a long time, and can be again. Ireland has beautiful Catholic provinces for a descendant of very Christian kings. King George is not yet so firmly seated on that throne that I cannot place Bourbons there, and if...."

Louis XVIII, interrupting with enthusiasm: "Oh, my beautiful crown of France, withered as your lilies are, how could I think of replacing them! Oh, rather the words King of France than omnipotence elsewhere!"

Napoléon: "If Ireland does not suit the Bourbon family, a greater empire, perhaps more worthy of it, is vacant in the North: Sweden, with Finland, only has a king devoid of posterity. Norway, which has just been taken away from it, might be reunited with it again, and even Denmark, if destiny wished it, might come to complete the ancient monarchy of the three Northern kingdoms. That septentrional tiara, Prince, is doubtless worth such a sacrifice."

Louis XVIII; "You know little of the hearts of kings, Monsieur, to try to attain them by such corruption."

Napoléon, getting to his feet angrily: "Abandon your terrible firmness to the Emperor of the French, Prince; where benefits cease, punishment might more easily commence."

Louis XVIII. Calmly: "My family is accustomed to martyrdom, General; I am ready for anything; there is still room for me in your ditch at Vincennes."

At the word *Vincennes* the Prince de Condé, who had listened to the conversation with a cold disdain, suddenly trembled, went pale and let his hand fall on to the pommel of his sword. Then, tears having trickled down his cheeks, he raised his hands to the heaven and went out, crying: "Oh, my God!"

Napoléon had not missed any of those movements, and, having become calm again, he said to Louis XVIII: "Your Highness cannot remain in France, and England has become France. My minister will make my intentions known to you."

As he finished speaking he left, precipitately, remounted his horse, and, without addressing a single word to the generals who were accompanying him, he returned to the town of Aylesbury at top speed.

## Chapter VI
## *THE ISLE OF MAN*

The Emperor went to Glashow, where the parliaments of Scotland and Ireland were gathered. As he had already done for the King of Poland, Poniatowski, he handed the scepter to King George in the presence of the members of those parliaments, and in a rather brief speech, he assured the two kingdoms of the enjoyment of their constitutions and their privileges, with the modifications that the system of Europe had imposed, he said; and the first was the emancipation of Catholic Ireland.

That investiture of the double kingdom assured him of a suzerainty in fact, although it was not officially promulgated.

From Glasgow he had the Duc de Bassano, the ministerial Secretary of State, write the following decision to Louis XVIII:

*Napoléon, etc.*

*Has ordered the following:*

*The buildings, park and dependencies of Hartwell House are united with our private domain.*

*Within a delay of one month, counting today, the Comte de Lille and his family, as well as the persons accompanying them, will go to the Isle of Man, which will become their place of residence.*

*Given at the palace of the University of Glasgow, 22 July 2014.*

*Napoléon*

*On behalf of the Emperor:*
*The Ministerial Secretary of State*
*Duc de Bassano.*

A letter from the Duc de Bassano accompanied that decision, full of respect for the illustrious exiles, informing them that the residence in question was an effective property of the island, and that so long as the Bourbon family remained on its territory, no French authority would pertain there or have any action.

Louis XVIII affected to refuse even the appearance of a sovereignty over that island; Messieurs de Montesquiou and de Blacas administered it, without even rendering an account that he did not want to receive.

Thus, a kingdom of sorts was, as it were, imposed on the man who called himself King of France. There was in that moderation on the Emperor's part an adroit tactic that could not escape Louis XVIII; so, while accepting that exile, which he could not avoid, he still protested by means of one of the noble declarations that are so well-known

The Isle of Man is about ten leagues long by five wide. It is fertile enough; Douglas is its capital, a port and town of about three thousand inhabitants. Other towns of lesser importance are found there; the entire population is about forty thousand souls.

It was in that island, a long time afterwards, in 1824, Louis XVIII having died, that his brother, the Comte d'Artois, was proclaimed King of France, without Europe knowing anything about it, under the name of Charles X.

## Chapter VII
## THE REPUBLIC OF SAN MARINO

A rather bizarre conquest came to break the glorious monotony of all these great revolutions, for the distraction of Europe and the amusement of posterity.

A few leagues from Rimini, in the kingdom of Italy, is the tiny republic of San Marino, populated by about six thousand inhabitants, having a territory two leagues in diameter.

The history of that tiny land shows the extent to which disdain might serve for the salvation of peoples. For more than eight hundred years, the inhabitants of San Marino had been constituted in a state of independence; it was a republic appointing its magistrates, a *provveditore* and a few other functionaries, and it seems, by virtue of a political joke, that other powers have always wanted to spare that nation.

In June 1815, however, the gamekeeper of a neighboring commune dependent on the French Empire having arrested a delinquent on a republican field, the act was considered as a violation of a foreign territory, which caused a great fuss in the locale.

The council was assembled and the importance of the event was gravely discussed there, along with the means of remedying it. The debate was long and energetic, and it was decided that a firm address full of the sentiments of liberty and dolor would be sent to the Emperor of the French to protest about the territorial violation and demand reparation.

That might have been bold and proudly appropriate if the Emperor had been willing, by virtue of the same sentiment of pity that the centuries had consecrated, to permit that reparation. But it would have been completely ridiculous if the sovereign were irritated by it—although that was not exactly what happened.

The Emperor sent word to the Prefect of Pesaro that he was to appoint a Maire for the commune of San Marino,

95

which would henceforth depend on the canton and the arron-dissement of Rimini, and to order the Commissaire of Police of the latter town to go to San Marino to proclaim that decree of the Prefecture.

Thus expired, by way of a legal declaration of the Commissaire of Police, the ancient Republic of San Marino.

## Chapter VIII
## PROMOTIONS

The Emperor left England and returned to Paris in the early days of the month of August.

On the fifteenth of that month, his birthday, he issued a decree in which, in memory of the great events of the receding two years, principally the conquest of England, he summoned to high dignity some of the great functionaries of the State.

Eugène Beauharnais was named King of Italy.

In his favor, Napoléon detached that title from his own crown. The new king conserved for the Emperor the government of the kingdom of Italy, without gaining anything from the magnificent favor but a more complete dignity, without any augmentation of power.

Napoléon had taught Europe that he could take possession at will of the title of king; he also wanted to teach it that he could resign and abandon it at his pleasure.

The Duc de Cadore was created Prince of Oldenburg.[56]

That was the recompense for the peace treaties that Monsieur de Champagny had concluded with great skill since the celebrated Treaty of Vienna. It was another just homage rendered by Napoléon to that minister, as distinguished by his severe probity as his elevated faculties, the only one for whom he had a deference that was almost tantamount to veneration.

---

[56] Jean-Baptiste de Nompère de Champagny, Duc de Cadore (1756-1834) had been an admiral before turning politician during the Empire, but after negotiating the Treaty of Vienna in 1809 and the Emperor's marriage he quarreled with the Emperor and retired; during the Hundred Days, however, he rejoined Napoléon, which led his temporary proscription by Louis XVIII.

In 1818, when the Prince Arch-Treasurer of the Empire died, the Duc de Cadore, Prince of Oldenburg, was promoted to that high dignity.

Comtes Montalivet, Mollien and Daru were created Ducs.[57]

Comte Roy, then president of the legislative body and later Minister of Finance, was created Duc d'Ilyrie.[58]

Six generals were named Maréchals de France: Belliard, created Duc de Mantua; Gouvion Saint-Cyr, created Duc de Ferrare; Molitor; Foy, created Duc de Tolosa; Clausel, created Duc de Calabre; Gérard, created Duc de Ravenne.[59]

---

[57] Jean-Pierre Bachasson, Comte de Montalivet (1766-1823) was one of the Empire's leading ministers, but was sacked after the Restoration; he supported Napoléon during the Hundred Days. The financier Nicolas François, Comte Mollien (1758-1850) left France after the Revolution but was brought back by Napoléon, who made him a Councilor of State under the Empire; he retired after the abdication; recalled by Napoléon during the Hundred Days, he refused thereafter to work for Louis XVIII. Pierre, Comte Daru (1767-1829) served as Intendant-General of Napoléon's military household, and succeeded Bassano as Secretary of State in 1811. He supported Napoléon during the Hundred Days but went on to serve in the peers' Chambre, defending the cause of democracy.

[58] In our history Antoine, Comte Roy (1764-1847) opposed Napoléon during the Hundred Days and remained in favor with the Bourbons, going on to a glittering career, which included several terms as Minister of Finance

[59] Agustin-Daniel, Comte Belliard (1769-1832) fought with Napoléon in the Egyptian Campaign, then with Murat, and finally at Waterloo, but was rehabilitated by Louis XVIII after a brief imprisonment. Laurent de Gouvion Saint-Cyr (1764-1830) was a dissenter from the Empire, but fought for it anyway, and was promoted to Maréchal in 1813 in our history too. He continued to serve during the Restoration, ns spite of trying (and failing) to help Ney avoid conviction. Gabriel,

Vice-Admiral Gantheaume was made Comte de Yarmouth and invested with the new dignity of Admiral, created in the navy by the same decree.[60]

Twelve brigadier-generals were appointed generals of divisions, and numerous other promotions, as well as decorations, were distributed in the army to those who had merited them in the recent military events.

The Emperor also wanted his mother to take the title of Empress Mother.

Madame Mère, as she was called then, recoiled before that magnificent dignity. She refused it at first, but Napoléon insisted, and made her recognize that the mother of so many sovereigns ought to have an imperial title herself. She was

---

Comte Molitor (1770-1849) joined Napoléon during the Hundred Days, was forgiven by the Bourbons and promoted to Maréchal in 1823, and continued in service after the July Revolution. Maximilien-Sébastien Foy (1775-1825) supported Napoléon during the Hundred Days and was wounded (for the fifteenth time) at Waterloo. Elected to the Chambre des députés in 1819, he became the effective leader of the opposition and wrote a history of the Peninsular War. Bertrand, Comte Clausel (1772-1842) also served in Spain, and took command of an army on the Spanish frontier during the Hundred Days, refusing to recognize the Restoration thereafter and escaping to America; he returned after the July Revolution, resumed his military career and was promoted to Maréchal in 1831, after taking charge of the invasion of Algeria. Étienne Maurice Gérard (1773-1852) served under all the governments from the 1789 Revolution to Louis-Philippe, despite supporting Napoléon during the Hundred Days, and as briefly Prime Minister in 1834. He also became a senator, very briefly, during the Second Empire.

[60] Comte Honoré Gantheaume (1755-1818) did not support Napoléon during the Hundred Days and was nearly lynched in Toulon after Waterloo. Louis XVIII made him a peer as a reward; he voted for Ney's execution.

crowned at Notre-Dame de Paris on 27 August; the Emperor asked the Pope to place the crown on his mother's head personally. The ceremony took place in the midst of great pomp, and for the first time, the cold and trembling hands of Pius VII were seen giving the blessing to the people. For some month that saintly pontiff had been weakening progressively, and he died a few days after the coronation of the Empress Mother.

In the same epoch, the inhabitants of Marseille thought the occasion favorable to renew a request to the Emperor that had not been granted to them the first time, which was to erect in the city's main square a statue to Charles Bonaparte, the Emperor's father. But Napoléon, who wanted everything to be extraordinary and more than human in him and his family, was importuned by that maladroit flattery; his father had only been an ordinary citizen. The present and the future belonged to him, Napoléon, but he could do nothing in the past. He felt that it was impossible for him to go digging up a grave in order to plant vain titles of king and emperor that could not germinate there. He responded with a second refusal.

## Chapter IX
## CARDINAL FESCH, POPE


Pius VII died on 15 September 1814; Napoléon thought about appointing his successor.[61]

It is certain that he thought about declaring himself the sovereign pontiff of the Catholic Church; his project had already led him to proclaiming himself the religious leader of Christianity. Under his new power, all the various sects of Christianity were reunited, free and independent in their worship, and all were reattached to the unity of a sovereign pontiff—but he doubted himself and thought that the time had not yet come.

The nomination of a Pope could not, however, be indifferent to him; he knew what weight religion and the influence of its ministers had in the hearts of peoples, and that in politics that force ought not to be disdained, either as an obstacle or as an instrument.

Doubtless, too, he had to reflect profoundly in that epoch on the bizarre exception of a single elective monarchy conserved in Europe; the residues of various republican forms that were so strangely mingled with the customs of the Catholic Church, a religion of omnipotence and authority, astonished and perhaps offended him.

In giving Poland its new constitution he had abolished the right of election and proclaimed that of hereditary sovereignty. But the innumerable obstacles that would have arisen to the destruction of the principal of papal election and the privilege of the cardinals stopped him. He dared not bring to it yet the only remedy that his genius deemed appropriate, that of attributing pontifical omnipotence to himself. He also hesi-

---

[61] In our history Pius VII did not die until 20 August 1823 and was replaced by Annibale della Genga, who reigned as Leo XII until his death in 1829.

tated as to whether, like Charlemagne, he ought to nominate the Pope himself, and if he did not pause for long on that idea, at least he wanted to direct as master the election of the sovereign, to whom he had previously rendered his Estates and a part of his temporal power. With that objective, while leaving the cardinals the magnificent privilege of choosing their pontiff, he wrote them the following letter:

*Illustrious cardinals,*

*The Lord has recalled to Him the venerable and holy pontiff Pius VII; Your Eminences are about to elect his successor.*

*Out respectful love for our holy religion imposes on us the duty to participate, in a way, by means of our wishes, in that pious and solemn election, and we have recognized that the interests of religion, like those of the Empire, as well as our particular wishes, summon to that signal sacerdocy our venerable uncle, His Eminence Cardinal Fesch.*

*We pray the Lord to enlighten and inspire Your Eminences in the accomplishment of that important duty.*

*From our Imperial Palace of Saint-Cloud, 7 October 1814.*

*Napoléon.*

All the cardinals of Europe were summoned to the conclave established in the imperial palace of Lyon. Napoléon's letter indicated more than a wish; it made his orders known. Every cardinal responded to it by giving assurances of his respect and submission.

Twenty-nine cardinals were present at the conclave; the assembly was presided over by Cardinal Alessandro Mattei of Rome, and the operations of the scrutiny commenced.

They did not, however, proceed with the unanimity of obedience that had been promised. The Italian prelates could not bear to see the tiara escape Italy, which had not happened since Urban VI in 1378, to be borne by a Frenchman. Some, moved by a sentiment of scruple and conscience, even thought it their duty to oppose the abolition of that custom, which had been consecrated by apostolic constitutions. They also knew that the right of exclusion enjoyed by the sovereigns of Austria and Spain had been taken away from them by a secret decision, and those violations of the forms of the election seemed to them to be sacrilegious. So, eight votes were given to Cardinal Bartolomeo Pacca of Benevento,[62] as a sign of energetic protest, but the other twenty-one votes obtained at the first session called Cardinal Fesch to the throne of Saint Peter.

The new Pope was proclaimed in Lyon, then in Paris, and finally in Rome, to which he went in December under the name of Clement XV. He took for his arms the imperial eagle of France.

Napoléon was deeply wounded by the division of the cardinals in the election, but, far from showing it, he wrote the following letter to Cardinal Pacca:

*The votes that called you to the throne of Saint Peter have proved to me the esteem in which the Sacred College holds Your Eminence.*

*This is also to indicate mine.*

*I inform Your Eminence that I am sending him the insignia of the great eagle of the Légion d'honneur and that I shall present him to His Holiness Pope Clement XV for the vacant seat of the archbishopric of Milan.*

*I pray God that he has Your Eminence in his holy and worthy protection.*

*Napoléon.*

The emperor had thought momentarily that the new Pope ought to take the name of Napoléon I, but he quickly aban-

---

[62] Cardinal Pacca (1756-1844) did everything possible to persuade Pius VII to oppose Napoléon and not to sign any concordat with him; Napoléon explicitly declared him an enemy.

doned that idea, which was dissolved by other intentions that he destined for the future.

## Chapter X
## THE PEACE OF 1815

Everything seemed finished and pacified in Europe. The Emperor, returned to Paris, resolved to employ the leisure of Peace and the immensity of his treasures for the embellishment of Paris and France.

The great Rue Impériale that we have already mentioned was almost complete.

A similar street, of the same width and the same magnificence, cutting the Rue Impériale almost at a right angle, was extended from Saint-Denis to Montrouge, thus dividing the capital into two halves. The street was named the Rue Militaire, because it did, in fact, leads to two military highways, to the south and the north, and above all because the great plain of Saint-Denis, which it traversed, became an immense Champ de Mars, extending from Aubervilliers to Saint-Ouen and from Paris to Saint-Denis. The Emperor had that large area defended by broad ditches lined with masonry, into which channels brought the waters of the Seine. That plan being overlooked by Montmartre, he also had a fortress constructed on that elevation, the works of which were undertaken and completed under the direction of General Marescot, to whom Napoléon, had, in that epoch, rendered his good graces.[63]

---

[63] Armand-Samuel de Marescot (1756-1832) was in command of an engineering corps throughout the Revolutionary wars and then in the Peninsular War; he was taken prisoner at Bailien, where he negotiated the French surrender; after being included in an exchange of prisoners he was tried by court martial and stripped of his rank, somewhat unjustly. In our history he was rehabilitated after the Restoration and remained loyal to Lois XVIII during the Hundred Days.

That new Champ de Mars had a diamond shape, with its longer diameter from Paris to Saint-Denis and the other two angles at Saint-Ouen and Aubervilliers; at the latter two points and at Saint-Denis immense barracks were constructed, each able to contain twenty thousand men. They were like three military cities guarding a capital. Cavalry quarters, which could accommodate twelve thousand men and as many horses, were also erected at Saint-Denis. Those barracks were also defended by earthworks of considerable importance, which did great honor to the arm of military engineering.

The citadel of Montmartre assured, by its position and the size of its fortifications, considered as impregnable, the defense and conservation of Paris, as well as mastering, by overlooking it, the new Champ de Mars and the plain of Saint-Denis.

While those military works were being carried out in the vicinity of Paris, the interior of the city also acquired numerous embellishments.

The Rue de Rivoli and the Bourse were completed.

Almost all the public squares were restored and ornamented with statues of Maréchals who were dead. That of Maréchal Lannes[64] was erected in the middle if the Place des Vosges, which resumed the more consecrated name of the Place Royale.

The Emperor ordered the recasting and reestablishment of the statue of Louis XIV on the Place des Victoires with the inscription:

*LUDOVICO. MAGNO*
*NAPOLEO. MAGNUS*

---

[64] Jean Lannes, Duc de Montebello and Prince of Siewierz (1769-1809) was one of Napoléon's ablest and most trusted generals, but he was fatally wounded by a cannonball at the Battle of Aspern-Essling.

The buildings of the Quai d'Orsay were finished and a sequence of symmetrical town houses similar to those in the Rue de Rivoli were constructed between the Rue du Bac and the Pont Louis XVI and prolonged beyond it to the palace of the legislative body.

Those residences were reserved for the ambassadors of foreign powers, who were thus lodged at the expense of the Empire, and each one bore the name and arms of the State whose ambassador it accommodated.

The quay from the Pont Louis XVI to the Pont d'Iéna was completed later with great luxury. It was named the Quai des Ambassadeurs.

The church of the Madeleine being completed, the Minister of the Interior suggested placing the Senate there, but Napoléon refused, without saying anything more. He would not have tolerated two political bodies deliberating face to face, almost within touching distance of one another. It suited his plans better for the Senate to remain at the Luxembourg; he had not forgotten Machiavelli's old maxim: to divide is to rule.

The church of the Madeleine was, in fact, consecrated to the worship of that saint, and became a parish church for a quarter that did not have one.

Versailles was repaired and furnished as if Napoléon were to reside there, but he rarely went there; Saint-Cloud, closer to Paris, seemed to be his favorite residence.

However, a singular action encouraged the thought that that Emperor might one day move into the royal residence of Versailles. The new Pont de Sèvres had been commenced, and was due to become one of the most beautiful stone bridges in the vicinity of Paris, but orders were given to discontinue the works. Instead of eternal arches, a wooden bridge was constructed at Sèvres, of an extreme elegance; at the same time, a military construction of sorts was placed at its head, on the Sèvres side, as if to defend it.

A few people remembered that Louis XIV had never consented to the construction of a stone bridge, that the construction in question had taken place under Louis XV, and that it was by means of that bridge that the population had come, on the fourth and fifth of October 1789, to remove Louis XVI and his family from Versailles.

A wooden bridge, on the contrary, defended by troops, could easily be cut or burned, and such an irruption would become impossible henceforth. Such was the reasoning of some, but no one ever knew whether that had been the Emperor's thinking.

The galleries of the Louvre were completed in their entirety, the private houses that existed in the interior being demolished. The triumphal arch at the Carrousel also disappeared. "It's a child's toy," Napoléon had said. Thus, the Place du Carrousel extended from the Louvre to the Tuileries, and that immense space was no longer divided by the railings forming the château's court of honor.

The Arc de Triomphe at the Étoile was continued, and was entirely clad in white marble.

At the same time, under the administration of Monsieur de Chabrol,[65] Paris was sanitized and increasingly embellished; the waters of the Seine, raised up to a greater height by pumps, were distributed into all the houses and to all the floors; the streets, broadened, were equipped with sidewalks; several public squares, planted with trees, were created in the city center, which grew incessantly in extent and population.

It was the same for the other cities of France. An imperial palace was constructed in Lyon, at the junction of the Saône

---

[65] A graduate of the École Polytechnique and an engineer with the Ponts et Chaussées, Gaspard de Chabrol was appointed Prefect of the Seine by Napoléon in 1812, and was responsible for paving several of the capital's streets and boulevards with Volvic stone as well as converting the city's nocturnal illumination to gas-lighting. His speech welcoming Louis XVIII back to Paris for the second Restoration is credited with coining the phrase "the Hundred Days" with reference to the period of Napoléon's brief return to power.

and the Rhône; but those various works were surpassed by those carried out in Rome and in Italy.

*Chapter XI*
## *WORKS IN ROME AND ITALY*


In March 1816 the Emperor went to Rome, accompanied by his court and ministers; he also took several members of the Institut, including Lagrange, Monge, Prony, Berthollet, Visconti, Denon, Millin, Percier and Fontaine.[66]

Comte Molé,[67] the director general of Ponts et Chaussées, also went there, and, surrounded by that other court of science and talents, Napoléon traversed Rome in all directions, more than once traveling the dangerous road to Terracina through the Pontine Marshes.

Then, when he had seen everything with that sweep of his eagle eye, which saw everything in order to remedy everything, he assembled a council and declared that he had two desires:

Firstly, that the draining of the Pontine Marshes should be completely effectuated; and secondly, that the Tiber should be diverted from its bed in Rome.

---

[66] The mathematicians Joseph-Louis Lagrange (1735-1813), Gaspard Monge (1746-1818) and Gaspard de Prony (1755-1839); the chemist Claude-Louis Berthollet (1748-1822); the antiquarian Ennio Quirino Visconti (1751-1818): the archeologist Vivant Denon (1747-1825); the antiquarian Aubin Louis de Millin (1759-1818): the architect Charles Percier (1764-1838); and the artist Pierre Fontaine (1762-1853).

[67] Louis-Mathieu Molé (1781-1855) served the Empire as Minister of Justice as well as in the indicated role, and continued his career under Louis XVIII, Charles X and Louis-Philippe, but abandoned politics in 1839 until he was elected as a député under the Third Republic. The 1851 coup drove him into retirement again.

Those two orders were received with admiration by the council, and welcomed with enthusiasm when they were known in Rome.

The mathematicians and engineers, headed by Messieurs de Prony and Monge, were charged with draining the pestilential marshes, cadaverous ruins of an ancient and excessive civilization, which, in a country then depopulated, infallibly consumed those who dared to reside there.

A system of canalization was devised and conducted over a number of points that extended as far as Terracina. Large areas were hollowed out in basins, in imitation of the London docks. The port of Terracina was greatly extended, and two years after the Emperor's arrival, that region, so beautiful under ancient Rome had reappeared, dried out, sanitized and brilliant, only requiring a population, which hastened from the towns and resuscitated it. Terracina, having become one of the most important ports in the Mediterranean, was able to contain and shelter a numerous fleet in its basins, and communicate deep into the interior via the canals that had been dug.

In the delirium of their gratitude, the people of Rome and Naples erected a statue a hundred feet high in honor of the Emperor, placed on the height of Mont Circello; it was covered with bronze leaf, and a lighthouse was established in the pedestal supporting it, as if a new benefit out to burn incessantly in sacrifice at the feet of the benefactor.

The environs of Rome, which offered a spectacle of sterility and desolation, were vanquished by the stubborn skill of the engineers; immense plantations were created there; raised aqueducts brought over their arcades, as if over innumerable triumphal arches, the waters that came to refresh and fecundate the region, and within the desert circle that surrounded the holy city for fifty leagues around, life, agriculture and numerous populations reappeared, as in the times of the Caesars.

In exchange for that benefit, an admirable devastation was committed in favor of France. Trajan's column was removed, transported to Paris and erected in the middle of the courtyard of the Louvre, which as paved in marble throughout its extent.

Rome mourned that loss, but it was so rich in antique columns, including the Antonine column and the countless obelisks that Augustus had once removed from the land of Sesostris, that it wept in silence over the action of a conqueror who had otherwise done so much for them.

It was, however, above all with the Church of Saint Peter, the sole marvel of the modern world, that Napoléon occupied his thought and his action. The envious successors of Michelangelo had wanted to outdo his plans, and, confusing the long with the great, had spoiled the great man's Greek cross, extending the nave of the church immeasurably, and inflicting the most insignificant of portals on its face.

Napoléon wanted, boldly, to restore to Saint Peter's the primitive grandeur that Michelangelo had created. But there is in religious monuments a double consecration of art and religion, which sanctifies their form and renders even their faults venerable. He therefore left the Latin cross, whose extent was regarded as marvelous by the Catholic faithful.

However, having made that concession to religious sentiment, he had the columns of the portal destroyed, and the rows of intersections that disfigured it. In their place three rows of superimposed unequal arcades were erected, above a line of ten smaller ones, and finally, on the highest row, twenty more crowned with an admirable attic and twenty-one colossal statues. Tuscan, Ionian and Corinthian columns separated and ornamented those arcades, whose ensemble was simultaneously reminiscent of the grandiosity of the Pont du Gard and the majesty of the Coliseum.

The Emperor drew up the plans personally that would serve for the deviation of the Tiber.

The profound excavations made along the line traced by his imperial hand discovered immense riches in antiquities, subsequently distributed in the museums of the Empire.

When the day arrived on which, those channels being finished, the Tiber—the old and young Tiber—was to quit its eternal bed for a unaccustomed bed, the Italian and almost Roman population of Rome was seen to leap into its cherished river, to bathe there amorously, and to plunge into it joyfully as if to prepare it for the great revolution.

At an agreed signal, cannons were fired and the bells of all the churches rung; the Pope, accompanied by the sacred college, gave his benediction to the people and the Tiber. From the height of a very elevated throne, the Emperor gave the order. The last barriers were broken and the river as precipitated, roaring terribly, into the unfamiliar channels, leaving its former bed dry, delivered naked to the gaze of its people.

Twenty thousand workers and soldiers were employed in digging in the abandoned bed of the Tiber. An administrative order reigned over those works, and the smallest discoveries were registered and placed in various depositories established by the administration.

Who could tell what the old Roman river enclosed in its entrails? For more than two thousand years, jealously, it had been swallowing all the riches of the Republic, and the city of Emperors and Popes. Every invasion of barbarians had accumulated treasures there. It was as if it were paved by the most magnificent sculptures. Everything reappeared: the marbles, the gold, the bronze, the statues, the bucklers and the weapons: another Rome, the ancient one, asleep in the noble mud of the Tiber, resuscitated to enrich French Rome.

The great work of Messieurs Visconti, Denon and Percier gives precious details of the diversion of the Tiber and the discoveries made in consequence.

Napoléon was present everywhere; he presided, with the simple and expansive joy particular to great minds, over those admirable works. He felt proud of the victories that he was winning over the past, and could not get enough of that city, which he was seeing for the first time. For, even though his expeditions had taken him, in several epochs of his life, to the gates of Rome and Jerusalem, he had always avoided until then entering within their walls, as if he feared contact then with the superhuman grandeur of the two cities, and dreaded that his glory might be obscured by theirs.

## Chapter XII
### MADAME DE STAEL

The Emperor left Rome after having filled it with his genius and his benefits; everything was done for the magnificence of Italy and for its happiness; he had nothing more to order there, and left the rest to time. In any case, a few muffled warning of a great movement in the north of Europe had attracted his attention keenly, and he thought that the return was necessary.

He went via Geneva, where the Baronne de Staël was languishing in exile.[68] He wanted to settle things with that celebrated woman; he knew what hatred she retained for him for persecutions endured, but he also knew the power that the imperial smile had and the first step taken by his power.

Madame de Staël usually resided on her estate at Coppet in the environs of Geneva, but she was in the city when an orderly officer came to inform her that the emperor had arrived and was about to come to her residence. A moment later, a carriage stopped and Napoléon got out.

The Baronne de Staël's position was very difficult. Caught almost unawares, still driven by discontent and per-

---

[68] Germaine de Staël (1766-1817) was the daughter of the statesmen Jacques Necker, who thought it politic to flee France when the 1789 Revolution broke out, but she thought it safe to stay until 1792, when the Terror prompted her to return to her native Switzerland, were she hosted a salon at Coppet that became famous and produced her own classic works, foundation-stones of the French Romantic Movement, including the novel *Corinne* (1805) and the study *De l'Allemagne* [On Germany] (1810). She returned to Paris frequently until 1804, when she commenced what she described as a long ideological "duel" with Napoléon and he ordered that she be kept away.

haps hatred, she was not prepared at all when Napoléon came straight toward her and, extending his hand, took hers and said to her: "Your genius is a power, Madame, and I have come to treat with you."

In the greatest surprise and overjoyed by that unusual mark of honor, Madame de Staël gave her hand to the emperor, who shook it and began to weep.

The emperor told the people accompanying him to leave, and remained alone with her for two hours.

It is certain that in the conversation that followed, he expressed his regrets for having been mistaken on her account; the she had been represented to him as a genius to be feared, but that a recent reading of her works in Italy had transported him with admiration; that he had seen Rome with Corinne, and that if, in fact, her great merit could have made him fear having her for an adversary, on the other hand, nothing was more to be sought than her amity.

Madame de Staël could not contain her emotion, and, throwing herself at Napoléon's knees, she told him that, in spite of her dolor, she had nevertheless professed for him a kind of hero-worship, and that his step, made at that moment caused her heart to overflow with joy and gratitude.

The emperor spoke to her about her book on Germany, of which his ministers had stopped the printing. "That was barbaric!" he exclaimed. "I want that book, Madame, to be printed at the Louvre by the imperial presses."

In talking to her, he called her Madame la Duchesse.

"Your Majesty has let a title fall," she said, smiling.

"I have raised it to your level, Madame," he replied.

Then he spoke about the Académie Française and asked her seriously whether she wanted to be a part of it. Madame de Staël replied with the same gravity that she would be happy to receive that honor. It seemed that he ought not even to raise the question of whether a woman could be a member of the Institut.

"You shall be, Madame," he said. "To avoid the preliminaries, I shall make your intention known personally, and you will see the Académie coming to you."

He went out then, and asked her whether she was returning to Coppet; Madame de Staël replied that it was indeed her intention. They left together, and the Emperor, offering her his hand to help her into the imperial carriage, said to those surrounding it: "I introduce to you Madame la Duchesse de Staël, Messieurs." Then he placed her by his side in the carriage, and, having stayed for an hour at Coppet, departed from there directly for Paris, to which Madame de Staël returned herself a month later.

On his return to Paris Napoléon summoned the Académie Française to the Tuileries and told its members that, the death of Bernardin de Saint-Pierre having left a seat vacant, the thought that the Académie would be honored by a choice such as that of Madame la Duchesse de Staël. The following day she was elected unanimously to that illustrious company.

Sometime after that, the reception session took place, witnessed by the Emperor and the imperial family. Madame de Staël's speech was sublime, as is well-known; it was full of literary boldness and profound views. The enthusiasm of the recipiendary for the Emperor burst out several times, and was shared by the assembly, which covered both of them with acclamations.

## Chapter XIII
## MOREAU

It seemed that Napoléon, having risen so high above everything, wanted, for want of empires, to conquer human beings.

Moreau,[69] since the judgment that had exiled him, was living in America, contemplating the great events in Europe with the insouciance typical of him, and scarcely thinking that he had seen the throne on which his enemy was sitting at such close range himself.

From Rome, Napoléon sent General Andréossy[70] to America to the victor of Hohenlinden, bearing and amicable letter and important propositions.

When General Andréossy reached Moreau he found the great man habituated to the most simple life, working in his garden, seemingly oblivious to world-shaking events.

---

[69] Jean Victor Moreau (1763-1813) was in command of the Army of the Rhine when the Battle of Hohenlinden was won, but then retired to Paris, where he became the focal point of those opposed to Napoléon's aggrandizement, allegedly under the influence of his ambitious wife; when the group was arrested, Moreau was banished and settled in America. In our history he returned to Europe after hearing about the retreat from Moscow and joined forces with the Crown Prince of Sweden and Czar Alexander in opposition to the beleaguered Emperor, but was fatally wounded at the battle of Dresden in August 1813.

[70] Comte Antoine-François Andréossy (1761-1828) was Napoléon's ambassador to Constantinople in 1812; he retired thereafter but returned during the Hundred Days and was one of the negotiators with the coalition in the wake of Waterloo, continuing his career on behalf of the monarchy thereafter.

He received Napoléon's offers coldly and said that he would not accept anything from him. But General Andréossy, who knew that that great character lacked energy and persistence with regard to personal matters, returned to the charge the next day. Moreau was to be created a Maréchal de France, Duc de Carniole and great eagle of the Légion d'honneur.

Moreau hesitated then; he missed his homeland; his wife and daughter talked about nothing but the joy of seeing France again. He floated for a while, still uncertain, and then accepted. General Andréossy profited from that resolution with insistence, and persuaded him to leave right away and embark on a French frigate that would take General Moreau's name if it brought him back to France.

That act of generosity on the Emperor's part was not without calculation; in that epoch, the army was renewed, a new generation of soldiers had arrived, having heard as if in the distance of the exiled general's glory, but they were no longer the army of the Rhine that would have shed their blood for an adored general. Moreau's glory was ancient, almost history, and his name could no longer have any effect on the masses. So the Emperor knew that he was no longer to be feared, and that there as everything to gain by bringing the illustrious general to his side at the moment of a great war that he suspected to be imminent.

Moreau arrived in France, and was immediately presented to the Emperor, Napoléon stood up, ran to him and embraced him. "Monsieur le Maréchal," he said to him, "my ambassador has forgotten to ornament you with the most illustrious of your tiles. Then he said, in a loud voice and with majesty: "I salute you, Prince of Hohenlinden..."

At the name of the victory that had made him so illustrious, Moreau bowed and seized Napoléon's hand; he was about to kiss it in gratitude when the other raised him to his feet; they embraced for a second time. From that moment on, Moreau's amity and devotion was gained by the Emperor.

An immense fortune was assured to him; a palace would be constructed for him at State expense in the Rue Caumartin, which would take the name of Rue de Hohenlinden. A victory sixteen years old could be named with impunity then. Napoléon would not have done any of that a few years earlier.

## Chapter XIV
## SARDINIA

In his voyage to Rome, in spite of pressing invitation from Murat, the King of the Two Sicilies. The Emperor had not wanted to go to Naples. He could already see a tortuous suggestion in the conduct and manners of that sovereign and an intention to behave with a certain independence.

That was certain to displease Napoléon, so he replied that the exclusive concerns of his empire obliged him to renounce a voyage to Naples.

At the same time that King Murat was soliciting from his suzerain the favor of receiving him in his capital, in a bold expression of his power and his liberty, he unbridled his ambition and thus tried to discover exactly to what extent he could act within the sphere of his own power without offending the Emperor grievously.

Napoléon's grandeur importuned the jealous soul of Murat. He wanted to be a conqueror in his turn.

Sardinia, then governed incognito, so to speak, by the House of Savoy, became the objective of his thought. He resolved to invade it. A Neapolitan frigate was given orders to capture a Sardinian boat; that led to a protest on the part of King Victor Emmanuel, which led in turn to a superb refusal to satisfy that prince on the part of Murat, which led to a war.

A naval combat took place off the coast of Africa near the island of Zimbe, a ridiculous parody of the giant combats of the Empire. A Neapolitan ship of the line, a frigate and a few brigs, the entire fleet of the Kingdom of the Two Sicilies, easily destroyed the even weaker flotilla of Sardinia. Murat, at the head of an army of thirteen thousand men, also made his invasion, also had his small decisive battle, and entered Cagliari as a conqueror. There, also dating a decree from a conquered capital, that presumptuous imitator declared that the

121

House of Savoy had ceased to reign over Sardinia, and that the kingdom in question was united with that of the Two Sicilies.

King Victor Emmanuel, thus dispossessed of his Estates, had succeeded in escaping to Corsica after his defeat in a fishing boat.

Without giving any notification to Napoléon, Murat had undertaken and completed his conquest, and he thought he ought to persist in that boldness and not let him know when it was concluded.

Profoundly irritated by that action, the Emperor retained it in his heart and bided his time. Nevertheless, via the intermediary of the Prefect of Bastia, where King Victor Emmanuel had taken refuge, he invited that king to come to France. Between Toulon, where he landed, and Paris he was welcomed with the honors due to a sovereign. The Emperor received him personally with studied respect, assigned him a palace, and after a few days, mingled him with the host of the other kings of his court.

## Chapter XV
## *THE NORTH-EASTERN LEAGUE*

If the Emperor did not show with regard to Murat what he was when he believed himself offended—terrible and inflexible—it was because the symptoms of a great revolution were then appearing to his eyes, where Europe still saw a pure and cloudless sky everywhere.

Russia, the great power that had previously believed herself powerful enough to struggle against the monarch of the South, and perhaps to overthrow him, was devouring the humiliation of the war of 1812 and shedding tears of blood over her beautiful provinces of Poland and Finland, removed from her domination.

After that same war, Sweden had seen one of her crowns fall from her head—that of Norway.

And Prussia, ever turbulent, inflamed with hatred against France, which could not forgive her for the unpardonable shame of Iéna and ten other defeats, was calling every day for vengeance and contemplating with envy and fury what Saxe and Germany had gained from her when the victor dismembered her provinces.

A new and mysterious coalition was formed between those three powers; proposals to join it were made with the greatest secrecy and in a rather vague fashion to the new King of Poland. Poniatowski rejected them with horror, and declared proudly that he would be the first to warn the Emperor of the French, to whom he owed everything.

Denmark, Austria and Scotland were also sounded in their intentions, in order to be aggregated to the alliance; all three refused, the first by virtue of gratitude, the second fear and the last weakness.

Only Turkey remained to be won in Europe, a blind power stationed proudly in the middle of the movement of the world.

Von Hardenberg sent Goltz to Constantinople, without any apparent mission, who was joined by Nesselrode and Posen in Belgrade, and all three obtained an audience with the Great Turk.[71]

That Sultan was inclined to peace and some amity with Napoléon, but the natural presumption of the Turks was excited by the offers made by the three powers and dreams of the glory of conquest.

Illyria and the Ionian islands, which had become French, were to be restored to Turkey, as well as Transylvania, which Austria would be obliged to surrender. Hope was also offered that Venice might be detached from the French Empire to become a Turkish province.

Mahmoud therefore entered into the coalition that history has named the North-Eastern League.

The operations of the four allied powers were planned as follows: a part of the Russian army would march on Warsaw and take possession of it, while the rest of the army, together with the combined military forces of Sweden and Prussia, would move into Westphalia and Bavaria; Turkey, for its part, would simultaneously embark its troops in the Kingdom of Italy, on the coasts of Ancona, and mount a land invasion via Illyria.

The operations of the four powers had been planned in the greatest secrecy in their cabinets. They were counting a great deal on the element of surprise.

But the Emperor Napoléon knew everything.

---

[71] Karl-August von Hardenberg (1750-1822) became chancellor of Prussia in 1810, and undertook far-reaching schemes of social, political and military reform, although his influence was soon eclipsed by Metternich. August von der Goltz (1765-1832) was his Minister of Foreign Affairs. Karl Nesselrode (1780-1862) was the Russian foreign minister. "Posen" remains enigmatic, the Swedish minister of Foreign Affairs at the time, in our history, being Lars von Engeström.

## Chapter XVI
## THE WAR OF 1817

The month of February 1817 was reached without any external manifestation having yet revealed the war plans of the North-Eastern League. Already, under Napoléon's orders, the Empire's fleets, comprised of those of France, England, Holland and Demark were gathered in the ports of Toulon, Barcelona and Genoa, and in February, all those fleets set sail for the Adriatic.

At the same time, land forces were held in readiness on the banks of the Rhine. One might have thought that Europe was expecting some prodigious result, so great was the silence, and, so to speak, the stupor of nations.

The Russian army commenced hostilities first, attacking Grodno in Poland and taking possession of the city. From then on, everything was ablaze: the four powers of the league and France, which drew the rest of Europe behind her.

The King of Poland attempted to retake Grodno, but in vain. The Maréchal Ducs de Bellune and Tolosa—Victor[72] and Foy—rushed to his aid and entered Poland with forty thousand soldiers.

The Prince of Hohenlinden, Moreau, with a hundred thousand French, English and Danish troops, occupied Mecklenburg and Denmark, heading toward Sweden.

The King of Italy, Eugène, with the Neapolitans, Austrians and Bavarians, and along with the corps of the Maréchals Prince de la Moskowa and Duc de Castiglione, entered Bosnia and Serbia.

The French fleet, divided into two squadrons, under the orders of the Admiral Comte de Yarmouth and Viceroy

---

[72] Maréchal Claude-Victor Perrin (1764-1841) was known familiarly as "Victor." He supported Louis XVIII during the Hundred Days but later refused to serve Louis-Philippe.

Missiessy,[73] appeared in the Archipelago and set sail for Constantinople.

The Emperor himself, at the head of the Grande Armée, traversed Bavaria and entered Prussia once again.

Then the tempest of war roared in all is fury—but it was brief, for almost simultaneously, in the course of April 1817:

Constantinople was bombarded and taken by our fleets, and Admiral Missiessy took the government for France.

The King of Poland and Maréchal de Bellune entered Moscow, while Maréchal Foy took possession of Petersburg.

Moreau, having crushed a part of the Swedish army at Wexio, had entered Stockholm as the master of Sweden.

For his part, the King of Italy had carved the Turkish army into pieces near Belgrade, killing twenty-five thousand men.

And on 21 April, under the walls of Berlin, the Emperor, with his Grand Armée, in the most extraordinary of victories, had annihilated the combined Swedish, Russian and Prussian armies. On the evening of that day, a stray cannonball struck Czar Alexander dead.

The rapidity of those victories, happening at the same time, confounded the famous North-Eastern League, which vanished like a cloud before the sun.

The Emperor did not deign to enter Berlin. He appointed the Maréchal Duc de Dalmatie governor general of the city and Prussia entire—after which he withdrew to Dresden, where the new arrived in rapid succession of those unprecedented successes, and it was there that the suppliant kings, their courts and ministers, came to meet him. Conquests and victories had never been so sudden, and the European power

---

[73] Édouard-Thomas de Burgues, Comte de Missiessy (1756-1837) undertook various missions in the Caribbean on behalf of the Empire, but incurred Napoléon's wrath for disobeying his orders; he is nowadays more celebrated for the supportive role he had earlier played in the American War of Independence.

of the Emperor had never been more assured. Everyone trembled before him; all were subservient or vanquished.

## Chapter XVII
## DRESDEN

On 8 May 1817, the Emperor made it known to the kings and ministers of the vanquished States that he consented to receive them. Early in the morning, the principal reception rooms of the Royal Palace of Dresden were crowded by the kings of Prussia and Sweden, the three Grand Dukes of Russia, wearing mourning for their brother, the Emperor Alexander, and Mahmoud's brother, accompanied by a numerous court. Napoléon made them wait for a long time, and that disdain was his first vengeance. At midday, the crowd was introduced. A single seat was in the room where the Emperor received them, and he did not even stand up when the kings and the others came in.

"What do you want with me?" he cried, darting a gaze flamboyant with anger at them.

The King of Sweden advanced, trembling, and said in a faint and respectful voice: "We request from Your Majesty the treaty that he pleases to grant us."

"No treaty," said the Emperor, in a thunderous voice. "Orders! Go!"

Never had he seemed so irritated and so scornful. He sensed that Europe was at his feet and that he could trample it as he pleased.

They all went out, with rage and shame in their hearts.

The Emperor ordered the Duc de Bassano to write to the Kings of Sweden and Prussia and the three Grand Dukes of Russia that they could not return to their States, of which the destiny had not been decided. The city of Prague was designated to them as a place of residence. They went there.

After the victory of Belgrade, the King of Italy traversed Serbia and Rumelia, and, also having entered Constantinople, received orders from the Emperor regarding that country. In consequence, he had Rumelia, where the remains of the Turkish army were, evacuated. The troops, and Sultan Mahmoud, were transported to Asia, on the other side of the Bosphorus.

That war, so great, in which half of Europe had battled the other, was thus ended in very little time by the most memorable victory. It was the last, and in the early days of June 1817, that part of the world was the entire and exclusive property of Napoléon, who could divide it as he wished, and let the dependent crowns fall as he pleased on the heads of vassal princes.

## Chapter XVIII
## POLITICS

The anger that the Emperor had manifested in the brief interview in Dresden, and in the two terrible words that he had hurled at the kings, was calculated, and had an interest.

It left the vanquished in a complete uncertainty as to their fate, and, in consequence, in a more fearful wait for the will of the man on whom they depended. And the latter gave them time to think about the way in which he would take advantage of that final triumph.

Napoléon knew that the hour had sounded in which there was no one but him in Europe, and all the others, kings or nations, were his subjects. Europe was entirely his; he could proclaim it; he did not hesitate to do so.

Russia and England were the only powers that his genius had been able to fear. They no longer existed.

You know how he had annihilated England.

As for the nation of the North, Russia, ever-reborn beneath her ice, he promised himself that she would no longer be redoubtable, and that he would abuse her in the measure of the smallest States. What a glorious sensuality there was or him, besides, in incessantly kneading and remaking empires, distributing crowns, renewing the earth, in order finally to realize the promise that he had once made himself, one day to be the most ancient of the monarchs of Europe. And in order that no one should misinterpret the striking actions of sovereignty that he was preparing, he took pleasure, before anything else, in annihilating the titles of Emperor and Czar that still decorated imperial heads, and passing a royal leveler over all other sovereign princes.

He alone would conserve the title of Emperor, and already he had made it known the esteem in which he held that of King when he stripped himself and gave to Eugène the title of King of Italy, about which he no longer cared.

Having become the master of Europe, the other title of Protector of the Confederation of the Rhine became derisory; he rejected that too; he got rid of it at the same time as the despotic mediation in which he let go of the Swiss confederation.

It pleased him, too, to make a batch of kings, as if to weaken that character by dint of rendering it common.

To give a greater brilliance to those changes, which were anticipated with so much anxiety, he delayed its execution by three months, keeping the kings prisoner in Prague and the peoples uncertain as to their destiny.

While he was preparing to reconstitute Europe, he returned to France, surrounded by his glory, marching in the midst of pomp and acclamations, welcomed almost as a god; but his genius had already lost its taste for triumphs, and no longer lived for anything but ambition and power.

## Chapter XIX
## TRIUMPH

I have been brief in speaking of those victories. What would be the point of describing them magnificently, when they were so rapid and simultaneous, that admiration, summoned simultaneously in Sweden, in Turkey, in Germany and in Russia, could not be recognized, so to speak, in that confusion of triumphs, when every day had two or three battles to consecrate, when the capitals were overpowered at the same time, and one could not even assign a date to each of those conquests?

What does the description of the battles matter, the number of the dead, the relative calculation of glory, which, before deploring the loss of ten thousand men of the fatherland, determines whether it is necessary to rejoice because a hundred thousand have succumbed on the other side?

What do the details matter of treasures removed, cannons captured, monuments of art torn from their native soil, innocent trophies of genius become trophies of war?

What does it matter? For all of that is summarized in two words: victory and conquest.

History, painters, gravediggers, artillerists, generals and almanacs record all those things, and place them with exactitude.

I have already announced that I am not writing history.

Thus, I shall not recall the triumph of Napoléon and his victorious Grande Armée when it deployed, sparkling with iron and pride, along the roads of France, like an immense serpent in the colors of gold and emerald.

The newspapers reported those fêtes, the joy that burst forth as they passed by, the population holding hands, and forming a single incessant hedge of cries, homages and enthusiasm all the way from Strasbourg to Paris.

And the triumphal aches! And the flowers with which the roads were strewn! And he young women in white, gathered like garlands of white roses, surrounding the heroes and kneeling before them.

And the cannons of the big towns, the bells and the rifles of the villages, and all the hills flamboyant with fires of joy!

And the universal delirium!

And the bodies of State that traveled twenty leagues from the capital in order to assure the great man sooner of their respect and delight! And the entry into Paris under the victory arches of the Étoile and Louis XIV; the streets with their carpets of flowers, the houses clad in fabrics like festival garments; and the heads appearing everywhere, from the highest windows and skylights, and he millions of mouths resounding with the endless cry: "Vive l'empereur!"

And him! The Emperor, overwhelmed by fatigue, glory and ennui, returning in the evening to the Château des Tuileries, where he could not sleep.

That is a triumph!

## Chapter XX
## THE ARC DE TRIOMPHE AT THE ÉTOILE

In accordance with orders received the previous year, the Arc de Triomphe at the Étoile was about to be covered in white marble. Already, Canova and Chaudet[74] had finished the model of the two colossal statues of Glory and Peace that, seated and leaning back, would crown the gigantic edifice with their majestic repose. The two sculptors were on the point of carving their marble. But the works were halted. Another material, more glorious, was to replace that one. Cannons without number had been captured from the enemy, useless machines since submissive Europe no longer had any more need of the death that emerged from their mouths for the great game that they had lost.

The Emperor ordered that the arch of the Étoile should be entirely clad in the bronze of the cannons captured in the recent war. So, from that time on, it was called the Bronze Gate—and eleven years later, the Golden Gate, when, in 1828, the bronze was entirely gilded.

The two columns of the Barrière du Trône, thin the grand Rue Impériale, were also covered with that vanquished bronze. One of them bore in letters of gold the names of the combats of that last campaign, and the other those of the generals who had been the most illustrious therein.

But those striking manifestations of Napoléon's power and glory seemed negligible, and vanished before the *Moniteur* of 15 August 1817, the new anniversary of his birth. He liked that similarity of date, as if he were dissolving history within himself, and as if his name were thus to envelop all the great revolutions of the world. This time, it was the subjugation of Europe.

I shall copy that *Moniteur*.

---

[74] The neoclassical sculptor Antoine-Denis Chaudet (1763-1810).

## Chapter XXI
## *THE* MONITEUR UNIVERSEL *OF 5 AUGUST 1817*

*Napoléon, Emperor of the French, sovereign of Europe.*

*The history of the last twenty years, all marked by battles, bloodshed, the convulsions of empires and the misery of peoples, has made Europe aware that a mortal vice existed in its constitution.*

*That multiplicity of States, powers and equal ambitions led incessantly to wars and disasters.*

*God had shown that the continent required a sovereign, and that such a republic of kings without a leader was not in His designs.*

*Providence, guiding us with its finger through our victories to the conquest of Europe, has visibly summoned us to that signal sovereignty.*

*In consequence:*

*On the report of our ministers;*

*In view of the deliberations of the French Senate, sufficiently garnished with kings and sovereign princes;*

*In view of the advice of our Council of State;*

*We have decreed and decree the following:*

*Article 1. Europe is divided into kingdoms and vassal principalities, under the immediate sovereignty of the French Empire.*

*Article 2. The French Empire alone conserves the title of Empire, and its sovereign that of Emperor, the other former monarchs and powers henceforth taking the title of realms and principalities.*

*Article 3. The division of Europe will be regulated by decree.*

*Article 4. The Emperor of the French will appoint the kings and princes of those various States.*

*Article 5. The principle of legitimate succession to thrones and principalities is recognized and established by the present decree.*

*Article 6. Nevertheless, the heads of those governments, realms and principalities, must receive the agreement and investiture of the Emperor of the French.*

*Article 7. The Emperor of the French takes the title: Emperor of the French, Sovereign of Europe.*

*Article 8. The kings, the sovereign princes of Europe and the ministers of our Empire will each execute, insofar as it concerns them, the present decree.*

*From the Imperial Palace of the Tuileries, 15 August 1817*

*Napoléon.*

### Second Decree

*Napoléon, Emperor of the French, Sovereign of Europe,*
*In view of our decree dated this day, creating the title of Emperor of the French, Sovereign of Europe,*
*We have decreed and decree the following:*

*Article 1. The titles of King of Italy, Protector of the Confederation of the Rhine, Mediator of the Swiss Confederation, will henceforth no longer be given to us; we have disposed of them and dispose of them by the present decree.*

*From the Imperial Palace of the Tuileries, 15 August 1817*

*Napoléon.*

## Third Decree

*Napoléon, Emperor of the French, Sovereign of Europe,*
*In view of our decree dated this day, creating the title of*
*Emperor of the French, Sovereign of Europe,*
*We have decreed and decree the following:*

*Article 1. Europe is composed of different States of the following formation and circumscription:*
*1. The French Empire, which contains France, Corsica, Holland, Hanover, Holstein, Oldenburg, Italy, Illyria and England.*
*Annexed to our Empire, becoming integral parts of it, are and will remain Albania, Rumelia, Greece, Morea, the Ionian islands and the Archipelago, Malta and Catalonia;*
*2. The kingdom of Spain;*
*3. The kingdom of Westphalia;*
*4. The kingdom of the Two Sicilies;*
*5. The kingdom of Portugal;*
*6. The united kingdom of Austria and Hungary;*
*7. The kingdom of Walachia and Moldavia, to which will remain united Bessarabia, Transylvania, Serbia and Bulgaria, and a part of Bosnia, the other part of that province, which borders Illyria, being united with the French Empire;*
*8. The kingdom of Switzerland;*
*9. The kingdom of Poland;*
*10. The united kingdom of Scotland and Ireland;*
*11. The kingdom of Bavaria;*
*12. The kingdom of Wurtemburg;*
*13. The kingdom of Saxony;*
*14. The kingdom of Baden;*
*15. The united kingdom of Denmark and Norway;*
*16. The kingdom of Sweden and Finland;*
*17. The kingdom of Russia, capital Petersburg;*
*18. The kingdom of Moscovia, capital Moscow;*
*19. The kingdom of Bohemia;*

20. The kingdom of Silesia and Posen;
21. The kingdom of Sardinia.

*Article 2. The sovereign princes of Germany conserve their possessions as they existed under our protectorate of the Confederation of the Rhine.*

*From the Imperial Palace of the Tuileries, 15 August 1817*

*Napoléon.*

## Chapter XXII
## THE PROMOTION OF KINGS

### Fourth Decree

*Napoléon, Emperor of the French, Sovereign of Europe,*

*In view of article 4 of the first of our decrees dated this day;*

*In view of our third decree of this day;*

*We have promoted and summoned to the dignity of kings the princes of our family whose names follow:*

*Article 1. Our brother Joseph Napoléon is named King of Spain.*

*Our brother Louis Napoléon, former King of Holland, is named King of Silesia and Posen.*

*Our brother Jérôme Napoléon, King of Westphalia is named King of the Two Sicilies.*

*Our brother Lucien Napoléon, former King of Portugal, is named King of Switzerland.*

*Our brother-in-law Joachim Napoléon, former King of the Two Sicilies, is named King of Sweden and Finland.*

*Our brother-in-law Félix Napoléon, Prince de Luques, is named King of Portugal.*

*Our brother-in-law Napoléon Borghese is named King of Westphalia.*

*Article 2. Promoted to the dignity of king and summoned to the sovereignty of States whose designation follows are:*

*1. To the realm of Austria and Hungary, the former Emperor of Austria;*

*2. To the realm of Scotland and Ireland, the former King of England;*

*3. To the realm of Poland, King Poniatowski;*

*4. To the realm of Bavaria, King Maximilien-Joseph;*

5. To the realm of Wurtemburg, King Frédéric;

6. To the realm of Saxony, King Frédéric-Auguste;

7. To the realm of Baden, Grand Duc Charles Frédéric;

8. To the united realm of Denmark and Norway, King Frédéric VI;

9. To the realm of Sardinia, King Victor Emanuel;

10. To the realm of Bohemia, Frédéric Guillaume III, former King of Prussia;

11. To the realm of Walachia and Moldavia, Frédéric Auguste, Grand-Duc de Moldavia,

Article 3. The Russias of Europe and Asia are divided into three realms: 1. Russia: capital Petersburg; 2. Muscovy: capital Moscow; 3. Siberia: capital Tobolsk. The delimitation of these three realms will be fixed by special decree.

Promoted to the dignity of king and summoned to the sovereignty of the States whose designation follows are:

1. To the realm of Russia, Nicolas. Grand Duc de Russie

2. To the realm of Muscovy, Constantin, Grand-Duc de Russie;

3. To the realm of Siberia, Michel, Grand-Duc de Russie.

Article 4. The kings promoted by the present decree will enjoy dignities and royal powers, for themselves and their heirs and legitimate male descendants, by order of primogeniture.

Article 5. In default of legitimate male heirs, the Emperor of the French has the power to appoint a king for the vacant throne.

Article 6. Before their advancement to the throne, the kings of Europe will take an oath of fidelity and homage in the hands of the Emperor of France.

Article 7. The Emperor will summon, within a delay of three months, a general congress of the abovementioned *kings, summoned with the purpose of taking the oath specified in the previous article.*

*Article 8. Will conserve their title of king, to enjoy the prerogatives and honors due to that dignity and to take their rank among the titular kings and before the sovereign princes of Germany, the honorary kings whose names follow:*
*King Charles IV, former King of Spain;*
*King Ferdinand VII, former King of Spain;*
*King Ferdinand I, former King of the Two Sicilies;*
*King Charles XIII, former King of Sweden;*
*King Jean VII, former King of Portugal and King of Brazil.*

*Article 9. Will conserve their title of king, in order to rank immediately after us and before the kings of the royal blood, our beloved sons:*
*The King of Rome;*
*The King of England.*

*Article 10. Will take rank before the kings our brothers, our uncle the Holy Father, Pope Clement XV.*

*Article 11. Will take rank immediately after the kings of our blood:*
*The King of Italy, Eugène Napoléon.*

*Article 12. The kings nominated above in article 1, 2 and 3 of the present decree will be ranked in the same order in which they are placed in these articles, with the modifications made in articles 9, 10 and 11.*

*Article 13. The empresses and queens of our blood and our family will be placed, in great ceremonies, at the rank that it pleases us to indicate, without the preceding decisions being able to nullify our future dispositions.*

*Article 14. The sovereign princes of Germany will take rank after the kings in the order that will be prescribed by a special decree.*

*Given at the Imperial Palace of the Tuileries, 15 August 1817.*

*Napoléon.*

## Chapter XXIII
## REFLECTIONS

Reflections naturally flowed from that celebrated *Moniteur* of 15 August.

Prussia was erased therein from the kingdoms of Europe, and its sovereign transported to the throne of Bohemia.

Turkey disappeared as entirely from the States of Europe, and the Emperor took for himself what was most brilliant and useful from the rubble of that State—which is to say, Greece, the Archipelago and Constantinople.

Russia was seen therein at the lowest degree of abasement. As much as Napoléon had been able to fear her, he had wanted to divide her, weaken her and render her devoid of weight in the balance of peoples. She was stripped of Finland, of all the Polish provinces, and, to complete the impoverishment, divided into three States devoid of strength.

Strange reversals in the destiny of nations! When, at the end of the eighteenth century, Austria, Russia and Prussia attacked the cadaver of Poland and tore it to shreds, who would have thought that the day would come when Poland would be resuscitated more brilliantly, while of her avid enemies, Prussia would be annihilated, Russia divided in her turn and superb Austria would lose Bohemia with the title and rank of Caesar!

Sardinia was found restored as a Kingdom and removed from Naples; the time had come to punish Murat for that imprudent conquest and to relegate him to a northern throne.

Holstein was reunited with France, and her sovereign, always a faithful ally of Napoléon, was largely recompensed by the title of king of the northern provinces of the former Turkey.

The Grand Duke of Baden was seen in the decree to have become the pettiest of the kings of Europe.

All the members of the royal family had been made kings.

Lucien was also seen here charged with a bizarre royalty: the former republican had become the king of a republic.

In addition to Bohemia and the imperial title, Austria also lost Transylvania. Those chastisements punished for her hesitation during the North-Eastern League; she was, in addition, the only power still important—an empire, in sum—and Napoléon wanted no other empire but his own.

Five dispossessed sovereigns kept the title of king, but in those royal promotions there was still the same forgetfulness of the former kings of France.

It ought also to be noticed in those decrees that in attributing to himself the right and name of Sovereign of Europe, and rejecting his other titles, the Emperor no longer mentioned the grace of God and the constitutions of the State.

If ever an act of power had been accomplished on Earth thus far, that was undoubtedly it.

## Chapter XXIV
## MARIE-LOUISE

The Empress Marie-Louise was about to give birth when a sudden deterioration in her health brought her to the brink of the tomb.

The new King of Austria, her father, was suffering greatly from the deadly blow that the decree of 15 August had dealt him. At the beginning of the century he had already been forcibly deprived of his imperial German crown, but today, after having surrendered his provinces, his armies and his daughter to Napoléon, he had to descend to the rank of a mere king and divest himself of the imperial purple. It was horrible for him to have ceased to be a Caesar twice. Let Napoléon demand even more provinces from him, take his Styria, his Tyrol, even his Hungary, provided that he left him his imperial Austria!

It was in the midst of that affliction, and in those terms, that he wrote Marie-Louise a most energetic letter in which he asked her whether she was suffering as much humiliation as her father.

Marie-Louise, whom Napoléon kept apart from politics, only saw it as a matter of emotion and filial sentiment. Her father's entreaties troubled her. A few people devoted to the house of Austria were still active around her, whose intimate advice excited and emboldened her weakness; nevertheless, she sensed vaguely that her participation, even suppliant, in her husband's designs was imprudent and might be disastrous.

Already, at the commencement of her marriage, when Austria, wanted at least to exploit to the advantage of her politics the immense present of an archduchess, had pressed the empress to make a few demands, she had been refused coldly, and severity had chilled Napoléon's tenderness for the first time.

She had done nothing similar since, but in this latest circumstance, the dolor of Francis I seemed so sharp, his instigations so pressing, that she dared to make another attempt.

Napoléon, one can be sure, expressed his indignation in the most violent manner. The Empress, thunderstruck by his wrath, fell in a faint at his feet, as if dead. The Emperor, having calmed down, had her picked up and helped, but the deadly blow had struck, and a month had not gone by when she gave premature birth to a son, who lived, while she died the same day in the throes of childbirth.

Napoléon mourned her, for he had loved her; the most magnificent funeral was held, worthy of her and the sovereign of Europe. And for the first time since the destruction of their old tombs of kings, the restored crypts of Saint-Denis reopened to receive the remains of the empress.

The son that she deposited on the threshold of life as she died lived in spite of his extreme weakness; the Emperor gave him the title of King of Greece.

After the death of Marie-Louise, Napoléon thought profoundly about what he ought to do. In his ascendant march to European sovereignty, he had often regretted the bad ambition of old that had made him aspire to a wife of imperial blood. Then, it was a favor, but since then, that blood had fallen well beneath him. Now, in fact, he could hardly bear that alliance, which retained him on the same plane as other kings. The death of the Empress, while tearing his heart, rendered him a sort of liberty, and ensured that from now on, he would no longer have anything in common with the other kings.

## Chapter XXV
## JOSÉPHINE

Napoléon remembered then the Joséphine whom the people called the good Joséphine even after her disgrace, for the people are not a courtier who measure their homage according to fortune, but often reserve it for misfortune. She had always been called Napoléon's good genius. Since 1809, the epoch in which the Emperor's false politics had caused him to reject her, she had been languishing, always sad and suffering, in her beautiful palaces of Malmaison and Navarre, from which she still followed with her tearful eyes the life and glory of the great man she had loved so much.

The death of Marie-Louise must have been, for the creole soul of the Empress Joséphine, a fecund source of burning emotions, and perhaps she dreamed then of a return to the throne from which she had once descended.

That hope was not mistaken. A few days after the death of Marie-Louise, the King of Italy came to see her mother and announced the arrival of the Emperor at Malmaison.

It is not known what passed in the long meeting between Napoléon and Joséphine. It lasted from ten o'clock in the morning to dusk. Tears and cries were heard, perhaps tears and cries of joy, but no one has ever been able to penetrate the secret of that imperial reconciliation. At any rate, the Emperor, while dining with the Empress Joséphine, declared before the officers of the house that there was still a reigning Empress.

Paris, France and Europe soon heard about that great event. Unexpected as it was, it produced various effects. Every royal family had hoped in secret to see one of its daughters mount and sit upon the throne of thrones. That new marriage dashed many hopes.

Pope Clement XV blessed the new union at Notre-Dame, and the Empress Joséphine was crowned for a second time.

But it was France, above all, that quivered in joy at the news. There was an instinctive enthusiasm and love for the good Joséphine that cannot be explained; her disgrace had caused that as much as her generosity, for nothing inspires so much interest and affection as the misfortune of beautiful and tender souls. Thus, she had numerous resounding voices for her, those of the poor, who rejoiced in seeing that inexhaustible source of grace and benefits risen so high once again.

The Emperor, in reorganizing the Empress' household, gave her to accompany her a queen of honor; that was the Queen of Wurtemburg. Princes of the royal blood became her gentlemen, and they were already so far from their former royalty that they solicited those favors, and the Emperor did not spare them. He loved placing them thus at inferior ranks, from which they could only see his imperial majesty at a distance, and in which they learned more clearly how much distance there was between the sovereign and the kings of Europe.

# BOOK THREE

## Chapter I
## *ALGERIA*

After those great events—the North-Eastern war, the promotion of the kings and the Emperor's marriage—there was a longer peace, scarcely interrupted in the month of June 1818 by the brief and glorious Algerian expedition.

Ever insolent, that nation of pirates had not feared to offend the imperial flag of Europe, which, since the recognized suzerainty of the Emperor of the French, floated from the mainmast of ships of all the nations. A French ship was pillaged by Algerian corsairs. Immediately, the expedition was ordered, activated with the greatest vigor, and the disembarkation of considerable forces was soon effectuated on the African coast. As cowardly as it is superb, Algeria surrendered after the initial hostilities, and the tricolor flag flew over its citadels.

The Dey's treasures, amounting to nearly three hundred million francs, were taken to France, and the Dey was brought himself as a prisoner. The Emperor did not want to see him, and had him told by his Minister of Marine that he had hesitated as to whether to have him shot. He was held for two years in the prisons of Vincennes, and then transported to Asiatic Turkey.

After that first expedition, the Emperor, to whom that conquest had been represented as one of the most important for the security of the seas, ordered its continuation over the entire Barbary coast, which was swept clear of pirates from Morocco to Egypt. The four Barbary empires became a French colony; Algiers was its capital; one of the Emperor's aides-de-camp was appointed Governor General of the city and the colony, which was given the name of African France. Immense treasures were also found in the cities of Tunis, Morocco and Fez, which were swallowed by the cellars of the Tuileries, where the Emperor had been piling up incalculable riches for a long time.

That conquest had been brief and glorious, but decisive. Nothing any longer remained of the brigands who had infested the Mediterranean for ten centuries. Commerce breathed, and France gained, in addition to a magnificent colony, a coastline that gave her almost entire possession of the girdle of the Mediterranean.

More than two million French and European families that had only known poverty in their homeland obtained concessions of land and were transported to Africa, where they populated the vanquished terrain. There was a kind of enthusiasm of emigration in the poor class, which permitted the Emperor not to realize his political determination to render that emigration obligatory for the banishment of selected citizens.

A triple organization, judiciary administrative and military, was established in African France. It was divided into départements, but without ceasing to be submissive to a colonial regime, the Emperor not having wanted to make it an integral part of the Empire.

## Chapter II
## PEACE, CANALS AND ROADS

That expedition was the only one that interrupted peace between 1817 and 1820. Perhaps it cannot even be said that that was a war; the Emperor did not want to consider it as such; he regarded it as a punishment inflicted on pirates.

During those four years of peace, he devoted himself almost entirely to the organization of a complete system of roads and canals in the Empire. He ordered the creation of military roads, all departing from Paris and progressing almost in a straight line to the most important cities of the extremities of the Empire. The most extraordinary, incontrovertibly, was that from Paris to Constantinople, the breadth and beauty of which are considered as marvels. The others, though less extensive, were no less admirable; they were the military roads from Paris to Amsterdam, to Calais, to Hamburg, to Geneva, to Toulon, to Rome, and the branch of the Constantinople road that went from Scutari, in Morea, to Lepanto. The military road from London to Edinburgh only ceded to the one to Constantinople in length, for all of them were uniform in breadth and formation.

Canals were also established throughout French territory, especially in France. It was suggested to the Emperor that he realized the project, already long discussed, of a maritime canal from Paris to Le Havre, to which he replied that it did not matter much whether the sea came to Paris, since it went to Le Havre and almost to Rouen. "Le Havre, Rouen and Paris," he added, "are a single city, of which the Seine is the High Street." That was almost as poetic as Pascal's statement that "Rivers are roads that move."

By means of the system of the canalization of rivers, those moving roads were connected from the Garonne all the way to the Elbe by a chain of artificial rivers linking them all up, making a kind of immense network of navigation thrown over the entire Empire.

At the center, the Imperial Canal was created, greater in width and able to carry large-sized ships. It departed from Bordeaux and Lyon to join up in the vicinity of Orléans and was prolonged, via Paris, as far as Amsterdam. All the other départemental canals were connected to it; it was also a military road for commerce.

## Chapter III
## LIFE AND DEATH

In the epoch of 1819, a great scientific research was undertaken, perhaps the greatest and most sublime of all: that of life, of the mystery of life and death.

Three men of the most powerful genius, Bichat, Corvisart and Lagrange,[75] conceived almost at the same time the idea of exhausting all the resources of medicine, all the secrets of physiology and all the forces of physics to arrive at a knowledge of that verity.

The multiple experiments reported in the work included countless dissections carried out in living beings, in which they observed, in the first moments of fecundation, the first movements of nascent life, and also, in subjects who were about to die, that last symptoms of life at the moment of its departure. The most profound researches were carried out in the erudition of all the centuries; physicians, philosophers, cabalists and mystics were consulted; every intelligence of all the ages brought its tribute of the new or elevated thought that it had had. Finally, those three great men, uniting their triple genius for that great work, were to achieve the result of the most sublime discovery made on Earth, and a communication to human beings with one of the secrets that God had hidden from them previously.

---

[75] The anatomist and physiologist Marie-François Xavier Bichat (1771-1802) was long dead before the alternative history deviated from ours, but the vague account of the discovery seems to derive from his particular theory of vitalism. Jean-Nicolas Corvisart (1755-1821) was a celebrated physician who became Napoléon's chief physician during the Empire. It is not obvious what the mathematician and astronomer Lagrange would have been able to contribute, but nor is it obvious why Napoléon had earlier taken him to Rome.

You will recall the enthusiasm that was produced, in the month of September 1818, by the report made by Bichat to the Institut on behalf of his two colleagues. They had discovered life; they had seen it arrive, appear, insinuate itself and burst forth in inorganic matter, and later abandon living matter, extinguishing itself and separating itself from every molecule; they had recognized that etheric flame emerging from bodies, when the body was chilled and another power succeeded it there: death.

More than that, they had found in the highest physics the very force of life. Masters of directing galvanic and magnetic currents at will, they were seen, in their miraculous experiments, to reproduce and stimulate vital phenomena; in sum, to create—for under the action of the forces they directed, vessels were seen to blossoming and being born in bodies previously inert, palpitations begin, and life itself escaping from their superhuman hands.

And as if it were only a simple corollary of their discovery, they also applied it to the general system of the universe. The individual life of each world, and the relative life of all of them—which is to say, the general system of the world—was no more than an effect of the great principle that they had discovered. By extending their discovery, they completed it, and proved that life is one, that of an insect as that of a sun and its subservient planets.

That immense work will make our era illustrous, as the discovery of America made its own illustrious, and doubtless more so, for hazard and a bold intelligence were able to discover existing lands whose mystery was distant; but nothing equals the magnificent result of three powerful geniuses asking God to account for one of His great secrets, and arriving by necessity almost far as Him in order to extract it from Him, discovering the system of humankind as Newton discovered the system of the world, and teaching the humans off Earth how the divine intelligence organizes itself for its goal.

A few months after that report, in June 1819, the great work appeared entitled *The Discovery of Life and Death in*

*Human and Organized Beings*, by Bichat, Corvisart and Lagrange.

Exhausted by that ultimate effort of human faculties, the three great men died soon afterwards. It seemed that humankind could not go beyond what they had learned on Earth; that their souls had done enough, and had no more to do than to depart for another world where they would see all the other mysteries face to face.

Lagrange died first, scarcely a month after the publication of the book; in his final moments, philosophy was seen once again to master his agony, in order to dream of unknown secrets. He was about to die, and his desolate disciples foresaw that in a few hours he would no longer exist; and yet, he was silent and calm before the perceptions of his intelligence; one might have thought that he was seeing things that could not be understood. Suddenly, one of them, Dr. Hallé, moved by a sentiment of despair and genius, imagined a heroic remedy that might snatch Lagrange back from that imminent death for a few days, and restore a little life to him. But Lagrange, thus brought back to earth, was indignant, and pronounced the sublime words: "What are you doing? Why are you disturbing me? I was studying death."

## Chapter IV
## THE COUNCIL OF KINGS

Napoléon had lowered the status the kings sufficiently, and did not think that they could dream of raising their heads again, but there was something divine in that dignity that consecrates, even in the midst of adversity, and does not allow too extreme a curvature.

He had wanted all the European kings created, reestablished or confirmed by his decrees of 15 August to assemble in council in the final days of the month of December. The Louvre and the Tuileries were completed then; in those palaces, magnificent apartments were attributed to them, and far from seeing the grandeur of royalty that they had left in their capital cities weakened, they rediscovered it with more ostentation and magnificence in the imperial hostelry on which a master forced them to descend.

For two consecutive weeks, which the people called the imperial fortnight, the Emperor assembled them every morning in a council over which he always presided, in which the most important social questions were raised, in the general interests of Europe and the particular interests of each State.

Around a long oval table those crowned heads were arranged according to rank and seated on thrones; at the extremity of the table, a throne like all the others, but placed on a slightly higher platform, appeared to be the seat of honor; it was the one in which the Emperor sat down when he was told that the assembly was complete.

The room where the council was held was knows as the Hall of Kings; it is located, as everyone knows, at the extremity of the great gallery of paintings, in the Pavillon de Flore, at the corner of the garden and he quay.

There was in that council of kings such submission, and such great confidence in the intentions of the Emperor, that there never seemed to be any but one will and, so to speak, one head, so much did respectful hesitation oppress those regally banded foreheads, uniformly.

However, the three councils held in the three years following 1816 had seen their attitude modified; the regal spirit, that cannot entirely quit those it has consecrated, recommenced illuminating them once again. Time, which always removes everything, even glory and power, had revealed their weakness and had made them more aware of the heavy burden of their subjection.

One day—it was 20 December 1819—in mid-council, Napoléon expressed an entirely new idea. He wanted, by virtue of I know not what disdain, to invite the kings to consent in that session to a kind of royal charter which would bind them even more tightly to the feet of the imperial eagle. The striking, albeit tacit, submission of the vassal kings was no longer sufficient for him. In the caprice of the moment, it appeared to be necessary to him that a solemn document emanating from them should inform Europe and each of their peoples of what was certain, patent and official in their servitude.

That was too much for the hearts of kings, accustomed to adversity but not to shame. A murmur escaped from their ranks, like the testimony of a dolorous amazement.

Napoléon shivered profoundly at that unaccustomed movement, but what was he not obliged to feel when the King of Bohemia, the former King of Prussia, rose to his feet and spoke in these terms:

"Your Majesty has sickened our hearts with a proposition that his profound wisdom had doubtless not weighed. He knows the relationships that exist between us and our peoples, between our peoples and their kings. He knows in what veneration our scepter ought to be held, and how the sanctuary in which God and Your Majesty have placed us must be sacred for the nations. And now our character will be withered; scorn will be raised against us; the measure of our humiliation will be complete, and it will only remain for us to die. Your Majesty is doubtless forgetting at this moment what kings are on earth."

Those last words, spoken energetically, were followed by the approval of the council. All of them rose to their feet at the same time, repeating that such were their sentiments.

Napoléon, scintillating with fury, also rose to his feet and, thrusting back his armchair forcefully, struck the council table so violently that it was broken. Then, striding back and forth and looking at them with blazing eyes, he shouted angrily:

"Kings! Kings! Oh, I know, they are sometimes slaves who desire to be rebels.

"Kings! They are children into whose hands I have put two playthings, a scepter and an orb.

"But that scepter, I shall throw into the fire, and it will crackle there like a vile piece of wood.

"But that globe is nothing but a light bubble, which my breath has inflated, and my breath can burst."

The King of Sweden, Murat, raised his head as if to reply.

"Silence!" he cried, in a thunderous voice. "Silence, King of Sweden! Silence, all of you!" And he added, in the ultimate degree of exasperation: "Well, if you have forgotten what you are, know what I am!"

## Chapter V

## THE SOLDIER KING (1)

As he pronounced those words he plunged a paper-knife that he was holding in his hand into the table, and, rapidly approaching the window overlooking the quay, he opened it angrily, and almost all the panes broke as it slammed against the wall.

He looked out, and, having seen a grenadier in a police cap who was going tranquilly to his barracks, just about to cross the bridge to go over to the other bank of the Seine, he called out to him loudly. At that familiar voice the grenadier turned round, removing his cap, and looked for the person who had called to him. He soon saw the Emperor at the window, flamboyant with fury, who shouted to him: "Grenadier, come here!" At the same time, the Emperor gave an order that he was to be brought to him immediately.

A moment later, the soldier came in, his pipe in his mouth and his expression a trifle ironic, although surprised by the summons.

As soon as he was there, the Emperor sent his pages and officers away, remaining with the kings and the grenadier.

"Your name?" he said to him.

The soldier extinguished his pipe, and, standing to attention, replied confidently: "Guillaume Athon."

"You age, your regiment, your homeland?"

"Forty-seven years, from Pithiviers, grenadier in the Imperial Guard, second regiment, second battalion, first company."

"Your service? Your history?"

"Thirty-one years of service; twenty-two campaigns, Egypt, Italy, Spain, Russia, etc. No history. I've been hit, I have sixteen wounds, but I'm still a soldier."

Perhaps the man's self-confidence astonished Napoléon, but he did not show it. The kings were waiting in a bleak silence.

"So much service deserves more," the Emperor went on. "You're no longer a soldier...I'm making you a king."

"King! As you wish, Sire."

At that response, made insouciantly and phlegmatically, the Emperor looked at him with a searching gaze.

"Yes, a king. There's a vacant throne; you can go and sit down on it."

It was the place of old King George, ill and dying in Glasgow.

"Good!" Having uttered that word, he was about to sit down with ease and lack of curiosity when the Emperor stopped him, took his hand and embraced him. "I consecrate you king," he said. "Go and sit down."

"I don't understand the rest," the soldier said, "but my general has embraced me." And two large tears formed in his eyes.

He took his place on the royal seat, and, looking at all his new colleagues with an icy expression, he sank back in the armchair, replaced his police cap on his head, and was perhaps about to go to sleep when the Emperor, standing up, said in a terrible voice:

"You know what I am, Messieurs, and now you also know what kings are. Go—the session is ended."

And he withdrew.

Slowly, the kings went along the great gallery of paintings in order to return to their apartments. Their heads were bowed sadly; they knew that they could do nothing against such a caprice coming from such a power. They even feared communicating their thoughts to one another, and, in the midst of that silence the long gallery only resounded with the gravity of their footfalls.

The new king, Guillaume Athon, was the last to leave. Having gone into the gallery he amused himself contemplating the paintings, his police cap tilted over his ear, sometimes whistling barrack-room tunes, albeit rather quietly.

The sight of the paintings entertained him, and he had not emerged from the section of the Italian school when the kings had already disappeared into the main hall—for he was one of those bizarre characters that nothing astonishes or causes chagrin, who cares as little about a kingdom as a slight wound, because he did not understand what the first of those words meant, and was not unaware that shedding his blood in war was his métier.

Curious, however, as soldiers are, he was no longer thinking about what had happened a few moments ago, since he was looking at the paintings. Then, seeing that he was alone, he took his pipe out of his pocket, along with a stone, flint and tinder, and he was about to relight his tobacco, without any further care, when someone stopped him by the arm and told him that the Emperor was asking for him. He turned round, and without making any reply, followed the officer who had interrupted him in his scarcely regal distractions.

## Chapter VI
## THE SOLDIER KING (2)

Violent as Napoléon's anger might have appeared, in general, it always had its measure, because he was so well able to bridle his passions that he only allowed them to surge forth when it suited his profound thought.

On the contrary, in the council of kings, that fit of rage had been sudden and uncalculated. A blind and unreflective anger had carried him away, and doubtless nothing in the world could have been a more legitimate cause than the insolence of kings who dared not remain slaves.

Later, however, when he was alone in his study, his passion calmed down and his reflection became cooler; he began to think, and saw exactly how far he had been dragged by it. Falling back into himself, he was afflicted, ashamed of his action and the outrageous caprice that had caused him to throw a scepter to a soldier. In any case, had he not gone too far? Curbed too far, the kings might rear up again terrible, and did he not have an interest in conserving, at least for the people, the respect that surrounds royalty? Regretting what he had done, and uncertain as to what he ought to do, he wanted to see his new king, Guillaume Athon, and a officer, having been sent to look for him, found him in the gallery of paintings, as we know, and brought him to the Emperor.

He came in, standing to attention respectfully in the doorway, but with his had high and his gaze steady, conserving the simultaneous noble and submissive attitude of a soldier before his commander.

"Someone bring a chair," said the Emperor, "and then leave us."

Left alone, they remained silent for a few minutes, the soldier king still standing.

"Would Your Majesty like to sit down?" the Emperor said to him, in a melancholy tone.

The soldier sat down, still looking fixedly at the Emperor.

"How did what happened in the council seem to you?" Napoléon asked him.

"In truth, Sire, I don't understand it, unless it was only a mockery made of an old soldier."

"No, it's serious. You're a king."

"King! Why?"

The Emperor paled at that singular question, and said: "Because it was my will."

"Your will can make me a king, when all your generals couldn't make me a corporal?"

"Explain yourself."

"I don't know how to read..."

"What does that matter?" Napoléon said to him, his heart aching more and more. "You've been elevated to the highest dignity on earth; you're a king. My choice is sufficient. Doesn't that please you?"

"No more than you, perhaps."

"What do you mean?"

"That, without understanding any of all this, it seems to me that it might have been better if Your Majesty hadn't made me sit down in the middle of all those...well, let's leave it there, and let me go back to my barracks, or the two o'clock roll call will go by, and I'll get three days in the guard room."

Those words, that indifferent firmness and that instinctive wisdom astonished the Emperor to the highest degree. He replied: "That can't be. You're a king; my word has crowned you, and nothing can remove that crown from you."

"All right," said the soldier.

They fell silent, the Emperor supporting his forehead in his left hand.

After a few moments, the soldier king was the first to speak, and his staring eyes were animated by a strange gleam. "I believe that my person is an embarrassment to your Majesty. Well, everything can be sorted out."

"How?" asked Napoléon, looking at him anxiously.

"Send me to the far side of the world...or further still...for if all this rigmarole were to end with a State prison for life...I wouldn't stay alive for two days."

The Emperor was amazed. "What do you mean?"

"That if it's necessary to pay for your title of king with my life, I'm ready."

"You value your life so little?"

"Bah! I've risked it twenty times for a lie, an insult, a kiss from a whore, and twenty times for nothing when I'd been drinking. I'm not talking about war; cannonballs have gone between my legs and crushed one of my ears; two inches more and it would all have been over, but that's the profession; I'm not talking about that."

"And your family?"

"I don't have one—no mother, wife or children."

"So you don't value life very highly?"

"It doesn't matter to me, and if it suits you...."

"Who told you that?" said Napoléon, anxiously.

"No one. Do you please."

"No: you'll live as a king, with your scepter, your court, palaces and treasures."

"All right!"

And they both fell silent again. A thousand sentiments were rending the Emperor's heart; the soldier king perceived that, and stood up.

"Sire, you need to decide. If Your Majesty wishes, I'll kill myself, and no one will know anything...or I can wait until someone..."

The Emperor looked at him, and there were tears in his eyes; he held out his hand to Guillaume Athon, who seized it and kissed it. The Emperor opened his arms, and the other threw himself into them; they embraced.

The soldier's firmness quit him then, and he wept too.

"That's twice Your Majesty has embraced me today," he said, wiping his eyes. "I could have a thousand lives that wouldn't be worth as much to me as that joy, and I won't be any happier if I live after that."

Napoléon looked at him with moist eyes.

"Adieu, Sire," he said, "adieu!" And he turned to go.

The Emperor, absorbed in is reflections, did not get up.

At the door, Guillaume Athon turned round again, and said, with simplicity: "Adieu, Sire; I'll go back to the barracks; and this evening…adieu!" And he disappeared.

There were many in the Grand Armée like him, simple souls, energetic and bronzed by the smoke of battles.

The following day, it was learned that the previous evening, at about nine o'clock, the body of Guillaume Athon had been found, struck in the heart by three thrusts of a bayonet. There was no indication of a struggle. It was assumed that he had committed suicide, for he was not known to have any enemies, and the wounds were all in the front. In any case, the unimportant event did not go beyond the barracks and the lieutenant's report to the colonel.

Nothing more was known about the man. The kings, on hearing about his death, kept silent about the day's events, and time continued in its course as if no blood had been shed.

## Chapter VII
## *REVISION OF LEGISLATION*

France was then, in 1819, flourishing to the highest degree, rich, populous and happy. The general system of roads and canals complete; monuments, bridges and public edifices of the greatest magnificence constructed; a strong administration protective of the citizens and their fortune; above all that an incredible glory—such was France, and, to a lesser degree, the dependent countries of the Empire.

The laws were as admirable as the rest. Still young, they had the energy of youth, and the authority of ancient laws. That was one of the finest results of the unjudgeable revolution that, like a giant placed between the old order and the new world, had its feet in blood and its head in the sky. The entire law had been renewed. Monuments of wisdom had been raised up by men who were often in delirium, and when Napoléon had returned from Egypt and had taken France, he had aggrandized and completed the legislation in all respects, and, to crown the edifice, had issued his codes.

And when he had seen his work, he did not rest.

He did not have the jealous pride that thinks that something done cannot be improved; on the contrary, successive laws came usefully to correct those codes. Thus, those of civil interests saw a few of their principles modified more than once, and the criminal codes their excessive severity.

In the month of February 1818 he published a new edition in which all those ameliorations had been included.

But he did more, for he was not unaware that the new legislation, since 1789, was not the entire law of France and that there were still, in the ancient French laws, important materials and sacred residues that ought not to be regarded as annihilated. He therefore wanted to reconnect those old legislative traditions with the new laws and bring back, so to speak, all the past of ancient France, in order to fuse everything in his unique work, and in order that the people of his time would no longer have to look backwards in order to search for anything but inert memories of old history.

Napoléon had said that "All of France must date from me," and he had arrived at the point of strength at which he could compress the past and drive it before him at his feet.

In order to arrive at that great result, he surrounded himself with the most illustrious jurisconsultants of France and Germany. He attributed a power to them near to that of the legislative power itself, and with that high delegation, he put into their hands the entire disposition of the archive of State and the libraries of Europe.

The commission thus instituted took the name of the Superior Council of the Revision of the Laws, and its mission was to collect and revise all the parts of French legislation, from the earliest times of the monarchy to the present day.

The Superior Council of Revision was divided into two principal sections. The first was charged with bringing together in a complete body all the ancient laws, as well as the capitularies, ordinances, establishments, edicts and declarations prior to 1789.

After having finished that first chronological collection, which was only a work of great historical compilation and a preparation for the reformative work, the members of that section would choose in those materials the laws still in vigor, classify them and redraft them in special codes, which by virtue of the skillful harmony of that fine work, would be coordinated with the existing codes and complete them with all the force still remaining in that old legislation.

By means of a third labor, the same section would prepare a decree of abrogation of all the laws that were not recalled in those special codes, in order that, recognized unnecessary to civil and political life, those ruins of times past would cease to hinder its march, to pass henceforth into the state of history.

The second section carried out a similar labor on analogous bases on the laws, edicts, decrees and decisions rendered since 1789, in also order to sweep away the unnecessary debris and reestablish in the midst of the confusion of those innumerable laws the rights of order and clarity.

Four years were sufficient for the completion of that great work worthy of Napoléon and the superior men to whom he had entrusted it. The two great chronological collections, from the fifth century to 1789 and from 1789 to 1820, were published separately, as historical documents rather than as a work of legislation.

But it was not the same with the combination of those special decrees, which were immediately submitted to the sanction of the two legislative bodies and promulgated in their ensemble in February 1824, under the title of the General Body of French Laws. The first edition, in ten quarto volumes, emerged at that time from the Imperial printing presses, and became French law.

Thus, France had its Digest and its Justinian.

The accomplishment of that work had given the highest impulsion to philosophical and historical studies of the law, and when Napoléon gave that magnificent and luminous legislation, to all parts, in France, Germany, England and even Italy, great works were in preparation on those matters.

It was in vain that Arch-Chancellor Cambacérès had said, wittily, to one of his collaborators during the promulgation of the first codes: "We have killed Roman law." Roman law was not dead; it was revived in the studies of savant jurisconsultants; they hollowed out its depths and discovered its sources. They also went to dig in the entrails of the Middle Ages to find the legislations of those times; they went to find in foreign nations the laws that had been imported by conquests. Norman laws were studied in England. Ancient French customs, so curiously explored, were studied in the Anglo-Norman islands or in the countries of America where they still subsisted, and German and Saxon laws, transported in their turn to England and southern Europe were interrogated in their new homelands. Then appeared, at the same time: in Germany, *Essays on Ancient Roman Law* by Niebuhr, *The History of*

*Greek Legislation* by Gans and *Views on Roman Law* by Savigny; in England, the magnificent work by Mr. Brougham entitled *General Concordance of the Laws of Europe*; and in France, *The History of French Law* by Monsieur Dupin, *Essay on Commercial Law in the Middle Ages* by Monsieur Pardessus and the works of Monsieur Thierry on the legislative establishments of the barbarians.[76]

Two other works were also connected with those, by their nature and by their date: the astonishing book *Considerations on the French Constitution* by Monsieur de Maistre, which Napoléon had seized and burned; and *The History of France through its Laws and Monuments* by Monsieur Guizot, an entirely new work in which historical verity was supported at every step by charters, monuments, medals, laws and, in general, all the contemporary acts that cast light and an incontestable authority on the facts.[77]

---

[76] Barthold George Niebuhr (1776-1831) was a statesman and financier who became Germany's leading historian of ancient Rome. The jurist Eduard Gans (1797-1839) did not become notable in our history until a later epoch. Friedrich Carl Savigny (1779-1861) was also a German jurist and historian. Henry Brougham (1778-1868) was Lord Chancellor of England in our history from 1830-34. The advocate André Dupin (1783-1865), sometimes known as Dupin aîné to distinguish him from his namesake Charles Dupin, became a liberal statesman in our history, holding his office under Louis-Philippe, and also served the Second Empire. Jean-Marie Pardessus (1772-1853) published a four-volume work on commercial law in 1813-17.

[77] The Savoyard Counter-Enlightenment philosopher Joseph de Maistre (1753-1821) considered monarchy to be divinely-sanctioned, and campaigned ardently for the Bourbon Restoration. The statesman and prolific historian François Guizot (1787-1874) played a leading role in the July Revolution of 1930 and is widely credited with originating the celebrated doctrine of the *juste milieu*.

*Chapter VII*
*CATALOGUE*


In continuing the history, it is impossible to pass over in silence the remarkable and powerful movement that was imparted to literature in the year 1820, which was prolonged and increased until 1830, and as the nature of his work scarcely permits me to interrupt the historical narrative and interweave it too frequently with literary considerations, I shall pause momentarily here, at the date 1820, when that movement of progress commenced, and, without worrying about the chronology that condemns me, and will be able to submit me to its yoke again in the next chapter, offer an abridged history of the immense works that were published during those ten years.

If there were a form even more abbreviated than the one I shall employ, I would choose it for preference, so much do I seek rapidity and brevity, and so much, above all, do I value the liberty of literary opinions; a historian first and foremost, and a critic hardly at all, I only want to bring together in this chapter the names of authors and books in a certain order—in brief, to draw up a veritable catalogue.


1820. In that year the publication commenced of the monumental encyclopedia known as the Encyclopedia of the Institut, because all the members of the four academies collaborated in the execution of the work, and imposed the law upon themselves of signing all the articles. No more important work has ever been confided to more expert men, and one can veritably call it the book of books. It was completed by the publication of its sixty-eighth quarto volume in 1828. Fifteen volumes of plates and seven of tables bright the total number to ninety volumes. The encyclopedia was printed with the greatest luxury by the imperial presses, and the Emperor's great liberality rendered its price accessible to the majority of fortunes.

1820. Appeared simultaneously:

*Philosophical Dialogues on the Universe* by the Comte de Maistre. 3 octavo vols.

*History of the Genius of Antiquity* by Paul-Louis Courier.[78] 5 octavo vols.

*The Book of Passions* by the Duchesse de Staël, 3 octavo volumes.

Those three works far surpassed all that France and Europe had been able to expect of the genius of their authors.


1821. Monsieur de Lamartine published his *Poetic Meditations*.

*General History of France* by M. de Chateaubriand.

The twelfth and last volume of that magnificent history, the most beautiful of national histories, was published in 1826; its frontispiece bore the new titles of Monsieur de Chateaubriand, created Duc d'Albanie and appointed Minister of State in that same year, 1826.

The ninth edition appeared in 1829.

*Tableau of the Heavens* by Herschel, 3 folio volumes. Atlas.

*Usages and Forms that Exist in Civil Society External to Laws* by Comte Merlin, 3 quarto vol.[79]

*Principles of Ideas* by Kant. 2 octavo vols.

*Philosophy of Numbers* by Lagrange. 2 quarto vols.

---

[78] The Hellenist Paul-Louis Courier (1772-1825) also became famous as a relentless opponent of the Bourbon Restoration; his career was cut short by his murder, for a motive never fully explained, by two of his servants.

[79] Philippe-Antoine Merlin (1754-1838) helped bring down Robespierre in the Convention, and then helped Cambacérès draft the Napoleonic Code; he was rendered destitute by the Restoration and then exiled after supporting Napoléon during the Hundred Days, but returned to France after the July Revolution.

1822. *History of the Establishment of Christianity* by M. de Lammenais. 8 quarto vols.

*Analysis of Arabic Literature* by Comte Sylvestre de Sacy. 6 vols.

*Transcendent Geometry* by Baron Poisson, quarto.

*Considerations on Epic Poetry* by M. Villemain, Councillor of State, 2 vols.

1820-1827. Continuation and conclusion of two great literary enterprises known by the names:

*Collections of the Historians of France.* 42 folio vols.

*Collection of Laws and Ordinances of the Realm of France*, pre-1789. 48 folio vols.

1823. *Description of the Ruins of Palmyra.* 2 quarto vols. Atlas.

*On Matter and Mind* by Broussais. 3 vols.[80]

*Chronological Geography or History of the Successive Revolutions of the Earth, Empires and Humankind and Discoveries that have been made on the Surface of the Globe, by a Scientific Society.* Large folio Atlas.

*Les Dix plaise,*[81] satires by Lord Byron, with the epigraph: "Forward March!"

1824. *Description of the ruins of Babylon.* 3 quarto vols. Atlas.

---

[80] In our history the controversial physician François Broussais (1772-1838) published *De l'irritation et de la folie* [On Irritation—in the sense of stimulation—and Madness] in 1828.

[81] I have left this title in French because I am not sure what it is supposed to mean, and am tempted to wonder whether the last two letters have been transposed by a misprint. (*Plaies* would signify "wounds.")

*Grammar and Dictionary of Hieroglyphs* by Champollion. 5 vols.

*Essay on the Calculation of the Strength and Genius of Humankind* by the Comte de La Place. 2 quarto vols.[82]

1825. *History of Greece* by Michelet, 4 vols.
*Philosophy of History* by the same, 2 vols.
*Philosophy of History* by Ballanche, 6 vols.[83]
*God*, a poem in 18 cantos, by Lamartine.
*Philosophy of Nature* by Geoffroy Saint-Hilaire, 3 vols.
*History of Human Knowledge* by Ampère, 4 vols.
*Dialogues of the Dead. Philosophical Essays* by V. Cousin, 2 vols.
*On the Influence of Paganism in Modern Societies* by Mignet. 2 quarto vols.[84]

1826. *General History of the Physical Sciences* by G. Cuvier, 8 quarto vols.
*General History of the Mathematical Sciences* by Biot, 6 quarto vols.
*Treatise on Philosophy* by Royer-Collard, 3 octavo vols.[85]

---

[82] Like several other titles in the list, this one is a subtle joke; in our history the mathematician and pioneering statistician Pierre Simon Laplace (1749-1827) remains famous for his classic study of *Mécanique céleste* [Celestial Mechanics] (1799-1825)

[83] In our history Pierre-Simon Ballanche (1776-1847) never finished his planned multi-volume work on the philosophy of history, interpreting human history as process of "palingenesis" defined within the context of Christianity.

[84] In our history, François Mignet (1796-1884) was best known for his history of the 1789 Revolution.

[85] The philosopher and statesman Pierre-Paul Royer-Collard (1763-1845) became famous in our history as the leaders of the Doctrinaires, who opposed the Bourbon Restoration and

*Richelieu*, historical novel by Sir Walter Scott; a book written in French and published in France.

*The Condition of Civil and Political Society in France under the Second Race* by Augustin Thierry, 3 vols.

*The King of Yvetot*, political novel by Ch. Nodier. A rare book, the second edition not having been authorized.[86]

1827. *The Holy Bible* translated by Cardinal de Frayssinous. 20 octavo vols.

*The Wars in Spain* by Maréchal Foy, 8 vols.

*History of French Literature* by Villemain, 6 vols.

*The Science of Laws* by M. Dupin aîné, 4 vols.

*Luther*, historical novel by V. Hugo, 2 vols.

*Theory of Mind* by M. Beyle de Stendhal. This overly witty book irritated Napoléon had caused him to exile M. Beyle to Rome, where he completed his beautiful *History of Italian Painting*, 1829, 12 octavo vols.[87]

1828. *History of Philosophy* by V. Cousin, 4 vols.

*History of Politics among Ancient and Modern Peoples* by A. Carrel, 4 vols.

---

effectively engineered the July Revolution. He was also the mentor of the twice-cited Victor Cousin (1792-1867).

[86] "The King of Yvetot" became a popular reference to a petty monarchy of no significance, celebrated employed as the title of a popular song by Pierre-Jean de Béranger (1780-1857). The reference here might be a sly comment to Nodier's status as "king" of the Romantic Movement's first famous *cénacle* and its supersession by Victor Hugo's

[87] Marie-Henri Beyle, alias Stendhal (1783-1842) witnessed the burning of Moscow, and the experience had a powerful influence on his classic novel *Le Rouge et le noir* (1830), whose hero learns under the Restoration not to look back with so much nostalgia on the glories that Napoléon might have attained—a circumstance that might not be unconnected with Geoffroy's decision to write the present novel.

*Historical and Geographical Description of the Interior of Africa*, 6 quarto vols. Atlas.

*Moses*, an epic poem in twelve cantos by V. Hugo, quarto.

*Maître Quinola*, novel by M. de Balzac.


1829. *History of the Emperor Napoléon prior to the Universal Monarchy*, by A. Thiers, 8 vols.

*Satan*, poem by Alfred de Musset.

*Songs* by P.-J. de Béranger.

*History of England* by Guizot, 9 octavo vols.

*Essay on Credit and Finance in the Universal Monarchy* by Comte Roy, Duc d'Illyrie, 4 octavo vols.


1830 *Diplomacy within the scope of everyone*, by a king. Octavo. This singular and ironic book appeared in an epoch when diplomacy had become an unnecessary science; it is generally attributed to M. Talleyrand.

*History of two centuries, 1440-1650* by Mignet, of the Institut, 3 vols.

*The Comedies of Menander*, recently discovered, translated by Sainte-Beuve, 4 octavo vols.

*Sursum Corda*, small duodecimo. The author of this admirable work, which had had so much influence on good mores and stimulated the elevation of minds so forcefully, remain unknown. A multitude of editions having succeeded one another, Napoléon, impressed by the results of the book, wanted at any price to know the author, but research and promises of magnificent recompense were equally fruitless. Nothing could shake the modesty of that human benefactor, and the mystery is still impenetrable.

*Jupiter* by Goethe. 2 vols. The last and strangest production of that illustrious writer.

*Critique of Civil Laws* by Troplong. 4 octavo vols.[88]

---

[88] The jurist and politician Raymond-Théodore Troplong (1795-1869), whom Geoffroy must have encountered in a pro-

I shall terminate the list here, to which I could have added the titles of many more publications of similar importance.
I have not included either works for the theater or other works
of which France retains the memory and posterity will not
forget.

---

fessional capacity after Troplong was appointed to the Court
of Cassation in 1835. He had not published anything significant in our world by the date cited, and it is probable that he
terminates the list by virtue of wordplay, his surname signify-
ing "too long."

## Chapter IX
## SAINT-SIMON, ABBÉ DE LAMENNAIS

There were two men that Napoléon did not like.

Alongside the literary development that we have just sketched out, a new mental tendency was revealed around 1823; philosophical and political at the same time, it sought to ameliorate the fate of humankind, especially the poor, and to give commerce and the sciences the application most useful to the progress of humanity.

It was the sonorous philanthropy of the eighteenth century, applied.

The Emperor examined that opinion closely, and studied its progress seriously. When he had recognized its utility, and saw that no danger accompanied it, he let it alone, or favored it by direction. At the head of the movement, the father and leader of that political philosophy, the Comte de Saint-Simon, was a man of powerful imagination, although more often than not ready to stray, but the first to posit the principle of the social perfection and amelioration of the fate of all human beings.

A limitless development of industry was the basis of his system, so it came to his mind ne day to coin the word "industrialism," which enjoyed great fortune.

Napoléon was impressed by certain works published by Monsieur de Saint-Simon between 1810 and 1822. Seeker of forceful men as he was, he fixed his gaze upon that innovator. But if he encountered near-genius in philosophy, he was scornful of his veritable capability; he wanted to make him a man of action, and he found that the thinker could not do anything but think. Appointed prefect successively at Avignon and then Nancy, Monsieur Saint-Simon only made mistakes, and showed himself to be a very mediocre administrator. After two years, the Emperor withdrew him from his functions and created a place for him as a director of industry, under the orders of the Minister of Commerce. But there again, the Comte de Saint-Simon, to inferior or perhaps too superior, to that position, only brought vague theories thereto, and a disorderly administration. The Emperor, increasingly disgusted with the man, in whom, alongside so many faults, he forced to recognize a mind of such great range, removed him definitively from all active service, to relegate him to the vain functions of a Councilor of State in extraordinary service.

Saint-Simon died tranquilly, greatly neglected by the Emperor, in June 1827.[89]

While he was alive, a group of young men who had chosen him, in spite of his refusals, for their master flaunted his name at the masthead of a philosophical doctrine that they fashioned in the manner of a religion. They made Saint-Simon into a kind of god, and called themselves Saint-Simonians. The Councillor of State, offended by that enthusiasm, found no other means of purging himself of that apotheosis than launching a lawsuit against his stubborn disciples, which occupied minds keenly, and which is still remembered.

If the Emperor, very irritated by the mistakes that we have mentioned, had ended up seeing the Comte de Saint-Simon with a continually marked displeasure, it was not the same with the Abbé de Lamennais.

That powerful genius, disdainful of a social movement that seemed to him to be leading the world to the abyss, of an

---

[89] In our history, the great pioneer of 19th-century utopian theory and coiner of the term "industrialism" Claude-Henri de Rouvray, Comte de Saint-Simon (1760-1825) was never entrusted with any practical responsibility; deeply disappointed by his failure to win many converts to his schemes, he attempted to kill himself in 1823 by shooting himself in the head but failed six times; even so, he still contrived to expire earlier than he does in Geoffroy's alternative history, in which the great tradition of French Utopianism that he founded, carried forward by Charles Fourier and Étienne Cabet, obviously becomes redundant.

imperial power that was not imposed upon him, ablaze with anger before the icy indifference of nations that were going toward forgetfulness of God and the faith, full of conviction, life and genius before those dying people who were descending into the tomb borne by philosophy, he, the Abbé de Lamennais,[90] outside that movement, that power and those death-throes, appointed himself the apostle of God, the Luther of the Catholic Reformation; and, stirring minds with the fury of his speeches, he awoke people who were slumbering in indifference, and who got up, dazed by that noise.

The Emperor, whose politics admitted religious progress, and ardently favored the beliefs of a religion that placed Caesar alongside God, authorized and even supported the illustrious father of the Church.

But only a short time had passed when he saw his anticipations surpassed by the overflowing rhetoric of the priest. Napoléon wanted to make use of all forces, but he wanted above all to remain master of them; he was not a man to let any power, no matter what it might be, exceed the range and action of his own.

He summoned Abbé de Lamennais to Saint-Cloud.

When the two men met, they contemplated one another for a few moments silently, for they had not seen one another before.

Napoléon, as everyone knows, had acquired a plumpness in that epoch that rendered his lack of height more obvious. At that moment he was clad in a gray frock coat, which he wore habitually.

---

[90] In our history, Hugues de Lamennais (1782-1854) wrote his classic *Essai sur l'indifférence en matière de religion* (1817) with the fallen Emperor very much in mind, having attacked him while in power for usurping papal authority in the appointment of bishops. Having allied himself with the Restoration he fled to England during the Hundred Days, probably unnecessarily.

179

The Abbé de Lamennais, who was even shorter, and remarkably thin, had not thought, even for the court, of abdicating the right to dress simply that every ecclesiastic has. A black cravat, tied like a string around his neck, and black woolen stockings were the only garments left visible by a long brown frock-coat in which he was enveloped.

The Emperor was the first to break the silence of the examination.

"Here are two men of short stature who might change the face of the earth," he said, with a smile, and, as if regretting having given the priest too much credit in the remark, added, proudly: "There's one, at least."

"Perhaps," replied the Abbé de Lamennais, coldly, and that word was spoken in such a way that one could not disentangle the doubt and presumption therein.

But the word had enlarged the stage. The Emperor, without pushing the gracious preliminaries any further, unveiled to the Abbé de Lamennais the mysteries of his politics: how he needed religion in order to affirm it; how that power dissolved in his own rendered it henceforth infallible. He added that he had cast his eyes upon him in order to aid him in a universal reformation of Christianity; that he was not unaware of the force of which his religious writings had rendered him the master. He told him that he could make him Pope. But, he added, he intended that the Pope would only be the second in that great power, and that he could not think of arrogating half of it.

The vehemence of the Emperor's speech, and the admirable eloquence that he had when he wanted to convince or seduce, found in Monsieur de Lamennais, however, a cold and respectful resistance. Personally, he was far from possessing such a magic of language. Sublime in his books, he found improvisation difficult and conversation somewhat embarrassing. Always overflowing in his ideas, speech was for him an imperfect instrument of collection.

Nevertheless, he had traced an invariable line in order to respond to Napoléon: that there were two forces in the world,

God and the emperor; that those two forces could assist one another, but could not be confounded; that it would be folly and sacrilege to see religion as a subservient support; and that, for himself, he only saw in that alternative the man who ought to be towed by religion.

They did not reach an understanding.

Napoléon became pressing, even terrible. Monsieur de Lamennais, head bowed, was as calm before seduction as before fear.

Then they conversed together about the highest matters of religion and politics, but his story knows nothing about the end of that conversation, as mysterious as the mysteries that are often stirred up there by great intelligences.

Monsieur de Lamennais thought that he ought to keep the secret.

After five hours of animated discussion, sometimes disturbed by the Emperor's anger, they separated, astonished and dissatisfied with one another.

Napoléon had seen that there was nothing to be done with Abbé de Lamennais. He could at least suppress the surge of his publications, but he left him tranquil in his person, and did not think of persecuting him.

*Chapter X*
*MURAT (1)*

The commencement of 1820 offered the Emperor a terrible opportunity to prove to the kings the real value of his suzerainty over Europe.

King Murat had quit the beautiful throne of Naples, in which Napoléon had left him for too little time, with a profound dolor. He pride had only understood the disgrace that had struck him when he saw himself relegated to an insignificant throne in the North. Sweden and Stockholm, that was what he had received in exchange for his two Sicilies and Naples, especially at the moment when his conquest of Sardinia reunited under his power the two largest islands in the Mediterranean, and a new kingdom.

But that imprudent increase in power, that indiscreet conquest, was precisely what had irritated the Emperor. Without saying so, he had wanted to make it known to the kings that not a single cannon shot ought to take place in Europe without his permission. So Murat paid dearly for the pretention of that conquest, and the parody he had tried to make of his brother-in-law. He went to brood about that royal exit—and his vengeance—under the leaden skies of Scandinavia.

His vengeance! For his proud soul did not rest for a moment without nursing its projects. Hatred had replaced henceforth all other sentiment in his soul, and it was the implacable hatred that succeeds and kills gratitude, and grows even on the benefits it receives.

Scarcely had he arrived in his new Estates than he set to work to prepare a future of vengeance. He tried first of all to renew the North-Eastern League smashed in 1816. His attempts were vain; the Kings of Russia, Bohemia and Muscovy were no longer able to be anything but subservient; their heads, still smoking from the lightning-strikes, bowed down before the eagle and no longer thought of raising themselves.

Denmark, Poland and Saxony, more faithful allies, rejected Murat's propositions more explicitly, and he remained alone with his impotent hatred.

The Emperor, however, was not unaware of any of those maneuvers. His innumerable and almost universal police had extended its roots everywhere. Everywhere, the cabinets and State of Europe were entangled in that immense net, and Murat's culpable propositions, no matter how secret he tried to keep them, were known to Napoléon. He did more, procuring the most authentic evidence, and, finally weary of the plotting of a king and a brother-in-law, he wrote to the King of Sweden personally in the harshest and most menacing terms; he reproached him for what he had dared to do, reminded him that he was the one who had plucked him from obscurity and put him on thrones. He let him know that his hand might withdraw, and that his fall would then become infallible. He concluded by summoning him to Paris to explain his conduct—or rather, he said, to receive a pardon.

Perhaps there was a lack of skill in addressing such a letter to a man like Murat. It was easy to divine that it would irritate his anger even more, for he was not a king to bow down so rapidly under humiliation. In any case, the throne of Charles XII and Gustav Vasa was not made to diminish the chivalric exaltation of the new sovereign who was sat upon it. So the King of Sweden replied with scorn to that letter from the sovereign of Europe.

Perhaps also there was a profound calculation on the Emperor's part, and he knew that the letter would put Murat in the necessity of an open revolt, giving him the right to punish him, for he seemed weary of that brother-in-law, and the conquest of Sardinia had not slipped his mind.

At any rate, the King of Sweden received the Emperor's letter with the utmost indignation. Having immediately assembled the Senate, he read it aloud to the members himself, after which he addressed the Senators and asked them whether it was possible for a king and a nation to tolerate such an outrage. As for himself, he added, he would rather lose his life twenty times than not avenge his honor. In consequence, he would declare himself released from all submission to his oath toward the Emperor of the French, and in a state of war with him. He protested his love for Sweden, and concluded by declaring that he could not believe that the Senate and the nation would hesitate for an instant to share the king's wrath and his vengeance.

The Senate trembled before the sovereign's communications, and thought about the events that might follow in consequence. Without making a definite decision, it let the king know that he could do anything, and that, if he wanted war, it was necessary for Sweden to want it.

After that session, the King of Sweden recalled his ambassador from Paris, and expelled the Baron de Cases, then the French ambassador in Stockholm.

What that news arrived in France, Napoléon had the following decree inscribed in the *Moniteur*:

*Napoléon, Emperor of the French, Sovereign of Europe. Has decreed the following:*

*Article 1. The King of Sweden, Murat, guilty of high treason toward the Empire, and of having violated his oath of fidelity to the Emperor of the French, will be brought before the Court of Kings to be judged.*

*Article 2. To that effect, the Council of Kings, convened extraordinarily as a High Court of Criminal Justice, will meet on 25 April next in the Imperial Palace of the Louvre, in order to pass judgment on the King of Sweden.*

*Article 3. The Prince Arch-Chancellor of the Empire, assisted by our procurator general of the Court of Cassation, will undertake the prosecution on behalf of the Emperor and the Court of Kings.*

*From our Imperial Palace of the Tuileries, 10 February 1820.*

*Napoléon.*

The Kings all came to Paris before the date fixed.

Murat, who believed himself to be safe within his kingdom, and who was preparing a desperate defense, was suddenly abducted by a company of his own guards, of whom he had no suspicion, but who remained secretly devoted to the Emperor. He was transported by them to the coast, and immediately embarked by force on a French vessel, which brought him to France. He arrived in Paris in the first days of April. Preparations were then made for the royal trial in the Louvre. The Emperor had commissioned the Minister of Justice to collect the charges and the responses given by the King.

King Murat constantly refused to respond to the Minister; he would make his explanations he said, before his pers.

The Minister having advised him to choose advocates, he looked at him with disdain. "Do you think," he said, "that this an affair of the theft of handkerchiefs? One does not plead, Monsieur; I shall speak."

## Chapter XI
## MURAT (2)

Nothing was more solemn than that trial and the formalities retained by it. The Emperor had even thought about holding that court of royal judges at the Panthéon, where, beneath the magnificent inscription: *To the Great Men, the Fatherland is grateful*, he saw something just and terrible in judging a culpable king. Then, by virtue of other considerations, it was in the Great Hall of the Imperial Museum that the sessions of the High Court were to be held.

That Great Hall, stripped for the occasion of the paintings that decorated it, was entirely hung in long draperies of red velvet embroidered with gold. At the back, on a stage, thirteen thrones were arranged; the one in the middle was raised above the rest, and was destined for the Emperor. On a less elevated parquet was the Arch-Chancellor's seat. Finally, lower down, facing the tribunal, was another empty throne. A few secondary arrangements completed the organization.

At eight a.m. on the twenty-fifth of April, the part of the room that had been reserved for spectators was filled with princes, senior officers of the crown, generals and other high functionaries. The people, for whom that publicity was an illusion, were not admitted, as if they ought not to appear at a solemnity too great for them.

At ten o'clock, a guard of honor introduced King Murat. He was in the uniform of a general and decorated with his Swedish orders. After having examined the hall for some time, in which his judges had not yet arrived, he sat down disdainfully on the throne reserved for him, facing the tribunal.

Shortly thereafter, a chamberlain placed at the door of the Apollo gallery announced: "The Court of Kings!" and twelve of the kings of Europe were seen to enter, two by two, among whom there was no member of the Napoléonic family. Their relationship with Murat had motivated their recusal.

The twelve kings were clad in their royal ornaments. They sat down on the thrones, in an order agreed between them in advance, or perhaps decided by the Emperor.

Scarcely had they taken their places than the High Chamberlain, standing at the door of the long gallery, announced in a loud voice: "The Emperor!"

Napoléon appeared. He had none of the imperial purple, but the simple military costume that he preferred and habitually wore. On his arrival, the kings rose to their feet, and even Murat, agitated by that influence, stood up, as if regretfully, and immediately fell back upon his throne. The Emperor went up to his place, saluted the assembly, and, having sat down, said that the Arch-Chancellor could begin.

It was thus that the singular procedure commenced. It was observed that Napoléon, as president of the tribunal, did not think it necessary to fulfill the formalities habitual in common affairs, such as asking the accused to name himself and interrogating him. That was because everyone was aware of who the king was, and such formalities were unnecessary.

It also seemed that the dignity of the accused would have suffered before the depositions of witnesses who were not of his rank, so Murat was only opposed by his acts, his treaties and letters. The Arch-Chancellor, in a luminous report full of respect for the majesty of the king who was about to be judged, exposed the grave affair—after which Napoléon, in a calm and emotionless voice, addressing Murat, said to him:

"Your Majesty knows of what he is accused; has he chosen a counsel, or does he want to explain himself?"

"Perhaps I should not have to," Murat replied, "for I do not recognize that anyone here has the right to attack my character or ask me to account for my diadem. A king, like all of you, I have no other place than in your ranks, not before you and in the position of an accused, and I decline as a crime and a sacrilege the audacious idea of judging me."

Then he stood up and, having covered his head, he continued with the greatest energy:

187

"What Monsieur the Arch-Chancellor has said is true. He might, however, have spared the word *conspiracy*, which does not apply to me. A king does not conspire, but he has designs, which God judges after him. If I have attempted to regenerate Europe and to render liberty to my brothers the kings, it is not for them to find it bad and to abase themselves to the extent of making hypocritical reproaches to me; and if the man that fate found, like me, a soldier, to make him a sovereign, is offended by my thoughts, he had only one way of summoning me to judgment; that was on the sole tribunal of sovereigns, the battlefield. Shame upon him who has refused war in favor of judgment!"

After having said that, the King of Sweden sat down again. With the same calmness, the Emperor said to him: "So, Your Majesty recognizes all the actions represented to him?" and, addressing the Duc de Bassano, the Minister of State charged with keeping those papers, he ordered him to set before Murat's eyes the treaties, letters and writings that emanated from him and were able to compromise him.

Murat replied: "I know all these papers and I do not disavow any of them."

"And Your Majesty can neither explain them nor defend them?" said Napoléon, with the same impassivity.

"I do not want to," said the king.

"And Your Majesty has nothing to add?"

"Nothing," said Murat.

Then, at a sign from the Emperor, the Arch-Chancellor stood up and made a fairly short speech in which he summarized the great affair. He tried to justify the word conspiracy, which had offended the king. Then, having established the proofs of the crime, arriving at the penalty that ought to be applied to it, he asked whether the actions of the King of Sweden were not outside all ordinary justice, and whether the laws of the people could attain the character of a king. He ended by saying that there was reason to believe that justice and the law ought, in this unusual circumstance, be combined and flow simultaneously from the court of kings, by fixing, in the august verdict that it was about to render, both the new legislation concerning the King of Sweden and a decision in conformity with the principles that the legislation in question would establish.

Scarcely had the Arch-Chancellor finished speaking than Murat, turning toward him, said to him in a loud voice: "Monsieur Cambacérès, that is the second time in your life that you have weighed the fate of a king in your hands, but you have strange accomplices today."[91]

The Arch-Chancellor bowed his head as a sign of respect.

The Emperor asked the King of Sweden whether he had any further observation to make.

"No!" Murat replied, with a new energy. "But think of this, kings who are listening to me, and who have arrogated the right to decide my fate: that you are degrading yourselves with your own hands; that your majesty is withering, that the seal of God is falling from your foreheads in this execrable mission that is imposed on you, and that you have no more than one step to take to surpass all the limits of baseness and crime. Go, slaves, go—and if you dare, return as assassins!"

Exhausted by anger, he fell back on his throne.

The Emperor alone had listened with indifference to that thunderous attack, while the twelve kings, their heads uniformly bowed, seemed overwhelmed by the weight of such courage.

The Emperor Napoléon, after a few moments of silence, and after having gathered together the documents that the Arch-Chancellor and the Duc de Bassano had deposited on the

---

[91] When he was a member of the Convention, Cambacérès had protested that it did not have the power to judge Louis XVI and that the king ought to have due facilities for his defense; nevertheless, when the votes were cast, he voted with the majority for the king's execution. Had he not done that, he would surely have fallen victim to the Terror, although he could not have known that at the time.

tribunal's table, said that the court of kings would deliberate the affair for the rest of the day, and the session was resumed on the following day, 26 April.

The session having been lifted, the Emperor and the kings quit the tribunal, and the King of Sweden was taken away by the guards that had accompanied him.

*Chapter XII*
*MURAT (3)*

The next day, the court of kings resumed its sitting. Murat seemed paler and more fatigued. His eyes were somewhat extinct, and the dejection of his physiognomy allowed the divination of the dolorous combats that his firm heart must have experienced during the sleepless nights preceding the day when his life would be decided. A great silence fell when the Emperor, having taken his place, said to Murat: "King of Sweden, you are about to hear the decision of the court of kings."

And, having deployed a parchment, he read in a slightly unsteady voice the following verdict:

"The court of kings, constituted by virtue of the decree of 10 February 1820, presided by the Emperor Napoléon, Sovereign of Europe, and assembled for the purpose of judging His Majesty the King of Sweden, Joachim Murat, accused of high treason toward the Empire, of having violated his oath of fidelity to the Emperor and of having conspired against the order established in Europe, after having heard the report of the Arch-Chancellor of the Empire and the responses and observations of His Majesty the King of Sweden, has decided:

"That the high treason of a vassal king against the Empire and the Emperor, Sovereign of Europe, is a crime punishable by the death penalty;

"That the violation of the oath of fidelity taken between the hands of the Emperor, Sovereign of Europe, under the terms of the decrees of 15 August 1815 by a vassal king, is a crime punishable by the death penalty;

"That the attempt made by a vassal king whose objective is to overturn the order established in Europe by the same decrees, is a crime punishable by the death penalty;

"After having proclaimed these principles, become law by the will of the court, and immediately having force,

"The court of kings, united in the Louvre under the presidency of the Emperor, Sovereign of Europe, has decided that the King of Sweden, Joachim Murat, is convicted of having committed the three crimes imputed to him;

"In consequence, the court of kings condemns him to the death penalty."

"Good!" said Murat. It was his final word, and he withdrew without adding anything, surrounded by the guards that had brought him.

The twelve kings descended from their thrones in the same order and in profound silence; they seemed consternated.

The Emperor left the room rapidly. He precipitated himself, so to speak, into the long gallery before anyone was able to read the dominant expression on his visage, and the people in the courtroom who had witnessed that extraordinary scene withdrew full of admiration and terror.

Napoléon, secluded in his apartments, was inaccessible to anyone. His sister, Murat's wife, tried in vain to reach him; she could not do so. The Empress Joséphine herself, accustomed to obtaining so much grace from him, could not see him. There was no longer any hope but in his own power; people wondered whether, in this circumstance, the Emperor might attribute to himself the right to grant mercy, although the other sovereigns had concurred in the decision that had condemned Murat. It was thought that such a striking opportunity to manifest the powers and rights of his sovereignty might be seized by him. That hope remained for the rest of the day.

## Chapter XIII
## MURAT (4)

There was, in fact, an immense struggle in Napoléon's heart between his sovereign justice and his former affection for Murat, between political necessity and the memory of twenty years of fraternity and glory. There was not one victory in Europe and Egypt in which that sublime soldier had not been at the Emperor's side, he being the genius of the saber as Napoléon was the genius of war. They had loved one another as brothers, and Napoléon had heaped him with his amity, giving him his sister, principalities and two kingdoms. But such a revolt, such audacity, seemed to have vanquished those memories.

Meanwhile, after the pronunciation of the verdict, King Murat had been taken by an imposing escort to the Luxembourg palace. He received his tearful family there. The hours went by in heart-rending scenes; the queen and her children uttered cries of despair, and covered him with tears and kisses. But he, with the vigor of his character, overcame all those dolors, received their adieux, embraced them a thousand times and, affecting an extreme fatigue and the need for rest, separated from them at about ten o'clock in the evening, and remained alone in the room that had been destined for his last night of captivity and his life.

Fatigue had mastered his senses to the extent that he could not resist torpor, and a few moments after the departure of his family, he threw himself into an armchair and fell into a profound sleep.

Scarcely an hour had gone by when the sound of a door opening woke him up with a start; he got up rapidly from his chair, and saw a lone man facing him, by the faint light of a candle, clad in a gray frock-coat, his head covered by the well-known hat; it was Napoléon, standing silently a few paces away, his arms folded.

At that sight, Murat's blood seethed, and circulated ten times, alternately ardent and icy, in his veins; the most violent sentiments agitated him, but the unexpectedness of the apparition and the uncertainty of what was about to happen held him voiceless, as if petrified.

The Emperor had followed all those convulsions of Murat's thought. He took a few steps forward, and said to him, in an affectionate tone: "It's me who is coming to you, brother."

At the name "brother," Murat trembled and bowed his head. All the energy of his hatred had collapsed before that word, pronounced in that place. His legs buckled, as they would not have done at the sight of the most frightful perils, and he felt his heart fill with emotion. Falling back into his armchair, he covered his face with both hands.

That scene had decided his fate.

Napoléon, deeply moved himself, took his hand warmly and repeated in an affectionate voice: "My brother! Murat! What can be done with him? What do you want?"

"Death!" exclaimed Murat, bitterly. "Death—and above all, a prompt death, for, since a moment ago, I sense that it will be infamous, having envisaged it so noble and proud."

"It's necessary that the husband of my sister and the father of my nephews lives," said Napoléon.

"Well," said Murat, excitedly, "since Your Majesty..."

"You are talking to your brother, not to the Emperor," said Napoléon, shaking his hand.

"Well then, Napoléon," he exclaimed, "I shall live, but in the guard, a simple grenadier, as I was thirty years ago, in order to reconquer with my saber and my blood your amity and my forgiveness."

"You're right! You're the best soldier in the world," the Emperor told him. "Politics does not become you, Murat, you have too much courage for it; it's glory that you need. Well, you shall remain a soldier between the kings and me, and you shall be more than them: my lieutenant in Europe and, if God will it, the world."

"Oh!" said Murat, and, dissolving in tears, he threw himself to his knees—but Napoléon did not give him the time. They embraced tightly, their tears confused. Never, perhaps, had such joy swelled the hearts of those two men, nor had tears flowed over such noble heads.

"Listen," said Napoléon. "Your sons will sit on the throne that took you too far away from me, and you will combine with the title of king that of Lieutenant of the Empire."

Murat could not reply, so full as his heart of gratitude and joy.

"But we can't stay here," added the Emperor. "Come with me."

They went out together and went through the rows of guards, who stood their stupefied by their passage.

On their return to the Tuileries, the Queen of Sweden and her children, the Empress and the imperial family, were immediately summoned, and a delirium of joy succeeded the delirium of dolor.

The next day, the Emperor's magnanimous decision was proclaimed everywhere to the sound of trumpets, and there were only twelve men who were troubled by that news: the twelve kings, who had not been able to sleep during that night of mercy.

*Chapter XIV*
*EUROPE*


Napoléon had finished with the old Europe that had, as he said, annoyed him for so long. The level had passed over the kings, raising up the weak and lowering the powerful, and he soared above that population of kings, at an inaccessible height.

One alone had dared to raise his head above that level, and that head had almost fallen. The others must have taken heed of the judgment, understanding more clearly that it was necessary not to step out of the class of kings to which they had been assigned in future.

The nations of Europe were no longer thinking of themselves; they regarded their kings as prefects, and the Emperor as a god. In their enthusiasm, they no longer knew what liberty was, having enough of two things, equality for all, and the ultimate power of one alone.

The French people, however, always marching at the head of those nations seemed to command them, as Napoléon did the kings; they were the patrician people; nearer to Napoléon, they arrogated more particularly the right to be his, for he was in their sanctuary, and the other nations were placed lower down.

Having done as much for the kings and the peoples, Napoléon also wanted to do something for Europe itself, to aggrandize it.

And that idea was certainly new. For if there is anything sacred in the history of the world, it is the mysterious and immemorial division of the Old World into three parts, Europe, Asia and Africa; it seems that it is a division made by God Himself. The world has seen empires change their name and extent a hundred times, live and die, burying the peoples that crumble with their memory into a mute past, and always, through those revolutions, the grain of sand where Europe ends and Asia begins, and the wave where the name of Asia expires and that of Africa begins to be murmured, have subsisted, without having been displaced, or their being stripped of their names.

It is not known whether it was the jealous thought of the Emperor to break that sacred division, and thus set the will of a moment in conflict against an eternal tradition, or whether, wanting to aggregate his conquests in Africa with the Empire of Europe, he decided no longer to leave such important colonies so close to the metropolis. It seemed that his avid power was not yet satisfied with the conquests of Constantinople and the occidental coasts of the Archipelago. He also wanted to assure himself if the entire littoral facing it, in order that the sea of the Archipelago with its hundred islands would belong to him in its entirety, and would be enclosed everywhere in his Estates. Without any further explanation, therefore, he removed the provinces of Asiatic Turkey from the Sultan, already expelled from Europe, and who could only protest against such an invasion. A part of Anatolia, from the eastern extremity of the Sea of Marmora to Rhodes, with Mytilene, Rhodes and Smyrna, belonged to Imperial Europe, and the strait of the Dardanelles no longer bathed two continents of the world as if, in separating them, it belonged to neither.

The following decree expressed the causes and effects of this determination:

*Napoléon, Emperor of the French, Sovereign of Europe.*
*Wanting to complete the political system of Europe and put it in harmony with our conquests in Africa;*
*Considering also the necessity of including the Archipelago and its coasts in the sovereignty of Europe;*
*Has decreed the following:*

*Article 1. Are reunited with Europe:*
*1. The northern part of Africa known as Barbary, from the Atlas Mountains to Egypt;*

*2. The occidental part of Anatolia, from the island of Rhodes to the oriental extremity of the Sea of Marmora;*

*Article 2. These States and countries are aggregated to the French Empire and have ceased to belong to Africa and Asia, taking the denomination of European provinces.*

*At Fontainebleau, 22 July 1820.*

*Napoléon.*

Thus having broken the old order of the world, Napoléon rested.

## Chapter XV
## SULLA

I have already said that in writing this history of Napoléon, I have not wanted to impose any rule, taking the facts that
I please and simply leaving aside certain important matters.
Guided by that same caprice when facts of a lesser interest
arrive in my mind, I might collect them, not fearing thus to fall
from the summit to the threshold of the edifice, for I have not
traced out my route and I leave to hazard the care of bring me
memories.

Thus far, in fact, I have scarcely talked about any but the
incredible events that pertain to the Emperor alone; it is as if I
have been forced to follow him in those historic heights were
thought wanders, and now I shall take advantage of the great
man's repose, recounting in this chapter an event of an inferior
order.

It is also a conquest of sorts, which did not fail to produce a great enough sensation, although its theater did not
surpass the dimensions of a mediocre folio.

One of the most celebrated curators of the Vatican library, Angelo Maio, had rediscovered in Rome, in old palimp-
sests, and collected, numerous fragments of a few ancient authors: the poems of Ennius, the Philippic histories of
Pompeius Trogus, and Cicero's *Republic* reappeared thus with
a few works of lesser importance. No political work was encountered except a fragment of the works of the Emperor Jul-
ian, for Cicero's *Republic*, a rather mediocre work by a very
elegant writer but a very poor politician, had shed little light
on that matter in antiquity.

But one discovery of immense interest followed those we
have just mentioned; Angelo Maio, an intrepid searcher of old
books, found in a folio manuscript that appeared to date from
the eighth century the commentaries of memoirs of Sulla written in Greek. They were appended to a Latin commentary by

Jordanes on Augustine's *City*, and those two works, written in the same epoch, had been, thanks to the rare intelligence of some monastic bookbinder, united in the same volume, and, as might be expected, the first leaf bore in large letters *Jornandis commentaria*, without any mention of the remainder.

Fortunately, Jordanes had been brief, and Sulla reigned over four fifth of the thickness of the volume.

It was a marvelous discovery. Roman history, so loquacious in Livy and so incomplete in the other historians, appeared in that book quite new, completely bare and fully alive; it was known from then on what Rome and the Romans were. Those twenty-two books of commentaries begun by Sulla in his youth, and to which he put the final touches, according to Plutarch, two days before his death, revealed, with the author's harshness of soul and style, and the scorn for men and convention that characterized him, the stormy city of Rome with its chronic warfare of the patricians, the people and the knights, the furious struggle of Sulla and Marius, and finally, Sulla's own history in the wars in Africa, Asia and Greece, when he enchained Jugurtha, crushed Mithridates and bloodied Athens.

But above all, what gave the discovery of those memoirs an extraordinary interest was the immodesty with which the dictator had combined all those actions with justificatory documents. Half of the work was reserved for those extraneous materials. Proclamations, lists of proscription, *senatus consulta* and the singular decree in which Sulla made himself dictator were found there. We saw for the first time the formulae of the documents of the republic, which lay clearly bare the secrets of Roman politics, those historical arcana on which the science of modern times sometimes exercises itself so amusingly. We learned how the Senate was formed and recruited, how public and private education existed in Rome and Italy; we discovered, curiously enough, what Rome's finances were, the state of the treasury and the budget of the republic. We found entire new details there about religion, mores, the administration and policing of cities—mysteries that previous-

200

ly produced the double evil of irritating an incessantly disappointed curiosity and demonstrating remorselessly the absurdity and ignorance of theorists.

Books IV and VII, jokily dedicated by Sulla to Venus and Silenus, contained a chronicle, sometimes very free, and details of a bizarre novelty. It is known that Sulla liked the table and was fond of wordplay, and that at sixty, his white hair did not protect him from the flirtations of Valeria, the sister of the celebrated orator Hortensius. So, in those two books, he gives free rein to his insolent gaiety and licentious remarks. In Book VII there is a song that begins with the words *Amica si Bacchum et te*, which Sulla represents as his own, and which, with the outrageous and curious anecdotes that follow it, complete one of the singular aspects of the portrait of the man, born of one of the greatest houses of Rome, having spent his youth in opprobrium, in the midst of hideous pleasures, mingling crime and vice, pursuing his career in blood, in which he did not slip, and finally master of the world, which he released when it pleased him; repulsive of face and terrible of gaze; a joyful guest and executioner at the same instant; having within him much of Sardanapalus and Cromwell, and fusing it all with a Roman soul, the only Roman of his epoch.

The Greek quarto edition of those Commentaries was published by Monsieur Crapelet;[92] it is rightly preferred to the octavo edition in two volumes printed in Parma by Bodoni.[93]

The savant author of Roman history, Monsieur Michelet, produced an excellent translation in 1824.

---

[92] The Parisian printer and historian Georges-Adrien Crapelet (1789-1842).

[93] The famous printer Giambattista Bodoni (1740-1813) was dead by this time, but his widow Margherita had taken over his business, presumably still under the patronage of Joachim Murat in Geoffroy's alternative history.

## Chapter XVI
## *THE DEATH OF NAPOLEON'S MOTHER*

Since she had been crowned Empress by Pope Pius VII, the Emperor's mother had been resident on the Palais de l'Élysée; it was there that she had created, in the midst of the conflagration of wars and the resonance of her son's grandeur, a refuge of repose and virtue. Very pious and very benevolent, she accomplished all of Christ's law by means of an immense charity. When Napoléon made her Empress, almost against her will, her heart was augmented, but she reserved a kind of tranquil family sanctuary where she was no more than a mother, and which was only penetrated by those kings and queens who were no more there than her children.

The Emperor visited his mother frequently; his affection for her had remained respectful and had something of obedience in it; he liked to set down his power in her presence and to consult her strong intelligence when he had exhausted his own. He received from her the advice and inspiration that only emerge from the souls of mothers. In exchange for that confidence, his mother had conserved for Napoléon, in the secrecy of her intimacy, the most tender familiarities; she addressed him as *tu*, as in his childhood, sometimes took him to task, opposing his ideas—and the conqueror opened his heart of bronze to that celestial soul, and came to refresh his seething head in that atmosphere of maternity and love.

In 1817, a serious accident had compromised her health and almost her life; she had broken a leg falling down a staircase in the palace; she supported that event with the angelic energy that was habitual to her, and it was with a smile on her lips that she greeted her children when they ran to her, consternated by that misfortune.

In July 1819, the Empress Mother went to Aix in Savoy, where she took the waters. Far from finding the relief therein for which she had hoped, however, those fatal waters, taken with imprudence, occasioned the greatest disorders in her health. On her return to Paris a terrible malady became manifest, and after a journey to Fontainebleau that she wanted to make, in spite of her suffering, in order to see Napoléon there, she returned to the Élysée. The malady made further progress, and soon all hope of saving her life was lost.

Informed, Napoléon immediately went to Paris, where his brothers and sisters arrived successively, and his uncle Pope Clement XV.

The Empress Mother, on her deathbed, had conserved all her strength of mind. In her bedroom or the drawing rooms that preceded it, there was an Emperor and an Empress, seven kings and seven queens, all her children; she summoned them by turns, especially her dearest, Napoléon and "the persecuted"—that was Lucien, for whom she had kept that appellation even when his grandeur had been raised to the level of the others.

She also summoned her grandchildren, and, surrounded by all of them, she consoled them, giving them her advice and her final instructions, and abandoned her burning hands to them, which they covered with kisses and tears.

She sensed the end approaching, and wanted to know its precise term. She was informed. Then she seemed calmer. She said to them, while they were kneeling or leaning over her: "My children, no death could be gentler than mine, and how I shall bless the Lord, who has done so much for you and for me!"

She was asked whether she was in pain.

"I'm not suffering," she said. "I'm only weak; it even seems to me that it's idleness," she added, smiling.

It was because the mortal fever that was consuming her had already devoured her suffering.

She turned to the Emperor. "My son," she said to him, "You're going to remain alone on earth, alone with the world. Soon, you'll no longer have your mother to bring you your tender submission. There's only her, dear child, to whom you owe deference and respect. Poor Napoléon, how alone you will be in the world where there are only inferiors in your presence!"

She summoned all her children. "Lucien, Pauline, Joseph, my dear children, Napoléon will be your father henceforth. You owe him everything; never forget that your grandeur is his, and belongs to him."

Then she said to Napoléon: "My son, Europe is yours. God, by whom you have done such great things, has reserved even greater things for you. Know that the entire Earth will belong to you, but never forget that it is God who has given you omnipotence."

In the intervals of her weaknesses and faints, she reminded them, effusively, of their early years, of how, left a widow and alone, she had felt the strength to guide them, and how her efforts had been blessed.

She asked for the last sacraments of the Church; Pope Clement XV was there, waiting. He approached her to administer them.

"Holy Father!" she said, emotionally. "What, yourself!"

"My beloved sister," said Clement XV, "I would act thus as supreme pontiff, if I were not doing it as your brother and your old friend."

The archbishops of Paris and Milan assisted the Pope in the holy ceremony.

The Empress mother raised herself up on her elbow and wanted to pronounce the prayers herself; her tongue was embarrassed, but her voice was not weak.

When the Pope had withdrawn, she said to Joseph and Napoléon, who had remained alone with her: "I'm better, my children; that ceremony has relieved me greatly."

She rested for some time, and, having awoken again in the midst of all her children, she asked them to leave her alone with Napoléon.

When she was alone with him she said: "My son, at the moment when I am about to appear before God, I assure you that my life has always been pure."

Napoléon was sobbing.

"Courage, my son," she said. "If you knew how happy I am dying..."

Then she confided a secret to him, which he kept religiously, contenting himself with telling his brothers that it was an admirable act of delicacy and generosity.

Afterwards, she showed him with her gaze an open book. "Napoléon," she said, read me the prayers for the dying."

The Emperor obeyed, but after a few seconds she said: "I'm tired, stop..." Then she sighed, and delirium took possession of her mind.

All her children came in. She stammered incomplete phrases and inarticulate sounds. At about eight o'clock she said, effortfully but distinctly: "Mother of Napoléon! I'm the mother of Napoléon! I was too proud! Forgive me my pride...my God...my children..."

They were her final words. Her respiration became more awkward and more rapid; another hour went by in that anguish.

At nine o'clock in the evening on 15 November, her breathing, which had weakened, suddenly stopped without any vestige of distress or dolor appearing. She had just expired.

Then all those sovereigns prostrated themselves around her death-bed, and their prayers, mingled with their sobs, saluted the departure of that admirable soul.

Her funeral was worthy of her majesty.

On 25 November, from the Palais de l'Élysée to the church of Notre-Dame, an innumerable cortege deployed in the middle of the streets and quays hung in black.

First of all the entire Imperial Guard marched at the head.

After that came the clergy of Paris, on foot, the carriages of the bishops, the carriages of the cardinals, and the Pope's carriage, draped in velvet; the funeral cart, splendid in its magnificence, surmounted by the imperial crown and drawn by sixteen horses caparisoned in violet and gold velvet; and the kings of Bavaria, Austria, Saxony and Poland, on horseback, holding the cordons of mourning.

After that came Napoléon, who was weeping. At his sides, and in the same line, were the seven kings, his brothers and brothers-in-law, all clad like him in mantles of mourning, barefoot and bare-headed.

Then came, in solemn order, the kings, the great officers of the crown, the Maréchals of the Empire, the Council of State, the Senate, the legislative body, a hoist of corps and authorities, and then the imperial and royal carriages, and finally an army of fifty thousand men.

The Archbishop of Paris, accompanied by eight bishops, received the body under the portal of the basilica, entirely hung inside with violet velvet.

The Empress Mother was buried in the middle of the choir of Notre-Dame; over her tomb a colossal seated statue was erected. It was thirty-seven feet high, and cast in a single piece of bronze. Since that time the main altar has been placed at the entrance to the choir under the cross.

Three other monuments worthy of her were erected in her memory. They are the Hospices Ramolino, Bonaparte and Fresch, each containing a thousand beds for the old, poor military personnel and the sick. They rose up majestically between the Champ de Mars and the Esplanade des Invalides, on the bank of the Seine, almost opposite the gigantic palace of the King of Rome.

Thus died, thus was honored, and thus was mourned that strong woman, that admirable mother, all heart and all soul. The mourning of the people, like that of her family, was profound and true.

## Chapter XVII
## PUBLIC DEBT

In the midst of conquests, the Emperor always had present to his eyes the hideous and continually bleeding wound of the public debts of Europe. The debt of France, including those of Holland and Italy, rose to about five billions, but it seemed small by comparison with the enormous debt of twenty-five billions that oppressed England.

He thought profoundly about curing that ill; for, after the idea of invasion and conquest, the thought of order and reparation soon followed in his mind.

It was in vain that in that era, by virtue of I know not what absurd paradox, political writers had tried to justify that evil and to sustain that public debt was a virtuous necessity of the social body. Napoléon saw those elevated questions more simply, and for that reason he contemplated them with more grandeur. He had collected from Abbé Raynal,[94] a master he had greatly admired once and had so completely denied since, the maxim that although credit is the life of private fortunes, it kills that of States.

Amortization was very insufficient. Ingenious as the mechanism was, its action was to pump out and dry up that cesspool of public poverty. Of bankruptcy he had a horror. The citizens had given that money to the State, the State owed it to them to conserve it or repay it honestly, for a State is an entity that has its grandeur and its honesty, its baseness and its shame.

---

[94] Guillaume Thomas Raynal (1713-1796), a significant contributor to the Age of Enlightenment, whose principal work. *Histoire philosophique et politique des établissements et du commerce des Européens dans les deux Indes* (1770) was banned in France.

He knew too that in France, money is a serious matter; that the French have changed little since Caesar's Gauls, when they yielded to the victories and despotism of the Napoléon of Rome, but revolted furiously when the latter wanted to surcharge them with a tax of a fiftieth of their revenues. He knew that he could ask them for their life and their blood without measure, but that he ought to show the greatest reserve in asking them for their money. Napoléon was covered with applause when he said to the legislative bodies: "This year I need a hundred thousand men, and I have reduced the charges of the nation by fifty million."

In the same epoch, a singular theory of legislation took hold of his mind. It is said that he found it in Germany and that, having developed it in his mind, it soon acquired the status of a desire, and in consequence a law.

That law concerned the law then existing in Europe in regard to testaments. For the Emperor, that privilege was absurd. Born solely in Rome, and perpetuated until our day, it was nevertheless for him an intolerable offense to good sense and the public good. How could it be, in fact, that a man, after his death, when everything had escaped him—his breath, his body, his thought, his life—still arrogated a posthumous right over wealth that he could no longer possess; that he conserved a new property when he no longer existed, and the exorbitant right to dispose of things that could no longer remain in his domain?

That abstraction consecrated by time appeared to him to be too offensive; it was, in any case, the source of shameful poverties and that cowardly and deceitful veneration with which the elderly rich are too often surrounded. It had even happened that social progress had already brought into play the execution of the thought that was hidden in the depths of good minds. The principle of substitutions, or testaments prolonged over several generations, had succumbed in the great revolution of 1789, and that political destruction of an abuse had been widely welcomed.

A new law was promulgated by the Emperor. Under its provision, every proprietor must see his rights end with his life, and die intestate, while conserving until then the right to use and abuse whatever constitutes property.

The legislation no longer recognized any but legitimate descendant succession, exempt from any hindrance, purged of all fiscal rights.

The Emperor thought, however, that he ought to preserve collateral successions in France, for the first two degrees, those of brother to brother and uncle to nephew; the others were abolished.

England no longer conserved in its law any kind of collateral succession; only direct succession remained there.

And all the successions of ascendants and collaterals that he annulled in families were declared vacant, acquired by the State and necessarily applied to the extinction of the public debt.

The exception relative to England was in relation to the greater enormity of its public debt.

The law based on those principles this comprised an enormous amortization of all the fortunes that the State collected, and the diminution of the Empire's public debts was rapid.

However new those theories and that imperial constitution might appear, they did not disturb minds. Along with the public debt, the taxes that sustained it diminished. Direct successions, previously impeded by enormous legal rights, were entirely freed. Property itself, free from laws and freer from taxes, saw its value increase. Nothing had been injured, except for the uncertain expectation of future successions. In sum, the peoples trembled, and accommodated themselves to the Emperor's theories and laws.

What is bizarre is that it seems certain that the advice of a woman was no stranger to some of Napoléon's political determinations.

# BOOK FOUR

## Chapter I
### *SPEECH TO THE LEGISLATIVE BODY*

Through these great revolutions the Emperor had thought he ought to conserve the Senate and the legislative body—not that he would have refrained from attacking them long ago the moment that it was entirely convenient for him to by-pass them, to give France and the Empire imperial laws without the monitoring of any other power, but perhaps the memory of the struggle between the sovereign and the people, of which the legislative body was the symbol, had made him conserve it, either out of respect for that memory or better to show that the people were no more today than the shadow of the immense reality of Napoléon.

On the other hand, in the Emperor's administrative machine, those two bodies of State had certain functions in finance and legislation that were not without utility; it would have been necessary, to replace them in that action, to create other councils originating more directly from the Emperor, but that had become unnecessary, for there was in the obedience of those two assemblies of elected men something enlightened, and even something like a reflection of the Emperor's nobility.

Finally, by not withdrawing from the peoples of the Empire the free nomination of their delegates to the legislative body, he found in the choices, free of partisan spirit, and ordinarily full of wisdom, the revelation of men of merit whom he did not yet know; that was like a supplement to the rapidity of his glance in the search for elevated capacities. And he did not find it inconvenient to appeal to his peoples to aid him in that investigation.

The Senate, augmented at the same time as the Empire, then counted five hundred Senators for life, each having a salary of forty thousand francs. The Emperor had retrenched and destroyed the former senatoreries, the institution of which seemed unnecessary to him and might needlessly give a local senator an importance that could be dangerous.

The Senate had become he magnificent retreat of all the great military men, scientists, litterateurs and administrators. Chosen with the most luminous severity by Napoléon himself, that foremost body of the State formed a sheaf of all French glories, and imposed the greatest veneration on the country.

But neither of the two bodies was political.

Thus, the Emperor, in opening their sessions every year by a decree, limited himself to that document, and appeared to have forgotten, since 1815, to appear in person at the opening session, which for seven years had only been solemnized by a speech by the Arch-Chancellor on the Emperor's behalf.

A decree of the last days of November 1820 made it known that Napoléon would open the session of the two legislative bodies of 5 January 1821 in person; the Panthéon was designated as the location of the session.

The kings of Europe were then gathered at the Louvre in the annual council of kings that we have mentioned; they were invited to remain in Paris until 5 January.

On that day, at noon, to the sound of a thousand canon shots that had been heard since the early morning from Montmartre, Vincennes, Saint-Denis and the Invalides, the sound of bells and the acclamations of a million spectators, the Emperor and his cortege went to the Panthéon. Such a spectacle had never been seen. In the midst of the magnificence of the cortege, the twenty carriages of the kings could scarcely be distinguished; but what attracted all gazes was the imperial carriage in which Napoléon, simply dressed, was alone with Joséphine: the two finest things in the world, grandeur and generosity.

The Place du Panthéon had become an enormous tent in which a host of people was crammed, and in order that they

212

could obtain a better view of what was happening inside, the portal had been widened for the day, its walls demolished, so that behind the columns of the façade there was no longer anything but a vast doorway that permitted eyes to see into the depths of the edifice.

In that circular profundity, a high platform had been constructed, where the twenty kings were seated on their thrones. Pope Clement XV appeared in their midst, clad in his pontifical vestments.

In front of that semicircle of kings, on a very considerable elevation, two thrones were placed. Napoléon took his place there with Joséphine.

On the two lower sides, on the seats to the Emperor's right was the Senate, and to his left, the legislative body. Two stages of the platform and the rest of the temple contained the queens, the high dignitaries, the Maréchals, and the senior State functionaries. The people and the army shared the tent set up in the square and a considerable section of the interior of the edifice.

There is no need to describe the sunlight of that beautiful day; it has become proverbial to speak of Napoléon's suns.

At one o'clock, he stood up from his throne and pronounced the following speech:

"Senators and députés of the legislative body,

"You know what I have done.

"In the seven years that I have not been able to find myself among you, I have occupied myself incessantly with the concerns of my glory and the grandeur of the Empire.

"Today, I have assembled you to report to you what I have accomplished, and thus to inform you as well as my army of what I want to do.

"During those seven years I have triumphed over those who were my enemies, in the north of Europe.

"I have conquered England. I have only to congratulate myself for having united that great nation with my Empire; my new subjects have shown themselves worthy of my subjects in France.

"I have placed London in the third rank among the cities of the Empire, after Paris and Rome; Amsterdam has been obliged to take fourth place.

"After that conquest, impotent and irreflective Europe wanted to rise up again; I suppressed it, in a matter of days, and permanently.

"But the last sigh that old Europe exhaled made me realize that it was necessary to organize that body, henceforth dissolved and lifeless.

"I have reconstituted it and I have established a new order; my decrees of 1817 informed you of my political will when I declared myself the supreme sovereign.

"It was then that I sent back to their tents the barbaric sons of Mohammed; they have abandoned Europe, today entirely Christian; Constantinople was the capital hat completed my Empire; it has become its fifth city.

"I have nothing but praise for my vassal kings.

"I have swept the coasts of Africa clean; the brigands have retired beyond the Atlas. I have also created an African France there, which commences at the Atlantic and finishes at Egypt.

"After having done as much for the Empire and Europe, I was able to do something for myself; I recovered the Empress Joséphine."

As he spoke those words, the Emperor seemed emotional, and his emotion was shared by the crowd. But the enthusiasm reached its peak when, at that moment, Joséphine threw herself at Napoléon's feet. The Emperor raised her to her feet and pressed her in his arms. Nothing could be heard but acclamations and cries of joy.

He continued:

"My happiness is as complete as my glory.

"I have wanted my people to have their share of that happiness, as they have their share of my glory.

"Since my last victories and three years of peace, my resources, in spite of the immense ameliorations with which I have endowed my empire, have accumulated.

"Far from asking you, therefore, Messieurs, to fix the revenue of State for this year, I declare that I can do without it.

"I give back to my people all the taxes; for a year, none will be levied under any pretext."

At the announcement of that unexpected liberality, which accorded nearly two billions to the people of the Empire, the enthusiasm was such that it appeared that the vaults of the Panthéon were about to crumble.

When calm was reestablished, Napoléon, turning to the kings, said to them:

"Kings of Europe, also make it known to your subjects that the sovereign of Europe has not forgotten them in his munificence; I shall return this year's tributes to them."

Addressing the senators and the députés, he continued: "Messieurs, that is what I have done; I can talk to you about the future.

"I am going to take possession of Egypt and conquer Asia.

"I ought not to go any deeper into that determination before you; my politics keeps its secrets; but I wanted my people to be informed...I have no fear that Asia will be."

The Emperor terminated his speech, and bade farewell to the assembly with a gesture.

The news of that war in Asia was unexpected, and penetrated the crowd with admiration. Acclamations succeeded those extraordinary words, and accompanied the Emperor, who set forth again with his cortege on the road the Tuileries, all the way to the Imperial Palace.

## Chapter II
## *EGYPT*

It has been said of women that their projects are often executed before being conceived; one could also say that of the Emperor, so much was the rapidity of his thought allied with the rapidity of his action.

So, the expedition to Egypt, scarcely announced at the Panthéon, was already prepared in the ports of the Mediterranean and the Adriatic. We are talking about the maritime expedition to Egypt, for the expedition overland, directed against Asia, was in preparation in the former Turkey, where a Grande Armée had been gathering for some time in the vicinity of Constantinople, on the frontier of ancient Asia, on the other side of the Bosphorus,

Napoléon wanted to recommence the expedition to Egypt to which he had once given the title of the Great Expedition, when he had made it with few soldiers, few victories and, in the end, with a few defeats and a forced evacuation—and yet, that first expedition justly retained that celebrated name in the minds of nations, because the Bonaparte of those days had grown to an unusual splendor in being able to balance by the surest triumph of science the less certain success of political glory.

Today he recommenced that campaign joyfully, now that he had Europe entire under his orders, and England, which he had once found as an enemy on the coasts of the Delta, was no more than a useful and submissive auxiliary.

He confided the command of the maritime expedition to Comte Sidney Smith.[95]

---

[95] In our history, Napoléon said of Sir William Sidney Smith (1764-1840), who rose there to the rank of admiral, "That man made me miss my destiny," because of the assistance lent by his H.M.S. *Tigre* and *Theseus* to the defenders of Acre (Saint-

"If Nelson were alive," he said, "He would command the fleet and I would disembark in the bay of Aboukir."

He had no fear of recalling the saddest memories of the first war, and recalling to the very places of their victories generals who had once been his enemies, so much did he regard former national individualities as presently dissolved in France and extinguished.

The fleets, composed of a fairly small number of warships and an immense number of transport ships, departed on the fixed dates from various ports in the Mediterranean, where they were assembled, and they came together at the end of February 1821 in the waters of the Nile.

The general disembarkation was effected on the second and third of March. A hundred and ten thousand infantrymen, thirty-two thousand cavalrymen and a considerable artillery made up the army thus transported to Egypt.

At the same time, the Grande Armée of the land, more than two hundred and fifty thousand strong, gathered in its entirety in the environs of Smyrna, and, in accordance with the Emperor's previsions. The general junction of the two armies was carried out during the first days of April in the plains of Aleppo in Syria.

For himself, Napoléon's face was radiant with joy when he placed his feet on Egyptian soil. Everything that he had promised himself in his mind when he had abandoned it twenty years earlier was realized, perhaps beyond his expectations, and now that he had reappeared there with his omnipotence, the dreams came back again, and it seemed to him that the destinies of the world were about to be accomplished in the Orient, and that he was already its master.

He directed the army toward Syria and, only keeping ten thousand men, he advanced at their head into Upper Egypt; it was like a military promenade, in which he came, with his old

Jean-d-Acre in French) in 1799, during the long siege in which Napoléon ultimately failed to take the town, finally being forced to abandon his army and return to France.

companions in arms, to recognize the battlefields where they had once fought.

It was, in effect, merely a stroll, and not a conquest. Egypt, which trembled at his memory, and at the mere thought of his coming, fell silently to its knees when he arrived, like the kneeling divinities of granite that had been its gods three thousand years ago.

He entered Cairo, where the Pacha of Egypt came to surrender. The next day, he took his ten thousand men to the pyramids. The old soldiers, who had lain down in their shadow during the first war, showed them proudly to their new brothers in arms, and the army waited anxiously for Napoléon to make them hear a few words as sublime as those he had pronounced before in confrontation with those colossal constructions.

But he was pensive before them; or, rather, he was not thinking about them; they seemed smaller to him now, and he did not say a word.

He did not press his march any further; one fact was sufficiently established, the silent submission of Egypt. That, in any case, was not his plan. Egypt is like a neutral ground placed between Africa and Asia, belonging a little to both; a country of passage that, by itself, would offer little interest to conquest if the conquest were to stop there. For Napoléon, it was a means rather than an end.

He soon quit Cairo, only leaving a rather feeble garrison there, a French governor and a tricolor flag, and with the rest of his ten thousand men he went to rejoin his army in Syria.

Before reaching the isthmus of Suez, he recognized with emotion the fortifications of Salahieh and Belbeys, which he had had built in the first war by the care of the leader of the engineering battalion, Monsieur A. Geoffroy.[96] Those works

---

[96] Napoléon's memoirs, in our history, simply refer to Geoffroy's father as "Citoyen Geoffroy," with no further details; it is not obvious why this passage says, incorrectly, that he died at Austerlitz.

still existed. Napoléon recalled that officer, whom he liked and who had died so young at Austerlitz; his heart contracted at that sight, the memory of that brave and savant military man came back to him, mingled with regrets. "If only Geoffroy were here…," he said, and passed on, rapidly. A few moments had gone by when the thought of his glory had not yet entirely chased from his mind the memory of the companion of arms who was no more.

## Chapter II
## SAINT-JEAN-D'ACRE

Islamism still subsisted, and was not so weak that it did not still carry an immense weight in the politics of the world.

When Napoléon had so easily expelled it from Europe, it had silently folded up its tents and had withdrawn, for it knew that its strength was not there. But its retreat was not an annihilation; after having passed over the strait, it had come to settle in Asia Minor, Syria and Arabia, where it found itself in all its power.

Europe was perhaps scornful and had not paid sufficient attention to that retreat; it had thought it saw in it a sign of destruction, but that sign was deceptive.

The Emperor had not thought thus; although he had been astonished himself by that silent flight, he was not unaware that, placed on guard at the gate of Asia, Islamism would reappear to him when the time came, terrible in energy and fanaticism, and that the great struggle would take place in Syria that would decide the conquest of the Orient and of the religion of Mohammed; so he had prepared large forces in order to confront enemies of whom he was far from scornful.

At the news of the arrival of European troops in Asia, Sultan Mahmoud[97] had solemnly deployed the standard of the prophet, and had summoned all Muslims in the name of God and Mahmoud to the defense of the land and the religion. In all the cities, the mosques were resounding to the voices of clerics, and the public squares with war cries. Never had fanat-

---

[97] In our history Mahmud II (1785-1839), who became the ruler of the Ottoman Empire until his death, kept that role until his death, obtaining a reputation as a significant reformer, although the successful war to secure the independence of Greece, fought in the late 1820s, was a crucial phase in the fragmentation of the Empire.

icism been exalted so swiftly and so inflamed; all hearts were uplifted, and the nation of Mohammed was suddenly ready to receive the enemy.

Among the Pachas, however, some, the governors of provinces in the vicinity of Persia, hesitated to come and join the sultan's army, which was nevertheless more than three hundred thousand men, and came together without them under the walls of Saint-Jean-d'Acre. Without misunderstanding the cowardly uncertainty of those governors, Mahmoud did not seem to pay any heed to their delay; his army seemed powerful enough in their absence to do battle when the time came.

During those preparations by the Turks, the French Grande Armée, under the orders of the King of Spain, had entered Asia. Having found no obstacles, it had advanced as far as Syria. The Sultan had, in fact, withdrawn his troops from Asiatic Turkey in order to unite them completely, as we have said, in the vicinity of Saint-Jean-d'Acre, and placed there, they prevented the junction of the two European armies.

After his short expedition to Egypt, Napoléon came to rejoin his army in the south of Syria; confident in his glory, he conceived the project of annihilating the Mohammedan army at a stroke by means of a surprise attack. He therefore resolved not to wait for the arrival of the King of Spain, and, following the coast in order to be supported and resupplied by his fleet, he advanced rapidly toward Saint-Jean-d'Acre. He had more than a hundred and thirty thousand men with him; he was, moreover, accustomed to winning victories with lesser forces than those of the defeated; he counted on the courage of his army, the surprise of his arrival and finally on fortune, and the seventh of June found him on the territory of Saint-Jean-d'Acre.

Part of the Mohammedan army was occupying the city, a heavily fortified situation, and the other part was camped in the plain, supported by the fortifications. It was in the south of the plain that the Emperor developed his army. Having arrived within sight of the city, he looked at it angrily. Saint-Jean-d'Acre was a dolorous name for him. It was there that he had lost Egypt twenty-five years before; but in revenge, it was there that he was going to win Asia.

He believed so, at least. And he was accustomed to victory.

The day of the eighth of June was spent by the two armies in dispositions for attack and defense, and in the occupation of the most favorable positions.

On the morning of the ninth, the Emperor's army deployed to the south of the city, brilliant, rested and avid for glory.

The Sultan's troops faced up to them, with their backs to the walls of Saint-Jean-d'Acre, whose enormous gates were continually vomiting forth enormous battalions. They were waiting impatiently for the signal to attack; their religious exaltation was inflamed to the highest point before the battle. It seemed, on seeing the agitation of that armed host, that it was, so to speak, like a single body pawing the ground, from which cries of "Allah and Mohammed!" escaped continuously. It was, indeed, the case that a great spirit was animating that mass of men, that the living idea of God and religion bound all of them in one sole thought and one single force.

The French army also had its faith, its glory—but that sentiment, cooler than that of religion, was not manifest by any cry. The army was silent.

At ten o'clock, battle commenced; the impact was terrible. Never in human tradition, as we know, had such a conflict been engaged. The Turks precipitated themselves confusedly, with so much violence, upon the French lines, that the army was shaken by it, and, unaccustomed to such disorder, the European maneuvers were broken by that first attack; the ranks were unable to rally thereafter. Then the battle became furious and terrible, a hand-to-hand combat, a furious and murderous conflict. Turks were seen, mortally wounded, still dragging themselves under the feet of the enemy who had struck them to pierce them with their daggers, and to die themselves with that final exhaustion of life and vengeance. For the French, it was as if there were a double army to fight, the one standing up and the one left behind on the battlefield, after having been mortally wounded.

On the other hand, the Turkish cavalry charged the disorderly French lines innumerably and from all directions, and wrought a frightful carnage there; the infantry, whose strength is in the mass, disunited and fragmented in all parts, could not defend itself and was overwhelmed.

However, Napoléon, desperate, succeeded at about two o'clock in the afternoon, by dint of energy and skill, in rallying the left wing of his army, at the head of which Maréchal Berthier had been mortally wounded, some distance from the battlefield. That section of the army had suffered less. Having taken command of it, Napoléon brought it back to the battlefield in order. The center, commanded by Maréchal Belliard, also rallied, and the right wing, which had sustained the heaviest losses in the commencement of the battle, at the sight of those reunited tops reappearing like a second army, recovered a new energy in its turn, tightened its ragged ranks, and it seemed that the battle, after the first astonishment of the irruption of the Turks, was about to recommence, and that European discipline would recover its superiority.

Then, suddenly, a rumor spread from rank to rank. The Emperor was wounded, it was said.

It was true.

At that news, the army stopped, in its stupor, and no longer thought of defending itself. It seemed that it had been struck in the heart in the person of its leader.

Napoléon was soon seen, pale and mastering a spirited horse, racing along the lines at a gallop, but his very presence, instead of rendering the troops their moral force, only confirmed them in their despair, for blood could be seen running down his thigh, where a bullet had struck him.

It was all over for that day. The Turks, bathed in the blood of their brothers and their enemies, but not sated with carnage, pursued the debris of the French troops, with retreated in disorder after having suffered terrible losses.

At about three o'clock, the French army, for the first time in twenty years, withdrew from a battlefield leaving a victorious enemy there.

The Emperor, without paying any heed to his wound, gathered the remains of his army a league from Saint-Jean-d'Acre, and effected his retreat in the direction of Jerusalem. His march, in the midst of enemies further emboldened by victory, was considered as one of the most admirable of which the military history of the world has conserved the memory; not a single man was lost. Even the bodies of the wounded who expired during the march were not abandoned by the vanquished army.

It is necessary to admit, however, that the Sultan's army, intoxicated by its triumph, paid little heed to pursuing the French in their retreat. For them, that victory was so great and glorious that the Sultan preferred to remain on the plain where he had won his victory and enjoy his triumph entirely rather than actively pursue the consequences.

At ten o'clock in the evening, the French army, exhausted by fatigue, called a halt about four leagues from Saint-Jean-d'Acre, near the village of El'mayr, of which the Emperor immediately took possession. He had his troops rest and, retiring himself to a local house, remained there inaccessible to anyone all night: a night of dolor and anguish for the great man, so unaccustomed to such catastrophes.

It is said that, at about one o'clock in the morning, Maréchal Molitor, then far advanced in Napoléon's amity, having wanted to bring him consolation, had tried to reach him in spite of the prohibitions, but when he arrived at the door of the room where the Emperor was sleeping he had heard sobbing and moaning, and had withdrawn in despair.

At any rate, at five o'clock the following morning, Napoléon summoned his generals. He gathered them in council and there, grave but not distressed, he said to them:

"We have been beaten, Messieurs." And after uttering a sigh and darting animated glances at all those present, he added: "But no one here has despaired of our glory and the conquest!"

As no one spoke, he stood up straight, more animated. "No! No one has despaired! I have my thought and my fortune as a guarantee of that. Remember Messieurs, that twenty-five years ago, a first check before this fatal city was followed by the conquest of Europe. This other disaster of Saint-Jean-d'Acre announces to me the conquest of the world."

As he addressed those words to them he looked at them attentively. And when they asked him for details of his wound he showed them his leg, whose slight lesion offered no disquieting character.

At that sight and those words, the generals recovered hope.

He had the troops assembled immediately, and passed them in review shortly thereafter. He traversed all the ranks, and his consolatory words drew them out of their affliction. All were reassured on seeing the Emperor calm and careless of his wound.

The results of that great disaster were calculated that day: the Prince de Neufchatel, major general of the army, the Maréchals Duc de Trevise and Duc Gouvion Saint-Cyr, and twelve generals of divisions of brigades were dead and had remained on the battlefield with more than thirty-five thousand men, all dead—for, in their barbaric fanaticism, the Turks had not wanted to take a single prisoner.

All the artillery had fallen into the possession of the Turks. Of a hundred and thirty thousand men, only eighty thousand soldiers remained at El'mayr; the rest had been killed or dissipated.

It was estimated that the Sultan's army must have lost more than twenty thousand men on that bloody day, but that mourning did not trouble for a moment the actions of grace that the clerics of the God of Mohammed caused to burst forth on the day after the battle, and in which were joined the frenetic songs of the soldiers and the inhabitants of the city.

It was, in fact, an immense and magnificent victory.

When they were informed of it, the Pachas of Bagdad and Erzeroum, who had been waiting until then in crafty inaction for the first results of the war, arrived, bringing their troops to the Sultan, who thus found himself at the head of an army even more powerful than before the battle.

It was the second time that the name of Saint-Jean-d'Acre had been fatal to French armies commanded by Napoléon.

## Chapter IV
## DAMASCUS

The European Grande Armée commanded by the King of Spain had arrived in the vicinity of Aleppo when it learned of the catastrophe.

At the same time as that news, King Joseph received from the Sovereign of Europe the order to advance on Damascus at a forced march, to which the Emperor would take his own troops in continuing his admirable retreat. He arrived there in the last days of June, and it was under the walls of that city that the junction of the immense forces of the King of Spain with the formidable debris of the army of Egypt finally took place. Napoléon, without admitting the disaster of Saint-Jean-d'Acre, without even making any allusion to it, immediately took general command of the troops, and his presence, and the energy of the orders of the day he had published, revived the constancy of the soldiers dejected by the defeat.

Still concentrated in the province of Saint-Jean-d'Acre, the Sultan's army had imprudently let slip the opportunity to prevent the union of the French armies. The intoxication of victory had been so long and so fascinating that it had seemed to them that it was all over, and that Europe, with Napoléon, had been annihilated during that day at Saint-Jean-d'Acre. So they only sent inferior forces, disdainfully, to trouble Napoléon during his retreat to Damascus; fortunate in a first great battle, they were no longer thinking that victory might be infidel to the standard of the prophet on another occasion.

Several combats, however, in which the vanquished army had obtained signal advantages during its march might have awakened doubt in them, and their impotent attempts could not hinder Napoléon's military operations and his junction with the forces of the King of Spain.

Two days after taking command, the Emperor assembled a council of war in which great questions were raised. All

227

voices seemed united in favor of laying siege to Damascus and taking possession of the city, the veritable key to Asia. King Joseph, in particular, supported that opinion strongly. Damascus, although very strong, he said, was at that moment occupied by Turkish troops that were not very numerous. It could be taken easily, and the French Grande Armée, with immense resources, would find an invaluable position there that would render it master of that part of Syria, so favorably placed between Europe and the Oriental expedition.

Everyone was impressed by the advantages of the proposition, and they were one waiting for the Emperor's assent. Until then he had remained silent, as if deep in thought, but, suddenly rising to his feet, he said:

"To stay before Damascus would be a mistake. It's necessary that the army march to Jerusalem. I'm not in a mood to waste my time and my fortune, like Alexander, before a new Tyr. It's necessary that the probable time of that siege has not elapsed when Asia is already conquered, and for that, we'll march to Jerusalem."

And as they were all amazed by the name of Jerusalem, and could not comprehend a decision that would make the army march backwards, away from Asia, he exclaimed: "Yes, Jerusalem! Do you believe, Messieurs, that your arms and my power are sufficient to conquer the world? Is it in this Holy Land that we will forget Providence and the God of armies? We're going to quit Damascus and march to Jerusalem."

The astonishment of the council had increased to the highest degree. They looked at one another in silence; they did not understand such unexpected words, of which the Emperor alone knew the import.

The defeat of Saint-Jean-d'Acre had revealed a new thought to his mind. He had seen his fatality and his glory buckle before the religious enthusiasm of the Turks, and seen that army, animated by an immense faith, vanquish his own. He considered that Asia, with regard to battles, no longer resembled Europe; that his savant marches, his skillful tactics and his military genius would no longer find the same enemies, and that the echoes of the Orient would not resound as fearfully to the sound of the name that won battles on its own in Old Europe.

In that mysterious land of Asia, a new force appeared to him: religious faith, fanaticism; an incalculable force because it is beyond humanity, and to which it is necessary to oppose more than tactics and glory. So, before that new world, he had a new thought.

After seven days of marching, the Grande Armée, having quit Damascus and followed the Jordan, crossed the river south of Lake Tiberias and headed for Jerusalem. Napoléon went up the Kidron, northwards, and after that movement the army deployed facing Calvary, which still hid the holy city from view; for Jerusalem, circled by the Kidron as by a girdle, seems to repose between two celebrated mountains, Calvary to the west and the Mount of Olives to the east.

Then, before that sacred city, whose name, pronounced from mouth to mouth stirred old sentiments in the hearts of four hundred thousand warriors, which were dormant there, Napoléon had the following order of the day, so unfamiliar to the warrior habits of the day, proclaimed in every corps:

"Soldiers of the European Grande Armée,

"When, having conquered Europe, I promised you the conquest of Asia, when I made you traverse Asia rapidly in order to lead you to this ancient and holy land of Palestine, I had not revealed my thinking in its entirety; I was waiting for today in order to do so.

"The goal that the Middle Ages could not attain with two hundred years of battles, bloodshed and reverses, it is reserved for you to attain.

"Soldiers, this crusade of France will be the last of the crusades of the Occident; Jerusalem will be delivered and the holy sepulcher purged forever of infidels and profanations.

"Soldiers of Europe, Christian soldiers, the earth in which the insulted bones of your forefathers have been buried for so many centuries will henceforth be a French land, a

Christian land, and the annihilated Turk will not even be a slave in these places where he has been the master too long.

"In the name of God and the Cross, brave soldiers of my army, let Christianity soon be finished with these fanatical sons of Mohammed.

"Tomorrow, the army will enter Jerusalem."

## Chapter V
## THE BATTLE OF JERUSALEM

At the approach of that formidable army, the Turks occupying Jerusalem did not try to put up any resistance, and evacuated the city, retreating toward Bethlehem.

As he had said, Napoléon entered Jerusalem the next day, and headed directly toward the Church of the Holy Sepulcher, the ruins of which had not been rebuilt since the fire of 1811. He did not pause there and, having entered the convent enclosing the sepulcher itself, he had himself taken to it, and bowed down for a few moments, as if absorbed in a profound and religious contemplation. Then, having climbed back up to the convent, he spoke to the religious guardians of the sepulcher, and announced his intention to rebuild the destroyed church and to make it the most magnificent of the world's monuments.

Other orders and other dispositions also brought forth the religious enthusiasm by which his heart and his politics had been suddenly gripped; he also wanted the army to file in its entirety before the holy sepulcher and traverse in the city all the points that Christian tradition regarded as the most sanctified. For himself, having gone up to the Mount of Olives at the end of the day, he contemplated his army snaking everywhere through the regular but narrow streets of the city, filling them all and animating with an unaccustomed life the Jerusalem that had seemed dead itself since a God had died there.

When the first uncertainty of the soldiers and officers, who hesitated before the sentiment of religion, so long forgotten, had yielded to a real and profound impression, it arrived that the European army veritably believed, in the environment of Jerusalem, in its divine mission. That sudden crusade, perhaps undertaken for an entirely different goal, found itself Christian. Religious exaltation had soon inflamed all of them;

231

it circulated through the entire army as if in a single body, and that body, in effect, had just gained a soul.

During the week that followed, the Emperor took care to sustain and stimulate that enthusiasm. Preachings simultaneously warlike and religious excited minds so disposed to that sentiment in the very theater of their beliefs, under the skies of Jerusalem. It was a strange marvel, that military nation transported to the Orient and suddenly transformed into levites of Christ. A sudden piety had inundated those desiccated souls, and that European army named itself with pride the Christian Army.

Napoléon congratulated himself on those dispositions, and did not delay in putting them to profit. Scarcely had that first week gone by than he talked about returning to Saint-Jean-d'Acre to avenge the defeat and to enjoy for a second time the conquest of Asia.

Already, the preparations for departure were beginning, and the army, in its enthusiasm, was demanding with loud cries to be led against the enemies of the cross, when it was learned that Sultan Mahmoud was advancing himself with all the forces of Islamism toward the holy city of the Christians, as if to cast down in a single destruction Jerusalem and the European army, with its leader and its Christianity. Such, at least, were the promises that the Sultan had solemnly made to his troops, and he assured them that he would keep them under the walls of Jerusalem.

The Emperor heard that news with joy, and refrained, in spite of the excitement of his soldiers, from informing them of the arrival of the Turks and setting forth to meet them. It suited him better to wait in repose for an immense army fatigued by a long march, abandoning a province where its strength was increased by the memory of victory, and coming of its own accord to offer battle under the walls of a city whose sight alone inflamed all the hearts that had become Christian in Palestine.

20 July 1821 was the day so ardently desired by the Christians and the Turks. Those two innumerable armies, like

two great peoples suddenly transplanted into the deserts of Palestine, deployed in a plain situated beyond the Kidron, to the north of Jerusalem. It was the second time that those enemies found themselves facing one another, the Turks with the same enthusiasm, heightened by their victory, the Christians having, more than at Saint-Jean-d'Acre, vengeance and faith—two forces that were confounded in their hearts with courage, and disposed them to the miracles of the battle.

The bells of the convents and churches of the city, mute for such a long time, made their peals heard continually. The songs of priests were repeated in chorus by the Europeans. In the midst of the ranks, new standards, bearing the sign of the cross, rose up alongside tricolor flags. Everything took on a religious aspect on that solemn day when, for the last time, the armies of Christ and Mohammed found themselves in one another's presence, about to decide, finally, the fate and religion of the world, as before, in the times of Charles Martel, in the fields of Tours and Poitiers.

But God was with the truth in the ranks of the Europeans, and Napoléon was the general who had given it to them.

That extraordinary victory is so well-known that it would be superfluous to describe it in detail. It was not a battle but a massacre. The Mohammedans were swiftly surrounded and crushed by the European army, superior in number. The religious enthusiasm seemed equal, but newer and more ardent among the French; the engagement was horrible and brief. In the first few moments Sultan Mahmoud was killed, and the standard of the prophet almost immediately captured by the Christians.

Scarcely were those two immense losses for the beliefs and fatalism of the Turks known than it was as if they were struck by delirium. In their vertigo, they threw down their arms and hurled themselves at the French ranks. The latter gave them no quarter; their warrior fury was inflamed to the highest degree. They remembered the cruelties carried out by the victors after Saint-Jean-d'Acre, and in their turn they promised themselves a barbaric vengeance; they had sworn not to take any prisoners and not to spare any enemy.

That day was nothing but a day of slaughter and one long murder. The Mohammedan army was entirely massacred, for not one wanted to flee. In their despair, they offered their breasts to the iron that pierced them, and the Christians, insatiable for vengeance and murder, did not rest so long as a single Turk remained alive on the field of extermination.

Napoléon let them do it.

His mute vengeance was as terrible as that animated and bloody vengeance. His defeat was washed away and his politics satisfied. Islamism, that terrible despot of Asia, was annihilated. Three hundred thousand Turkish warriors had died in the Battle of Jerusalem, and with them, Turkey had ceased to exist. On the French side, scarcely fifteen hundred men had been killed. In the midst of the vapor of blood, as if to intoxicate them further, the army was exalted by actions of grace; they cried that the hand of God had aided them; perhaps Napoléon also believed that himself. Occidental Asia was struck by the same thought at that news; it saw that Mohammed's reign was over, and that the new prophet Buonaberdi, as they called him, had come from the Occident.

## Chapter VI
## THE DESTRUCTION OF MOHAMMEDANISM

On the evening of the battle, before the army had rested, the Emperor entered Jerusalem with great triumphant pomp; he was at the head of the kings and generals of his army, accompanied by an immense cortege, in which were confused, in the midst of the military forces, the people, the priests and the monks of the convents. The city, suddenly illuminated, resounded with clamors of victory, religious songs, cries of sated vengeance and the continual and redoubled ringing of bells. Fires were lit on the surrounding mountains.

In the midst of these expressions and acclamations, Napoléon advanced toward the holy sepulcher, where the clergy of the convent received him, singing the *Te Deum* in thanksgiving. After having heard it, he took a few steps into the church; having arrived facing the sepulcher, he had an ardent brazier brought, and having broken and torn up the standard of Mohammed himself, he threw its debris into the flames. The priests, who had not been notified in advance of that sudden solemnity, joined in with it enthusiastically; the chanting of psalms and the perfumes of incense-burners accompanied that vengeful holocaust, and when everything was consumed, Napoléon withdrew in the midst of the same acclamations, and the army and the people cried at the sight of that symbolic sacrifice that the Mohammedan religion had ceased to exist on earth.

It had, indeed, had its day, and its end did not surprise its sons. The Mohammedan tradition had announced for a long time the arrival of another messiah, who would strike it dead. For the Muslims, in spite of their fanaticism, only saw their religion as a religion with a lifetime of its own, which had to come to an end; they could not doubt its future disappearance, and that double and inexplicable conviction of its verity and its fall did not seem the least certain mark of their blind and

235

irreflective fanaticism. The events that had just overwhelmed them informed them that the time had come, and for them the great victory of Jerusalem was the destruction of their belief and the accomplishment of prophecies.

The next day, in the morning, Napoléon returned to the field of victory; from a nearby eminence he contemplated silently the mountain of the three hundred thousand corpses of the vanquished, which seemed a single cadaver. He was moved; the spectacle seemed to absorb his soul in profound and singular thoughts.

Before the debris of Mohammedanism, he almost groaned over the destruction of the belief to which he had just delivered the final blow; he had no hatred against it; it was more a sacrifice to his politics than to his opinion. It is even thought that the religion in question, with its fanaticism, its Oriental coloration, its enthusiasm, its energy and its entire submission to a leader pleased him. Twenty years before, he had thought about putting on the turban and rejecting France, which had exiled him in his conquests; he had hesitated then as to whether, for lack of her, he might make himself a monarchy in the Orient. History had made known the veneration with which, in that epoch, he had protected Muslim beliefs, and with what equality, for which he was subsequently reproached, he mingled the names of Christ and Mohammed in Egypt, when his genius swayed between the empire and God of France and the empire and God of Asia.

But the world had experienced great revolutions since the first Egyptian campaign, and the final regret that Napoléon allowed to fall on the end of that false belief soon gave way to higher thoughts. The strangeness of that sentiment, however, merited being collected by history.

To facilitate the removal of that multitude of cadavers, the Emperor permitted the soldiers to strip them, as they removed them from the battlefield, of the incalculable riches in which they were clad. Only a few days had gone by when all the corpses had been transported to another plain further to the north of Jerusalem, where they were buried or burned. That was a new service rendered to the holy city, which was beginning to fear that deadly proximity, for pestilence would not have taken long to arise in the midst of those mountains of dead.

Thus master of all of Syria, the Emperor distributed his troops in the various cities of the province. The King of Spain returned to Damascus, which opened its gates. Napoléon finally entered Saint-Jean-d'Acre, which could no longer close its own. The army corps under the command of the King of Westphalia was directed toward Aleppo, and the army rested for some time in those provinces, occupied henceforth without any obstacle.

Meanwhile, the King of Italy, who had remained in Jerusalem with fifty thousand men, soon received the order to enter into Arabia and march directly on Medina and Mecca.

Those cities were still two nuclei of Mohammedanism, which Napoléon had resolved to extinguish without delay. The greatest powers were attributed to King Eugène. The approval of all his actions and those of his army were assured in advance, and that was nothing less than permission for barbarity and destruction, two necessary means in the Orient, and which are like the common law of the land.

The King of Italy only took twenty-five thousand troops with him, selected from his army; he entered Arabia and arrived at a forced march before Medina. At his approach, a few Muslim troops, remaining faithful to that sanctuary of their faith, attempted a vain resistance; they were exterminated. The French army immediately entered the city, with tricolor flags and standards bearing the sign of the cross deployed and only halted outside the celebrated mosque where the three tombs of Mohammed, Omar and Abu Bakr were. The king immediately had them destroyed before his eyes; the white marble of the prophet's tomb was pulverized, and that debris, as well as the formless remains found in the tombs, were profaned and thrown into the temple with the lacerated and destroyed ornaments of the religion.

237

After the accomplishment of these holy profanations, the King of Italy had the doors of the edifice closed, and in spite of the protests of the inhabitants, had all the parts of it set ablaze. Protected by the troops, the immense mosque required five days to be consumed. The king disdained to conserve any of the innumerable riches that were found there; he wanted everything to be annihilated by the flames, and a few insensate individuals who, in fanatical despair, still wanted to oppose what they called a sacrilege, were hurled into the flames themselves, to perish there with their faith, their temple and the tomb of their prophet.

After the fire had gone out, King Eugène had the calcined ruins swept away by his troops, and had an enormous quantity of earth brought, which was spread over the site where the mosque had been. He ordered that the new terrain be plowed and that maize should be sown there, in order to cause even the vestiges of what had been Mohammed's tomb to disappear.

When that was finished, he quit Medina and advanced toward Mecca. That cradle of the prophet had even more to suffer than the conquest of his funereal city. Mecca, the mother of cities, as the Mohammedans called it, the metropolis of their faith, situated in the middle of an ingrate land and sterile mountains, only lived, so to speak, and artificial and religious life. The fecundity of other lands was brought into its bosom by caravans and pilgrims, and to topple the superb Masjid al-Haram, the Great Mosque, was to destroy the sources of its existence and annihilate the city itself.

Far from giving the King of Italy pause, that thought excited him further; his own was the destruction of the infidels and their religion. The fatherland of Mohammed seemed to him to be a filthy city, for the religious emotions of Jerusalem had exalted an implacable fanaticism in his mind, and the Emperor knew that when he chose him for that expedition.

King Eugène had the temple sacked and pillaged; he did not even respect the ancient kaaba, which was said to have been built by Abraham. He removed the silver frame in which the famous black stone had been enclosed for so many centuries, which Mohammed himself had respected, and which the tradition of the Arabs, among other fables that they attached to it, revered as having fallen from the sky in the times of Adam. That was the only trophy he conserved in the midst of that destruction, and he sent it to the Imperial Museum in Paris, where it can be seen today. Then he had the magnificent mosque set ablaze and mined, which collapsed and disappeared in the double exterior and subterranean conflagration.

More powerful and more irritated than Medina, because that destruction was a death sentence for it, the city of Mecca opposed uprisings and an energetic resistance to the French troops, but that manifestation was also more fatal. The blaze was not limited to the temple; the King of Italy, to punish the city, allowed the flames to spread and propagate. Soon, all the quarters of the city that had given birth to Mohammed were inundated, which then seemed to render its last sigh.

For a month, the flames, which no longer encountered any obstacle, formed a kind of ocean of fire, in which the great city gradually dissolved; but that flamboyant destruction, which satisfied the pious vengeance of the King of Italy, was more terrible than useful. Deprived of its mosque and its pilgrimages, Mecca, the city discrowned of its religion and its prophet, in the middle of that desert wilderness, would perhaps have perished more slowly, but irredeemably. However, that more rapid destruction annihilated the religion that was henceforth no longer able to recover the birthplace or the tomb of its prophet.

Thus the final blow was delivered to Mohammedanism, and it did not rise up again.

After a three-month campaign in which he had to combat a few Wahabite tribes, which soon surrendered, King Eugène took his forces back to Syria. He learned that the Emperor had just quit the province, and he caught up with him on the banks of the Euphrates. The Emperor welcomed him and his army with great eulogies, and the details of his expedition were solemnly proclaimed in the midst of the French troops.

If I have devoted long pages to that destruction of the religion of Mohammed, it is because that event was the most considerable in the Emperor's expeditions and conquests; Mohammedanism was the only force in the world that could struggle against his own; it was broken. Napoléon was soon the master of the world.

## Chapter VII
## THE RUINS OF PALMYRA

It is only in the Orient that one can work on a large scale, Napoléon often said. The old mother of peoples, Asia, is always the queen of the world. Everything in her has been or is great: her population, her extent, her monuments and her catastrophes. The Sovereign of Europe himself only came to impose his conquering monarchy after the monarchies of the Assyrians, the Persians and the Romans, after the conquests of Alexander, Genghis Khan and Tamerlane; but he came in his turn to close that series of conquests by causing to flood over Asia the French and Napoléonic monarchy, more powerful than all the rest, and it is useful, before following him any further, to pause momentarily cast an eye over the power that Napoléon then had in Asia.

Conqueror of Arabia and Asia Minor, suzerain of Asiatic Russia and Siberia, master, by virtue of the union of English and Dutch colonies, of Hindustan, he only found half the continent as yet beyond his domination: Persia, the Chinese Empire, Tartary, and India beyond the Ganges.

All those states were conquered successively, and, one can say, without great efforts. Two years elapsed after the battle of Jerusalem were sufficient to complete the entire success of the expedition. Volumes of history could scarcely describe the marvels of those two years; for myself, I declare that I do not aspire to reproduce so many details here. It was easier for the Emperor to conquer than it is for his historian to write, and that rude leader soon left history far behind, which, overwhelmed by fatigue, could not follow him.

And, as Plutarch said in his biography of Alexander of Macedon, that Napoléon of olden times: "I beg my readers not to make me a criminal if, instead of recounting in detail all those celebrated actions. I content myself with relating the greater part of them in summary. May I be permitted instead

241

to penetrate the signs of the soul, in order to grasp the most marked features of character, and to paint the life of the great man according to those signs, leaving to others the detail of combats and striking deeds."

The care that the Emperor took in deflecting his armies away from the most illustrious locations of Alexander's victories has been noted; he seemed, in fact, to be avoiding them; the battlefields of Issus and Arbela—or rather Gaugamela— were left far from his route, and the curiosity of his generals could not be satisfied.

The assembly of scholars who were following his expedition begged him to traverse the ruins of Palmyra and Balbek. He consented to that request all the more easily because his own thoughts had directed the army's march toward the coast, in order to link up with and accompany the European fleet, which had received orders in that regard.

We are assured that the mysterious solitude of Palmyra struck his mind with astonishment; he was surprised, in contemplating that forest of columns suddenly rising up in the desert, the magnificent palaces still recognizable, and the gigantic debris in a place where not even the debris of a people still breathed. He saw that ruins last longer than nations, and that traditions sometimes crumble before stones.

Little is known about the history of Palmyra. Placed for some time in the desert as a commercial halt between the Persian Gulf and the Mediterranean, so long as the merchants had consented to it, it had been one of the most flourishing cities in the world, with its temples, its porticos, its endless avenues of colonnades, its heroes, its queen and its philosophers; but when commerce, that capricious earthly abstraction, had abandoned it scornfully, as it had Babylon, Tyr, Carthage and Venice, Palmyra became a cadaver devoid of movement and noise, but still conserving the admirable attitude of its past life.

The scholars collected drawing and fragments of its monuments avidly. Another of the inestimable fruits of the conquest was the description of the ruins of Palmyra and Balbek, which, published since in Paris and London, differed in a few respects from the first description published in London in 1753 by Robert Wood.

Either because Napoléon wanted to let his army rest or because he wanted to allow the marvelous news of the Battle of Jerusalem and the destruction of the religion of Mohamed to spread through as-yet-unconquered Asia, he relented his march toward Persia. It was also known that large armies were gathering in the north of Hindustan, and perhaps he measured in his delays the time already foreseen at which the junction of all his military forces would be effected.

Thus, while India carried French armies toward its northern frontiers, the Empire's fleets lined up from the Persian Gulf to the China Seas, the vassal Russian armies approached independent Tartary, and central Asia could hardly breathe on seeing itself surrounded on all sides, the Emperor, having traversed the desert and its ruins, advanced with his army toward Bagdad, which surrendered, conquered before even perceiving him, and, having reached the Euphrates, went down the river as far as the city of Hillah.

## Chapter VIII
## HILLAH

Toward the end of October 1821, the army occupied the various cities of the Pachalik of Bagdad, and spent the winter there. The Emperor traveled those provinces personally in all directions, creating a new administration there, distributing a justice hitherto unknown, and most of all destroying the last debris of Mohammedanism that still remained there. He had the ashes of Ali thrown to the wind, and razed the walls of the mosque of Meshed Ali in which they were enclosed.

During the five months that he remained in the countries between the Tigris and the Euphrates, he took pleasure in researching curiously the dubious locations where Nineveh, Babylon and Seleucia had once existed, sometimes staying in Bagdad but more often in Hillah.

Hillah is a fairly small city situated on the Euphrates, twenty-five leagues south of Bagdad, mediocre in construction, devoid of commerce, monuments and picturesque sites. It was difficult to comprehend why Napoléon had chosen that particular site for his temporary residence. He had transported there, with part of his military forces, an army of scholars: Humboldt, Dolomieu, Niebuhr, Champollion, Quatremère de Quincy, Prony, Malte-Brun, Monge, Millin and others, whom he had chosen for his great scientific expedition and brought with him on this campaign, whose secret they did not know, although they suspected that they were going to conquer ruins.[98]

---

[98] The scholars here named but not so far cited are the geologist Déodat Gratet de Dolomieu (1750-1801), long dead in our world; the Orientalist Jean-François Champollion (1790-1832), who deciphered hieroglyphs with the aid of the Rosetta Stone; the archaeologist Antoine-Chrysostome Quatremère de

He had realized, in fact, that the ruins of Babylon ought to exist in the vicinity of Hillah, without their veritable situation being known for certain; some placed them to the north of the city, others to the south, but still on the banks of the river, but all of them only brought suspicions, although the Emperor, having arrived near Hillah, said to them: "Messieurs, we're close to Babylon. Find Babylon for me."

But it seemed that Jeremiah's prediction had been fulfilled, and that that city, which once overwhelmed the plan with its immense mass, had been dissipated entirely like a handful of sand. The scientists were increasingly hesitant; the slightest brick found in the sand revealed Babylon to them; some wanted to see the original Nineveh there, or at least the second city of that name, and they exhausted themselves in research devoid of discoveries.[99]

Napoléon, who found the game worthy of his repose, also searched for traces of the great city, and having gone up the Euphrates three leagues from Hillah, he applied himself to reconnoitering an immense, uncultivated, singularly uneven plain, through a multitude of eminences and little sandy valleys. It extended over an area of four or five leagues square, and appeared to have been disturbed by volcanoes, or by civilization, as powerful as volcanoes in shifting earth and drying it out beneath ruins, mortally injuring its fertility. The plane

---

Quincy (175-1849); and the geographer Conrad Malte-Brun (1775-1826).

[99] Joseph de Beauchamp believed that he had determined the precise location of Babylon in the vicinity of Hillah prior to the 1789 Revolution, and subsequent excavations seemed to prove him right. Claudius Rich produced a map of the site in 1811; in our history the latter published his *Memoir on the Ruins of Babylon* in 1815, and several other British explorers visited the site prior to 1821, excavating numerous artifacts, but presumably that did not happen in Geoffroy's alternative history; even so, his implication of uncertainty and controversy must have seemed slightly unwarranted at the time.

was divided by the Euphrates into two equal parts; to the west it descended in a steep slope from a mountain of singular conical form that rose up more than a league from the river. The plain, as well as the mountain, bore the name of Bel; but, as the denomination Bel, Bal or Baal is found in more than twenty places similarly along the banks of the Euphrates and in various and distant locations, the uncertainty, far from being destroyed, was, on the contrary, augmented by a tradition that placed the ruins of Babylon much further to the south of the city of Hillah.

Napoléon did not take long to resolve those doubts in favor of the northern plain that we have just mentioned. He took pleasure in climbing to the top of the mountain of Bel, which, covered from its base to its summit with old cedars and green trees of a prodigious height and vigor, seemed even more picturesque in the midst of those fields of desolation and sterility, and there, resting on the summit of the hill, he drew plans of the sinuosities and the places where his imagination reconstructed the greatest city of antiquity; or he rode around the vicinity of the hill and the uneven terrain on horseback. He was seen both animated and silent, and in the fire of his gaze a challenged was glimpsed, which his mind brought to the earth that hid the secret in its entrails.

On 2 December 1821—that date has been conserved because of the singularity of the event that it recalls—the Emperor left Hillah in the morning, taking with him old Dolomieu, Prony and Champollion.

Day was beginning to break when they arrived on the bank of the Euphrates in the plain of Bel.

"Messieurs," Napoléon said to them, as they reached the top of a sandy eminence that overlooked a large part of the plain and found themselves facing the hill of Bel, "this immense plain is Babylon."

"Your Majesty is doing as Alexander did," young Champollion said to him, "and cutting the Gordian knot."

"Which I couldn't untie, could I?" Napoléon replied, smiling and, pinching his ear in a familiar manner, he added:

"That's my jealous scholars, who don't want to forgive the profane the slightest erudition. What about you, Prony?"

"It might be, Sire," said the great engineer, "but I don't know. By my count, that makes more than ten Babylons we've discovered in two months."

"And you, Monsieur Dolomieu, have you more faith in my words?"

"Even less, Sire," said the old geologist, who conserved all frankness before the sovereign, as a privilege of his white hair. "Your majesty is mistaken; Malte-Brun has definitely found the ruins neat Kefot. Call this plain Nineveh if you wish, or Ctesiphon; my Babylon is my friend's."

At that time Dolomieu had taken into his closest amity the savant geographer Malte-Brun, in recognition of his devotion during the return from Egypt, and the grave illness of which the geologist had nearly died in 1801.

"So," said Napoléon, "you leave me without support, and the discoverer and the believers are confounded in my person alone. It's therefore necessary to convince you; but until then, Messieurs rebels, remember that I told you in advance about the discoveries I'm going to make."

And leading them to the very locations, he indicated the places where, according to him, great marvels were hidden: the hillocks that contained the largest temples, the two palaces on opposite banks of the Euphrates. He specified the two places where the entrances ought to be fund of the tunnel under the river that connected the two palaces by way of a subterranean vault: a prodigious construction forgotten for three thousand years, which had recently been renewed in London under the Thames and in Bordeaux under the Garonne. He designated the place where the temple of Bel would be discovered, and, so to speak, named the edifices for them. In an immense valley to the east, according to him, the lake hollowed out by Semiramis had existed; nearer were the canals she had constructed; here the walls, there the gates of the city—and where they saw nothing but a sea of sand and stone, it seemed that

247

Babylon was entirely reborn in the Emperor's picturesque description.

After a journey and detours that had lasted more than five hours, the three scholars, who protested by their silence against what their conscience doubtless called the imperial romance, were brought back by Napoléon to the mountain of Bel. Having demanded careful attention from them, he said: "And what do you think this is?"

"A mountain rising between four and five hundred meters," said Monsieur de Prony.

"I've measured it myself," said Napoléon. "It's one thousand six hundred and fifty feet high. Notice how conical and regular it is."

They examined it attentively, and were, indeed, surprised by the geometric form.

"What do you think that mountain contains, Dolomieu?"

"I don't know," said the geologist, "but that conical form makes one think that an enormous granite rock forms its nucleus, and that it's the last element of the mountain chain that extends to the east."

"And you, Messieurs?" said Napoléon

But they did not reply.

"It's necessary to tell you, then," As they listened, with great attention, he said in a loud voice: "It's the Tower of Babel."[100]

They were stupefied, and a few minutes' silence was broken by a burst of laughter from Champollion.

"Hum!" added Monsieur de Prony, more gravely.

As for Dolomieu, raising his spectacles over his forehead in order better to see, no longer the mountain, but Napo-

---

[100] As long ago as 1616 Pietro della Valle, one of the first explorers who thought that he had discovered the site of Babylon, identified the mythical Tower of Babel with a location called Tel Babil, and had two paintings made of it, which became well known after being reproduced in a book by Athanasius Kircher.

léon, he moved closer to the Emperor and looked at him for some time with an inexpressible astonishment.

"Yes, Messieurs," the Emperor said to them, earnestly, "that mountain and its forests hide the ruins of the ancient Tower of Babel; we'll find within its flanks the oldest titles in the world. During the two months that I've been exploring this region, my thought has been fixed; it's no longer a suspicion that I'm exposing at hazard, it's a prophecy for which I'm incurring the responsibility, but of which I shall have the glory. Now," he added, smiling, "we can quit Babylon."

He took the three scholars back to Hillah, and on the way he made known to them the intention he had of ordering immense excavations in the plain and the mountain, and sustained his pretention of discovery so ardently that all three of them arrived at the city shaken, if not convinced.

*Chapter IX*
*BABYLON*


Scarcely had he returned from that exploration then the Emperor imposed a new contribution on Asia Minor and Arabia, but it was no longer treasures that he claimed as master—he was overloaded with them—but men. At his orders, innumerable hosts of workers soon arrived, successively, from neighboring lands; the soldiers of the expedition were also employed in the same endeavors, and thus combined, in a very short time, that immense army of workmen rose to at least two million men. It was with that number that Semiramis, according to Diodorus, had built, or at least aggrandized, Babylon; Napoléon required no less great a multitude to resuscitate that city and reconstruct its ruins.

The works commenced immediately. Two hundred thousand men were exclusively occupied in uncovering the flanks of the mountain of Bel, and the rest were dispersed over the plain where, according to Napoléon, the gigantic cadaver of the city reposed. He was everywhere, animating with his orders and gestures, directing the digging and the operations, and revealing with an admirable discernment the places where the monuments lay, which, soon uncovered, confirmed his revelations.

The European and Asiatic engineers united their combined efforts, and soon created marvelous machines animated by the waters of the affluent river, by steam and mechanics; all the camels of Arabia and the beasts of burden of Asia were also employed, and all those combined forces tripled the action, already so powerful, of the population of laborers.

The rapidity of the execution was no less extraordinary than the inception of the project and the combination of so many means. Two months had scarcely gone by, and immense mountains of sand and earth rose up at the edges of the plain. Babylon, disengaged from the masses that had covered it for thirty centuries, reappeared in the open air; it felt its entrails open and breathing, its streets struck once again by the sun's rays, and its valley finally reborn to the world.

It seemed, on seeing it rise up day by day, that it had lost nothing, so well had the indestructible construction of its walls, in that preservative climate, kept their form beneath a depth of two hundred feet of sand and earth. And scarcely had it returned to life that it already had all its tumult and agitation, as if it had rediscovered its population of old in the millions of men who repopulated it as they resuscitated it.

Inspired by Herodotus, with his book in hand, Napoléon rendered their names to all those debris. The quays were recognized almost in their entirety; some of the hundred bronze gates were found—the gates of which the Lord had said, in speaking to Cyrus, according to the testimony of Isaiah: "I shall march before you and I shall break the gates of bronze."[101] Another Cyrus had discovered their debris.

They followed the traces of the enclosing wall; the great regular square of which antiquity speaks reappeared, as well as the forty towers still rising above the walls; for the eternal mixture of bricks and bitumen had conserved them as in the earliest times. From the hundred gates the fifty principal streets departed in all directions, incredible in their length and width, cutting one another at right angles with an admirable regularity; and those streets also reappeared with their houses, whose upper stories had almost all been destroyed.

Only one construction had disappeared, and that was the marvelous bridge of which history has given such strange descriptions; it no longer existed, but the pillars of its arches were found under the water, and it was easy to reconstruct the enormous stones of which they had been formed, still linked together by chains of cast iron and lead.

---

[101] *Isaiah* 42: 2. The standard, but atypically inaccurate, citation from the A.V., reads: "I will go before thee, and make the crooked places straight. I will break in pieces the gates of brass, and cut in sunder the bars of iron."

The aqueducts were rediscovered almost intact, and they could have received the waters of the mountains that they went to rejoin at great distances, but the Emperor did not extend the clearance beyond the extent of the city.

In the midst of those discoveries, one above all appeared to strike the admiration of Europe and Asia: that was when the vaulted road that Semiramis had had constructed under the Euphrates, and which connected the two palaces she had erected on opposite banks, was finally found, after the most stubborn research. For thirty centuries the waters of the Euphrates, which it had been necessary first to divert in order to construct the subterranean bridge, has flowed over it without destroying it, and without even causing any deterioration.

When the approaches were definitely established, Napoléon, without waiting for an entire clearance, was the first to go into it, and he boldly traversed the entire width of the river. He took by his side the same scholars that we mentioned in the previous chapter, and who followed him with an admiration equal to their terror. The great man, in the double depths of earth and water, was still joking with them about their incredulity, and when they reached the middle of the tunnel he said, smiling: "Well, Messieurs, are we in Babylon?"

But they did not reply, so amazed were they.

The Emperor also emerged first from those vaults, and, climbing a long spiral stairway that rose up to the other bank, he went into the palace of Semiramis, whose ruins offered little of interest.

If anything, however, could surpass those prodigies, it was doubtless the works excavated on the mountain of Bel. Napoléon, who had placed his greatest hope for discoveries there, watched over them himself with a constant attention, and directed them with an extraordinary activity. A week had not one by when the conical mountain, stripped of the forests that covered it everywhere, appeared as a great bald pyramid, whose forms seemed even more regular. Then the excavations were driven more profoundly, especially between the middle and the top. Soon, after enormous labor, a wide road as laid bare, paved with bricks and bitumen, which appeared to rise up in a spiral around the mountain.

That discovery guided the work; the traces of the road were pursued all the way to the summit and descending again to the base. That immense spiral, diminishing its coils progressively as it neared the summit, embraced the gigantic edifice, which gradually reappeared as the earth under which it was buried was removed; at every moment they saw new arcades and endless vaults reborn, as if standing out, superimposed one atop another to incredible heights. Architectural forms of which none had had any idea previously were revealed to astounded artists. Rooms without number succeeded one another in its flanks and were opened and explored; at every step they presented antiquities and fragments of every kind, which belonged to epochs of which humans had not even conserved the traditions.

A series of stone tablets charged with sculptures and hieroglyphs was discovered in that prodigious monument; they appeared to date back to the earliest times after the Deluge, and Champollion, who studied them for a long time, ended up discovering their precious mysteries. He read on those symbolic pages antediluvian writings and traditions, which finally revealed in a certain manner the history of the earliest times of the world, ruining many theories, and confirming, by completing them, the narrations of the sacred books.

Thus the Tower of Babel reappeared, after the forty centuries that it had been buried by a double envelope of earth and forests. Books and atlases have collected and published the details of its discovery; we shall content ourselves with saying that the diameter of its base was five stades, or a quarter of a league, and that its height was more than six stades. The emperor, who was the first to go up it on horseback following the exterior spiral road, took more than nine hours to reach the summit, and there, on a platform about twenty feet wide, he summoned Prony, Dolomieu and Champollion, and said to them, in a mocking tone:

"Well, Messieurs, are we at this moment on the summit of the Tower of Babel?"

They could do no more than admire, and old Dolomieu, in a kind of delirium, at that place, in that country, and before that prodigy, prostrated himself as if in adoration before Napoléon; but the latter lifted him up, smiling, and made another joke about his granite nucleus.

## Chapter X
## THE DEATH OF GENRAL RAPP

In the spring of the following year, Napoléon entered into Persia with his army, and completed its conquest in less than two months. It would be almost as accurate to say in one day, for Persia, weakened in all parts by the invasions of Tartars, Russians and Afghans, could not oppose a serious resistance. Its forces were concentrated near Tehran, and a single day was sufficient for Napoléon to destroy that army, take possession of the capital and conquer that empire.

He took the Sophi prisoner, ordered that he should be transported to Europe with his children, and divided Persia into two military governments.

The conquest of Afghanistan was more difficult, and retained Napoléon in that region until winter. That nation, newly constituted and still little known, was nevertheless very powerful. With the energy of a young and free people, victorious until then, its soldiers occupied a territory favorable to defense, bristling with mountains everywhere, and back up, as if against an in eradicable frontier, to the highest mountains in the world, the chain of the Himalaya. Mountain people, they had courage and obstinacy, and the Emperor, although certain of reducing them, took rather a long time to do so, and was only able to succeed after repeated difficulties. Having finally rendered himself master of the southern provinces, however, and later of Kabul and Kandahar, the remainder was unable to resist and was forced to yield.

As the most significant act of his conquest, Napoléon continued to destroy Mohammedanism in the vanquished lands. The protestant sect of Ali had obtained no more mercy from him in Persia; he had annihilated it without return along with its mosques and clerics.

Those conquests as well as that of the kingdom of Kashmir, really only formed a single campaign, that of 1822, and did not present anything remarkable. Asia, struck a death-blow at Jerusalem, was still struggling, as if in the last convulsions of its agony, but it could no longer rise up.

A single catastrophe signaled that campaign. General Rapp perished, the victim of an infamous treason, which was not long delayed in being avenged in a terrible manner. General Rapp had been charged with invading and occupying with his division the northernmost province of Afghanistan, that of Balkh, which is the ancient Bactria. The submission of the country seemed complete, and the general, with fifteen hundred men, was himself in Balkh. He had been greeted as its master, and he believed he had an ally in that perfidious city; every day brought new fêtes, in which the inhabitants deployed their Oriental luxury in order better to celebrate the conquests of the French.

On 22 July, the most magnificent of those fêtes was announced in the morning by the sound of trumpets. On the delightful banks of the Dehaz, in the midst of the enchanted plains that surround the city, an immense banquet had been prepared for the French troops; the most exquisite wines of Persia flowed in abundance; the young women of the seraglio, whom, in their religious effervescence, the French soldiers had immediately freed when they destroyed the cult of Mohammed in the cities, mingled with the victors and further excited, with their gazes and their songs, the joys of that seething youth.

For their part, meanwhile, the inhabitants of the city had gone in great numbers into the plain; they maintained themselves at some distance from the victors and their devoted themselves to secret conversations; a hidden fury, which one might have thought satisfied, broke through the sinister gravity of their features at intervals. That was because unexpected news had just spread through the city of Balkh; they had learned by word of mouth that that Napoléon had been assassinated in Kabul and that his army was fleeing in disorder toward Hindustan.

The inhabitants of Balkh did not want to be left behind in that criminal progress. Those exquisite wines contained the most subtle of poisons; those women, who were also in on the secret, were fascinating the soldiers and pouring out the liquors in abundance, from which, on a religious pretext, they persisted in abstaining. And when, at the end of the banquet, fifteen hundred voices, with a common accord, drank a toast to the Emperor and the Grande Armée, the barbarians welcomed it in a profound silence and with a barbaric voluptuousness.

Only a few seconds had gone by, however, when cries of pain were already succeeding those cries of joy; the unfortunate soldiers could no longer get up from their seats, and were struck as if by a devastating death. It was a frightful spectacle, and General Rapp, who was the first to divine the crime, drew his sword and, in a dying voice, cried: "To arms!"

But there was no longer time, for at the same moment, thousands of sabers and daggers suddenly gleamed in the hands of the inhabitants of Balkh; they invaded the banquet, and hurled themselves with frightful howls upon the unfortunates, whom the poison killed before the blades. Their rage knew no limit; they struck furiously, and a few hours had not elapsed before they had cut the throats of all those who could still writhe in agony.

They cut off the head of General Rapp, and, having placed it on top of a pike, they exposed it on the highest of their minarets, and threw the bodies of the other Frenchmen into the plain, without sepulchers, and soiled by the most abominable profanations.

The intoxication of that crime had a prompt awakening. The news of the Emperor's death was false. Napoléon was with an army corps, closer to Balkh than the barbarians had believed. When he received notification of the crime he arrived at the city at a forced march. He had it surrounded by his troops and refused to enter it. Deputations came to him shedding tears and wearing mourning; old men came to throw themselves to his feet, begging for mercy for their city, which tradition named the most ancient in the world—in vain.

"Its time is finished, then!" cried the Emperor; and he delivered some of those delegates to execution, and after having the others mutilated, he sent them back with the bodies of the dead to inform the city that it had neither hope nor pardon.

Napoléon's anger did not burst forth with violence; it was the fury of concentrated vengeance. His brave soldiers and his friend Rapp had been assassinated in a cowardly fashion, and he only hesitated over the choice of the most terrible punishment.

When he had settled the matter in his thought, he ordered that the gates of the city should be walled up, in order that no inhabitant could escape therefrom. And having brought forward his artillery, he had them set fire to the ancient city in a thousand places. Bombs, Congreve rockets, grapeshot, fireworks and incendiary materials were launched into all its parts.

In vain, for two days, cries of agony escaped from the midst of the roar of the fire and the muffled crackle of the flames. He did not try to put them out; it was necessary that everything be consumed, the city and its inhabitants, and even the ruins—everything save for the memory of the crime.

The action of the fire lasted a fortnight in all its violence, and left nothing but a mountain of hot ashes. Then Napoléon seemed satisfied with his vengeance; he ordered the remains of the soldiers, which the barbarians had abandoned in the plain, to be collected, and having constructed a tall pyramid with the calcined debris of the city, he had the following words inscribed on its site:

*HERE LIES GENERAL RAPP*
*AND HIS BRAVE FRENCH SOLDIERS*
*AND THE INFAMOUS REMAINS OF THE CITY*
*THAT ASSASSINATED THEM*

## Chapter XI
## THE LION HUNT

Napoléon was exposed to a great danger himself in that campaign when, in the early days of September 1822, while in Kabul, he wanted to take part in a lion hunt, which were very common in that epoch.

To the east of Kabul extends a broad plain, intercut with woods and thickets. It was there that a lion had been seen. The Emperor, accompanied by a few aides-de-camp and a considerable troop of Afghan hunters, commenced its pursuit.

Exhausted by such great labors, Napoléon had little leisure to devote himself to hunting, but when he could, he went about it with an enthusiastic activity. It was his favorite sport, and the thought of hunting the king of beasts increased that pleasure, and grave him something new and greater.

Three leagues from the city, terrible roars informed them that the dogs were on the track of the lion. Immediately, the hunters, who had until then been beating the plain with precaution, ran forward; but the Emperor, carried away by his ardor, spurred his horse to the greatest gallop, and leaving behind his companions, who could not keep up with him, went into the forest, where he was soon alone, and out of the sight of his friends.

Meanwhile, the furious lion had traversed the plain and the clumps of trees with which it was scattered with enormous bounds; shots from carbines and rifles that did not reach it only irritated its rage; it had torn apart the dogs that were pressing most closely on its heels, and having made immense detours, had sent the others astray. No longer hearing their baying or any gunshots, it had gone to ground in a distant part of the wood, where, near a mass of rocks, it rested, panting, its mane bristling, its eyes and mouth bloody.

Suddenly, the sound of a horse's hoof beats resounded; a rider entered the wood rapidly and headed for the rock.

It was Napoléon.

Close to the lion, alone, and in that extreme peril, the Emperor seized the moment when, with one bound, it launched itself toward him and, aiming with the greatest composure, he fired his rifle at it—but the bullet went through the mane without wounding the animal, which, furious, threw itself upon the Emperor's horse, plunging its claws into its breast and knocked it over, lacerated and dying.

The Emperor had also been knocked down but, detaching himself promptly, and preserving his calm on mind in that dangerous situation, he backed away toward the rocks from which the lion had departed, in order to wait for it there.

During that maneuver, the lion slaked its fury on the unfortunate horse; it had opened its breast and raked its flank with its claws, and was bathing its fiery tongue in the hot blood of its victim. And yet, without abandoning the horse, it followed Napoléon's slow and assured march with its gaze. While retreating, he examined his terrible adversary's slightest movement with the greatest attention.

He had just attained the rock, and was leaning against it, when the lion quit the horse, which had just expired, stood up, raised its head, its mane bristling, uttered a single but frightful roar, and bounded toward the Emperor, who drew his hunting-blade in order to receive it.

The weapon was inadequate, without a doubt, and the Emperor, having immediately understood that, threw it away at the moment when only a few feet separated him from the lion.

Instead of the blade, he struck it with his gaze, assaulting its eyes with all the energy and fixity of his stare; their two gazes engaged, so to speak, without quitting one another, and without any of the four eyelids blinking.

At that steely gaze the lion reared up in surprise, and roared terribly. As if its progress had been paralyzed, however, and an unexpected power had just issued a command, it stopped, foaming with rage and confusion, before Napoleon, who oppressed it with that singular force, overwhelming it with the gaze with which he had thus far only cowed humans.

Napoléon saw that the charm had succeeded, and that the lion recognized his power. Then he applied himself to giving his eyes the seductive gentleness that he knew so well how to secure its effect.

The lion, still held by that gaze, responded by a duller roar; it had lowered its head, which it supported on its paws, and having lain down, as if in arrest before the Emperor, it was doubtless waiting for the moment when those eyes looked away to devour its victim.

But Napoléon was not a man to yield in that contest. He did not want to content himself with that first success but to carry it through to the end. Alternately mastered and gentled by his stare, the lion appeared to become calmer and weaker. Its mane settled on its neck, the blood disappeared from its eyes and its tongue, softening, lolled like that of a breathless dog, refreshing the fire of its lips. And, crouching further and further, it lay down on the ground and placed its enormous head on its paws, which no longer displayed the redoubtable claws.

Then Napoléon thought that the time had come. He advanced toward the lion with a firm tread; it raised its head sharply, but the Emperor's eyes, incessantly fixed upon its own, became caressant, as if voluptuous. The animal shuddered with pleasure under that gaze, and the Emperor was only a few paces away when it came to him, agitating its tail as a sign of joy and swaying affectionately. Then, having reached his feet, it curled up and lay on its back, extended its enormous paws in the air, playing with ne of Napoléon's hands; he dipped the other into the coarse tresses of its mane.

They remained thus for some time, like old friends. Napoléon, not placing overmuch trust in that sudden affection, was nevertheless embarrassed by it, and did not know how to withdraw and terminate the scene, but the noble lion seemed to have forgotten everything; it eyes, having become yellow and moist, were half-closed, and gazing at the Emperor softly.

He played with his companion as if with a kitten, and its velvety paws, devoid of claws, stiffened and extended toward him amorously.

It must have been a marvelous spectacle to contemplate, that union, and such strange games.

Finally, Napoléon, after a few minutes, thought he had mastered the animal sufficiently to stand up and call it to him. The lion followed him tranquilly, head lowered, like a faithful dog, and they both emerged from the wood where that scene had unfolded.

All was not finished, however, and the Emperor feared, with good reason, encountering in his path the hunters, whose noise and tumult would have awakened the animal's fury.

Hazard permitted that the first person offered to his gaze was a servant who, thrown by his horse, was searching for the Emperor on foot. Napoléon, showing him the lion, signaled to him to approach without showing any fear. Stupefied, the man obeyed, and the lion, having looked at him momentarily, turned its head away and appeared not to pay any further heed to him.

The servant told him that the hunters had gathered some distance away, waiting for the Emperor and very anxious about his disappearance. Napoléon sent him back, instructing him to tell them that the lion had been tamed, and to order all of them to dismount and to rejoin him on foot, silently.

A short while later, the hunters and the Asiatics, obedient to his orders, arrived without noise. The lion, still caressed by the Emperor, pressed him with its head, and was not alarmed by the newcomers, so much confidence did it have in its friend. It therefore walked in their midst, but as they reached the summit of a small hill that masked a village, at the sight of the dwellings, the cries of children and the tumult that was audible there, the lion raised its head proudly.

Its mane bristled again, and, pulling away rudely from the hand that was still caressing it, bowled over two of the Asiatics with a single bound, and in a matter of seconds it had disappeared over the horizon, without having done any harm and without having been pursued—for Napoléon had protected the noble animal's retreat, by means of his prohibition.

They returned to Kabul, and everyone was amazed when Napoléon recounted that marvelous scene; and the Asiatics, who were beginning to believe that Napoléon was a god, asked one another: "Is it a man, then, that lions obey!"

*Chapter XII*
*CONTINUATION OF THE EXPEDITION TO ASIA*

During that long campaign, the Emperor distributed to his troops enough favors and advantages not to leave them time to regret the fatherland. Although he did not care about imitating Alexander in his great deeds, he had nevertheless studied his history profoundly, and especially his faiths; but he wanted above all to be himself, original—in sum, Napoléon—and not the reflection or the copy of another. The stupid flatterers who took it into their heads to compare him to other great men were lucky when they got away with scorn or sarcasm; the King of Annam came off badly, as we shall see, by virtue of his historical allusion. Napoléon only wanted Alexander to be recalled in order to draw comparisons between his own great wisdom and the Macedonian's imprudence.

In the course of their campaigns, the European soldiers had acquired an immense booty. He did not want them to remain burdened in their march, or that he might be forced at some point to have their riches burned, as Alexander had, when he had attracted the censure of his troops. In the cities through which his armies passed Napoléon had ordered the organization of large military depots; the soldiers brought their riches there and the imperial administrators gave them receipts in exchange that each of them could keep without being weighed down. The goods deposited were, moreover, conserved religiously, registered carefully, and became the property of families in case of the soldiers' death. Thus assured of the conservation of their fortune, the troops only had one desire: to march forward in order to augment it, and to extract from future conquests more of those singular letters of exchange in return for victory.

During the conquest of Afghanistan, and in the same epoch, the King of Spain overcame Baluchistan without difficulty. Although courageous and energetic, the inhabitants of those countries were not jealous of their independence, and easily adapted to a conquest that, without wounding their interests, placed them under the denomination of a man whom renown depicted to them almost as a god, before victory gave him to them as a master. Those events occurred in July 1822.

In the following month of November, Napoléon, with twenty-five thousand men, traversed the mountains of Persia and headed toward Tartary. He called that expedition "an invasion of barbarian territory." It was the land from which, in the fifth century, the Huns, the Alans and other barbaric nations had come to invade Europe, and political dreamers were sure that in those same little known regions immense populations still lurked—a "seed-bed of people," they were called—ready to flood into European civilization.

The Emperor had little faith in those previsions, and he had said: "The only means of preventing invasions is to make them."

Only one important battle signaled that expedition; on 23 December the numerous but undisciplined army of the Tartars was annihilated under the walls of Bukhara. The Emperor took possession of that city, traversed the desert as far as the Aral Sea, and three months later he returned to Samarkand, where he stayed for a few days.

He found the capital of Tamerlane's vast empire in ruins; it was almost uninhabited. It was the same with Tartary entire; the country, exhausted by the emigrations of the fifth century, had not been able to reproduce its former population. A few million wretched human beings were scattered through those vast countries; they were subdued after a few combats, and the Emperor made Tartary a military government, the capital of which he placed in Bukhara.

On emerging from Tartary, the Emperor traversed the Belour mountains, subduing petty Tibet in passing but without going up to greater Tibet. He entered Hindustan, which in that epoch was entirely a French possession; followed the line of the Himalayan mountains to the south, traversed Bengal, and the month of September 1823 found him in India, beyond the Ganges.

A few months sufficed—the time spent in marching—to conquer the kingdoms of that peninsula; only the Burmese put up a brief and vain resistance. The kingdoms of Cochinchina, Siam and Annam were conquered in advance, and the peninsula of Malacca was occupied without a shot being fired by Maréchal Gérard.

In all those lands, the Emperor persisted in the same system of political and religious conquest; he annihilated the traces of former domination, and had the kings and entire royal families transported to Europe; and everywhere, too, on the crests of pagodas and fortresses, he planted the cross and the tricolor flag.

As he was about to be thus transported by a French ship, the King of Annam requested an audience with the conqueror.

"What do you want with me?" Napoléon said to him, on entering the room where the interview took place.

Without making use of an interpreter, the King of Annam stood up proudly and said to him in bad French: "That you treat me as a king."

"You have read history," the Emperor replied, with a mocking smile, and, turning his back on him, he addressed his generals, saying: "This imbecile thinks that I've come three thousand leagues to play a farce." And he went out again without saying anything further to the unfortunate prince—who was, in fact, treated like the rest of the vanquished kings, taken aboard a ship and transported to Europe.

When Napoléon was at Amarapura, the Burmese brought him two living unicorns; those extremely rare animals had been considered until then to be fabulous. Naturalists studied them carefully; it was realized that they were merely a species of antelope of very considerable stature, whose two horns, very straight, were entwined in a spiral and stuck together, standing up from the middle of the forehead and only presenting the appearance of a single horn.

They were transported to France, the climate of which seemed to suit the life of those quadrupeds perfectly. They bred on our soil, where the race multiplied rapidly. Their mores were mild, they were easy to domesticate, and the strength of that graceful animal has already been seen in application to industry and luxury; its elegant and elevated proportions approach those of the horse, to which it is even preferable in some respects.

If we return our gaze to history, we see that by the beginning of 1824, all of Asia was conquered with the exception of China and the islands of Japan. At that time, Napoléon's Empire surpassed in extent and power the celebrated and temporary empires of Tamerlane and Genghis Khan.

## Chapter XIII
## THE DECREE ON MENDICITY

From the extremities of Asia, the Emperor did not forget Europe, and especially France. The administration of the Empire was everywhere that he was; his decrees were dated from Tehran, Samarkand, Delhi or Calcutta. It was a bizarre thing for the man who obtained the concession to construct a factory on some French or Italian river to see that imperial permission arrive from a city in Tartary or Hindustan. It was particularly from Siam, where Napoléon remained for the longest interval, that a large number of those decrees were rendered, among others the well-known and celebrated decree concerning the abolition of mendicity, whose principal dispositions we shall analyze.

Every individual recognized as a pauper or who, being found begging, was declared such by the tribunals, was immediately inscribed in the Register of Paupers, and from then on placed at the disposition of the government, which could transport them at will to any point within the Empire, or even to the colonies. More often than not the State divided them between the various communes of the French Empire, where they and their families were maintained in a fixed manner, at the expense of the State and the commune.

Each town or village was, in accordance with its revenues, charged with a proportionate number of paupers and obliged to lodge, clothe and nourish them. On the other hand, the paupers, thus saved from misery and hunger, remained under the surveillance of the administration; they remained at its disposal, unable to move away from that residence without permission, and under severe penalties; they were also, in certain cases, obliged to carry out certain work of public utility, principally the maintenance of the roads, canals, and State or common property.

Such an organization of paupers, which thrust them into an inferior class while providing for their needs and their existence, gradually obliterated mendicity, while stimulating labor. The shame of being recognized as a pauper increased to the point that it was necessary to have descended to the utmost degree of misery to solicit one's inscription on the register.

Idleness, which adapts so well to alms, recoiled before that new situation, because although in that order of things one found the resources of life, one lost liberty therein. Work and exile from the native soil became obligatory, at the whim of the administration; families, so often careless of the poverty of their members, feared that helotism, the opprobrium of which was reflected upon them, and hastened to come to their aid.

Soon, things reached the point that mendicity was almost extinct over the surface of the Empire, and the number of paupers, which, in the first census taken by the government amounted to nine million five hundred thousand, had diminished by more than two-thirds within two years.

The Emperor declared in that sovereign and reglementary decree that it should extend its application to all the States of Europe. He made little use of such general decrees, but he did not hesitate on that occasion, because he wanted to destroy mendicity, or at least reduce the number of paupers, throughout Europe.

## Chapter XIV
## *THE DESTRUCTION OF EGYPT*

Another decree, no less extraordinary, was similarly dated from Siam.

Old Egypt, once so calm, seemed to have been prey to continual agitations for some years. Seditions had arisen in Cairo and the cities bordering the Nile. Some of those revolts had been serious, and French garrisons, unable to repress them because of their small number, had been massacred. Finally, in one last convulsion, the Egyptians had cursed the name and power of Napoléon and proclaimed their independence. The false news of Napoléon's death spread through the Orient, which had occasioned, as we have seen, the massacres of Balkh, appeared to have determined that insensate insurrection.

And yet, in that epoch, the Emperor was thinking of vivifying Egypt by immense projects; two railways lines were about to be constructed in the isthmus of Suez, with a branch line to Cairo. The two navigations of the Mediterranean and the Red Sea were about to be linked by those two passages of commerce, and the lands that would have surrounded by their proximity the new route from India to Europe would have found a new life and flourished among the nations. On learning of the sedition of the country, however, the Emperor felt the keenest indignation; he swore a mortal hatred against it.

"Ingrate Egypt!" he cried. "A terrain devoid of faith and a fatherland, which is not even worth the trouble of being conquered, and which ought to perish after such a treason."

It was then that he accomplished the strange punishment of a nation condemned to death, irredeemably, which was about to be erased from the surface of the Earth.

He ordered that the Nile be redirected above Thebes and that, confined to a new bed, it would flow henceforth through the desert into the Red Sea. Thus diverted, the river, from

Thebes to the Mediterranean, abandoned its old bed, dried up and pestilential. The westerly winds soon brought their sand-storms, and reestablished the rights of the desert and death in those plains, which had been exempt from them since the Creation; there was no longer any life in those regions, once so flourishing, now desolate and burning. And while a new Egypt was created on the new banks of the great river between Thebes and the Red Sea, the ancient one gradually disappeared, sinking into the waves of sand and sterility, beneath which it was entirely engulfed in a few years.

After that, Napoléon cut through the isthmus of Suez; he recalled the nations of workers that he had employed in the uncovering of Babylon, and with such a force the immense works were soon completed. In 1825 the strait of Suez had replaced the isthmus of Suez; its breadth was considerable, Napoléon having wanted to hollow out a sea and not a canal with lock-gates, as he had been advised to do; in vain he was told that the levels of the two seas were unequal; he said that he would level them. And indeed, when the last barriers were removed and the two roaring seas precipitated themselves upon one another, their fury was brief; marrying their waves, they found a level, and with the waves the fleets of India and Europe soon arrived, which traversed the new Napoléonic strait with sails deployed and their prows superb.

Africa thus found itself the largest island in the world.

## Chapter XV
### CHINA AND JAPAN

Everything is singular in China. It seems that it is a world apart, cast into another dimension; everything there is particular, strange and original. The soil, with an unexpected fertility, has its own productions, its natural history, its mines and its rivers, resembling nothing in the rest of the globe.

God made for that nation a separate creation of humans, whose physical organization and coppery coloration are found nowhere else; they have developed a language whose forms only exist there, and a writing even more extraordinary, since the hieroglyph of every word is a new sign therein. Their religion, a confused theism drowned in a vague and ostentatious morality, is unlike any other. Finally, their remarkable political organization is entirely dissimilar to the other politics of the Earth; and in order that everything should be extraordinary in its mores, that innumerable nation, with frontiers so extensive, which delivers millions of human beings to the commerce of Asia and Africa, of which they occupy the borders, introducing their skill and their counters everywhere, remains jealous of its interior; it closes its gates and expels foreigners; it only wants with the rest of the world, from which it differs so much, the eccentric commerce that expires on its shores or at its great wall.

However, along with that national susceptibility, China is careless of its independence; it does not know what liberty is. Destined to be conquered, like ancient Rome when it offered itself to the highest bidder, it abandons itself without defense and almost without regret to anyone who wants to be its master. For forty centuries, its history has been nothing but the chronology of its defeats and tranquil submissions, for it was sure of finding in its advanced civilization a slower but no less certain victory over conquerors who unfailingly dissolved in its national superiority, and who, after arriving as barbarians, became Chinese after a number of years.

Renown had brought them rumor of Napoléon, and it was no longer in doubt for them that his intention was to conquer Asia in its entirety; China therefore, raised no obstacle to that. Three armies landed by the European fleets in the south, the center and the north of the country, near Canton, on the banks of the Blue River and in the depths of the Yellow Sea some distance from Peking, took possession almost without firing a shot of the principal cities, and extended Napoleonic domination successively over the various provinces, and soon over the whole empire. The Manchu Tartars, their last masters, after a lone and derisory resistance, were destroyed and disappeared, and the conquest of that great empire proved to be one of the easiest and most rapid.

But the Chinese were mistaken when, in their scorn for liberty, they allowed the Sovereign of Europe to come to them, opening the gates of their cities to him without dread. For them, Napoléon was only a twenty-second dynasty to register in their annals after all the others; but Napoléon was a man who did not want to be after anyone. If he had been able to destroy history and the past, he would have done so, and would have extended his victories there. He therefore made them aware for the first time that this was a revolution. They discovered that the man from the Occident would not make concessions to the religions, mores and laws of the people he vanquished, but arrived only to smash them, bend them out of shape and make himself their master, and that his inflexible will had decided to reduce all the nations, whatever they were, to the level of his general politics.

The Chinese empire expired in that final domination. Henceforth, it was no more than a province of Asia, and an ordinary fraction of the world, into which the iron hand of the master entered violently.

Only the islands of Japan remained at the extremities of Asia, and the great conquest, comprising the destiny of the world; they were occupied at various points and almost with-

273

out resistance by numerous army corps. Having reached its terminus, the expedition to Asia was completed.

It had lasted four years.

# BOOK FIVE

## Chapter I
### *A PRETENDED HISTORY*

Everyone knows the goal toward which this history is proceeding: the Universal Monarchy. That was where Napoléon was leading it, though his innumerable victories, feats so striking and events so marvelous that history takes fright, and has trouble trying to envisage them in order to reproduce them.

For my part, I am weary of those conquests, and in spite of the fairly considerable sobriety of victories that the reader might have noticed in these pages, I am nevertheless somewhat overwhelmed by the weight of that glorious and veridical history; but at least I can render the testimony, in the midst of my enterprise, that I have always thought about the honor of my country and the glory of the Emperor, and have omitted nothing that might heighten either of them; for that, I have only had to turn to the past, to see it and to write it, and it has transpired that I have written a monumental narrative.

After having rendered the testimony of having been truthful in what he has recounted of those grandeurs, may the writer not express his indignation for the culpable romancer who must have taken it for his task to insult a great man and vilify his homeland, by fashioning for posterity I know not what ignoble and detestable invention, the shame of which ought to fall back on its author?

You have divined me, and have sensed that I want to talk about the fabulous history of France from the taking of Moscow until our days, that history welcomed by I know not what caprice, that one finds everywhere, reproduced in all its forms, so widespread that in centuries to come, posterity might wonder whether that romance might not be history.

For myself, my heart feels the necessity to flagellate that odious fable; and, suspending my great history between Asia, which has just fallen, and the rest of the world, which is about to succumb in its turn, I shall relate to you where the anonymous author of that lie has dragged his imagination.

He has said what Napoléon and Europe were until 1812, but when he reaches the appearance of the French before Moscow, this is what he invents.

Moscow burns, and the Russians go to Saint Petersburg to sing a *Te Deum* because their city has been captured and burned. As for Napoléon, he finds nothing better to do—him, the man of activity and genius—than to stop there for thirty-five entire days trampling the ashes of the burned city; and, as if the Emperor had only done so many things to witness that distant fire of joy or distress, he soon makes his retreat toward France; and when he wants to flee that country a frightful catastrophe overtakes his armies in the ice of the Berezina, while the Emperor, wrapped in his cloak, leaves his soldiers there, freezing and dying, departs in a carriage with the Duc de Vicence, and returns to Paris.

Then begins the year 1813, which the anonymous hand has made so fatal for the Empire and the Emperor.

Prussia betrays Napoléon and joins forces with Russia; Austria, which gave him its daughter, and to which he had given life three times, also abandons him and enters into the Northern coalition. And Napoléon, who fights in vain at Lutzen, who is crushed at Leipzig, leaves his Frenchman in thousands, his brave generals and his Poniatowski dead on the battlefields of Germany.

That triple alliance draws after it Germany and the rest of the North; they all invade the frontier in 1814, and enter France!

Horrible impostures!

Then everything dissolves, he says; the enemy gains more and more ground, its victories and defeats drawing incessantly closer to Paris: Arcis-sur-Aube, Montmirail, La

Ferté, and eventually Paris—combats everywhere, finally in Paris, which is entered.

Oh my God, but all that is as false as it is absurd!

Then the Senate, which trembles and goes pale when an usher cries at its door: "The Emperor!" treats him as a Commissaire de Police treats a thief; its judges him, it expels him, it breaks him. And Napoléon, doubtless accustomed to obeying that Senate, especially when he is insulted by it, does likewise; he expels himself, he breaks himself, he abdicates.

Then all the allies, for all Europe has become allied since these things—England, Spain, Holland, Sweden and Bavaria all want to be in it—abduct Napoléon from the middle of France and throw him as sovereign into a tiny island, Elba, I believe, within telescope range of Italy, a few leagues from France, in order that all their great politicians can sleep more tranquilly, thus freed of their prisoner. All of them fall upon France and devour her; they tear into shreds what a hundred conquests had brought her of riches and monuments; they tread down the lava that they have poured over her, and place for guardian of those remains an old race of kings that had quit France twenty years before.

That is called a restoration; and once that word restoration has been found, the author, who doubtless likes it, sets about applying it to all the neighboring kingdoms: Ferdinand has his restoration in Madrid and expels Joseph; another king has his in Naples, from which he expels Murat; the King of Holland also has his, but there is no king to replace there when he comes back, for the empire extended until then.

The author, however, in the middle of that culpable romance, contrives one rather great thing. Napoléon stands up on 1 March 1815 and, kicking away his island with one foot, sets the other in France, marches for twenty days amid unanimous acclamations, enters Paris, finds the bed still warm from which his advent has chased away the king, sleeps in it, and wakes up on the morning of 21 March still Emperor of the French and France.

As if that great invention had exhausted him, however, the author immediately buckles and falls even lower; he can no longer do anything but create horrible disasters. He invents I know not what funeral name of Waterloo, to which he immolates a hundred thousand Frenchmen, and, unable to imagine anything new after that infamy, repeats the same calumnies, relates another invasion of France by her enemies, even more restorations, and overturns Napoléon for the last time, casting him away on another tiny island in the Atlantic, two thousand leagues from Europe, where the great man dies a few years later of a stomach schirrus.[102]

That is what the liar has made of Napoléon and history, and, in spite of that unprecedented confusion of absurdity and shame, I know not what caprice has welcomed it with an interest for which I can hardly account. These things have been repeated complaisantly in conversations and books, and it has reached the point when I know not what vague credence has given them a kind of appearance of reality. But it is a duty for a historian of courage to repudiate all these tales, and to declare loudly to the world that that supposed history is not history, and that that Napoléon is not the true Napoléon.

---

[102] A scirrhus is a malignant tumor. Napoléon's father had died of a similar affliction, and so did several other members of his family, so we can now assume that he had a hereditary vulnerability to the cancer in question. In the world of the present text, obviously, whatever environmental stimulus triggered the tumor in our world did nor materialize until a much later date.

## Chapter II
## NEW HOLLAND

I shall resume my veritable and great history.

After having assembled a part of his fleet in the gulf of the Yellow Sea, Napoléon set sail on the first of January 1825. It was a great and memorable event, that departure of the conqueror and his vessels, leaving Asia, of which he had nothing more to ask, after four years of occupation, success and conquests. As the ships drew away, Napoléon contemplated that vast continent incessantly, which diminished and faded away into the mists of the horizon. He seemed still to retain from the last of his glimpses the final appearance of those countries, become his. With them he had gained half the world, and he was already no longer hiding his thoughts when, losing sight of the coast, he exclaimed: "Adieu, then, Asia; with you I have accomplished half my work."

He did not consent to follow the advice of his naval officers, who had traced the route of the imperial fleet through the China Sea toward the Strait of Malacca, in order to enter the Indian Sea and from there head toward Europe. His adventurous will wanted to brave the dangers of fraying a route through the reefs and archipelagoes of Oceania. His directed his ships forwards, straight toward the middle of the Sea of the Moluccas. His fortune and the skill of his pilots protected the vessels miraculously through those amphibious regions, which dart their sharp and cunning arrows from the sea-bed, while the most rapid currents surround them, roaring, and increase the dangers further. However, he paused in Borneo, landed in Batavia, traversed the redoubtable Sea of the Moluccas, and went to rest his flag and his fleet in the Gulf of Carpentaria.

What a strange spectacle it was, that apparition of the Napoléon of Europe and Asia on the wild coasts of New Holland! But there was an enigma there irritating the sagacity of the sovereign of the old world. That virgin country, of which all that was known was the perimeter, embroidered with the illustrious names of French navigators, offered a strange mystery to history and geography. Only the coasts had been visited, without anyone having been able to push discoveries more than a few leagues inland. It seemed that nature had forbidden humans access to that unknown world; she had surrounded it with obstacles, and a short distance from the coast, continuous mountain chains rose up everywhere: immense natural walls that protected those countries from discovery forever.

Forever? Until the man had arrived who, after having vanquished men, was also able to dominate nature. That insurmountable barrier would be surmounted in its turn when Napoléon wished.

The fleet having touched land at the southernmost extremity and deepest part of the Bay of Carpentaria, the emperor disembarked two thousand of his troops, with abundant provisions, and, heading directly southwards, declared that he also wanted to make discoveries.

As they advanced toward the center of the island, the ground rose, and arduous mountains loomed up on the horizon, appearing to be merely the continuation of circular chains, part of which had received the name of the Blue Mountains, near Sydney and Botany Bay. Although they appeared impracticable, the novelty of the enterprise inspired so much energy in the little army that they had soon surpassed them, and in the month of June 1825 it had reached the highest passes and found itself on the opposite, southerly slopes.

Having arrived there, the Emperor and the army had the strangest of spectacles; instead of the lands that they had thought to discover, a great Mediterranean sea extended before their eyes, a new ocean, in the middle of which, in the far distance, countless flaming hills and volcanoes rose up, the eruption of which was soon recognized to be continuous.

Napoléon, struck by surprise at that sight, was all the more inclined to continue and complete his discovery. On the shore of that still-virgin sea, he had the first ship constructed ever to sail upon its waters. He was the first to set foot upon it and embark on those unknown waves.

A small fleet was soon created, with a surprising celerity; it scattered over that sea, reconnoitering its coasts and sinuosities, and approached the volcanoes and islands, all uninhabited, but some of which were charged with an admirable vegetation. Napoléon amused himself by giving the larger ones the names of his most cherished generals, but when he was asked in his turn to give his own name to the sea, he refused, for he had long since made a mental decision to retain his own name for himself, or perhaps for a world, as he disdained to shrink it to the narrow proportions of a sea or a continent.

He gave that Mediterranean the name of the New Sea.

The geographers and mathematicians of the expedition reconnoitered and measured its extent, which is about seven hundred leagues in its largest dimension, and five hundred leagues wide. No channel appears to connect it to the ocean; it thus occupies the center of New Holland, which surrounds it with its land in the manner of a ring, or like an immense vase containing its waters.

On the interior slopes of the mountains, no new object appeared to merit the attention of the voyagers. Here and there they encountered a few wretched and brutal peoples of the Malay and negro races that share New Holland. Natural history discovered a small number of new animals, always offering the bizarre types already identified in those regions, and had to recognize in other realms some rare but nonetheless extraordinary caprices of nature.

That great geographical question henceforth clarified, the Emperor continued his navigation over the New Sea, landed on the south-east coast, crossed the Blue Mountains, until then uncrossed, and entered the young and beautiful city of Sydney in the finest days of September. Newly founded, it already offered at that extremity of the globe, the advanced civilization of the foremost cities of Europe.

The fleet left in the Bay of Carpentaria had received orders to rejoin the army of discovery on that coast; it had arrived ahead of Napoléon, and he was therefore able to embark immediately for Europe. Before lifting anchor, however, at the moment of separating himself from the greater number of his ships, he divided them into several squadrons, and gave them the mission to spread out through the archipelagoes of Oceania, in order to subdue them all and to plant his tricolor standards on every island in the Pacific.

For himself, having only kept five vessels with him, he quit the magnificent port of Sydney a few days after arriving there, and set sail toward the Cape of Good Hope in order to return to Europe.

## Chapter III
### SAINT HELENA

The crossing from Sydney to the Cape was only remarkable for its rapidity. Napoléon, who felt the keenest desire to see France and Europe again, only paused in African territory briefly. He had already decided on the continent's future conquest, but by his armies alone, without him even taking part in it. He had I know not what horror for that great peninsula. It was in Africa that he had known for the first time in his military career what defeat and flight were, and now that he had arrived at the height of his power, he disdained to cover his former misfortunes there with victories. He knew, moreover, that the continent was filled by his name and his renown; that its less traveled depths resounded with his praises; and that in those spaces the nations, as if drawn by an inexplicable instinct, were summoning the vanquisher of Asia, with his laws and his religious faith. Napoléon knew, therefore, that he had only to have the country traversed by a Cross surmounted by one of his eagles for black Africa to come to kneel and bow down before that double sign of the God of heaven and the King of the earth.

The news he received at the Cape of that disposition of the African nations delighted the great Emperor, but could not detain him longer. The armies for which he had reserved the mission of traversing Africa in every direction in order to subject it to him had not yet arrived from Asia; the fleets that were to transport them were still in the Indian Sea. There was no point in waiting for them; he was so sure of his soldiers and of Africa, victors and vanquished. That conquest, in his view, was more a passage than an expedition, and he believed that in those barbaric lands, the sound of his name would have as much power as his presence.

He left the Cape of Good Hope and, favored by the winds, soon found himself in view of the island of Saint Helena.

We ought to pause here for a few moments and speak about the extraordinary impression that the sight of that tiny island in the middle of the Ocean produced in Napoléon's soul. At the moment when, the sailors having signaled the island, General Bertrand came to tell him that Saint Helena had appeared on the horizon, the Emperor went pale, a cold sweat suddenly spread and shone on his forehead, and one might have thought that an unknown danger, a fearful apparition, had chilled his soul and his blood.

"Saint Helena!" he said, in a somber tone, and let his head fall on to his breast, as if oppressed by a poignant dolor.

The kings and generals looked at him in amazement, unable to understand that alarm. The weather was calm, the navigation rapid and fortunate, and the approach of Saint Helena, a port of call for ships on the great voyage to India, was one more pleasure for the sailors and the army, who were about to renew the water and foot supplies and touch land.

Admiral Duperré, the captain of the vessel, came to obtain the Emperor's orders, and asked him when it was necessary to land.

"Never!" replied—or, rather, cried—Napoléon.

All of them were petrified with astonishment, and almost with terror.

"Let the vessel draw away from the island as soon as possible, without landing there."

He was obeyed. The vessel, steering westwards, traversed the sea as if with indignation and drew away from the island rapidly.

Meanwhile, the Emperor seemed to overcome that incomprehensible emotion. Up on deck, with his telescope directed toward Saint Helena, he was contemplating it with a somber attention that no one had yet dared to interrupt, when old Dolomieu, who saw nothing anywhere but science and its effects, imagining that the Emperor's attention was also purely mineralogical, said: "But that land is really only the product of more than twenty extinct volcanoes."

"I shall renew them."

Dolomieu did not understand any more than the others and was about to ask the Emperor, naively, what he meant, but, seeing the profound calm that everyone seemed to be maintaining, he kept silent himself, by a sort of instinct.

When the vessel, sailing north-west, had lost sight of Saint Helena, Napoleon seemed relieved; he became calm again, as if he had rediscovered the liberty of his mind, and even seemed to have entirely forgotten the emotion that had gripped him so suddenly.

A year later, the meaning and object of his words became comprehensible, but not their motive, when the Emperor, returned to Europe, having sent a squadron to Saint Helena, had all the inhabitants taken aboard the ship with all their riches. The island, thus depopulated, was mined in every direction, filled to its greatest depths with powerful artificial volcanoes, which assembled everything that the latest physics had been able to muster of the forces of compressed gas in terrible vapors and destructive powders, and when it was all disposed, the squadron drew away to put fifty leagues of sea between it and the accursed isle. The explosion of all the mines burst with such a resounding blast that even at that distance, the people on the ships heard it and were frightened by it; and the sea, uplifted by an immense turbulence, brought them a terrible residue of agitation and turbulence.

The vessels returned immediately after the explosion to the location where Saint Helena had existed, but it was only to see the final collapse of a few calcined remains, which seemed only to have lasted until then in order to display their death-throes in the face of their executioners. Finally, those fragments were carried away by the sea in 5 May 1827. Everything was consumed; the Ocean having labored with its waves the place where the island had existed, no vestige of it any longer remained, and ships were henceforth able to traverse without danger that space where, since the Creation, land had incessantly reigned until then.

What, then, had been the motive for that condemnation to death of an island by a man? Was it a caprice, a memory, horror or superstitious dead? Who can tell?

## Chapter IV
## AN APPARITION

The imperial squadron, on quitting Saint Helena, arrived so rapidly in sight of Cape Verde, and the navigation was so fortunate, that one might have thought it as a triumphal march over the Ocean, and that the silent and obedient waves also regarded themselves as vanquished.

Level with Cape Verde, however, the sea appeared to recover its independence; a rightful tempest blew up, with lasted for several days. The vessels, dispersed by the winds to great distances, hoped in vain to reassemble; incessant rain and continual obscurity rendered the navigation as uncertain as it was difficult, to the point that the pilots and naval officers, in the midst of those disorders of nature, could no longer recognize the route that they ought to follow, nor determine their position at sea.

Some of them thought that the imperial ship had been driven southwards, and could not be far from Ascension Island; others thought that it was closer to the coast of Africa and the Senegambia; a few sustained that the tempest had driven the vessel all the way to the seas of Brazil.

The Emperor, as calm in the battle of the elements as in the midst of the tempests of war that he had so often stirred up on land, contemplated with I know not what satisfied emotion that tumult of the Ocean, as if the sublime agitation in question found its measure in the grandeur of his soul.

However, they continued to be unaware of the veritable position of the vessel, the other ships had disappeared, and the greatest uncertainty, mingled with terror, reigned in all minds.

Suddenly, a sailor placed on watch in the crow's nest shouted that he could see land on the horizon.

Immediately, the naval officers directed their telescopes at the point indicated. They sought solicitously to recognize the coasts that would resolve the doubt into which they were plunged.

But that reconnaissance was futile; the distant land did not offer to their eyes the aspects of any known coast; it was like a new island in the middle of the Ocean—or rather, that apparition did not resemble anything that land had yet displayed on the horizon of the seas.

More than that; as the ship advanced toward that point, and the land grew in its extent, the apparition became more and more extraordinary; it struck them all with surprise and almost with fright, for it was no longer a land that was rising thus, but a phantom, a giant Napoléon!

It was him! With every instant that the inflated sails drew the vessel toward that point, the giant grew continuously, developing increasingly with its prodigious forms an incontestable resemblance to the Emperor. It was him: his historic head stood out at the summit of the mountain; he seemed to have his arms folded over his breast, and to be reposing, as if sitting on a rock.

The apparition still seemed to be more than thirty leagues distant, when the crew had already recognized, in its admiration, the image of Napoléon.

A few young matelots, more fearful and more superstitious, approached him, and wondered whether it might be the rising sun that had paused behind the vessel to project and fix upon the firmament the immense shadow of Napoléon.

The Emperor did not know what to think himself; his heart leapt with a supernatural joy; it seemed to him indubitable that there was something more than terrestrial in it, which might well be a transition from the world down here, of which he had already had enough, to the world beyond, of which he dreamed.

The ship advanced rapidly, and, the statue-mountain rising up to the clouds, it was realized that it was more than ten thousand feet high, and that its base was bathed by the sea.

The resemblance of its forms with those of the Emperor was so remarkable, and such was the artistry with which it had been constructed, that from the instant at which, from more than forty leagues away, the first sailor had shouted "Napolé-on!" on perceiving it, that resemblance had been incessantly augmented, until the crew, arriving at its feet, looking up to see it in the heavens, cried with even greater amazement: "Na-poléon!"

On landing, and only then, the naval officers recognized that the land was Tenerife. The statue was the peak itself, the forms of which had been miraculously sculpted, in order to bring forth from the mountain the colossal image of the Sovereign of the Old World.

It was the trophy of glory prepared for Napoléon by Europe, as it could no longer make a triumphal arch for such a noble head. For five years, the treasures, the enthusiasm and the arms of Europeans had been working furiously on that mountain, and had shaped it in the form of the Emperor. The most illustrious artists, with David at their head, had been summoned for that marvelous enterprise, and for five years, armies of sculptors, employing the cannon and the mine as often as the chisel, had been constantly occupied on that prodigious monument, which they had just completed.

The Emperor found on the island the kings of Europe, his ministers and his court. All of them had come that far to meet the sovereign, absent for six years, waiting for him in the shadow of his statue

The most profound secrecy had been maintained with regard to the Emperor and his family, and that surprise increased his emotion. So he expressed his gratitude and admiration loudly for such a singular homage.

He stayed on the island for ten days, often walking around his colossus, contemplating it with pride and amour, as a brother and master.

The four vessels scattered by the tempest had experienced the same astonishment at the sight of the peak of Tenerife thus transformed; they had headed for the island, where they found the imperial vessel.

To complete those marvels, and as if nature had wanted to participate in that homage, the volcano produced flames and fury during the Emperor's sojourn on Tenerife. Night, above all, caused a sublime spectacle to appear: the statue stood out against the sky, cut out by the moonlight; the volcano darted its flames at the summit, as if to crown Napoléon's head with a plume of fire, while red liquid lava flowed over his breast, designing a broad sash there, a river of crimson and flame.

And when he was sated with that glory, he quit the island with his court and his vessels, and headed for Europe.

## Chapter V
## *RETURN*

That returns to Europe was, like everything else, a marvel.

He returned the Sovereign of Europe, the conqueror of Asia, the master of the seas, the dominator of the Old World, the great man, the hero, the demigod...the god!

It was thus that he was named, that he was celebrated, that he was adored.

He returned after six years of absence and unprecedented exploits; his Europe, widowed of him for so long, was asking for him with enthusiasm, and France, his dear France, leapt with joy at the announcement of his coming.

I do not know whether one can call a triumphal march the twelve days that went by between his disembarkation at Marseille and his arrival in Paris. How can one put a name to and describe the delirium, the frenzy of joy, the continuous acclamations and the inflamed exaltation that greeted him, pressed him and drew him on during those two hundred leagues of marching? There were millions of men and women on the roads, and a multitude of inhabitants of Paris and the cities of the North had come all the way to Marseille in order to be the first to see him, to accompany him and follow him.

The most extraordinary scenes signaled that enthusiasm; we shall relate a few of them.

Two leagues from Aix, a village of three hundred inhabitants named Ormoy-les-Aix, within the walls of which the Emperor was to pass, set fire with a common accord to the narrow and ignoble houses that composed it, and, the ruins having been cleared away promptly, a broad road strewn with flowers and bordered with green and garlanded trees suddenly opened a new route for the sovereign.

At Aix, a woman of high rank was seized by such a great joy when he appeared that she fell dead, crying: "Vive l'empereur!"

Throughout the Midi, acts of a frenetic admiration took place. People threw themselves under the wheels of his carriage shouting to the men drawing it: "Advance, then! We want to die before him and for him!" For, since Marseille, the people, unable to tolerate a horse being harnessed to that sacred vehicle, had attached themselves to it in crowds, and there were bloody contests to obtain that honor.

At Valence, Napoléon having got down in order to rest momentarily, the carriage was removed and destroyed, torn into a thousand pieces; the wood, the copper and even the iron were broken under that enthusiasm like the most brittle glass; the innumerable fragments of that great relic were distributed among the crowd, while a magnificent carriage, sent in homage by the city of Lyon, was substituted for the one that had just been annihilated.

But in Lyon, above all, that delirium was at its peak; there were entire streets whose pavement was covered with the richest and most precious silk and velvet fabrics. As the carriage advanced, people threw gold and silver under its wheels, women tore off their jewelry and their scarves with cries of joy and spread them on the ground, and the emperor, his heart swollen with joy, advanced thus on a chariot drawn by a people over that rubbish-heap of gold and silk.

It was remarked, as a characteristic feature of that enthusiasm, that none of those god and silver coins were stolen or taken away by anyone, but, after the emperor's departure, they were collected respectfully and poured into the treasury of the commune. The silk and velvet fabrics that the passage of the crowd and the tracks of the wheels had badly damaged, were all the more sought after, and the most brilliant women adorned themselves with them with pride. They were called "pavement fabrics."

At Chalon-sur-Saône, a triumphal monument of a new and gigantic form appeared in the distance a long time before the emperor had arrived at the gates of the town. It was a colossal globe on which the geography of the Earth was designed; its dimensions were extraordinary and one of its poles seemed to be plunged in the ground.

When Napoléon came close to that singular trophy, he read these words in letters of gold: *To the Master of the World.*

"Not yet," he said, smiling at those surrounding him.

"But soon!" replied an unknown voice, for which he searched in the midst of crowd, but could not recognize.

The Emperor became serious; he walked toward the globe, which opened as he approached; he traversed it with a sentiment of admiration and pleasure, for the immense enclosure of the sphere was resplendent with light, flowers, marvelously adorned women and a delightful and enthusiastic music.

At Auxerre, a young man threw himself into the midst of the people preceding the Emperor's carriage; he was armed with a pistol, with which he shot himself in the head.

Napoléon, having approached the unfortunate man, who was still alive, asked him with interest what had occasioned that act of despair.

"I wanted His Majesty to notice me," said the young man, and expired.

*Chapter VI*
*AJACCIO*


The Emperor's entry into the capital of Europe further surpassed in pomp and enthusiasm everything that he had seen thus far, and it would be temerity to attempt to recount what even those who witnessed it could scarcely believe.

Among the tributes that were poured at his feet, which the people and the kings strove to render worthy of him, Napoléon distinguished especially that of the inhabitants of his native town, his compatriots, the Frenchmen of Ajaccio.

All of them had come together in an immense deputation, without anyone lacking; the women, uniformly clad in white with tricolor belts, were preceded by the men; the children came next, and on the carts that followed were the old, the sick and those who could not walk with their fellow citizens, in order that they could all be present at that meeting.

The garden of the Tuileries was filed by that population. The Emperor came down from the palace and received them on the steps of the Pavillon de l'Horloge, and Colonel Fesch, the Maire of Ajaccio and a relative of Napoléon, having advanced a few paces, prostrated himself respectfully and made this speech:

"Sire,

"We have also come to bring Your Majesty the homages and the tribute of respect and enthusiasm of the inhabitants of our town, your town, of Ajaccio.

"Ajaccio, Sire, was too glorious, for having seen Your Majesty born in its bosom, not to think of manifesting it to the world by a great decision.

"Sire, we have decided that no one in future can any longer be born where you have seen the light of day.

"We have all abandoned our habitations and destroyed our town; at this moment our brothers in the other towns in Corsica are building those voluntary ruins into a tall pyramid, which will display to the heavens and to times to come the evidence of our resolution.

"At the foot of that pyramid the words will be read: *AJACCIO, where NAPOLÉON was born.*

"Sire, it would have been necessary for you to see the unanimous joy with which we quit the houses of our forefathers, and with what enthusiasm we witnessed their destruction! There was but one thought, yours, that absorbed all others in enthusiasm and love.

"Sire, while we are all in Paris, our brothers in Corsica are building us another town, near to the one we have proudly and freely sacrificed, and we request that Your Majesty grant the new city the name of Napoléon."

The Emperor did not reply immediately, but a tear glistened in his eye. He embraced Colonel Fresch effusively, and cried in a loud voice: "My friends! My Compatriots! I should like to embrace you all!"

At that moment, the ranks of the inhabitants of Ajaccio broke, and they threw themselves at the Emperor's feet; he traversed that crowd with a tenderness that he could no longer master.

He said to them again: "You have given me a town; I shall give you another, and it will be worthy of you and of my name, which I give it."

At his orders, rapidly given, the new Ajaccio, named Napoléon, rose up as if by a prodigy, and after some time all its inhabitants quit France, heaped with favors and presents from the Emperor, and entered into the town that Napoléon had had constructed at his own expense and with the greatest magnificence.

From that time on, Napoléon appeared to be reconciled with Corsica, which he seemed to have forgotten or scorned until then; but that great testimony of the love of his compatriots revealed in him the keenest sentiments, and Corsica was henceforth one of the provinces he cherished the most.

*Chapter VII*
## *THE AFRICAN EXPEDITION*


As soon as the year 1894, when the Emperor had completed the conquest of Asia in China and Japan, he had projected the conquest of Africa. He knew that in that country, nature was his only enemy, because, for some years, labored and uplifted by rumors of the glory that the name of Napoléon had spread over them, the Africans, for from opposing obstacles, were only waiting, with a sort of calm fatality, for him to come, in order to submit.

That expedition, which was not the least extraordinary event in Napoléon's lifetime, is too well known and too admirably recounted in the history that has been given to the public by the King of Silesia, Louis Napoléon,[103] for me to weigh these pages down with it; I shall therefore only offer a rapid glimpse of it, mingling it with facts that I have chosen more at hazard than because of their veritable importance.

Before commencing that conquest, the Emperor already possessed numerous States in that continent, especially the greater part of its perimeter. Thus, the Barbary States, Egypt, Nubia, the coasts of the Mozambique Channel, and the Cape of Good Hope, an almost continuous chain of establishments along the coasts of Guinea and Senegambia, and all the islands of that part of the world, already belonged to Napoléon's empire. Only the interior of Africa remained unknown and independent of his power. Two years would suffice for an exploration and a conquest that were equally complete.

---

[103] Nor the subsequent Napoléon III but—as noted in passing in Chapter XXII of Book Two—his father, Louis Napoléon Bonaparte (1778-1846), whom Napoléon made King of Holland from 1806-10, and who married Hortense de Beauharnais, Joséphine's daughter from her first marriage.

Five expeditionary armies landed almost at the same time on five different parts of the African littoral. The first, the principal expedition, commanded by the King of Silesia, Louis Napoléon, the commander in chief of the other four armies, descended on the coasts of Senegal. Maréchal Molitor occupied the Congo; departing from the Cape of Good Hope, the Prince of Hoenlinden had to subdue the southern extremity of Africa, going north as far as Monomotapa; the Duc de Bellune was charged with the conquest of Kaffraria; and Maréchal Belliard had to take possession of Abyssinia and Darfur.

A single system linked and dominated those five expeditions; it consisted of two ideas: the establishment of Christianity and conquest. It was formulated by two names: Christ and Napoléon. It had for its symbol the Cross at the top of a tricolor flag.

That simultaneous invasion of a continent had been planned with so much artistry that two years sufficed or its accomplishment, and saw the commencement and the termination of the conquest over the five different objectives to which it was extended.

At all those points, and in all the countries that they traversed, the armies were welcomed by the Africans with cries of "Napoléon!" Elsewhere, there was no contest, no battle and no resistance; the European troops advanced without fear into the interior of the region, and everywhere, at their approach, the kings at the head of their peoples and the chiefs preceding their tribes came to kneel before the cross with tricolor flames. All of them said that the prophecies of times past were accomplished; all of them brought their idols, the divinity of which was exhausted, they said; they trampled them underfoot deliriously, and burned them of their own accord before the victorious cross. The Mohammedan sects rejected their Islamism, and the impulsion was so violent that the nations came to meet the French spontaneously in order to abjure their religion and their independence sooner.

All asked for Napoléon, and the absence of the divinity increased the mystery further.

The European armies admired the welcome and submission that the mere name of their Emperor occasioned. Everywhere they were fêted, everything was brought to them in abundance, the unaccustomed rigor of the climate as lessened for them and obstacles flattened by the Africans, who served them with an exalted devotion.

The roads of Africa, which became military roads under Napoléon's soldiers, were then rendered free for discoveries. That great and mysterious part of the globe was subsequently furrowed and traveled in every direction; the veils that covered it fell at every step; its rivers, without commencement or end, found their sources and their mouths; the dubious lakes, the unknown seas and the uncertain or unknown cities, finally appeared and gave their names and secrets to the conquerors, and in the two years that had sufficed for those five expeditions, Africa was as completely explored and known as it was submissive.

Begun in the month of June 1825, that immense conquest was fully concluded in March 1827, and the following May, the King of Silesia having assembled all the kings, chiefs and sovereign princes of all the countries of Africa in Timbuktu, which he had chosen for his residence, he made them solemnly swear an oath of fidelity and submission to the Emperor Napoléon, the new sovereign of Africa.

The King of Silesia soon declared in the same city, on behalf of the Emperor, decrees that divided Africa into thirty-two "circles," or provinces, to the command of which he appointed thirty-two French generals from the expeditionary armies. Having done that, with a provisional administration uniformly established, Mohammedan religion and idols destroyed, the Cross and the Imperial flag flying over all the towns and the smallest villages, and the name of the Emperor having become sacred and repeated everywhere, King Louis Napoléon assembled in the Niger delta the part of his armies that he did not want to leave in Africa, and embarked in August 1827 for Europe, after having gained a continent for his brother.

## Chapter VIII
## AFRICA


As I have said, I shall not weigh myself down with the details of a conquest in which ideas were the only weapons, in which a name and a Cross were sufficient to subdue everything.

From the midst of the most bizarre facts, the most curious discoveries and circumstances full of interest, I shall select a few details that I deem to be appropriate. Free, above all, in my historical march I am collecting what pleases me, and taking up what best suits my thinking.

Geography had important discoveries to record; the junction was determined of the chains of the Mountains of Kong and the Mountain of the Moon;[104] it was recognized that they formed a single great chain, the veritable vertebral column of Africa, commencing in the west near Senegal, traversing the continent, which it thus divides into two plateaux unequal in extent and elevation, and fading away, without discontinuity, in the vicinity of the strait of Babel-Mandeb. Admitting those natural divisions, one of them was named Northern Africa and the other Southern Africa.

The three great rivers of Africa were mapped from their sources to their mouths.

---

[104] Both of these mountain chains turned out to be fictitious, the former being indicated on a map drawn by Mungo Park and the latter reported by Greek and Roman geographers, but their non-existence was still unknown in 1836. Unsurprisingly, the rest of the geographical details invented by Geoffroy are also wide of the mark of the actualities eventually discovered in our history.

Firstly, the Nile, which has its source in the Donga, descends from the Mountains of the Moon and empties into the Mediterranean.[105]

Secondly, the Niger, which sees its source born on the northern slopes of the King Mountains, in the Senegambia, flows northwards, divides into two branches, one of which flows north-westwards, swells and is lost, under the name of the Senegal, in the Atlantic, above Cape Verde, while the great Niger, continuing its immense course north-eastwards, flows eastwards under the name of the Quorra and Djoliba, traverses several lakes, including Lakes Débo and Sudan, and, after having bathed the walls of Timbuktu, suddenly turns southwards, goes through the chain of the Mountains of Kong, which lower at that point and open a passage for it, traverses Guinea majestically and comes to pour its immense waters at Cape Formosa, in a multitude of branches and rivers, forming a delta there of extraordinary extent.

Thirdly, the Zaire, or Congo, and the Zambezi only form at first a single river, which has its source in the center of the southern slopes of the Mountains of Kong and Mountains of the Moon, descends southwards for three hundred leagues, divides at Houllah and extends its two great branches in two rivers no less considerable than the Niger, one of which casts its waves into the Ocean on the coast of Guinea, taking the name of the Congo, while the other, heading eastwards, goes under the name of the Zambezi to empty into the Mozambique channel.

They are the three great rivers of Africa, henceforth known and without mystery in their source, their course and their end. The existence of an interior sea was suspected in the continent, and a few European voyagers had already recognized the shores of Lake Chad, but they had only seen it as a large lake. The new observations assigned to it such an extent that it far surpasses that of the Black Sea, and that interior mass of waters received the name of the Chad Sea.

---

[105] Except that Napoléon has redirected its course.

What excited the highest degree of admiration and surprise however, was the knowledge of the mysterious city of Tombut or Timbuktu, of which some told such marvelous tales, while others had diminished its grandeur and enfeebled its importance as they pleased. Timbuktu, occupied by the French army under the command of the King of Silesia, was finally known and counted among the greatest cities of the globe. Its population rose no more than five hundred thousand souls; several quarters were well built and several edifices were remarked there of a bizarre and colossal architecture. Its fine port on the Niger is the busiest in Africa. It is the center of the continent's commerce. Numerous canals that circulate in the city further augment the importance of the port, and in the shops and markets that border those interior canals the European soldiers had as much surprise as joy in finding the merchandise of their European cities.

One of the most touching scenes moved he entire army, when the authorities of Timbuktu brought King Louis Napoléon two white prisoners detained in the city. They were recognized with joy as two celebrated voyagers whom their compatriots and homelands had despaired of ever seeing again: the surgeon Dickson, a friend of Clapperton, and Major Laing, whose death had been announced in Europe.[106]

The rumor also spread that Mungo Park was still alive at Boussa in the kingdom of Bergou; the King of Silesia sent a detachment to that town as soon as possible to gather information about the unfortunate voyager. They arrived just in

---

[106] Captain Hugh Clapperton's expedition in Africa, to which Thomas Dickson was attached, arrived in 1825, but Dickson was never heard of again after setting off from the Bight of Benin for Dahomey. Clapperton received reports from Timbuktu in 1827 that Major Alexander Gordon Laing, an earlier explorer, had been there the previous year, but that he had been murdered in his tent. Clapperton did not make it to Timbuktu himself, or back home, reportedly dying of dysentery at Sockatoo in the same year.

301

time, for Mungo Park was still alive, but his head was weak, his intellectual faculties having abandoned him along with his physical faculties; a dolorous old age, which chagrins and suffering had advanced, retained him on his death-bed. The sight of white men and the sound of European languages caused him to experience a convulsive sensation of joy, but the very shock was too violent for him. He recovered the complete usage of his senses for a few moments, showed a few manuscripts and a few remnants of is collections that he had been able to save from his enemies, and expired the on same day in which his eyes had seen compatriots again.[107]

Those manuscripts were a great help in the reconnaissance of the country situated around Timbuktu and Boussa.

The interior of Africa revealed new and most curious facts of natural history. Pliny had been right to say *Africa semper aliquid novi offert*.[108] At every step nature deployed all the unknown magnificences of her reign: bizarre plants, minerals whose existence was unsuspected, animal species of entirely new families—and industry, which followed the conquest, but these new marvels to profit.

Finally, history itself was, so to speak, rediscovered in Africa; populations unknown to the world, which as similarly unknown to them, retained treasures thereof. Oases strewn in the desert had conserved the old traditions of times past, like intellectual Herculaneums. Perhaps we shall talk again later about the oasis of Boulma, found in the Donga, but one cannot

---

[107] The great pioneer of African exploration Mungo Park was last heard from in 1806, and subsequent British expeditions believed that they had found evidence of his death in that year, recovering some of his alleged effects, but not his journal, perhaps leaving just enough uncertainty to permit this wild conjecture.

[108] "There is always something new out of Africa." The final *offert* in Geoffroy's version is not in Pliny, but was often added when the phrase was quoted as a proverb, and it might well have existed as a proverb before Pliny quoted it.

forget the discovery of the oasis of Theot in the deserts of Libya, where a colony of Egyptian priests was found, whose origin went back to the first pharaoh, and who, to escape persecution and death, had traversed the desert and finally ended up in that island of verdure in the middle of the sea of sand. Having taken refuge there, forgotten for more than three thousand years, that sacred colony had lived, conserving traditions of the language, the religion and history of Egypt; strangers to the movements of the external world, which did not exist for them, they had conserved their civilization of old pure, without augmentation. They rendered with fidelity the deposit of the past; they delivered the old secret of hieroglyphs and other Egyptian languages, and the veils of mystery fell with that discovery.

## Chapter IX
## TWO KINGS

News of the conquest of Africa did not arrive in France until more than a year after the Emperor's return. Since that return, Napoléon had resumed the immense government of Europe, to which he had just added those of Asia and Oceania. New ministers, functions and administrations had been created; those institutions, however, did not have the decisive and fundamental character that Napoléon had the habit of imprinting on all his actions; there was thought to be something provisional and temporary about them that was not his way. The people who made those remarks were not judging the Emperor; they were, on the contrary waiting, certain as they were that everything had a reason and a cause in his profound will.

During the conquest of Asia, Napoléon had placed Prince de Talleyrand at the head of the civil and political government of Europe and the Maréchal Duc de Dalmatie had been charged with the military government. On returning to Europe and seizing power again, the Emperor had been so full of satisfaction at the sight of the flourishing and happy Europe that Prince de Bénévent rendered to him after five years of absence—and equally satisfied with the continual relations that the Duc de Dalmatie had, with so much skill, established with the victorious army of Asia, always aided with his measures and conquests by the Maréchal's previsions and envoys—that he resolved to manifest prominently the contentment he had felt with their services.

At about the same time, in September 1826, the Duc de Parme, Prince Cambacérès, the Arch-Chancellor of France, died, leaving vacant one of the greatest dignities of the Empire. That elevated position became the object of all ambitions; the most illustrious individuals and the highest functionaries of the State and Europe sought it with the keenest ardor. It is even said that the King of Sardinia, in soliciting that dignity from the Emperor, had offered to resign his royal majesty in exchange.

The *Moniteur* of 2 October 1826 removed all the doubts; it contained the following decree:

*Napoléon, Emperor of the French, Sovereign of Europe, Sovereign of Asia and Sovereign of the islands of Oceania;*

*Waiting to testify to Prince de Bénévent and Maréchal de Dalmatie the great satisfaction that we have felt for their eminent services during our expedition to Asia;*

*We decree the following:*

*Article 1. Prince de Bénévent is named king;*

*He will take his rank among the kings of Europe and participate in the deliberations of the Council of Kings.*

*Article 2. Maréchal de Dalmatie is named king.*

*He will take his rank among the kings of Europe and participate in the deliberations of the Council of Kings.*

*Article 3. Monsieur Dupin aîné, advocate, member of the legislative body, is named Arch-Chancellor of the Empire, in replacement for the Prince Duc de Parme, deceased.*

*Given at the Imperial Palace of Fontainebleau, 1 October 1826.*

*Napoléon.*

*On behalf of the Emperor*
*Duc de Bassano.*

This Napoléon increased the number of kings while weakening their character; henceforth, they only formed, veritably, the first of four bodies of State, which could henceforth be arranged in this order:

The kings;

The Council of State;

The Senate;

The legislative body.

The appointment of Monsieur Dupin greatly astonished the court, but did not surprise the nation.

*Chapter X*
*A SESSION OF THE ACADEMY OF SCIENCES*


On Monday 23 October 1826, the Académie des Sciences was assembled for one of its ordinary sessions. Geoffroy Saint-Hilaire was president, Comte Humphry Davy vice-president and Cuvier and Delambre, perpetual secretaries, were at the bureau. Monsieur Ampère was occupying the tribune at that moment, where he was reading a memoir of the greatest interest on his admirable theory of electric currents. The Academy was absorbed in the attention commanded by the work in question, of one of the highest intelligence of our age, when a murmur suddenly spread through the assembly and an extraordinary agitation seized all the members at the arrival of a stranger, who, clad in a black suit and decorated with the order of the Légion d'honneur, appeared at the door of the room, entered mysteriously, made a gesture of silence that suddenly cut short the murmur and, having gone to a table, found an empty chair and sat down there.

Meanwhile, Monsieur Ampère, that man of genius is whom there was as much of Leibniz as La Fontaine, and whose extreme distraction is as well-known as his high intelligence, had not noticed that movement, soon diminished by the interest of his reading, and doubtless also by the care that the stranger who had just arrived had taken to calm it.

Having read the paper, Monsieur Ampère deposited it at the Académie's bureau and collected from all parts the expressions of admiration that his good work merited so thoroughly.

Those expressions had retained the honorable academician for a few minutes, who only returned to his place thereafter.

What was his astonishment, however, to see his chair occupied by that stranger, whom he did not know. Slightly piqued, Monsieur Ampère went around the chair which had been taken; he coughed with embarrassment and affectation,

307

and sought, with the naïve urbanity that was one of his characteristics, to make the usurper understand the necessity of quitting the usurped seat. Either because he did not understand, however, or because he did not want to understand, the stranger remained where he was.

Monsieur Ampère, becoming increasingly bold, began to murmur more distinctly; he said to his neighbors, in an indirect fashion but loudly enough for the unknown man to be able to hear it, that it was strange that someone should take a person's seat like that, without any formality—but as he encountered silent smiles everywhere, he experienced a veritable discontentment and said in a loud voice:

"Monsieur le Président, I ought to point out to you that a person foreign to the Académie is occupying one of our seats and has taken his place among us."

That declaration occasioned a considerable murmur, and Monsieur Geoffroy Saint-Hilaire replied to Monsieur Ampère: "You are in error, Monsieur; the individual to whom you make allusion is a member of the Académie des Sciences."

"Since when?" said Monsieur Ampère, quite astonished.

"Since the fifth of Nivose, year Six," replied the stranger.

"And in what section, if you please?" said Monsieur Ampère, with a certain irony.

"In the mechanics section, my savant colleague," replied the stranger, smiling.

"That's a bit strong," said Monsieur Ampère, and, picking up an Annuaire de l'Institut that was close at hand, he opened it with alacrity, and read under that date the name of Napoléon Bonaparte, member of the Académie des Sciences, in the mechanics section, 5 Nivose, an VI.

It was the Emperor, who had come from the height of his rank to bow his head under the level of science. Very troubled, Monsieur Ampère dissolved in apologies: he had very poor eyesight; he had not recognized the Emperor...

"That's the inconvenience, Monsieur," the Sovereign said to him, "that there is in not knowing one's colleagues. I never see you at the Tuileries; we must strive to get you to come."

Those words, spoken with an extreme benevolence, reassured the illustrious geometer, who, having found another empty chair, went to sit down in it without any further protest.

Monsieur Geoffroy Saint-Hilaire asked the Emperor if he would permit the session to continue.

"Of course," said Napoléon. "There's nothing new; the assembly is more complete, that's all."

Monsieur le Comte de Laplace appeared at the tribune and read a paper to which Napoléon appeared to listen with a keen interest.

An engineer foreign to the Académie succeeded Monsieur de Laplace; he read a discourse on subterranean bridges constructed under river-beds. Monsieur Brunel recounted the marvelous works that he had just completed in London.[109]

After that reading, the president of the Académie had to appoint a committee to report on that paper. The Académie experienced a profound surprise when Geoffroy Saint-Hilaire sad in a loud voice: "I nominate as members of the committee that will examine Monsieur Brunel's work His Majesty the Emperor, Messieurs Monge and Poisson."

All eyes turned to the Emperor, who, half-rising from his seat, said that he accepted that mission with pleasure.

The memorable session was then lifted. The Emperor remained for a few moments in the midst of the illustrious scientists, who surrounded them with their gratitude and their

---

[109] The reference is to the Anglo-French engineer Marc Brunel (1769-1849) rather than his eventually-more-famous son Isambard (1806-1859), although Isambard was the former's assistant in our history when he began worked in 1825 on a tunnel under the Thames between Rotherhithe and Wapping. In our history the project was not completed in the 1820s, work being suspended in 1828 after two serious accidents, but Marc Brunel eventually completed it, without his son's further involvement, in 1843.

309

homages. He conversed with a few of them on the most sublime matters of science, and then climbed into his carriage and
returned to the château.

## Chapter XI
## THE EMPEROR'S VOYAGE

At the end of 1826, Napoléon left Paris, having conceived the project of visiting the four capitals of his empire: Rome, Constantinople, Amsterdam and London.

He went to Rome first. Near Genoa, someone pointed out to him, on a sheer coast between that city and Livorno, a rock that advanced into the sea and served as a reference point for the ships of the two cities. The ancients, he was told, had intended to build a colossus there, which would have been visible at even greater distances.

Michelangelo had had the same idea

Finally, during the expedition to Asia, that thought, perpetually reproduced, had had a commencement of execution, but the far more extraordinary enterprise of the peak of Tenerife had caused that one to be abandoned and forgotten. Only the upper part of the rock had been sculpted, and the rest retained its natural form.

The Emperor examined the monument with interest, but he prohibited its completion imperiously.

Since his first voyage of 1816, Rome had recovered its former grandeur. Sanitized, repopulated, brought back to life, it then counted more than five hundred thousand souls. Habitations were reconquering the spaces left deserted in its immense enclosure, and those new constructions, occasioning continual excavations, had revealed the most curious antiquities and caused admirable monuments to reappear.

The Pope, the Emperor's uncle, was waiting at the People's Gate with the entire population of Rome. The welcome that those two august persons gave one another was noted; they embraced cordially, and the old etiquette of the Holy See was forgotten before the Sovereign of the Old World.

After staying in Rome for a few weeks, Napoléon went to Ancona, where he embarked for Venice. On seeing that

311

queen of the seas, now dethroned and enslaved, he took pity on her, and was moved by her misery; he remembered, as a remorse, that it was him, at the end of the previous century, as a general, who had terminated the long existence of that noble republic, and killed at a stroke its commerce, its power and its life. He expressed aloud his idea of restoring its grandeur, and as his compassion always went forward with his politics, he wanted, by restoring to that queen of the seas some of her ancient privileges, to recall her to the commerce of the Mediterranean, and refound at that point one of the most important ports of the French monarchy.

From Venice he went to Constantinople.

The spectacle of that capital was a sight to confound thought, since the Turks, raking with them their religion and their usages, had abandoned it. It was now a Christian city. Saint Sophia had become a cathedral again. There was a prefect of Constantinople, four Maires and administrators, as in the rest of Europe. A large number of French families had taken up residence there, and French had become the usual language spoken there. One could not think without surprise of what the city had been twelve years before, when Turkish despotism possessed it, in contemplating what it had become since Imperial civilization, succeeding so much barbarity, had changed and refounded it. At that moment the Italian theater was putting on the most brilliant performances: Lablache, Rubini, David, Tamburini and Mesdames Sontag, Malibran, Pasta and Mainville-Fodor were singing, with an extraordinary success, Rossini's magnificent opera *Napoléon* and Meyerbeer's *Asia liberata*. The Emperor went to several of the performances.

On the ruins of the Eski-Seraï, in the inner city, Monsieur Scribe had had a vast theater constructed, which he directed, and where he put on his comic operas and vaudevilles. That kind of spectacle, already acclimated to the Orient, obtained a great success there.

During his sojourn in Constantinople, the Emperor laid the first stone of a Bourse and an Imperial Court; those two monuments were constructed facing one another, in the great square of Al-Meidan.

The sojourn was also signaled by a very important discovery. During the taking of Constantinople the treasure of the seraglio had been found, but they had been surprised by the mediocrity of the things that had been left there and it had been supposed with some reason that the Turks, vanquished, had taken measures to disappear in god time and remove the greater part of their riches.

It was Napoléon himself who resolved the problem. Astonished by the singular construction of the part of the seraglio called the treasury, he ordered its demolition, and when the cleared soil of the buildings had been excavated, marble stairways were found at a depth of a few feet, which appeared for the first time and led down to subterranean galleries similarly lined with marble and ornamented with a multitude of silver lamps, extinct for more than ten years. In those galleries were chests and cupboards enclosing the immense treasures acquired and accumulated by the Mohammedans since the commencement of their monarchy.

They remained struck with admiration before that prodigious quantity of the riches of all ages. The inventory alone was something fantastic, like the marvels of tales of the Orient. And if the Emperor experienced some joy at that discovery, it could not compare with that of the scholars of Europe when they learned that manuscripts of the great authors of antiquity thought lost forever, with no hope of their ever being recovered, had been found there, intact and marvelously conserved. Among the most important discoveries, counted in the first rank are poems of Orpheus and comedies by Menander, the histories of Sanchuniathon and Pompeius Trogus, the history of Sallust, and the complete poems of Varius, Virgil's friend.

After that discovery, and after having repaired a few of the aqueducts of the city—especially the aqueduct of Justinian, almost entirely ruined—the Emperor left Constantinople in April 1827, and following the military route, returned rapidly

313

to Paris, which he only traversed in order to go to London, and from there to Amsterdam. Those two cities had lost nothing of their grandeur, but they offered nothing new to his gaze and his politics.

Napoléon returned from that great visit made to his capitals in June 1827.

## Chapter XII
## *PRESENTIMENTS OF PEOPLES*

If human beings sometimes set aside the cold reasoning that sometimes deceives them with its vain calculations, they would be struck with astonishment by the thought of the mysteries that surround and crowd them, but they reject them proudly because one cannot account for them.

Thus, they only accept half of nature, which for them is material, measurable in its dimensions, visible in its aspects, or at least discussable in its existence; but if one tells them that a fact has arrived from a nature higher than their own, passing through a higher region that reason cannot attain, they deny it scornfully.

Is not, however, one of those supernatural things, of which history has collected frequent and authentic examples, the rumors that suddenly spread, announcing in advance great events before they can be known, even before they can be realized. Thus, prophetic voices were heard in Rome and throughout Italy during the days preceding the death of Caesar. Thus, unknown couriers traversed the towns of Picardy and Flanders, crying that Henry IV had been assassinated, a few days before the murder was committed.

It was the same throughout Europe; voices were murmuring to all minds the words "universal monarchy." All souls were gripped by those words; everyone was talking about it with a holy conviction. The world, they said, is henceforth acquired to the domination of the Emperor; no land on the globe is any longer outside his power. The work is complete.

They spoke thus, and yet they only knew, as yet, of the sovereignty of Europe and the conquest of Asia and Oceania. They knew that Africa was presently being overrun, and doubtless conquered, but that was not certain, and no news had arrived of any change in the political situation of America with regard to the Emperor. There was reason to believe, on the contrary, that the incessant revolutions in the New World were occupying the nations exclusively, and that Napoléon, entirely preoccupied with the old continent, was not thinking about them.

Nevertheless, the telegraphs had been seen agitating their mysterious arms relentlessly for some time; it was announced that ambassadors had been disembarked at Cadiz and Brest; and finally, that all the kings of Asia and Europe, the Senators, the members of the legislative body and the grandees of the State had been summoned to Paris at the same time—and that combination of circumstances had doubtless revealed to the prescient nation of the French the great event that was about to be accomplished: the Universal Monarchy.

## Chapter XIII
### PREPARATIONS ON THE CHAMP DE MARS

A decree from Amsterdam dated 14 May 1827 had summoned to a general assembly, presided by the Emperor, the Council of Kings and the bodies of State. That solemnity was fixed for 4 July. Already, a tent as magnificent as it was immense was being prepared on the Champ de Mars; it was backed up against the palace of the École Militaire, which formed one of its sides, and it extended to the middle of the Champ de Mars.

All Paris witnessed the construction of that temporary edifice. They saw with admiration Napoléonic luxury burst forth there on all sides. A throne, of unusual elevation, rose up as high as the first floor of the palace, and the balcony windows were no longer anything but doors leading to that throne. The steps that descended to the ground were covered in velvet, gold and precious stones.

To support the canvas roof that covered the tent to a sufficiently great extent, recourse was made to novel means. Balloons filled with hydrogen gas were attached to various points and their ascendant force, skillfully calculated, lifted the fabric and sustained it in the air with a marvelous harmony.

Thrones, amphitheaters and ornaments of the greatest sumptuousness were disposed inside the tent; velvets, marbles, precious metals, gemstones and the rare flowers came every day to accumulate there in order to prepare the empty tent worthily for the still unknown solemnity.

Meanwhile, the kings and all the people seemingly invited arrived in a host. Paris was overflowing with strangers deploying in the capital of Europe the costumes and usages of all the countries of the globe.

The Emperor, who had returned on June 20, had not appeared since then; it was said that he was shut away in his

317

cabinets with the kings and ministers, absorbed in the most important endeavors.

## Chapter XIV
## THE FOURTH OF JULY 1827

That day, like all imperial days, was beautiful and pure, so much was God in accord with Napoléon.

From three o'clock in the morning on, the cannons of the Invalides, and the fortresses of Saint-Denis and Montmartre, the palaces of the Kings of Rome and England, were hard without discontinuity; it seemed that there was only a single blast, the sound of which lasted for nine hours, so closely did their thunder succeed one another. It is said that three thousand three hundred shots were fired.

The tent that we have mentioned was covered with scarlet silk; the gas balloons that lifted it up were attached to the ground by gilded columns, around which draperies were folded, leaving the interior of the enclosure open and freely visible.

Fifty thrones, placed much lower than the Emperor's, dominated the rest of the seats of the assembly, where more than ten thousand people could be seated.

Those thrones and seats had been occupied for more than an hour by a host of kings, princes, senators, members of the legislative body, ministers, grand functionaries, Maréchals, generals and delegates of all the nations, when midday sounded, the windows of the palace opened, the Empress, preceding the imperial family, came down to sit on a platform a few feet below the throne, and Napoléon seen appeared.

The acclamations that welcomed him are indescribable.

He was not wearing the imperial costume, but simply the familiar coat and hat he wore at war.

He sat down on his throne, his head covered. The most profound silence fell. A few seconds later he stood up, and pronounced the following speech with enthusiasm:

"Kings and peoples,

"I am the master of the world. My sovereignty has no limits on the Earth; I have attained the great goal of my thought, the Universal Monarchy.

"You know how I have become the Sovereign of Europe, how I have conquered Asia and the isles of the Pacific.

"I want to tell you how I have become master of the rest of the world.

"Africa entire, traveled by my armies, has recognized my sovereignty everywhere. The King of Silesia, followed by the kings of that continent, has returned; he has brought me news of that conquest.

"America, which was dissolving in its revolutions, has understood my power, its position and the decrees of Providence. The leaders of the nations of the New World have met in Panama, and all of them, with unanimous accord, have come to submit to my sovereignty.

"Thus has been accomplished the immense event of the Universal Monarchy.

"Kings and peoples of the Earth, I am glorifying myself and you; placed so high between God and human beings, I tell you this: my heart is full of joy and pride.

"That power, which no mortal has attained, and perhaps even imagined, since the commencement of the world, with the aid of God, I possess.

"But that grandeur will not make me forget my designs.

"Master of all lands, sovereign of all human beings, I want increasingly to think about the happiness of all.

"Today, a new order of things begins.

"In my anticipation of this event, the unity of my power summons the unity of organization.

"The Universal Monarchy founded on Earth is hereditary in my race; there will henceforth be no more than one nation and one power on the globe, until the end of time.

"Kings and peoples, you have aided me to arrive thus far; take part in my glory as you have taken part in my endeavors. Be as proud and happy as me, and with me.

"You above all, France, my beloved daughter, be glorious in that grandeur, and along with the title of universal monarch, I shall always keep that of Emperor of the French."

The Emperor concluded his speech there. At those last words, with a spontaneous and unanimous movement, the kings, the assembly and the immense people prostrated themselves before him. That instant when, above those million people, the only one standing, he alone was gazing at the heavens, must have appeared to him sublime.

He soon withdrew, superb and emotional; innumerable acclamations pursued him into the palace, and until dusk, nothing was heard anywhere but the cries "Glory to Napoléon!" "Vive l'empereur!" and "Vive le monarque universel!"

## Chapter XV
## *THE UNIVERSAL MONARCHY*

The universal monarchy! How often those words were pronounced without the understanding of the idea they enclosed. How often those words were stammered and coldly repeated by children, adults, pedants and kings, who did not know what the universal monarchy was, any more than infinity or God, the names of which their mouths incessantly murmured.

Thus, when, in his conquests, a man had united the shreds of several empires and had previously stood up to be master of some slightly enlarged little corner of the world, he had then rested, panting and out of breath, in his power until his imminent death, and blind historians had cried in loud voices their mysterious phrase, universal monarchy, in the face of that incomplete monarchy.

Only two intelligences, before Napoléon, had sounded the abysms of that phrase, one being Alexander of Macedon, who, having reached the shores of the Indian Sea, wept bitterly and took the gods to task for the spaces that he lacked.

The other was that abstract being, simultaneously people and centuries, Rome—Rome, none of whose children, even Caesar, understood the phrase, but which, in gathering together the thoughts of Romans in all ages, had incessantly dreamed of the domination of the world.

But he, Napoleon, the third, the most recent in time, the first, or rather the only one, had conceived the idea, had incarnated it and had created the Universal Monarchy.

## Chapter XVI
## AMERICA

The Emperor had only indicated in his discourse the last revolution of America; the following day, the circumstances were known; they were researched with the keenest interest, for that submission made Napoléon a universal power, and completed the world for him.

For more than twenty years, America, the land without a past, without races, without fatherlands, which, to replace its murdered children, had begged Europe for its surplus populations and Africa for the merchandise of its vanquished; the land that, without having had a youth, had arrived at decrepitude in the midst of innumerable evolutions; was dissolving and heading for complete ruin.

It could then be divided into two quite distinct parts, Spanish and Portuguese America, and the America of the United States. The rest—which is to say, the former English and Russian possessions in the north and the totality of the Antilles, except Saint-Domingue—was already under the direct or mediate power of the Emperor.

During the first wars in Spain and Portugal, Brazil and the other States of the South had raised the standard of independence and attempted to shake off the metropolitan yoke, but those attempts, poorly conceived by mediocre individuals, and only produced a perpetual state of civil war in those lands without leading to decisive victories or defeats.

Only one man of elevated genius and admirable character, Bolivar, had, in 1820 and 1821, liberated New Grenada in two victories and founded a new republic in Central America named Colombia, after the great Columbus. As great a politician as a captain, he had organized the new State and, for two years, had governed it with a remarkable administration; but, harassed by ingratitude and the mischief-making of his fellow citizens, he had lost his taste for power in his homeland, had left it for another, and had retired to Jamaica, where he lived tranquilly in obscurity.[110]

Then Colombia, like Brazil, Mexico, Peru, Paraguay, where the mysterious Dr. Francia had just died,[111] Chile and the rest of the Spanish possessions fell back into the abyss of anarchy, misery and civil wars, and all those nations were torn apart mortally, like bodies killed by fever and gangrene.

In the north, the United States presented a no less deplorable spectacle; so energetic and so strong in its federation when it as a matter of defeating a common enemy, in peace and repose that nation had felt egotism insinuating itself into diverse interests, disuniting and corroding the parts of the powerful ensemble. Laws of finance and commerce solicited by the northern States and rejected by the southern provinces began that struggle of interests, a conflict soon irritated, which changed into furious hatred and wars all the more horrible because the enemies were brothers and interest was their case. The American congress split; two or three new federations had attempted to establish themselves, various seats of government were founded, and the young republic of Franklin and Washington perished.

---

[110] In our history the Venezuelan soldier of fortune Simon Bolivar (1783-1830) created the State of Gran Colombia (much larger than the present-day Colombia, which is only a fragment of it) in 1821, and was elected president, but was then engaged in a battle to liberate Peru from the Spanish, which he continued in our history until 1825, when the Republic of Bolivia was created, under his presidency. Gran Colombia began to fall apart in 1826, eventually forcing Bolivar to step down as president in 1830, shortly before his death.

[111] In our history the first leader of Paraguay following its independence from Spain in 1811, José de Francia (1766-1840) was still alive and in power—having become increasingly autocratic—when Geoffroy write the present text.

The great rebel of the Antilles, the island of Saint-Domingue,[112] after having resisted a French expedition during the early days of the Empire, succumbed subsequently under the multitude of its sovereigns; anyone could be emperor, president, leader or king in that African America, and the negroes, too rapidly passed from slavery to politics, murdered one another in order to achieve civilization.

In spite of so many symptoms of dissolution in the continent, the Emperor, occupied in conquering the Old World, seemed to have completely forgotten it; no demonstration, speech or action had revealed his thinking in regard to America.

Undoubtedly, his profound sight was considering the agony of its nations from afar, and his wisdom was biding its time. Perhaps, too, unknown agents dispersed in those countries were revealing in their discourse the deadly state of affairs and the only possible remedy: alliance with the Old World and submission to the Emperor.

Already, at all points of the continent, people were beginning to say that only Napoléon could save America, and that it was necessary in any case to anticipate an imminent conquest. America could, by a voluntary and opportune submission assure itself of advantages that a military conquest

---

[112] Slaves in the French colony of Saint-Domingue on the island of Hispaniola staged their own Revolution in 1791 but accepted French rule in 1793 when the French abolished slavery. Conflict with the former slave-owners soon led to further rebellion, intensified when it became clear that the French intended to re-establish slavery, and the French were forced to withdraw in 1803, leaving the independent republic of Haiti to be proclaimed the following year, unrecognized by other nations. In our history, Charles X sent French troops to reconquer the former colony in 1821, pressurizing President Boyer into accepting an economically ruinous treaty that demanded a huge indemnity in exchange for independence, prompting Boyer's exile and a long succession of coups.

would have lessened. In any case, there was no salvation for it outside the Napoléonic monarchy.

Such were the words and thoughts that developed in all parts. Whether they had been sown or germinated of their own accord, they became considerable enough for the governments no longer to be able to recoil before them. Soon, senates and camps were assembled everywhere; a rapid and skillful diplomacy harmonized their discussions. Finally, a general congress of all the sovereigns, presidents, generals and legislators of the States of America was convened in Panama, and met on 7 March 1827; the independent island of the Antilles was invited, as well as the chiefs of the not very numerous savage tribes that had not yet been exterminated on the continent.

Six sessions sufficed for a great decision.

Seven hundred and forty members of legislatures, kings, leaders or generals were present at the congress.

The deliberation was brief. There was consent without conflict, enthusiasm without debate.

On 17 March, the president of the congress, General Jackson of the United States,[113] read the decree unanimously accepted, which put the constitutions, the possession and dominion of America and Saint-Domingue in the hands of the Emperor Napoléon, Sovereign of Europe, Asia and the islands of the Pacific.

That document only reached Napoléon a few days before 4 July 1827, and he kept it secret in order to announce it with greater pomp at the great assembly in the Champ de Mars.

The States of the Pacific had, as we have already said, been traveled and conquered by the vessels of the Asian expedition. Thus, there no longer remained a single parcel of land

---

[113] The reference is to Andrew Jackson (1767-1845), who was the President of the U.S.A. in our history from 1829-1837, having been narrowly beaten in the 1824 election by John Quincy Adams—a controversial defeat that led his supporters to found the Democratic Party.

outside Napoléon's power, and the entire surface of the globe was embraced by the words *Universal Monarchy.*

On the morning of 5 July 1827, that day's *Moniteur* appeared, as thick as a folio volume, so many supplements had accumulated, and the newspaper had never merited more its title of *"universel."*

It contained thirty-one decrees. The one that preceded them all was conceived as follows:

*Napoléon, Emperor of the French, Universal Monarch of the Earth:*

*To the kings and nations of the world, greetings.*

*For the first time since the commencement of time the entire surface of the globe is submissive to a single domination.*

*The Universal Monarchy is founded.*

*God has accomplished by that unprecedented event, the destiny of the world.*

*War is destroyed; the time of peace has come.*

*A new order of things is beginning; the old order is finished; the fatal diversity of nations and powers is dissolved henceforth, and until the end of time, in a perpetual unity.*

*God has placed in me and my race that unity of power and monarchy.*

*Let the kings and the nations join with me in rendering Him glory.*

*It is before Him and in His name that I have decreed the following:*

*Article 1. The continents, islands and seas that cover the surface of the globe compose the Universal Monarchy.*

*Article 2. Christianity is the sole religion of the world.*

*Article 3. The Universal Monarchy resides in me and my race in perpetuity.*

*Article 4. The seat of the Universal Monarchy is Paris, the capital of the world.*

*Article 5. The world is divided into four parts: Europe; Asia, with which are united the islands of Oceania; Africa; and America.*

*Article 6. The four parts of the world are divided into kingdoms.*

*Article 7. France alone conserves the name of empire.*

*Article 8. War is henceforth forbidden to kings and peoples.*

*Article 9. Slavery is abolished.*

*Article 10. The kings of the world are, under our sovereignty, charged in what concerns them with the execution of the present decree.*

*Given in Paris, 4 July 1827.*

*Napoléon.*

*For the Universal Monarch:*
*Napoléon Joseph, King of Spain.*

*Sealed by the Great Seal of the Universal Monarchy,*
*Duc d'Amalfi, Arch-Chancellor.*

The following decrees fixed the limits of kingdoms in the four parts of the world, and subdivided them into départements and other administrative divisions.

The third fixed the religious administration and convened a synod.

The fourth appointed the kings for the kingdoms of Asia, Africa and America.

The fifth declared all the islands of the world, except for Japan and the islands of Europe, French colonies.

The sixth fixed the relationship of kings and peoples with one another, and their relationship of obedience with regard to the Universal Monarchy.

The seventh proclaimed the new and universal constitution of the world.

The eighth founded the general administration of the Universal Monarchy and the particular administration of kingdoms.

The ninth instituted the Council of Kings, meeting once every three years in Paris in a two month session, presided by the Universal Monarch.

The tenth gave the four parts of the world the capitals of Paris, Calcutta, Timbuktu and Mexico. A directive Senate, appointed by the Emperor and presided by a king chosen by him, would sit in each of the last three cities.

The fifteenth fixed the military estate of the globe, created four constables and raised the number of Maréchals to a hundred.

The other decrees concerned customs, finance, justice, taxes, the sciences and all the interests of human beings and States.

One can judge the extent of that *Moniteur* and its decrees by recalling that the second edition that was published thereof contained no less than six octavo volumes.

## Chapter XVIII
### GENERAL OUDET

On the evening of 4 July, the Emperor was told that General Oudet was soliciting a private audience with the Universal Monarchy with the greatest urgency.

Those surrounding Napoléon protested against that request; they exposed the imprudence there would be in the Emperor receiving General Oudet alone; already the most animated were murmuring against what they called a dangerous clemency. "Oudet," he said, "far from being appointed general and commander of armies, should have been thrown into a State prison." Some, the most cowardly, spoke of military execution, and recalled abundant already-ancient anecdotes that had signaled General Oudet's hatred for the Emperor; how, in 1804, he had emerged from the ranks and come to insult Napoléon publicly; how, at Wagram, in the midst of cries of glory, he had made audible that of "Vive la liberté!"; how he had been suspected of founding secret societies within the army conserving belated republican ideas, and thus fomented the hatred of soldiers against the Emperor.[114]

Those murmurs made Napoléon smile. "Those stories are very old," he said. "I forgot that childishness twenty years ago. Since then, I've made Oudet a general; he's an excellent military man; his conduct in Jerusalem was admirable. I shall see him."

---

[114] The introduction of this character is anachronistic; in our history General Jacques-Joseph Oudet (1773-1809) was fatally wounded at Wagram. The rumor that he founded a lodge of the Masonic secret society of the Philadelphes in the army is due to an *Histoire des sociétés secretes dans l'armée sous Napoléon* published anonymously in 1815 and attributed to Charles Nodier, allegedly a member of the society in question, which is probably fanciful.

The audience was granted for the following day.

Napoléon was working in his study with the Minister of Justice and the Grand Maréchal of the palace when General Oudet came in.

"I'm delighted to see you, General," the Emperor said to him. "What do you want with me?"

"I had hoped for an audience," said Oudet, parading his gaze over the two ministers.

"I hear you. Messieurs," the Emperor said to the Minister and the Duc de Frioul, "the general and I need to have a private conversation."

The great judge left, and Duroc, looking anxiously at the Emperor and Oudet, went out after him, as if regretfully, and murmuring.

"Now we're alone," said Napoléon.

"Yes, alone!" said Oudet, hotly. "I can say everything, and you can hear everything; we're alone with one another, you, despotism incarnate at the summit of power, and me, liberty dying and vanquished."

"What is all this, my dear Oudet?" said Napoléon, with a mocking smile.

"It's the last sigh of liberty, the last speech of an independent man."

"Let it be short," said the Emperor, frowning.

"As long as it pleases me, for at this solemn moment speech and time are mine, and you'll listen to me until the end."

"Insensate!" said Napoléon, and was about to ring a bell.

"Wait!" said the general, seizing the emperor's arm with one hand, and taking a pistil from his pocket with the other.

"Wretch!" Napoléon exclaimed. "What—a crime, Oudet!"

"A crime!" said Oudet, calmly. "So you no longer know me, Bonaparte? A crime! It's me that this pistol will attain before I leave here; it's my liberty that will die—but before then I want you to hear one last speech."

At that moment, the Duc de Frioul entered precipitately, having heard the Emperor's exclamations.

"Leave us alone!" aid the Emperor, firmly.

And Duroc went out for a second time.

"Yes, Bonaparte, it's necessary that I die; I can no longer live in the midst of your despotism; you have gone back on your promise to your mother; you have stifled liberty under heaps of glory, and its very name has been forgotten in your empire.

"You know that, because the police know everything, and I'm not unaware of their steps; I had galvanized a few hearts in your army to make them quiver secretly in the name of liberty. Well, they have all frozen again on hearing your name; they've abandoned me, and I scarcely have a few faithful friends remaining. But don't worry; they'll die with me, and then there will no longer be any thought of liberty in the world.

"But I wanted at least one protest more to be heard in the midst of glory.

"In old Rome, you would not have had a popular triumph without the outrage of a citizen having preceded your chariot. Well, here it's me who will be your insulter, in the midst of this superhuman grandeur with which you're crushing us. I tell you this, Napoléon: you're nothing but a tyrant; you have killed liberty. Shame on you! And let all free men die!"

Calm but pale, Napoléon listened with composure, and, interrupting Oudet benevolently, he said: "I knew everything, Oudet. I knew about your conspiracies, but I held you in high enough esteem not to punish you, and to raise you to dignities in accordance with your merit."

"Take back those dignities, then, in order that I can die without gratitude, and freer!"

And he tore off his epaulettes, ripped away his red sash and threw the debris at the emperor's feet.

"Well then, why not quit the army to go and live somewhere, free and tranquil?"

To these words, General Oudet replied with the greatest excitement: "Live free! Where? You don't know yourself, then, Napoléon, what Universal Monarchy is! Tell me a corner of the world that's free! Tell me the ocean wave that isn't yours! Tell me where there's a particle of air in the atmosphere that isn't poisoned by your universal despotism! And how do I know that if I dig into the entrails of the earth in search of a tomb I won't find the Universal Monarchy even in its depths?"

The Emperor became animated at those words, but it was with an interior joy; he had never felt his power better than in that imprecation of an enemy, and a smile spread forcibly over his face.

Then Oudet said: "Smile, Napoléon! Triumph! Triumph! For you are the master of the world, and you have killed liberty…and I shall die with it!"

He fired his pistol into his mouth and fell dead.

The noise was heard; the alarm was sounded in the palace. Napoléon had the body taken away, and said: "That was a brave man, but a madman."

He was buried the following day, and that evening, over his freshly-dug grave, five men committed suicide: two officers, a sergeant and two soldiers. They were the residue of the phalanx of free men, and there was no longer on Earth either a human being or a word to express the idea of liberty.

# BOOK SIX

## Chapter I
## *THE JEWS*

All the peoples were vanquished; all had submitted to the leveling of Napoléon's sovereignty, without a doubt, for if a single fleet or army had remained outside that law, the Emperor's name would have sufficed to suppress it in no time at all.

And yet one people still existed who could doubt the conquest, ungraspable as a nation, everywhere on Earth and nowhere, circulating, living among other peoples, finding homelands everywhere but without a fatherland of its own, with no soil or land on which to confer the name of their nationality.

The Jews, that mystery nation, which entered Egypt as a family and emerged as a people, captive in Babylon, vanquished by Alexander, the cradle of a god that it had killed and cursed, and spreading over the surface of the globe in order to accumulate wealth there, to march at the head of the world's commerce, and drag everywhere the fatal law that disperses it and conserves it.

A nation of exiles, but indestructible, faithful to the divine constitution of Moses: the Moses who had kneaded them into a nation with his powerful hands, so marvelously that, lacking the soil that they had already populated, they would remain a people even though they had lost their fatherland, that their nationality could live on in them, and that they would not cease to be Jews in foreign lands.

If Napoléon thought for a few moments about the Jews, perhaps it was while he was contemplating that admirable constitution, when he was thinking about re-kneading and reconstituting the world.

335

As a matter of conquest, he did not worry overmuch about the character of foreigner that the Jews insisting on conserving in the midst of nations that allowed them to be born and due. It was sufficient for him that the nations were subjugated, and the Jews subject with them to the common law.

However, the Emperor felt a keen satisfaction when he learned that the religious leaders of that people, explaining their traditions, had thought of assembling their brethren in order to deliberate on the state of the Jewish nation.

That celebrated assembly of Jews took place in Warsaw.

It was a curious spectacle, that of a nation convened in its entirety, represented in what it had of the most considerable of illustrious men, gathered in a northern city to deliberate its existence and decide whether it ought to abjure its ancient worship, annihilate its old constitution, accept an enemy religion and dissolve into foreign nationalities.

But such was the empire of ideas that had gripped the world, that those old sentiments, so profoundly anchored in the hearts of Israelites, weakened and loosened in the midst of the general current. The time, they said, had arrived, the traditions were accomplished; and fear and admiration swept away the last of their doubts.

The Sanhedrin hasted for more than a month. It was the last of those assemblies. In the final session, all the Jews, with unanimous assent, abjured their religion, declaring that the time of Israel was accomplished, and all, with a common accord, accepted the Catholic religion, sacrificing their law and their faith to it.

Only one among them, Samuel Manasses, the rabbi of Strasbourg, protested with the greatest violence against the decision of his brethren, and, in a moment of exaltation, cried: "Let Christ signal his verity and his power, then! For myself, faithful to the law of my forefathers, I blaspheme him loudly, and I defy the God of the Christians!"

Either because the exasperation with which Manasses had pronounced those final words had broken the equilibrium of his existence, or because the finger of God had touched him, he fell down, foaming at the mouth, mortally struck. He was surrounded, but he was already dead.

That extraordinary circumstance dealt the final blow to the Jewish religion; it expired that year with the cult and constitutions of Moses.

After that great sacrifice, the Jews pressed Napoléon insistently for the restoration of Jerusalem and Judea, but the holy city was refused to Christians who were too new to possess the sanctuary of Christianity.

The island of Cyprus had just been devastated by the plague; the inhabitants that the scourge had not afflicted had abandoned the island in fear to return to Asia Minor. The Emperor accorded that island to the Jews. They soon repopulated it and made it the center of their commerce and their wealth. It was the first time since their dispersal that they had gathered together on a national soil; they built a new Jerusalem there, but the island, called New Judea, did not cease to be part of the French Empire and to be directly submissive to imperial administration.

## Chapter II
## UNITY (1)

Meanwhile, the Universal Monarchy extended its great system of unity over the world.

The unity of legislation was established first.

It was the same with the unity of weights and measures, and monetary unity: a single money was current throughout the world. The effigy of other sovereigns was not conserved thereon; one side presented the Emperor's bust with the words: *Napoléon, Emperor of the French*; and the other a globe with an eagle with spread wings and the inscription: *Universal Monarchy*.

The system of education was renewed and extended uniformly in accordance with the skillful restoration that was primarily due to the remarkable works of Messieurs de Fontanes,[115] Guizot and Brougham.

Education was public and gratuitous. Six degrees of schools took the children of the poor and rich at the beginning of their thought, in order to lead them successively to the most transcendent knowledge. Impartial examinations admitted the capable to the superior degree.

Public instruction, thus renewed, was more rapid in its course, and given everywhere in the French language.

The Emperor was particularly insistent on establishing that unity of language. All legislative, administrative, civil or other documents, pleas, declarations, all speeches and all writings having a public character were necessarily in the French language. At first, the existing generation had difficulty complying with that law, but the one that followed, fashioned in the schools to the universal language, took that new language

---

[115] Louis Marcellin de Fontanes (1767-1821) was president of the legislative chamber from 1804-10, but accepted the Bourbon Restoration in our history.

back to the family, where it was introduced as master, replacing other languages everywhere.

Agriculture and commerce, directed by a special senate established close to the Emperor, gained, if not a unity impossible in various conditions and climates, at least a harmony and a balance useful to all.

Sciences, letters and the fine arts also had nuclei of unity in the capital of the world; three superior councils dominated other counsels of the second class spread over all parts of the globe. By their continuous correspondence they brought back to the common center the efforts and results of genius, to make them radiate from that hearth and spread out to the extremities of the Earth.

A universal library was created, composed of the imperial library, completed in what it lacked by all the libraries of the world. The multitude of books, manuscripts and prints that accumulated there was such that the Emperor conceived the plan of reuniting the immense riches of museums that were overloaded and placing them in a library and museum city. Versailles was chosen for that destination; that town, by virtue of the prodigious extension of the capital of the world, was already linked to Paris and considered as one of its suburbs; it thus found itself the city of arts and letters, and gathered those marvelous collections in the immensity of its palaces and galleries.

## Chapter III
### UNITY (2)

A universal postal system, singularly activated by the creation of canals, railways, steamships and steam locomotives, established an extraordinary rapidity and regularity in communications.

The magistracy was uniformly organized. Each part of the world had a court of cassation, and every State imperial courts and tribunals of justice similar to those of France.

Above those courts, a Senate of Justice was created, a universal high court composed of twenty members and presided by the Arch-Chancellor. It had the power to summon to it and remake the decisions of the four courts of cassation; it alone could arrogate that supreme jurisdiction, and no one could seize its claims directly. It also had the power to issue reglementary edicts in certain matters, and its edicts, submitted to the Emperor's approval, had the force of law.

Each State had a court of accounts whose works were approved in the last resort and registered by the high court of accounts sitting in Paris.

The division of the globe became the same as that of the French Empire. Every State was divided into départements, arrondissements, cantons and communes, having administrative and judiciary authorities with the same attributions and names as in France.

That new division let to a universal census, concluded in 1829. It gave the following statistical result of the population of the globe: Europe, 302,500,000 inhabitants; Asia 455,000,000; Oceania, united with Asia, 33,590,000; Africa 182,000,000; America 58,000,000. Total: 1,031,090,000 inhabitants.

The population of the French Empire in Europe amounted to 112,960,000 inhabitants.

Not included in that last figure were the populations of the French colonies in Asia, Africa and America and the totality of the Oceanic islands all directly linked to the French Empire and not submissive to vassal kings.

Paris, whose outlying districts had invaded Sèvres, Saint-Denis, Saint-Mandé, Vincennes, Montmartre, Vaugirard and Montrouge, and whose diameter was no less than five leagues in any direction, counted a population of 3,600,000 souls, in addition to the multitude of foreigners who flocked here from all parts of the world.

London, by contrast, had decreased slightly, and no longer had more than 1,100,000 inhabitants. Calcutta, the capital of Asia, had 1,700,000, Timbuktu 600,000 and Mexico 420,000.

Of those four capitals of the world, Paris and Calcutta were part of the Empire and the other two, although situated in the middle of basal kingdoms, only depended upon it, remained under the direct sovereignty of the Emperor.

All public debts were combined into one; the Emperor resolved to extinguish them, and thanks to a powerful legislation, extraordinary contributions and imperial liberality, it was amortized in a few years, and then extinct.

Indirect and direct contributions were established with uniformity.

Military organization had something particular, all the forces resting in the hand of the Emperor, and each kingdom had a Maréchal or a French general commanding on behalf of the Emperor.

It could also be said that military forces were abolished in the vassal kingdoms, so much were they reduced. National guards replaced soldiers in the maintenance of internal order.

The Emperor, however, conserved his immense army.

It was the same with the navy, innumerable in the French Empire, restricted in the other kingdoms.

The diplomatic system was no longer anything but a fiction and a ceremony. Napoléon had ministers next to every king, and every king had an ambassador, always of the royal blood, close to the Emperor.

A penitentiary system, ameliorated and rendered uniform, was established. New Holland was exclusively reserved for the penalty of deportation. Between two surrounding fleets, on the ocean and the interior sea, it received the deportees of all the States of the globe.

## Chapter IV
## UNITY (3)

Printing and bookselling were submitted to the sole and powerful action of Napoléon. Armed with the principle of the freedom of the press, he steered that liberty in the direction of his power, and no one knows what might have happened if the thought thus reproduced and poured out in all parts of the globe had risen toward him other than as incense, and if, afflicted by it, he had been wounded by it.

There was an official world newspaper, entitled *The Earth*; it bore the Universal Monarch's orders everywhere.

The *Moniteur* was conserved solely for the French Empire.

Another periodical, *The Globe*, occupied exclusively with science, literature and the fine arts, appeared every week by government order, and spread a complete and transcendent education throughout the world.

Understandably, there was no longer any question of politics. Politics is only a word, devoid of value and meaning, where complete and universal power exists; politics is only a transitional science appearing at the ruination of States, when everyone is occupied with those ruins, makes speeches about them and offers plans or their reconstruction; it is also a science that, dreaming about the relationships between nations, seeks to harm some and favor others; but in a world constituted by a single government and with such power, the word "politics" is no longer anything but nonsensical.

There was one politics, solely permitted to the Emperor, and that was the police, an immense network enveloping the world, which everyone sensed and no one dared perceive.

Napoléon also subjected to universal regulation: theaters; telegraphs, all terminating in Paris and radiating from that city to all the extremities of the globe, marvelous machines, permitting the slightest word murmured at the utmost limits of the world to be heard; the clergy and the infirm; his household and court; the seal of the Universal Monarchy, representing an eagle gripping a globe; the code of recompenses, placed facing the code of penalties; titles of nobility; the Légion d'honneur and new orders of chivalry, among which was distinguished in the first rank the Order of Kings, representing a globe with two crossed scepters and the words *Nemo nisi rex*—an extraordinary distinction accorded to kings alone, and with extreme reserve; inhumations and general salubrity; and numerous other matters that all regulated society, reducing it to simple forms and to the unity that rendered it light and comfortable in Napoléon's hand.

The most singular of those attempts at unity of which history has conserved the trace is doubtless the idea of Napoléon to struggle against nature and climates, and to cause the disappearance of the variety of races and colors existing among human beings. Human beings, with such diverse forms, colored white, red, black and yellow, with intelligences and thoughts so contrary, importuned him; he wanted to make a single humankind, and having gathered to that effect a council of the greatest philosophers and mathematicians in the world, he submitted the following problem to them:

Was it possible, by means of mathematically determined alliances between the various human races, to arrive after a number of generations with a unity of race and color; and in what epoch could that complete transformation of humanity be effected?

To such an unexpected question, the scholars did not know what to reply, so great was their amazement; however, having recovered somewhat from their surprise, they established that seven generations would suffice for that recasting of humankind—but they added at the same time that the mathematical formulae justified on paper by the calculations were quite impractical.

Regretfully, Napoléon renounced that singular pretention.

*Chapter V*
## THE ECUMENICAL COUNCIL

There is no doubt that the Emperor thought of signaling his advent to the Universal Monarchy by a solemnity as marvelous as the circumstance manifestly warranted. He wanted a new coronation; but as he required, in order that nothing should be lacking in that pomp, the presence of all the kings in the world, he put off the date of that coronation for nearly a year, and fixed it for 20 March 1828.

The rest of the year 1827 went by in the satisfaction of omnipotence and glory.

Paris, inflamed by the presence of its master, and proud of being the capital of the world and the queen of cities, celebrated that winter in pleasure and luxury, in intoxicating joys and follies.

Suddenly, however, in the midst of the resonance of festivities, the news of a universal council came to occupy all minds.

An ecumenical council opened on 6 December 1827 in the church of Notre-Dame, with Clement XV as president; the patriarchs of the Orient and eleven hundred Catholic bishops and archbishops were in session therein. The principal leaders of all the sects and Christian protestantisms were also summoned, by order of the Emperor.

It was said that the Universal Monarch was going to take part in those deliberations. Napoléon did not appear in the council, however; he even left Paris ostentatiously while it was being held—certain in advance, it was said, of the result of the meeting, he traveled around France, where the Two Seas Canal had just been completed, uniting and confounding the waters of the Atlantic and the Mediterranean.

The sessions of the council were held in secret, and that mystery augmented popular respect. Every morning the crowd knelt down with veneration on the square of the parvis, which was traversed on foot, in order to reach the cathedral, by the Pope at the head of his army of prelates.

The council's decisions revealed subsequently what had been discussed there.

One great fact, and one alone, the veritable object of the assembly, was the unity of the Christian Church, absorbing and dissolving all the deviations, divergences and defections that had desolate Christianity since its birth. The time had doubtless come for that great peace of Christianity, for, with a unanimous accord, all the dissident commissions came to prostrate their foreheads, their submission and their doctrines at the feet of the leader of Catholicism.

It was on 16 December that that union was proclaimed; Pope Clement XV fell to his knees on the pavement of the church and, raising his arms to the heavens, cried, in the midst of the religious exaltation of those priests: "O my God, thanks be rendered to you, for today your holy word has been accomplished, and there is no longer on Earth any but one voice to bless and adore you."

That sublime goal having been attained, those fathers of the Church went further, and, in their luminous intelligence, comprehending the future of the religion, henceforth based on those unique and indestructible foundations, they requested a reform of a few points of worship.

The French language was henceforth the language of God, as it was of the world. There was no sacrilege in that decree. If the essence of Catholicism is unity and universality; if, in the midst of the confusion of tongues and "minced" States, as Monsieur de Maistre put it, the necessity of a universal religious language had been recognized, in order that, at the same moment, the same words would raise up all over the globe the same prayers and express the same aspirations of souls, as the philosopher called them, now that the Empire and the French language were universal, that tongue ought to be accepted as an accomplished fact, as the expression of human worship of God.

Other fairly numerous modifications were made to the ceremonies, without affecting the dogma.

The decisions of the council were promulgated at the end of the year, and some were put into execution at the beginning of the year 1828.

Finally, two religious singularities were judged and condemned by the council, to which all power had been given over religious ideas on Earth.

The first relates to the Baron de Jantenne, a litterateur known for a highly esteemed book on Greek mythology, which caused him to be appointed Prefect of Athens. That very favor caused the doom of Monsieur de Jantenne; his excited head, entirely filled with the mythological world of the Greeks, could not resist that new position. In the milieu of that Greek land, the placed inhabited and protected by the gods of his studies, singular hallucinations gripped him, he went mad and posed as the prophet of Jupiter and his gods.[116] A man of good faith and folly, he was preaching the renewed religion of Jupiter, Mars and Mercury; he set up altars and reestablished statues; in the restored Parthenon he offered sacrifices to Minerva. He had a few lunatics for disciples, was rendered desperate and locked up in the Chateau de Sept-Tours, where he died a short while later; with him died the infertile seeds he had sown, and the Parthenon became a ruin again.

The other schism was entirely Christian; it had gained the most elevated and the most tender souls among the faithful, those of poets and women, who, modifying the offices of the Church themselves, had substituted for the old songs of the Catholic rite the delightful songs of poets of Christianity. As one of them said: "they prayed with their words, they adored with their songs," and that sect, so pure in its error, so innocent in its sin, was already spreading when the condemnation

---

[116] I have left the names of the gods as Geoffroy renders them, although Monsieur de Jantenne must surely have posed as a prophet of Zeus and offered homages to Ares and Hermes.

of the Council came to strike it, and found it docile and re-pentant.

Thus, all was finished; idolatry and Mohammedanism had disappeared, Protestantism was submissive, the schismatics had rallied, and the Christian religion, one and reformed, reigned without division over the world and in all hearts.

Napoléon was informed of that result in Marseille, and rejoiced in it as in the greatest conquest.

## Chapter VI
## *THE SCIENCES*

In the years that saw the Universal Monarchy born and those that followed, the science, letters, the arts, and even nature herself, produced great discoveries and the most magnificent results. I have named nature because one might have thought that she came spontaneously to offer herself and bring her marvels.

Steam, in the most various applications, created supernatural forces and multiplied a hundredfold the forces already known.

There were vehicles that traveled with the rapidity of lightning along the railways, going from one extremity of the empire to the other between two sunsets. There were vessels with ten, sixteen and twenty paddle-wheels animated by numerous steam-engines traversing the plains of the Atlantic in less than a week to carry the Monarch's orders to America.

There were new machines, living on that steam, raising colossi and rocks, hollowing out the earth, stopping or launching waves, flattening mountains, and, combined with powders, even commanding the atmosphere, from which they expelled clouds and dissipated tempests by means of prodigious detonations.

Electric telegraphs were established: metallic wires of immense length, departing from the Tuileries traversed the Ocean, rivers, seas and mountains, to reach the other great cities of the world. In every State, the capital was itself the center of a similar communication system; the conductive wires, whose quivering and shocks had become a language, suddenly brought all the news, transmitted instantly, from however far away, to the Emperor. Everyone knows that the rapidity of that transmission is such that the electrical commotion excited in Calcutta, New York or Cairo is received and perceived in Paris in an inappreciable time. Thus, Napoléon, at the same instant, heard all human speech, knew all the events and sent his orders to the extremity of the globe, and held in his hand, so to speak, all the wires of the magical network that surrounded the earth.[117]

Aerostatic balloons, enlarged and multiplied, gave veritable wings to humans, who were able to steer them. The last result, so ardently sought, was due to the combination of magnetic and electrical forces.

Glass, so resistant and so brittle, softened under the fingers of chemistry; it folded like supple wax, and could thus be applied to usages of life and, furthermore, to usages of death. A mummification as simple as it was complete could protect the bodies of great citizens, and a transparent layer of glass enveloped them and preserved them forever.

Medicine discovered marvels; people whose death had been certain were recalled to life; blindness could be cured; deafness found in artificial ears the most subtle energy of audition; and, doing more than curing, new means came to give the senses forces and developments hitherto unknown. Glass lenses gave sight microscopic discernment and the range of telescopes; gases brought the sense of smell new resources to enjoy odors with unknown sensations. Hearing could be augmented to a high degree; even taste acquired a greater delicacy; and science, in this augmenting the pleasures of human beings, brought them a little closer to happiness.

Vaccines were discovered for the majority of maladies, and medicine advanced, with the word prevention overtaking that of cure.

---

[117] Although hypothetical descriptions of electrical telegraph systems had been published in the 1820s, it was not until the 1930s, in our world—shortly before Geoffroy wrote his text—that the first experimental systems were constructed, so the developments described here are futuristic. The "telegraphs" to which the text has previously referred are of course, Claude Chappe's famous semaphore signaling system, of which Napoléon made extensive use in our history.

A marvelous inutility long thought impossible, the squaring of the circle, was discovered in singular circumstances.

In a college, a facetious professor posed the problem to his pupil. The sage replied that it was impossible, the skillful approximated it, a child found it. The master encouraged the former, and as he had read that the problem was impossible he punished the idiot who had found it, with all the more vigor because he could not demonstrate the absurdity of the discovery.

The child, proud of what he had done, kicked the ground, and doubtless cried "*E pur si muove*," or something similar. The master put him in detention. But the Académie des Sciences, informed of these things, demanded communication of the child's work; it turned out that it was simply the real and true discovery of the squaring of the circle, which had been thought to be impossible—and the child was named an associate of the Académie.

The water of the sea was rendered potable; an electrical discharge, combined with a few other physical forces, disengaged it from its salts and its bitterness, and the frightful counter-sense of a man expiring of thirst in the middle of the Ocean was corrected.

The earth was hollowed out in its depths; gulfs discovered near Timbuktu and deprived of water permitted descent to five leagues beneath the surface; fire was discovered there.

Astronomy made some progress, but people already knew all that was useful, and the discovery of the planet Vulcan and the fourteen satellites of Uranus provided a name and two new facts without rendering any service to humanity.

The Emperor gave a particular impulsion to the progress of a science of which he was fond, geography, perhaps the most important of the sciences since it contains them all, describing nature and humans at the same time, and because its mission is to recount the history of the prodigious and incessant victory of humankind over nature.

That beautiful science was however, neglected and almost unknown, having not yet rendered a sufficient testimony.

The maps were mediocre, the books incomplete, and geographers could scarcely find a rank in scientific assemblies.

But Napoléon had spoken for it, and in response to his voice the men appeared, and excellent works were published; Buschings and Danvilles described the Earth in its smallest details,[118] and at the same time raised philosophical geography to its rightful place. The conquests served that work admirably, for, if Alexander has been named the foremost geographer of antiquity, one could say as much for Napoléon in modern times, with better entitlement.

The Great Imperial Atlas was completed in 1831. It contained, in eighteen volumes in *grand aigle* format, the universal description of the Earth, on a uniform scale, with a multitude of plans of cities and individual maps whose details were more developed.

The intellectual sciences made giant strides. The language of numbers of which Leibniz dreamed was found and applied. Thought had its algebra; it could be expressed and formulated, understood by all, independently of sounds and words, which reproduce it so imperfectly.

Finally, thought itself was able to enlarge under certain forces and rise to the level of genius. The art of stimulating it or calming it in minds was found. Sometimes powerful, sometimes somnolent, the will disposed of it and was able to make that tyrant a docile slave.

---

[118] The exemplary geographers cited are Anton Friedrich Busching (1724-1793) and Jean-Baptiste Bourguignon d'Anville (1697-1782).

## Chapter VII
## VOYAGES AND DISCOVERIES

The phrase Universal Monarchy implied the possession of known and unknown lands; no island or new land could appear without bringing with it that original enfeoffment to which humans and nature were subject with regard to Napoléon.

The Pacific Ocean gave a few more names to geography.

The austral continent was sought in the southern seas; vessels, as they got closer to the pole, saw the ice increase, but always sea before them, nothing but sea.

But the pole, which insurmountable ice protected in the south, was not unattainable in the north, and its discovery was not one of the least marvels of our age.

Vice-Admiral Parry, of the French navy, contrived in a fifth voyage to traverse the North Sea and finally discovered the famous North-Western Passage, which had been denied because no one had been able to find it. His vessels had passed through the Davis and Barrow Straits, entered the Polar Sea, having discovered the Parry Strait,[119] and had emerged from the Arctic Ocean via the Behring Strait when, seeing the enthusiasm of his crew, after acquiring such glory, he dared to propose even more: a campaign toward the pole itself.

---

[119] In our history too, William Edward Parry (1790-1855) discovered a Parry Channel and came close to discovering a North-West Passage; he made an attempt to reach the pole in 1827, when he had already published accounts of three previous voyages in search of the fabled passage, and he set a new record for the most northerly point then attained, which stood for half a century, but did not attain the rank of rear-admiral in the British Navy until 1852.

The mariners welcomed their admiral's proposal with acclamations, and, the vessel *Conquerant* having been chosen, he headed northwards in a straight line.

Incredibly enough, as they approached the ultimate degrees of latitude, the *Conquerant* advanced more easily in the midst of the eternal ice; free spaces among the mountains of ice opened a passage for them; the cold seemed, if not to diminish, at least not to increase. Eventually, on 28 February 1828, a land covered with snow, in the heart of which rose up a multitude of fir trees of rather mediocre height, suddenly stopped the ship; it was impossible to go any further. Observations revealed, however, that there were no more than twenty leagues to traverse to reach the pole, the object of so much desire. Was it necessary, then, to abandon such an attempt at that point? Admiral Parry did not hesitate; he ordered a landing, and scarcely had he proposed continuing the journey commenced on foot than everyone replied: "Forward ho!"

They marched for three days and two nights through that immense forest, but after that time they quit it, and it was then that the polar mountain appeared to them.

It was no more than half a league away, and appeared to rise up more than five hundred meters, and mathematical calculations determined that the pole was at the foot of the regular conical mountain.

It would have been difficult to doubt it; that mountain of native iron, the regularity of its form, its elevation and its existence in those deserts of ice were too extraordinary in nature not to be the signal of some predestined place: it was the Pole!

Admiral Parry was the first to climb the mountain, and, having arrived at the summit, he planted a tricolor flag there, raised his hands to the heavens and cried:

"In the name of God Almighty and the Emperor Napoléon, his monarch on Earth, I, Vice-Admiral Parry of the French Navy, have set my foot on the pole, and I have planted there the flag of my sovereign. *Vive l'empereur! Vive le monarque unversel!*"

The crew, ranged in battle order at the foot of the mountain, responded with the same acclamations; and the echoes of the pole, which awoke for the first time, repeated in muffled fashion those cries of possession and glory.

## Chapter VIII
## THE BURIED CITIES

The city of Pompeii had long since reappeared in its entirety; ashes alone had enveloped it, and it was only necessary to sweep them away to discover it.

It was not the same with Herculaneum; the liquid lava, in flowing through the streets and interstices, had gripped the monuments and habitations within its recooled rock as if in scales; it was necessary to strip away that solid envelope laboriously, and ten years was scarcely sufficient for its entire resurrection.

But that time and those labors were more than recompensed by the admirable things found in the entrails of the city; Roman life reappeared there as present as on the day of its destruction. The laws, the usages, the games, the mores, the people themselves, as if petrified in the lava rock, rendered the secrets of their existence, and, confronting the century of old and that of today, seemed to retrench eighteen hundred years of the course of time.

Mexico also had its Herculaneum. Fourteen leagues from Mexico City there was a broad uncultivated area called Grana. That word signified "city" in the ancient Mexican language. Tradition had conserved at that place the memory of a great city long disappeared. A first excavation, due to hazard, caused monuments of an unknown character to appear. The excavations were continued, and the Emperor, notified of the event, had them extended and completed. In that new tomb, the civilization was found of a people and an epoch whose traces had disappeared; nevertheless, it was necessary to recognize that the civilization had been quite advanced, and that the epoch in question was very remote, perhaps even antediluvian. What gave strength to that opinion as the discovery of a sculpted marble tablet representing the two hemispheres of the terrestrial globe, a veritable world map, in which the continents and the islands as well as the seas had contours and forms quite different from those that they had conserved since the last cataclysm.

A few discoveries of that sort, but of lesser importance, made in Siberia and Abyssinia, also produced curious results.

Bizarre discoveries! Singular mummies of cities of old, which Providence had conserved in their tombs in order that all the ages of the past could, so to speak, act out their presence for the Universal Monarchy!

This chapter would not be complete if we did not recall the reappearance of a primitive people preserved by a kind of burial in the oasis of Boulma. We have already mentioned that oasis during the conquest of Africa, reserving the provision of a few brief details for later.

A son of Shem had, in the first years that followed the Deluge, brought his God, his family and his traditions to that island. For four thousand years, unknown to the world whose existence they did not even suspect, his descendants, small in number, had lived in the middle of the desert, conserving the traditions, the mores and the language of the first humans. A family rather than a people, they had not felt the necessity of progress. The usages of the earliest times of the world had been sufficient for their life, and the language of Adam and Noah for their thought. They did not know laws, they had no history but their traditions; they had lived without literature, without arts, without war, without civilization, without swords and without passions, unaware that those things were necessary to other humans.

When they were discovered they numbered four hundred and fifty, two hundred of whom were women. Their astonishment when they saw other human beings, with usages and a civilization monstrous to them, is indescribable. They soon got used to those strange novelties, however, and when the civilized men had sucked the juices from their traditions, their language and their existence, they made them part of that civilization, and so, the inhabitants of Boura, after three years, had mores, passions, a literature, arts, a commerce, weapons and a sub-prefect—in a word, a civilization like the rest of the world, poor folk!

## Chapter IX
### POPULAR ERRORS

People had seen Napoléon surpass by such an extent what imagination could attain of greatness, they had seen him so high, so far from them, so far above humanity, that they believed him to be more than a man, and something other than a man.

The most widespread belief was that he had two souls; some went even further and attributed three or four to him, and once emerged from that unity, anyone could, in the grip of superstition, overbid others with the multiplicity of divine essences animating the great monarch.

Similar follies had already been said in antiquity of the poet Ennius, and the old author also had two souls, by the count of the Romans; that was forgotten after the death of the poet, and even more so after the death of his poems.

The Emperor declined that spiritualist compliment and seemed to set little store by it.

No more did he want the divinity that a few new Christians of India came to offer him. Those converted Indians had rediscovered a residue of idolatry in their hearts; they had already fashioned statues of the new god Napoléon; he had as many arms and heads as the most monstrous of the idols of Brahma, and they had thought they were rendering him more magnificent homage thus.

The god mocked them, and the prefects of India scolded those amateurs of apotheosis so harshly that they soon returned, confused and trembling, to Christianity.

If the Emperor had not determined in his mind to spread Christianity over the Earth without resistance and without exception, perhaps he would have accommodated himself to those homages, but the divinity that was offered to him arrived too late; it disturbed his politics and was merely ridiculous.

## Chapter X
## LETTERS AND FINE ARTS

Literature and the fine arts rose to the height of these great things; books multiplied, always more worthy of peoples and the monarch; poetry, history, philosophy and dramatic literature produced masterpieces and profoundly agitated souls that were increasingly capable of sensing and comprehending them.

Music, the sublime, mysterious art that comes to grip the soul without passing via intelligence, which is felt without being understood, which intoxicates and cannot be defined, made sublime progress. It was no longer the privileged sensation of the rich and scholars but the joy of all; it had spread everywhere; the air seemed to be full of its voluptuous exhalations. Universally popular songs were heard over the entire surface of the globe, and it is necessary to place at their head the one named "The Song of the World," for which Rossini provided the music and Lamartine the poetry, a hymn commencing: "Napoleon, you see the world..."

An imaginary language, not expressing ideas, but so melodious that it bathed hearts delightfully when it was herd, was invented for music, and in the new operas, thus written, the pantomime, more excited, explained what music and inexplicable words could not make comprehensible.

Spectacles were equally extraordinary. They even surpassed the bounds of civilization; spectacles of gladiators were established in Asia and northern Europe; the Emperor forbade that horrible pleasure.

Thought, having become more rapid, had need of instruments that matched its celerity; stenography became common writing and typewriters pianos of inscription, painting with the greatest rapidity thought scarcely sprung from the soul.

A science that might be called the mathematics of history, statistics, arrived at the highest degree of perfection. Its results were formulated in laws, and thanks to them, legislation and morality became exact sciences. History itself received an immense development that was imprinted on administrative action.

In every commune, the municipal council and Maires were charged with collecting details of all historical traditions, singular facts, physical circumstances, customs ancient and modern, and the most extensive details regarding mores, language, slang, fêtes, songs, literature, monuments, biography, events, religious customs, agriculture and commerce in the locality. At least one day of the council sessions was devoted to such works, which excited more love of the native soil, the importance of which grew in this historical research.

As one went from the smallest communes to the most ancient and the most populous, those precious documents offered a greater interest. Those that had conserved their ancient legislative customs, the charters of their rights and heir archives, did not fail to gather them together with the greatest care.

Those masses of documents were transmitted to the general councils of the départements, in association with which historical commissions were created charged with bringing them together and coordinating them; and the work of those commissions, assembling in a common center, brought to that unique hearth the materials of universal history.

While historical studies received that remarkable impulsion, literature, by contrast, moderated its impetus; more difficult in itself or more fearful of opinion, it was less fecund; but its works, more original and more laboriously prepared, often attained a great glory. It did not adopt new forms however; only one innovation struck minds, and that was when Lamartine published, in 1830, his poem in blank verse on Napoléon; those lines were so beautiful and so harmonious that, without having proscribed rhyme, they shared poetry with it.

Sculpture, like painting, grew and found new methods; the latter rediscovered the secret of the colors of Jean de Bruges and Rubens, which had been lost.

A new architecture was born; it was no longer Greek or Gothic, but French and universal.

Everything became great in that great century.

One day, the King of Sweden, Lucien Napoléon, reminded the Emperor of the century of Leo X,[120] adding that a similar gathering of geniuses was impossible; the Emperor asked for a week to respond.

A week later, united in the salons of the Louvre were Chateaubriand, Walter Scott, Lamartine, Beethoven, Byron, Manzoni, Niebuhr, Goethe, Geoffroy Saint-Hilaire, Madame de Stael, Béranger, Courier, Thiers, de Maistre, Villemain, Victor Hugo, Robert Brown, Volta, Lamennais, Cuvier, Canova, Ingres, Thomas Moore, Gay-Lussac, Kant, Berzelius, Poisson, David the sculptor, David the painter, Champollion, Thénard, Dupin, Delambre, Gérard, Brougham, Lawrence, Humphry Davy, Lamarck, Chaptal, James Watt, Rossini, Jenner, Herschel, Haüy, Paesiello, Humboldt, Thorwaldsen, Fourier, Royer-Collard, Thierry, Guizot, Ampère, Laplace and other great intelligences of the world.

"This is my century!" he said, pointing to that gathering.

---

[120] Pope Leo X, born Giovanni di Lorenzo de Medici (1475-1521) was the second son of Lorenzo the Magnificent; elected Pope in 1513, "his" century was the sixteenth.

## Chapter XI
### THE CORONATION

Two circumstances had delayed the coronation of the Universal Monarch, initially fixed, as we have said, for 28 March 1828; on that date, all the kings of the world had not yet arrived; a few, retained by contrary winds, had passed the deadline given to them by the King of Kings. Then again, the prodigious cathedral that the Emperor was having constructed in Paris, on the ruins of the old Palais de Justice and the Place Dauphine, was not yet finished.

We shall say a few words about that monument.

It was the most magnificent, the vastest edifice in the world. Napoléon, departing for his expedition to Asia, had laid the first stone. Eight years of relentless work had not sufficed to terminate it in its entirety, and a few more months were indispensable for its ultimate completion. It was, it was said, the Cathedral of the World. It had three times the extent of Saint Peter's in Rome; its architecture was known to be original and sublime, not imitated by any other monument on Earth. Of its two facades, one—the principal one—developed before the Pont Neuf, which had been entirely reconstructed in granite and marble, and had become, by its magnificence and size, the finest monument of its kind. Everything was in harmony in the vicinity of the church and the river, and anyone who stopped on the bridge or in the square facing the temple and the palaces that surrounded it, had the greatest spectacle that it was possible to see.

The works were pushed forward with a new activity; the church was entirely completed in the month of June 1828. The following second of July, Pope Clement XV, with a great deal of pomp, dedicated it under the invocation of Saint Napoléon, who became the patron saint of France and the world.

363

Meanwhile, all the kings had arrived in Paris, and Napoléon, who had faith in dates, chose 15 August 1828, the anniversary of his birth, for the ceremony of his coronation.

The most extraordinary preparations were made.

The Saint Napoléon Church, ornamented with all the riches of the Earth, as sparkling with gold and precious stones.

A floor had been constructed over the Seine from the Pont Neuf to the Pont des Arts; it was also supported by the quays of the two banks. The river had disappeared in that area; that immense improvised plaza continued all the way to the portal of the new church and was covered with blue velvet dotted with bees and golden globes throughout its extent.

At noon, the doors of the Louvre, facing the Pont des Arts, opened. The thunder of cannons and bells burst forth from all parts, and the cortege began to emerge from the palace.

All those who were taking part in it were on foot.

It would require an entire book to give details of that exceedingly orderly host of troops, people from the four parts of the world with their national costumes, heralds of arms, generals, magistrates, sovereign princes, ministers, great dignitaries and officers of the Empire and the Universal Monarchy.

After that population of peoples came the corps of the hundred Maréchals of France, and then the four constables of the Monarchy.

Finally came Napoléon, on horseback, covered in imperial purple and ermine, with an épée in his belt and carrying a globe in his hands.

He was followed, in the most imposing order, all on foot and clad in regal ornaments, by:

The kings of the imperial blood;

The kings of Asia;

The kings of Africa;

The kings of America.

Then came the queens, in the same order.

After that was seen another population of princes and grandees, no less numerous than the one marching at the head of the procession.

Having arrived on the floor constructed over the river, the cortege spread out with a magnificent order and pomp, and headed at a solemn pace toward the church.

Before arriving at the portal, Napoléon dismounted; he took a few paces forward, and, the Pope having received him and harangued him, he went into the church.

Another population was already inside the immense edifice, and their acclamations, combined with the chanting of the priests and the tumult of the music and the artillery, formed a confusion and a noise intoxicating for the heart of a master.

In the depths of the cathedral a long series of thrones was arranged; slightly above those was one on which the Empress Joséphine had already taken her place before the arrival of the cortege; and higher still was the throne reserved for the Monarch of the World.

Everyone took their places and the ceremony commenced.

Pope Clement XV, surrounded by sixty cardinals and a large number of archbishops and bishops, officiated.

At a certain moment in the office he turned to Napoléon and called him by his name.

The Emperor came down a few steps and, finding himself thus on a level with the last steps of the altar, he advanced toward the Pope.

Then His Holiness Clement XV invoked the Lord; he spread holy oil over Napoléon's forehead and, having taken a crown of particular form from the altar, he presented it to the monarch and said to him:

"God consecrates you by my hands, Universal Monarch of the Earth. May His name be adored, and may yours be glorified."

Napoléon, who had bent his knee, stood up, took the crown, and, having placed it on his head, climbed back up to his throne, where he sat down.

A cardinal came to present him with another crown, which the Emperor placed on Joséphine's head.

All the kings then came to the foot of the throne to renew the vow of fidelity and submission on their own behalf and that of their peoples.

When the last ceremonies were complete, the cortege left the church, and, resuming the same route, went back to the palace in the same order, and with the same solemnity.

## Chapter XII
## *CONSTELLATION*

In the evening of that day, after the memorable events and the extraordinary pomp that had signaled it, and the marvelous firework display had concluded, the people, still dazzled, slowly withdrew in the semi-calm tumult, mingled with fatigue and admiration, that follows fêtes, especially flamboyant evening fêtes, when the illuminations die down, the fireworks have finished and the atmosphere, momentarily troubled by all those little earthly lights, begins to recover its calm, to sweep away the last clouds of smoke raised by the fireworks, and, having become mistress of nature again, deploys the purity of a beautiful night and causes her stars to scintillate in the immensity of the heavens.

Suddenly, a new prodigy appeared in the firmament.

Was the universe, then, taking part in Napoléon's grandeur and the festivities of the Earth?

Was it the testimony of God manifesting His protection and joy?

Or was it one of those disorders ordered by the hand of the Lord, a catastrophe arriving in its time and in accordance with His thought?

The sky was seen to ignite in the middle of the constellation Orion; masses of flame seemed to be in contention, setting space ablaze; thunder, which seemed to be arriving from the extremities of the world, made itself heard and came to expire in the ears of the Earth.

The conflagration lasted for five minutes; there was something so strange in its flames and convulsions that the people of Paris stopped, stupefied, and contemplated that other fire in the celestial vault fearfully.

Soon, it too ceased, and while eyes were still searching the area of space, which had become dark, they found that a new aspect existed in the heavens; a revolution had just taken

367

place in the stars. Two stars in Orion's belt were extinct and had disappeared, and humans who searched with their sight and their telescopes could no longer find them in the sky henceforth.

Those two worlds had just ended, with their atmospheres, their planets and the beings who doubtless lives with them.

Two stars had disappeared; the constellation Orion no longer existed; a new one had formed from its remains, and it was necessary to recognize and name it.

The peoples still wanted to see there something of Napoléon, and the Universal Monarch was not far from taking that disorder of the universe for God's treaty of alliance with him.

And when, a few days later, science came to give him account of that catastrophe and ask him what it was necessary to make of that destroyed constellation, Napoléon arrogated its debris to himself, and, proud of having something to clarify in the heavens, he gave it his own name, Napoléon.

## Chapter XIII
## CLÉMENTINE

Just because kings prostrate themselves, the nations adore you, the world belongs to you, nature makes you a holocaust of its worlds, God glorifies you, the Earth is no more than a footstool, and you are Emperor and Universal Monarch, Napoléon, do not lose your head, for humanity beats beneath your grandeur, and dolor, higher still, overhangs your joys.

We have mentioned Queen Clémentine, the only daughter—the beloved daughter—of Napoléon.

The people had seen her that day, on a platform, witnessing the coronation ceremony, tall and beautiful, reflecting in her great beauty all her father's features, parading over the ceremonies a gaze that was as soft as it was noble, as pure as it was profound; the people contemplated her lovingly, knowing what inexhaustible treasures of bounty and intelligence there were under those angelic forms, and that for her, nature had created the most beautiful face to veil the most beautiful soul.

Her intelligence understood her father's thought. Daughter of Napoléon, she had received from him life and genius, but to that grandeur she added all that there was of sweetness in a woman's soul, all the riches of candor, tenderness, simplicity and virtue, and all that shone in her eyes and was resplendent in her ravishing face.

Such was Clémentine, as her father always called her, depriving her of her royal title, and even of the name of Napoléon, to make her an idol apart, in order that she should have her own cult, in order that the unfortunate might invoke her, and the fortunate bless her.

She was at the coronation, where she shared the gazes, but her presence saddened that great day of glory. Pale and suffering, her languishing head was tilted over her bosom, and when her eyes lit up with joy in seeing paternal grandeurs, one sensed that it was an effort, and that a hidden evil was devouring the emperor's daughter.

Alas, it was a day of death as well as a day of celebration. Consumed for a long time by a pitiless malady, she died at that moment. God who doubtless has His reasons for giving and removing so suddenly from the world a rapid glimpse of his angels, reclaimed her.

On returning to the palace, an ardent fever had gripped her, and while the people, so forgetful, were animated by their celebrations, the contests of flames burst forth in the night between earth and the heavens, and the great city manifested its joy and the glory of the master of the world, there were indescribable dolors in an alcove in the Tuileries, endless tears and a hopeless agony.

A horrible night followed that day! The man consecrated by God, the Universal Monarch, expiated his sublime enjoyments at the bedside of his poor daughter; he lifted her pale and feeble head in his arms; he covered her in tears that he could not hold back, and watched with anguish the succession of her sighs, as if he trembled to feel the last one exhaled.

And she took command of her pain! Mistress of her agony, she spared Napoléon from it. She kept her eyes on his, and all of heaven was in her gaze; she spoke to him, and all of heaven was in her speech. She consoled him for her death, she spoke about God, she spoke about the Emperor and his peoples, for she mingled the happiness of all with thoughts of God and her father; then she prayed, her weak head leaned forward, and her icy lips came to kiss Napoléon's hand.

Napoléon! The man who the morning had seen so close to God, who had placed his throne facing altars and had shared the adoration of peoples, now threw himself to his knees, prostrated himself, his forehead on the floor, he wept, he implored, he pleaded with God for his daughter, no longer having anything of the emperor about him, entirely a father and a supplicant.

He cried: "O, my God, conserve my Clémentine and take back the world from me!"

But God took back Clémentine, and left him the world.

At seven o'clock in the morning, Clémentine suddenly raised herself up; her face became animated; a flame traversed her gaze; she held out her arms to her father, tried to stammer a few words, and rendered her last sigh.

It was the last effort of life, which finds the strength to die.

She was lying there like an alabaster statue, for her soul had just returned to God.

Napoléon was taken away from that spectacle. His grief had no limits; he, so proud, so powerful, so high above the earth, choked in his sobs, uttered cries, called out to his daughter, asked for her on his knees. He was, in sum, a father, that man.

The people learned that a distance of a few hours separated that celebration and that death, and because the entire Earth was summarized in the Master of the World, like his glory and his power, his grief was universal.

## Chapter XIV
## OMNIPOTENCE

It was necessary to return to power. Only that could triumph over dolor.

But that terrible event had taught Napoléon that he was not the master of death. He thought about his own, and had a tomb built.

He chose Mont Valerien, around which Paris had extended its suburbs. On the summit he had the base of a pyramid constructed, as indestructible and greater than the greatest of the pyramids of Egypt, and in order to impose an aspect even more colossal upon it, the rest of the mountain was sculpted, following the ridges of the corners of the pyramid, all the way to the Seine. Enormous constructions consolidated that base, and the monument, in its ensemble, became the most extraordinary edifice on earth, a veritable Babel Tower of death.

The pyramid, in its full extent, as covered with white marble, and on the face that overlooked Paris was inscribed, in golden letters of prodigious dimension, a single word: NAPOLÉON.

After having taken that care, the Emperor seemed relieved, and occupied himself more liberally with the world.

In 1830, he embarked on a steamship of a new form, which took him to America in seven days. He wanted to visit Mexico, and later Timbuktu, his two capitals that he did not yet know.

The famous north-west passage, although discovered, was nevertheless impracticable for navigation. The Emperor visited the isthmus of Panama personally, and ordered its destruction, to make a strait and open the Southern Sea to the European navy.

After having stayed in America for a few months and visited the subterranean city of Grana, he set sail for Senegal, and went up the river as far as Timbuktu.

His African peoples, told of his coming, came running from all the extremities of the continent.

The spectacle of those black peoples, already converted, speaking the French language, civilized but having conserved in their admiration something of their expressive and fiery enthusiasm, pleased Napoléon. He spread benefits over them in profusion, founded cities, embellished Timbuktu, left numerous monuments in his passage, and having traversed Sudan and Guinea, embarked on the Niger all the way to Cap Formose, from which he returned to Europe.

On his return, he gave a new name to his grandeur. He left the titles of "Sire" and "Majesty" to the kings, abandoning them entirely, and wanted something else for himself.

People addressed him as Lord, and called him His Omnipotence.

That superb satisfaction given to his grandeur, he wanted even more to continue his reorganization of the world.

But already, he was lacking human things, and he could no longer ameliorate the past and solemnize his glory.

He therefore completed his task, which had become too facile, sweeping away obstacles, breaking unnecessary mechanisms, destroying the complications that time had accumulated an clarifying his order of things with an ever-increasing simplicity and enlightenment.

At the same time, Napoléonic monuments rose up all over the world, which bore toward the skies the gigantic testimony of the admiration of peoples.

Paris, above all, became a city of marble and bronze, filled with countless columns, obelisks and triumphal arches, and as that queen of capitals wanted to surpass all the manifestations of the other cities of the earth, it erected the Napoléonic Column in the Place de la Concorde.

That column was erected in 18 August 1831. It is entirely made of white Carrara marble. The shaft, a monolith a hundred and eighty feet high and twenty feet in diameter, is crowned with a capital of the Corinthian order and surmounted by a solid gold statue of Napoléon twenty-eight feet high. The entire monument, including the pedestal and the statue, is no less than two hundred and fifty feet tall. Its surface is covered in bas-reliefs, which, from base to summit, reproduce the life of Napoléon from the conquest of Italy to the Universal Monarchy.

Who has not admired that sublime column, rising with the funerary pyramid of Mont Valerien, at the end of Napoléon's career, like the ancient pillars of Hercules, as if to say that there is no longer anything beyond, and to transmit to posterity the two indestructible testimonies of his life and death?

Having arrived at that terminus, the time has come to conclude this book.

I hesitate myself before the history of those last years, full of the grandeur and the felicity of humankind, but which were not the best of Napoléon's life.

The Master of the World had, in fact, in that epoch, reached the peak, but he had also reached the end. He had mastered humans, exhausted things, and used up the world without being able to use up himself. Having risen so high, he bore the burden of his elevation, for he had found nothing at the summit but humanity, with its poverty and its impotence.

Having nothing more to do, because he had finished everything, nothing more to desire, because no desire as any longer possible for him, too far from things and people, he found himself alone in the universe.

He knew then that it is only God who can find, in His divinity, the means of supporting eternal solitude.

Would it be permissible to sound the last thoughts of that great soul, the master of the earth, the king of kings, the universal monarch, having no other future, and perhaps no other hope, than death?

## Chapter XV
## *THE DEATH OF NAPOLÉON*

On 21 February 1832, in the evening, Napoléon was struck by a sudden apoplexy. The efforts of the art were futile. From the first instant, his tongue was paralyzed, and he was unable to pronounce a single word. The malady was increasingly augmented, and soon took on an extremely grave character, albeit without the invalid appearing to experience very great suffering.

Two days later, on 23 February, at seven twenty-two in the morning, Napoléon expired, at the age of sixty-two years, six months and eight days.

## SF & FANTASY

Adolphe Alhaiza. *Cybele*
Alphonse Allais. *The Adventures of Captain Cap*
Henri Allorge. *The Great Cataclysm*
Guy d'Armen. *Doc Ardan: The City of Gold and Lepers; The Troglodytes of Mount Everest/The Giants of Black Lake; The Abominable Snowman* (anthology)
G.-J. Arnaud. *The Ice Company*
André Arnyvelde. *The Ark; The Mutilated Bacchus*
Charles Asselineau. *The Double Life*
Henri Austruy. *The Eupantophone; The Olotelepan; The Petitpaon Era*
Honoré de Balzac. *The Last Fay*
Barillet-Lagargousse. *The Final War*
Cyprien Bérard. *The Vampire Lord Ruthwen*
S. Henry Berthoud. *Martyrs of Science*
Aloysius Bertrand. *Gaspard de la Nuit*
Richard Bessière. *The Gardens of the Apocalypse; The Masters of Silence*
Chevalier de Béthune. *The World of Mercury*
Albert Bleunard. *Ever Smaller*
Félix Bodin. *The Novel of the Future*
Pierre Boitard. *Journey to the Sun*
Louis Boussenard. *Monsieur Synthesis*
Alphonse Brown. *City of Glass; The Conquest of the Air*
Émile Calvet. *In a Thousand Years*
André Caroff. *The Terror of Madame Atomos; Miss Atomos; The Return of Madame Atomos; The Mistake of Madame Atomos; The Monsters of Madame Atomos; The Revenge of Madame Atomos; The Resurrection of Madame Atomos; The Mark of Madame Atomos; The Spheres of Madame Atomos; The Wrath of Madame Atomos* (w/M. & Sylvie Stéphan)
Félicien Champsaur. *Homo-Deus; The Human Arrow; Nora, The Ape-Woman; Ouha, King of the Apes; Pharaoh's Wife*
Didier de Chousy. *Ignis*

Jules Clarétie. *Obsession*

Jacques Collin de Plancy. *Voyage to the Center of the Earth*

Michel Corday. *The Eternal Flame; The Lynx* (w/André Couvreur)

André Couvreur. *Caresco, Superman; The Exploits of Professor Tornada* (3 vols.); *The Necessary Evil; The Lynx* (w/Michel Corday)

Camille Debans. *The Misfortunes of John Bull*

Captain Danrit. *Undersea Odyssey*

C. I. Defontenay. *Star (Psi Cassiopeia)*

Charles Derennes. *The People of the Pole*

Georges Dodds (anthologist). *The Missing Link*

Charles Dodeman. *The Silent Bomb*

Harry Dickson. *The Heir of Dracula; Harry Dickson vs. The Spider*

Jules Dornay. *Lord Ruthven Begins*

Alfred Driou. *The Adventures of a Parisian Aeronaut*

Odette Dulac. *The War of the Sexes*

Alexandre Dumas. *The Return of Lord Ruthven*

Renée Dunan. *Baal; The Ultimate Pleasure*

J.-C. Dunyach. *The Night Orchid; The Thieves of Silence*

Henri Duvernois. *The Man Who Found Himself*

Achille Eyraud. *Voyage to Venus*

Henri Falk. *The Age of Lead*

Paul Féval. *Anne of the Isles; Knightshade; Revenants; Vampire City; The Vampire Countess; The Wandering Jew's Daughter*

Paul Féval, *fils. Felifax, the Tiger-Man*

Charles de Fieux. *Lamékis*

Fernand Fleuret. *Jim Click*

Louis Forest. *Someone is Stealing Children in Paris*

Arnould Galopin. *Doctor Omega; Doctor Omega and the Shadowmen* (anthology); *Harry Dickson: The Man in Grey; Harry Dickson: Tenebras*

Judith Gautier. *Isoline and the Serpent-Flower*

H. Gayar. *The Marvelous Adventures of Serge Myrandhal on Mars*

G.L. Gick. *Harry Dickson and the Werewolf of Rutherford Grange*

Raoul Gineste. *The Second Life of Doctor Albin*

Delphine de Girardin. *Balzac's Cane*

Léon Gozlan. *The Vampire of the Val-de-Grâce*

Jules Gros. *The Fossil Man*

Jimmy Guieu. *The Polarian-Denebian War* (2 vols.)

Edmond Haraucourt. *Daah, the First Human; Illusions of Immortality*

Nathalie Henneberg. *The Green Gods*

Eugène Hennebert. *The Enchanted City*

Jules Hoche. *The Maker of Men and His Formula*

V. Hugo, P. Foucher & P. Meurice. *The Hunchback of Notre-Dame*

Romain d'Huissier. *Hexagon: Dark Matter*

Jules Janin. *The Magnetized Corpse*

Michel Jeury. *Chronolysis*

Gustave Kahn. *The Tale of Gold and Silence*

Gérard Klein. *The Mote in Time's Eye*

Fernand Kolney. *Love in 5000 Years*

Paul Lacroix. *Danse Macabre*

Louis-Guillaume de La Follie. *The Unpretentious Philosopher*

Jean de La Hire. *The Fiery Wheel; Enter the Nyctalope; The Nyctalope on Mars; The Nyctalope vs. Lucifer; The Nyctalope Steps In; Night of the Nyctalope; Return of the Nyctalope*

Etienne-Léon de Lamothe-Langon. *The Virgin Vampire*

André Laurie. *Spiridon*

Gabriel de Lautrec. *The Vengeance of the Oval Portrait*

Alain le Drimeur. *The Future City*

Georges Le Faure & Henri de Graffigny. *The Extraordinary Adventures of a Russian Scientist Across the Solar System* (2 vols.)

Gustave Le Rouge. *The Dominion of the World* (w/Gustave Guitton) (4 vols.); *The Mysterious Doctor Cornelius* (3 vols.); *The Vampires of Mars*

Jules Lermina. *The Battle of Strasbourg; Mysteryville; Panic in Paris; The Secret of Zippelius; To-Ho and the Gold Destroyers*

André Lichtenberger. *The Centaurs; The Children of the Crab*

Maurice Limat. *Mephista*

Listonai. *The Philosophical Voyager*

Jean-Marc & Randy Lofficier. *Edgar Allan Poe on Mars; The Katrina Protocol; Pacifica 1, 2; Robonocchio; Return of the Nyctalope;* (anthologists) *Tales of the Shadowmen 1-12; The Vampire Almanac* (2 vols.); *The French Fantasy Treasury* (3 vols.)

Ch. Lomon & P.-B. Gheuzi. *The Last Days of Atlantis*

Camille Mauclair. *The Virgin Orient*

Xavier Mauméjean. *The League of Heroes*

Joseph Méry. *The Tower of Destiny*

Hippolyte Mettais. *Paris Before the Deluge; The Year 5865*

Louise Michel. *The Human Microbes; The New World*

Tony Moilin. *Paris in the Year 2000*

José Moselli. *Illa's End*

John-Antoine Nau. *Enemy Force*

Marie Nizet. *Captain Vampire*

Charles Nodier. *Trilby and The Crumb Fairy*

C. Nodier, A. Beraud & Toussaint-Merle. *Frankenstein*

Henri de Parville. *An Inhabitant of the Planet Mars*

Gaston de Pawlowski. *Journey to the Land of the 4th Dimension*

Georges Pellerin. *The World in 2000 Years*

Ernest Pérochon. *The Frenetic People*

Pierre Pelot. *The Child Who Walked on the Sky*

Jean Petithuguenin. *An International Mission to the Moon*

J. Polidori, C. Nodier, E. Scribe. *Lord Ruthven the Vampire*

P.-A. Ponson du Terrail. *The Immortal Woman; The Vampire and the Devil's Son*

Georges Price. *The Missing Men of the* Sirius

René Pujol. *The Chimerical Quest*

Edgar Quinet. *Ahasuerus; The Enchanter Merlin*

Henri de Régnier. *A Surfeit of Mirrors*

Maurice Renard. *The Blue Peril; Doctor Lerne; The Doctored Man; A Man Among the Microbes; The Master of Light*

Restif de la Bretonne. *The Discovery of the Austral Continent by a Flying Man; Posthumous Correspondence* (3 vols.)

Jean Richepin. *The Crazy Corner; The Wing*

Albert Robida. *The Adventures of Saturnin Farandoul; Chalet in the Sky; The Clock of the Centuries; The Electric Life; The Engineer Von Satanas*

J.-H. Rosny Aîné. *Helgvor of the Blue River; The Givreuse Enigma; The Mysterious Force; The Navigators of Space; Vamireh; The World of the Variants; The Young Vampire*

Marcel Rouff. *Journey to the Inverted World*

Marie-Anne de Roumier-Robert. *The Voyage of Lord Seaton to the Seven Planets*

Léonie Rouzade. *The World Turned Upside Down*

Han Ryner. *The Human Ant; The Superhumans; The Son of Silence*

Louis-Claude de Saint-Martin. *The Crocodile*

Frank Schildiner. *The Quest of Frankenstein*

Pierre de Selenes: *An Unknown World*

Norbert Sevestre. *Sâr Dubnotal: Vs. Jack the Ripper; The Astral Trail*

Angelo de Sorr. *The Vampires of London*

Brian Stableford. *The Empire of the Necromancers (1. The Shadow of Frankenstein; 2. Frankenstein and the Vampire Countess; 3. Frankenstein in London); Eurydice's Lament; The New Faust at the Tragicomique; Sherlock Holmes and The Vampires of Eternity; The Stones of Camelot; The Wayward Muse.* (anthologist) *News from the Moon; The Germans on Venus; The Supreme Progress; The World Above the World; Nemoville; Investigations of the Future; The Conqueror of Death; The Revolt of the Machines; The Man With the Blue Face; The Aerial Valley; The New Moon; The Nickel Man; On the Brink of the World's End; The Mirror of Present Events; The Humanishere*

Jacques Spitz. *The Eye of Purgatory*

Kurt Steiner. *Ortog*

Eugène Thébault. *Radio-Terror*
C.-F. Tiphaigne de La Roche. *Amilec*
Simon Tyssot de Patot. *The Strange Voyages of Jacques Massé and Pierre de Mésange*
Louis Ulbach. *Prince Bonifacio*
Théo Varlet. *The Castaways of Eros; The Golden Rock.; The Martian Epic* (w/Octave Joncquel); *Timeslip Troopers* (w/André Blandin); *The Xenobiotic Invasion*
Pierre Véron. *The Merchants of Health*
Paul Vibert. *The Mysterious Fluid*
Villiers de l'Isle-Adam. *The Scaffold; The Vampire Soul*
Gaston de Wailly. *The Murderer of the World*
Philippe Ward. *Artahe; Manhattan Ghost* (w/Mickael Laguerre); *The Song of Montségur* (w/Sylvie Miller)
Willy. *Astral Amour*

Victor Margueritte. *The Bacheloress; The Companion; The Couple*

## NON-FICTION

Stephen R. Bissette. *Blur 1-5. Green Mountain Cinema 1; Teen Angels*
Win Scott Eckert. *Crossovers* (2 vols.)
Georges Grison. *The Heads that Fell in Paris*
Jean-Marc & Randy Lofficier. *Shadowmen* (2 vols.)
Randy Lofficier. *Over Here*
Brian Stableford. *The Plurality of Imaginary Worlds*